WASICHU

Wasichu (waSHEchew):Lakota word for white man

Praise for Brierley

WASICHU is a remarkable tour de force, bold in concept and brilliant in theme. An excellent read of what the West has become."

---Clive Cussler

Barry Brierley is truly one of the most exciting, prolific writers of our times. He has proven this time and time again with his novels, like EDGES OF TIME.

He has surpassed this with THE BALLAD OF BASS REEVES. The reader is immediately immersed in the tapestry of the 1880's landscape and the struggles, love, friendships, family and the courage of this true American hero.

--- Gay Gilbert, Producer

In EDGES OF TIME "Brierley's writing is so vivid I felt I was there. His words paint a picture that transports the reader to that time and place. After 30 plus years working with writers developing scripts,
I have known few who can translate vision to screen. Brierley is one of those few. I love everything he writes."

--- Gay Gilbert, Producer

TIMELESS INTERLUDE AT WOUNDED KNEE is one of those wonderful books that is read in one sitting -- not because it has little to say, but because it's said so well that it's hard to put down. The book is so well researched that Brierley's Lakota Sioux leap to life in the reader's eye as they face their darkest hour."

--- The Writer's Showcase

Barry Brierley is the Tom Clancy of Indian historical adventure. His diligent research shows through on every page. I learned more about the Sioux culture reading these thoroughly entertaining novels than I have in any textbook.

*--- Marshall Terrill,
Author of Steve McQueen, the Last Mile*

In YESTERDAY'S BANDIT, (Butch Cassidy's Pursuit of Life and Honor) I believe that Brierley has captured Butch Cassidy's true character. It is a fun read for young and old. I especially encourage the younger generation to read this book to help give them insight about morals, justice and family values.

*---Bill Betenson,
Great nephew and researcher of Butch Cassidy*

ALSO BY BARRY BRIERLEY

WASICHU'S RETURN

TIMELESS INTERLUDE AT WOUNDED KNEE

WHITE HORSE, RED RIDER

YESTERDAY'S BANDIT (BUTCH CASSIDY'S PURSUIT OF LIFE AND HONOR)

SPIRIT RIDERS

EDGES OF TIME

BASS REEVES, AN AMERICAN HERO

WASICHU

A novel by...Barry Brierley

Copyright © 1993 by Barry Brierley

*All rights reserved.
No part of this book may be used, reproduced or transmitted in any manner whatsoever, including photocopying, recording or by any information storage and retrieval system, except for quotations in a review, without the expressed written permission of the author.
Library of Congress Catalog Card Number:93-79837*

*DAKOTA Indians—fiction
PS3552-R4554W37
1993*

2ND TRADE EDITION 2015

Published by
BEAR BOOKS
111 E. Main Street
Florence, Colorado 81226

Printed in the United States of America.

**Cover art by Barry Brierley
Designed and illustrated by Barry Brierley**

brierleybarry@yahoo.com

This is a work of fiction. Names, characters, places and incidents are the product of the author's imagination and are used fictitiously.

ISBN 1-889657-02-06
978-1-889657-02-8

ACKNOWLEDGEMENTS

Many people have given of themselves in the preparation of this manuscript. To all my friends and family who took the time to critique my efforts, I thank you.

A whole chapter could be written about the work, dedication and love that was involved in the writing of WASICHU. Very special thanks to my wife, Barb. Her tireless editing, encouragement, and cooperation were instrumental in the creation of my novel. If not for her, this book would not be complete.

This book is dedicated to all Native Americans and especially to the memory of my late friend, Joe four Bears, who was so proud of his people and his heritage. He once said to me, "If only we could have lived back in those days … wouldn't it have been great?"

Illustrations

Pg 11
BEGINNINGS

Pg 27
Part I . . . BUTTE

Pg 49
Part II ... Lakota

Pg 93
Part III... OKUTE

Pg 133
Part IV... ENEMIES

Pg 241
Part V... ROSEBUD

Pg 285
Part VI .... DECISIONS

CRAZY HORSE, Oglala Sioux... leading his warriors at the Battle of the Rosebud in June, 1896:

"Hokahey! Follow me! Follow me! Today is a good day to fight, today is a good day to die!"

MANY HORSES Oglala Sioux... Helped promote the ghost dance in 1890 at Standing Rock. When the ghost dance failed he confided these words to a white friend:

"I will follow the white man's trail. I will make him my friend, but I will not bend my back to his burdens. I will be as cunning as a coyote. I will ask him to help me understand his ways, then I will prepare the way for my children. Maybe they will outrun the white man in his own shoes..."

ARVOL LOOKING HORSE... Lakota Medicine Man and Keeper of the Sacred Pipe (from <u>Life Magazine, Special Issue; The Wild West,</u> April 5, 1993.)

"The buffalo faces the wind, no matter if it's hot or cold. The time has come for the Indian Nations to learn from the buffalo. We must turn and face the wind... the Sacred Hoop is mending."

PROLOGUE

~~~~~~~~~~~~

Sturgis, South Dakota... 1989

Ever since leaving the Black Hills in 1980, I had felt as though I was being pulled there by some unknown force. When it finally did come to pass, I became afraid.

We arrived there for a vacation. My wife, Barb, was with me and, at times, I feared for her safety. The fear came from a fear of the unknown, not because of any tangible menace. It's just that at the time I felt caught up in a vortex beyond my control.

Everything was normal for the first few days, but as soon as we drew near the northeast edge of the Hills, it was as though my rental car had a mind of its own. We headed straight for the town of Sturgis. Back in 1980, before I had met Barb, I had lived about five miles out of town in a housing development situated along the spine of a ridge.

Sturgis is a small town of about four thousand people. With no major industry nearby the town's livelihood was partially dependent on tourism. Being away from the usual flow of tourists because of its location, Sturgis became a bit reliant upon the income generated by their annual Motorcycle Rally. People come from all over the United States to participate in the many festivities. But once the Rally is over the town immediately reverts back to its pleasant, sleepy status.

With six or seven weeks to go before the next Rally, there should be no special reason to be going to Sturgis, yet I felt compelled to do so. As I am a Wildlife and Western Artist, it is normal for Barb and me to travel to many out-of-the-way places for photos and research. This time, however, there was nothing there for me, yet I felt drawn to the area.

We left the freeway and I drove down the familiar streets to the shopping area. I was just pointing out a place we could have lunch when I saw it. The sign read:

LA PETITE GALLERY
PAINTINGS, BOOKS, ARTIFACTS
JEWELRY, POTTERY

With three out of five; paintings, books and artifacts being some of my favorite things, I just knew that lunch was going to have to wait. Besides, Barb liked to snoop in places like that as much as I did.

Approaching the establishment I noticed that it had that cluttered, historical ambience that I loved and probably needed, if self-gratification can be considered a form of sustenance. As we were about to enter, I stopped. Suddenly, I had the strangest feeling. It was a feeling akin to having accomplished something of importance. Yet, I couldn't imagine what could have triggered this eerie, undeserved feeling.

Barb's tugging on my arm snapped me out of my reverie. I told her that I'd join her in a moment or two. Being used to my occasional quirky behavior, she went inside without me.

For some inexplicable reason, I felt that I couldn't leave the front of the store. In a moment I felt my gaze being pulled toward the showcase. Books and paintings took up most of the space in the window but there was also a Native American display of beaded items, two catlinite pipestone pipes, some rugs and jewelry. A sign proclaimed: "Your Native American Reservation Outlet." The sign and the Indian display brought back some fond memories but also some sad ones.

WASICHU

Of all the friends I have made in my life, my brief relationship with Joseph Four Bears was probably the most impressionable. He was a full-blooded Minneconjou Sioux from the Cheyenne/Sioux reservation north of the Black Hills. He and I had worked together during a brief time period when I wasn't working as an artist. Our relationship was one of those rare fusing of minds, the type of friendship that is as immediate as it is permanent. Joe has been dead about nine years now. But I think of him from time to time as though he were still alive.

Memories began to flood my senses of Joseph's stories and anecdotes of the Lakota and the many fascinating nuances of the Sioux culture. Most memorable of all were the vignettes of individuals among the Lakota.

All at once my mind was void of thought and I was drawn, like a magnet draws a nail, to a spot in one of the windows closest to the street.

The door to the shop was recessed. The sidewalk leading to the door was bordered by long, showcase windows. There were books, beaded fetishes, a pipe and beaded pipe bag, blankets, paintings... and something else. It was that unknown 'something' that I felt driven to discover. There was something behind the feathers attached to the pipe. I couldn't see what it was, but somehow I knew that I was supposed to see that 'something.'

When I all but burst through the door, both my wife and the proprietor gave me startled looks. The owner, who was staring at me as though he'd seen a ghost, was a huge bearded man who was peering at me over the top of his reading glasses. He had been showing Barb a pair of earrings before my frenzied entrance and interruption. He straightened and quietly asked, "Barry... you want to see it, don't you?"

I didn't have a clue what 'it' could be, but I knew I had to see it. Besides, I was so flabbergasted by the fact that he knew my name, I would have agreed to anything. Not trusting my voice, I nodded. Barb was probably thinking that I knew this complete stranger from when I had lived there. All at once I realized that I must have really looked stressed out because Barb was staring at me as though I had finally cracked. I silently vowed to pull myself together and try to act normal.

With another penetrating look over his glasses, the owner moved past me toward the showcase. Realizing that it was going to take him time to circumvent all the many items displayed within the window's confined area; I hurried outside so that I wouldn't have to wait for him to bring 'it' inside to show me.

I wasn't the least bit surprised when he went directly to the pipe. For the first time I noticed that right above it there was a flat area on the blanket where something had been sitting. Having spied the empty flat area above, he reached behind the pipe's feathers. Seeing me at the window brought forth another noncommittal glance and a strange smile. Holding his hand near the glass, he opened his fist. Looking even smaller within the planes of the proprietor's large hand, was a stylized carving of a horse. It looked to be about two inches long by one and a half inches high. It was carved out of pipestone and appeared to be very old. I found myself staring at the artifact as though mesmerized. I knew that I had never seen the piece before, yet I felt linked to it in some obscure way.

Hearing a hoarse, rumbling cough, I looked up. The proprietor, who later proclaimed to be the one and only 'La Petite,' jerked his head toward the shop and then began to carefully weave his way through the maze of artifacts and paintings.

Much to Barb's chagrin, I was unable to completely satisfy her curiosity about my behavior. How could I explain that I was being manipulated as though I was a puppet with

WASICHU

strings... and that I was unable to stop?

Luckily for me, La Petite arrived with the carved horse and captured all of her attention. Since we both harbored special feelings for objects carved out of catlinite, Barb and I fondled and stroked the artifact until the proprietor felt compelled to say, "It's not for sale."

Although I knew the answer, I looked up at him and asked, "This horse isn't carved in Lakota style, is it? It's some other tribe, right?"

La Petite grimaced, ran his large fingers through his graying beard, and said, "No, it wasn't done in Lakota style. But the owner is definitely a Lakota. He's a young Minneconjou Sioux and that artifact has been in his family for generations."

Judging from the covert looks that the proprietor/art dealer was giving me, I assumed that he wanted to talk to me alone. He gave me another meaningful stare as Barb handed him a smile, along with the carved horse. Turning to me she grinned and grabbed my arm saying, "Let's go eat."

Taking Barb aside I told her that I'd like to ask La Petite about Joseph's family and some other things. Knowing how much I enjoy talking with my peers and fellow book lovers, she agreed to meet me later for lunch.

The man waited until Barb was all the way out of the store before turning to me and saying, "I mean no offense to your wife, but what I have to tell you I don't want anyone else hearing. It's bad enough my having to tell you. The most important thing for you to understand is that what I'm about to tell you is the absolute truth, as far as I know. But, don't try to understand anything else, all right? We're talking Indian beliefs here, man."

La Petite sat down and began to study the artifact in a distracted manner as he spoke to me.

"I have a young man that has worked for me for a number of years. His name is Marlon Spotted Horse; he's a

Sioux from the reservation up north."

He looked at me then continued.

"He's really been a help to me in acquiring Lakota beadwork and artifacts."

Holding the horse carving up, he said, "This belongs to him. He claims that it's mystical, you know... spirits. I think it's all a bunch of hogwash, myself, but that's neither here nor there. He believes, and that's what counts."

La Petite smiled and slowly shook his head, saying, "I have to admit that he's right so far. You did come just as he said you would."

At that point I was getting nervous. I'd never heard of this Lakota person before and somehow he thought that he was responsible for my coming back to Sturgis. How could that be? Before I could torture myself any further with more unanswerable questions, La Petite continued his monologue.

Marlon's family has been friends with the Four Bears clan for years. Before Joseph Four Bear's death he used to talk about you all the time. Marlon's mother said that judging from what Four Bears had said about you, you sounded a lot like her late husband's friend. Four Bears had told her that you truly were interested in their history and culture and seemed to have a compassion for the plight of the Sioux people."

I held up my hand like a cop stopping traffic as I said, "Whoa... what is this all leading to... money? I don't have any. Mrs. Spotted Horse is right though, I am sympathetic to their plight, as she put it. But that doesn't put any groceries on the table, does it?"

As La Petite was about to speak, I interrupted with another pointless question.

"How did Mrs. Spotted Horse's husband die?"

The big man pawed at his beard as he replied, "He was killed during a Special Operations Group screw-up late in the Vietnam war."

WASICHU

Hauling himself out of his chair, La Petite stepped through a door that apparently led to a back room. Confused and befuddled, I dropped into his chair. In less than a minute he was back carrying a bulky rawhide bag with geometric Lakota designs and symbols painted in red and ochre across its broad sides. He unceremoniously stepped forward and dropped the weighty parcel square onto my lap. Looking down at me from his great height, La Petite sighed and exclaimed, "There, it's over! The responsibility is now yours, man. I'm out of it."

Being even more confused, I asked, "What is this? I don't understand."

La Petite grinned and replied, "It's a manuscript... or perhaps I should say manuscripts. They were written by a man named Christopher Raven, Spotted Horse's friend in Vietnam, and a young Sioux called Little Hawk. They, as well as Marlon and his mother, would like you to rewrite their manuscripts into book form and try to get them published."

I was stunned. Looking up at the art dealer as he towered over me, it suddenly hit me that this man's name actually means "tiny" in French. It makes about as much sense as the rest of this mess, I thought.

"Why me? I'm an artist... not a writer."

La Petite grunted and said, "Your late friend, Four Bears, had told Mrs. Spotted Horse that you had told him that someday you would like to write a book about the Sioux Indian Wars. They feel that this book, or books, would probably stand a better chance at being published if written by a white man."

"I don't get it," I replied, "why not this Raven guy?"

The dealer's laughter boomed off the walls. He grinned down at me and with a glint in his eye said, "If you want to believe what's written in there... and what these Lakota have told me... you could say that this Raven fellow is a bit incapacitated from time to time."

This last remark was followed by more inane laughter which was, thankfully, interrupted by the chimes on the front door announcing the arrival of a customer. As La Petite went on his merry way to help his potential buyer, I opened the bag.

I stared in awe at the stack of leather bound ledgers, bundles of coarse paper wrapped in tanned skins. There was even some type of scraped skins that weren't thoroughly tanned so that they remained stiff, yet smooth enough to write on. As I delved into the hodge-podge of written material, I lost all sense of time and place. I no longer heard La Petite's baritone rumble, nor did I hear or see anything else. I was captivated by the vast assortment of items within the package. Some of the writing had been done with a ballpoint pen, but the bulk of the writing had been done in a crude pen and ink and some type of dye, or had been painstakingly printed with graphite or charcoal. The sheer volume of the work astounded me.

There is enough material here, I thought, for two or three books. I began to read scraps here and there. My head spun as I read about a fight between Crazy Horse and General Crook at a place called the Rosebud... then detailed descriptions of the fight at the Little Big Horn. I marveled at the boy, Little Hawk, telling of how this Raven guy saved him from a grizzly, of Raven's love for Blue Feather. I read of the fighting spirit of Bear's Foot and Wolf's Spirit and of their friendship with Raven. I kept running into historical names that blew me away: Hickok, Sitting Bull, Two Moons... Custer.

I sat still for a moment. I was reeling, dizzy with excitement over the potential of all that raw material enclosed inside the bag.

As I stood up, I lost my grip on the leather sack and it fell to the floor. When I picked it up a metallic tinkle came

WASICHU

from inside. I pulled out a pair of G.I. dog tags; a leather pouch was attached Glancing at the tags I saw the name RAVEN, CHRISTOPHER stamped into the dull tin. A photo was in the pouch and had been folded, separating the color image of two men. At first they looked like pirates with their black bandanas on their heads, but as soon as I saw the AK-47 weapon in the hands of the guy with the gray eyes, I knew this must be Raven. The other man was obviously Joe Spotted Horse, the Lakota Indian. I had difficulty tearing my gaze away from the photo. Returning the picture to the bag, I then found a piece of leather inside that had a message scratched onto its soft surface: "IF YOU CHOOSE TO WRITE IT, FORGET THAT YOU ARE A WASICHU AND BE TRUTHFUL. THAT IS ALL I HAVE TO SAY."

With the bag of manuscripts tucked under my arm and my head still ringing with Raven's sardonic message, I stumbled to the door.

"Hey!"

I stopped. La Petite had just come out of the back room. I had been so engrossed I hadn't noticed him walk by me when he had entered it. He leaned on the counter and peered over his glasses at me.

"Are you going to write it?"

I nodded and said, "Thanks for everything."

As I turned to leave, La Petite's final question stopped me in my tracks.

"What's the name of the first book going to be? Maybe I'll buy a copy."

Thinking of Raven's message, I slowly turned and faced him. I grinned and said, "Wasichu."

B.B.
Mesa, Arizona ... 1989

Beginnings...

Vietnam...
Summer, 1968

ONE
~~~~~~

The blood started at his hairline, slowly breaking a trail through the dirt and sweat. It moved down and across his broad forehead. Moving faster, it gained momentum thrusting through and over the brow. The red slick trail quickened as it mixed with perspiration, moving down and around a short, slightly curved nose. Rushing across a narrow ravine of tightened lips, it slowed as it reached the ledge of a strong jaw. The blood pooled, slowly dripping off the chin onto a spot over the right chest, obliterating the name and initial stenciled there, C. RAVEN.

The ambush had caught the squad moving single file on an unusually straight portion of the trail. An American antipersonnel mine, called a claymore, had initiated the attack. Because of the lack of curves in the trail, the North Vietnamese had been able to effectively aim the mine and use it like shooting cannon down a sidewalk.

The eight-man squad made up of two American Special Forces advisors and six Vietnamese irregulars never had a chance.

Along with the mine detonation the North Vietnamese had delivered a withering cross-fire. Using their infamous AK-47 assault rifles set on full automatic, they laid down a field of fire that they felt would be impossible for anyone to survive.

The gunfire had stopped. The heat rested on the soldiers' shoulders like a wet blanket. They waited for the badly wounded to die.

Raven lay there, arms and legs akimbo in a lifeless appearing sprawl. The knowledge that at any moment his sham could be discovered and he would be captured, or shot, was having a claustrophobic effect on his psyche. Wet with humidity and sweat, he could feel the fear beginning to work on him. The only sounds he heard were the normal vocal or wing noises being made by the insects.

The blood running down Raven's face was not his own. The body of Nuong was partially covering Raven's. The South Vietnamese had taken so many rounds that he had been blown off his feet, sweeping Raven to the ground with him in a ghastly embrace.

When the ambush had been triggered, Raven inadvertently had been the last man in the single file. He had moved from the middle of the file to the end, checking his men's gear. He had stopped at the end so that he could help Nuong readjust his pack, and while making the adjustments, Raven's body had been partially shielded by Nuong's when the claymore had gone off. Hit in the helmet and thigh, Raven had been taken out of the annihilating line of fire when Nuong's body had knocked him down.

With his peripheral vision, he saw them as they moved into the open. Raven couldn't tell how many there were, but he could see that they were a unit of NVA regulars.

Raven felt a twinge of anguish as he thought of Johnstone, who had been near the front of the file. A tightening band of pain gripped his leg, clearing his mind. The pain surged and subsided as though an animal had his leg in its jaws and was alternating chewing and shaking. Having no other options he waited for the pain to subside.

The only movement among the eight bodies was Christopher Raven's eyes. He blinked them furiously as he struggled to free them of blood and sweat. His fear intensified as he watched the NVA move closer. He was sprawled in such a way with another man's body beneath his head and shoulders, that by looking through the corner of his eye, he could see most of the trail and the bodies scattered along its length.

The soldiers sounded relaxed and confident as they moved among the bodies, softly jabbering in Vietnamese. Suddenly their voices took on a more excited, vibrant tone. A loud shattering burst of automatic rifle fire rent the air!

The burst was so startling that it nearly thrust Raven to his feet. His nerves were frayed so thin that the gun fire came within an eyelash of pushing him into a wide-eyed panic.

The flat crack of a pistol shot bounced off Chris' eardrum. His mind reeled. Sweet Jesus, he thought, they're killing the wounded!

Teetering on the brink of hopelessness, Raven's bleeding, sweating body was completely rigid. Frozen with fear, he watched his murderers moving down the line, each step bringing them closer.

In his near catatonic state of mind, Chris' peripheral sight and growing mania visualized the NVA killers as dancers. Growing ever nearer in a graceful tableau of death... step, two, three, four... point, shoot! Step, two, three... as his mind refused to accept the reality, his fantasies intensified. The dancers floated through their routine in a chorus line of horror. His tormented mind became their choreographer. 'Wait... you're not together!' his mind shouted, 'It's all wrong... too much noise... oh, God, the blood!' His vision blurred while his mind blanked.

Reality returned in a vortex of terror at the exact moment that an NVA officer stepped from his peripheral vision to full front view. His entry into Raven's sight triggered a minute reflex response in his eyes.

Had he been watching for it, the officer could hardly have missed it. He didn't. He inexplicably said in perfect English, "This one's alive!" Raven's stomach lurched. He felt the blood leave his head as a wave of dizziness swept over him.

The unmistakable, metallic sound of the slide-action of an automatic pistol being pulled back and released resounded in Chris' ears. It told him that the pistol was now fully cocked and ready to fire.

The terrifying implication of the sound brought Raven's head and eyes up and alive, searching for and finding the NVA's face. He saw everything with absolute clarity... the narrow, Asian face... the sun helmet with a red enamel star. There was a chip out of the red enamel and the metallic gold color glistened in the light where the enamel should have been. At the tip of the Viet's nose was a drop of sweat. Raven watched it with mindless fascination. Will it fall or will it stay? Mentally shaking his head, he stared into the cold black eyes of his executioner.

His charade over, Specialist Fourth Class Christopher Raven, U.S. Army Special Forces, could feel the rage begin to build inside of him. It wasn't a mindless rage. Raven's brain was working furiously trying to sort out any and all probabilities that would enable him to survive his situation. There just weren't any.

Defiant, angry gray eyes locked in with the Viet's emotionless black ones. As pain surged through his leg, Chris said through clenched teeth, "Fuck you! You haven't got the balls, you chicken-necked bastard!"

Raven watched the hate flood into the soldier's eyes as he brought the automatic up, arm fully extended. Chris stared into the round, black muzzle and the cold, black eyes of death. He was consumed by a helpless rage.

A large, wraith-like figure seemed to materialize right at the Viet officer's feet. A dark, sinuous arm shot out, balled fist smashing into the NVA's temple! The punch was delivered with such power that the much smaller man virtually flew through the air.

Even before the Viet's slight form had hit the ground Raven's ears were assailed by the booming, hammering

WASICHU

explosions of his rescuer's pump shotgun. The twelve gauge shots were coming so closely together that they blended, sounding like one long deafening explosion.

Chris could see men falling, coming apart, obliterated by the shotgun blasts. Adding to the shotgun's clamor was the ripping cross-fire of several M-16's punctuated by the much heavier reports of an M-60 machine gun. It was only a matter of seconds before the shooting stopped and the quiet returned.

The only movement was the shimmering heat waves hovering above the tall grass and underbrush. Finally several American soldiers stepped into the open and carefully approached the downed enemy.

Grimacing from the pain in his leg, Chris shifted his body so that he could see better. Wiping the blood and sweat from his eyes, he looked over at the officer's inert body. At first he couldn't tell if he was dead or just unconscious. Then he noticed the unnatural position of the head and realized that he was dead.

The man who had saved his life was nowhere in sight. Troops were all over the area. They were checking Raven's squad for survivors and making sure that all the NVA were either dead or out of commission.

Raven suddenly raised himself onto his elbows and looked at the bloody tattered remnants of his squad.

"Johnny? Nuong?"

His voice, loud in the aftermath of the firefight, spun heads of several of his rescuers. They quickly averted their gaze and continued with what they were doing.

Finally admitting to himself that they were dead, Raven felt the weight of grief settle onto his shoulders. He thought briefly of Johnstone's family.

"Shit!" he exclaimed.

Leaning back, Chris pushed away his anguish and relaxed. He felt the rays of the merciless sun beating down on his exposed face and neck. Damn, he thought, what can I say? It's great to be alive.

Feeling a sudden resurgence of grief for his dead friends, he closed his mind to it and pushed it back out of sight, saving it for a more private moment.

Raising himself up onto his hands, Raven tried ineffectively to make his leg more comfortable by adjusting the pressure pad on his wound. One of the soldiers that had been checking the bodies, looking for live ones, had given him the bandage.

Settling back, Raven closed his eyes to the intense sunlight and tried to ignore his rising discomfort. In a flashback of unusual clarity, he could see again the moment of his rescue, only in much more detail. It was as though it had been permanently etched onto his retina.

The tall, bare-chested figure rose out of the waist high grass, dark skin and tiger stripe dungarees blending and fusing with the grass and underbrush. His longish-hair, black and shiny as any Vietnamese, framed a dark, fierce visage. His movements had the fluid grace of a dancer yet with the speed of a cat. For Raven, the most unforgettable part of the rescue was the man's facial expression. It expressed joy... fierce, undiluted joy.

Shifting his body a little, Chris leaned all the way back. This guy obviously loves combat, he mused. Maybe he's one of those guys who aren't happy unless they're living on the edge. As he felt himself beginning to drift, Raven had time for one more lucid thought, whoever this guy is, I'll never forget what he did for me.

The combined weight of Chris' grief and his wound shut down his mind and he closed his eyes. Ignoring the heat, he drifted away on a cloud of sorrow and mixed emotions.

Consciousness gradually pulled Raven back to the surface. He felt weightless, slowly drifting as though he was floating on a sea of pain.

WASICHU

Sound, light, pain, all began to blend into a fleeting montage of, savage imagery: gunfire, screams, half-naked warriors... sweeping, brown fist striking sallow flesh, a spinning, green disk, three black eyes staring!

Chris' eyes were going in and out of focus as though they were a camera lens being played with by a child. Slowly his sight began to return to normal. As his vision cleared, so did his fevered mind. He could see a medic kneeling beside him fussing with the dressing on his leg. The drop of sweat dangling from his nose brought back the horror. For just an instant, the medic's face became that of the dead NVA officer. The medic looked up and the image was gone.

Noticing that Chris was conscious, the medic said, "I see you're back. How ya doin'?" His homely, typically American face crinkled into a lively grin.

"You were lucky twice today. Not only did you survive the ambush, you also were goddamn lucky with this leg wound. Another half inch to the right and that fuckin' bullet would've blown out the main artery in your leg. Bleedin' to death ain't the worst way to die, but you're still just as dead."

As he talked, the medic continued to work on his leg, tugging and poking at the bandage with a skill developed for speed rather than dexterity. Raven, his mind finally lucid, grimaced and said, "Tell me, Doc, what did you do back in the world?" Chris' throat was so dry that his voice sounded like dry leaves rubbing together. "Let me guess. Did you butcher hogs, or maybe pound dents out of fenders? One thing for sure, you sure as hell weren't in the medical profession."

Chris softened his jibe by flashing the medic a smile. Holding his hand out for the soldier's canteen he muttered, "What do ya say, how about some water?"

Shaking his head, the smiling medic flipped him his

canteen and said, "You cowboys are all alike... bitch, bitch, bitch!"

Right in the middle of his answering smile, Raven remembered. He interrupted the medic who had started to ramble on about the dubious ancestry of Green Berets in general, and of Raven's in particular.

"What about my squad? Did anyone make it?"

Raven's face set into a mask. He knew the answer. By not saying anything, the medic confirmed his suspicions. Both remained silent. Each sensed that it was best not to say anything. Still, the medic's boyish face seemed to pinch together, and he gave a slight shake of his head as he concentrated on finishing wrapping Chris' leg.

Raven noticed that the pain in his leg had lessoned. He could still feel the pain, but the edges of the soreness had been rounded and softened. Must have gotten a shot, he speculated.

On the side of the medic's helmet cover was a rendering of an eagle. Chris stared at the pen drawing of the bird's gaping beak. When he saw the same thing on another soldier's pot, he recognized it for what it was... the symbol of the 101st Airborne Division, 'The Screaming Eagles.'

Chris thought, 'Paratroopers...my God... to think that my life was saved by some dog-faces with baggy-pants.'

Having finished with Raven's dressing, the medic began to put away his gear. He grinned and asked, "What do ya think of our wild Indian? From what I hear, he pretty much saved your ass."

It was like his words flipped the switch on a projector that was rerunning a film in Chris' mind. Once again he could see the Indian in all his wild disarray, working the slide-action of his snub-nosed shotgun and wearing that fierce grin.

Reality returned in a rush and Chris replied, "Yeah, he saved mine and totally kicked theirs."

WASICHU

For the first time, Raven looked the area over. Troopers were scattered all over the clearing in many different attitudes of repose. It was obvious that they had set up an LZ and were waiting for a chopper. Heat waves were shimmying above the tall grass. He could feel the sweat trickling down his side.

The medic's voice drew his attention. He had begun to ramble on about how "our Indian" managed to appear and disappear almost at will and how he had the highest body-count in their company. When he started talking about Nam in general, Raven let his thoughts drift.

Wiping the burning sweat from his eye, he thought of the ambush and of how lucky he had been. Being single and still alive, while his married buddy was taking up space in a body bag, was causing guilt to gnaw at him. He remembered the countless times that Johnny, in loving pride, had flashed the photos of his wife and two children.

With a conscious effort he pushed his ludicrous guilt out of his mind and, instead, thought about how good it felt to be alive. He wiped the sweat from his eyes and vowed not to bitch about the heat.

Seeing the medic rise to leave, Chris said, "Hey, Doc, before you go, there was one thing I wanted to ask. When the Indian took out that NVA officer did he…?"

His boyish grin lit up his face as he interrupted, "Hey, ask him yourself. What am I, a fuckin' secretary?"

He winked at Raven and hollered, "Hey, Chief!" gesturing at a nearby group of lounging troopers.

The medic gave Chris a slap on the shoulder and said, "Take care, cowboy."

Slinging his medical bag over his arm, he walked off.

"Later, Doc." Raven said.

He propped himself up on his elbows to see better. He saw the Indian stand up and leave the group. Chris was again impressed with the way the man moved. He's like a cat, he thought. When put outside, a cat always stops, looks in all directions and smells the air. Satisfied that there's no immediate danger, he moves on, occasionally stopping and looking behind to be sure that there is no threat from the rear.

The tall Indian moved in the same manner, he thought, but there was a difference. A cat's appearance doesn't show its lethal nature. One look at this Indian should convince just about anyone. He might as well have a sign around his neck, proclaiming, 'Danger... approach with caution!'

The trooper moved toward Raven with an effortless, self-assured grace. Chris guessed that he was about six-feet-two, a hundred-and-ninety pounds. He had dark skin with strong, handsome features. Raven mentally shook his head as he thought, 'the man is a walking arsenal.' Dangling from his right hand was the snub-nosed shotgun. His other hand was draped over the handle of a huge fighting knife. A bandoleer of shotgun shells was slung across one side of his deep chest, while a bunch of grenades were hanging from the other like a cluster of apples and oranges. Below the grenades, a Colt .45 automatic was riding his hip.

Raven was surprised when the trooper walked right up to him. He didn't think he'd recognize him with the blood cleaned off his face. In one fluid movement the Indian stopped, swung his Winchester pump across his lap, and squatted down next to him. Using his thighs for a gun rack and his knees as a table top for his forearms, he looked into Chris' eyes and let his body relax.

Raven felt impaled by a pair of eyes that were as black as midnight and hard as glass. Not one flicker of emotion showed on the Indian's face. The old adage, face like a wooden Indian, flashed through Chris' mind.

Suddenly, he smiled. It was like a ray of sunshine breaking through a wall of thunderheads. The contrast of the white smile on the dark face was startling. Raven was so

WASICHU

disarmed by the transformation he was speechless.

Nodding toward Raven's leg wound, he said, "I see you are going to make it. Is that right, man?" The man's voice had a whispery softness in its tone. His slight accent caused the word 'man' to be 'mon.'

Answering his nod, Chris replied, "Thanks to you."

There was a slight pause that Raven read the man as being shy. He wondered how shyness could be possible in a man of such decisive action. He decided to see if he could rattle his cage a little.

"Can I ask you something? It's been bothering me."

Raven caught his eye and held it. The Indian flashed his disconcerting smile again, followed by a small shrug, and said, "Sure, why not?"

Letting a little indignation show in his voice, Chris asked, "When you took out that NVA, how come you hit him with your fist? Why didn't you just bust a cap on the skinny son of a bitch?"

Eyes still locked with the Indian's, Chris went on, "I don't understand. You know, I was just a trigger squeeze away from becoming a pile of fucking fertilizer."

The Indian's gaze didn't waver. What had begun as a tease had turned into something else. Just talking about the incident had brought back the fear that Raven had camouflaging with anger.

Still looking into Chris' eyes the Indian began to speak. His voice was so quiet that it seemed to flow from his lips like smoke.

"You, being a wasichu (white man), will probably find this hard to understand."

He jabbed his chest with his left thumb as he said, "I am a Lakota and among my people we …"

Raven had stopped him with a raised hand and a sardonic look on his face.

"Just a minute… I think I know."

The Indian watched Raven's face. He saw the conflicting emotions: disbelief, anger, fear of what could have been. Then he saw the resolute look of acceptance pass across the white man's face. This is a man that is different from most, he thought.

Raven's eyes became animated as the realization hit him. With a savage grin he shook his head and said, "I don't believe this shit." In a surge of unrestrained enthusiasm, he pointed his finger as he said almost accusingly, "You're a Sioux Indian. You weren't just punching that 'dink,' you were counting coup. My God, I don't believe it."

Immediately upon hearing Raven's outburst, the Indian's eyes had opened wide and his hand had leaped up and briefly covered his mouth. The gesture was so obviously a show of surprise that, had he noticed it, Chris would have thought it hilarious.

Instead, he was so enamored by his discovery that he was blind to everything else. The fact that a man would use a century old Indian practice in Vietnam was so unbelievable that he threw his head back and laughed.

Some nearby troopers looked up. Seeing Raven they just shrugged and resumed what they were doing. Most soldiers thought that Green Berets were crazy anyway.

Seeing the seriousness of the Indian's demeanor, Raven calmed down. He was worried that he might have been close to becoming hysterical. Biting down a final chuckle, he thought, why in hell am I laughing? I could have been killed out there just because this guy wanted to play wild Indian.

Chris noticed that the guy was upset. Why, he wondered, what's the big deal?

All at once the trooper's black eyes were boring into Chris' gray ones as he asked, "How do you, a wasichu, know this?"

Deciding to show off a little, Raven replied, "The

same way I know that the Shoshone Indians were also known as the Snake Indians, or that Crazy Horse was an Oglala Sioux, and Captain Jack was a Modoc. It's no big deal. I used to read a lot. I've also read that among the Sioux, or Lakota, that counting coup, by striking the enemy with your hand, was considered the ultimate show of courage."

Raven couldn't put his finger on it, but he sensed that something was happening. All of a sudden he felt a strange rapport with this 'wild Indian.' He felt so at ease with him that he began to talk about himself. After a bit he even began to talk about when he was raised in an orphanage and foster homes.. Anyone that ever knew him, would not believe that he could be so candid.

Raven took a deep breath. He saw that the man's incredibly black eyes were still watching him so he said, "So not having any family gave me a lot of time for reading. Being here in 'Nam, I don't read much. Just keeping my ass in one piece is pretty much a full-time job."

During his spiel, Chris could have sworn that he saw a twinkle lurking in the dark, watchful eyes. Then the twinkle was gone and the trooper looked away and said, "I do not read here. This is a place for war."

He looked down for a moment. When he looked at Chris again the twinkle was back, and when he spoke, Raven could actually see his eyes soften.

"Most of my free time is spent writing to my family. I miss them."

He looked away momentarily, long enough to shake off the thought of his family, then looked back into Raven's eyes and offered his hand.

"Joe Spotted Horse."

Their hands met and held.

"Christopher Raven. I'll never forget that you saved my life, man."

Becoming progressively louder was the distant thud

of an approaching helicopter.

Still grasping Raven's hand, Spotted Horse shouted to be heard as he said, "Nor will I forget the wasichu that looked death in the eye, yet still had the courage to spit in that eye."

There was a sudden surge of activity as troopers scurried here and there preparing the LZ. Adding to the discomfort of everyone's sweating bodies was the cloud of dust and dirt kicked up by the Huey's arrival. Also arriving was the medic. Between him and Spotted Horse they were able to get Raven onto a stretcher and get him into a position for loading.

Raven, who had been busy scribbling, tore a page out of his notebook and handed it to Joe Spotted Horse. Shouting to be heard, he said, "If you think you can ever break that habit of counting coup and would like a shot at Special Forces, you can contact me at that base. I got a little pull, I can get you in. Think about it, man. We'd make a hell of a team."

The hammering din of the landing chopper drowned out Spotted Horse's reply. It seemed unlikely that they would ever meet again. But for some reason Raven had a feeling that their lives were going to be inexplicably linked. As the medic and the Indian crabbed their way, carrying Raven's stretcher toward the open door of the chopper, Chris sensed that this was not an ending... but merely a beginning.

Part 1
Butte

TWO

South Dakota... Spring, 1976

While half-stepping down a low hill, he saw the South Dakota landscape spread out before him like a green and tan patchwork quilt. The county road he was on cut through the sections of farmland with the absolute precision of having been drawn with a steel drafting tool.

Upon reaching the bottom of the grade, Christopher Raven lengthened his stride. As he moved into the ground-eating pace of the professional soldier, he shifted his backpack so that it rode higher on his back, giving balance to his forward impetus.

Six years of war and two years of drifting had eroded much of Raven's idealistic veneer but had strengthened his more solid beliefs. His lean face still retained its youthfulness, yet within the pale color of his eyes, there was revealed a subtle splinter of anguish. It had been three years since Joe Spotted Horse's death, but the pain was still alive and feeding on Raven's guilt-ridden soul.

Since his discharge from the army the pain had been a deterrent keeping him from reaching this point in his quest. Chris now felt prepared to face his demons and to fulfill a promise.

Looking across the prairie he precipitously smiled. There, rising like a boil on the earth's surface, was a butte. Beyond the butte and to the right was a towering dark mass of blue-gray hillocks; they were known by just about everyone as the Black Hills. It was the butte that was of primary interest to Raven. Ever since his friend's death he had known that one day he would find the sacred Bear Butte of the Sioux and Cheyenne. Upon finding it he would climb to its summit and perform a ceremony in memory of Joe Spotted Horse.

Years earlier in 'Nam, after they had become a team, Joe had made Raven promise that if he didn't make it back 'to the world' he would perform the ceremony that had been done for Joe's father and for his grandfather, from the very top of Bear Butte.

Being an orphan, Chris respected almost anything that pertained to family and had vowed that one day he would keep his promise. Now, seeing what he thought was Bear Butte in the distance, Raven felt an increase in his resolve to fulfill his pledge. As the afternoon began to slip away and the butte loomed much closer, Chris topped a small rise and saw some buildings in the distance that were crowding the lonesome stretch of highway. By the time he closed with the cluster of buildings, the sun was a red ball sitting to the left of the dominating silhouette of the butte. As he drew closer, the buildings evolved into a gas station, a cafe, a feed store and a tavern. The only place that looked open was the tavern. Loud music and occasional laughter spilled out into the street where a couple of pick-ups and an old beat up Chevy waited to be taken home.

Raven was about to walk on by when he spied an Indian sitting on a bench that leaned up against a wall of the bar. As he took the two steps leading up to the veranda-like porch, Chris saw that the Indian was very old and very drunk. Moving closer, he saw that the old man was barely conscious. He was dressed in filthy, cast-off clothing, yet still had enough pride to maintain the traditional braids and wear Lakota moccasins. Raven felt a twinge of pity as he shifted his pack and blanket-roll to a more comfortable position and squatted down in front of the old man. Looking at the haggard, withered face made him remember Joe's anguish when he had spoken of how alcoholism, indolence, and lack of traditional pride was destroying his people. Chris' eyes softened as he reached down and gently shook the old man's foot.

Suddenly, voices were raised inside the bar as tempers flared. An authoritative baritone voice came clearly through the door.

"I want you two outta here! We don't need none 'o yer trouble, hear?"

Raven ignored the voices as he saw the Indian's rheumy eyes peek open. Speaking softly in Lakota, Raven said, "Tell me uncle, am I near the Sacred Butte?" A spark of life ignited behind the dark eyes as the old Indian leaned forward and raised a shaky hand and pointed toward the distant butte. Chris smiled.

He looked up as the door came open with a bang and two hard-eyed cowboys stomped out onto the porch. Seeing Raven crouched by the Indian, they stopped.

What they saw was a lean six-footer dressed in dusty, faded blue jeans, a drifter in need of a shave, a haircut and a damn good reason to be talking to the Indian.

The first cowboy looked at his friend and slurred, "What the fuck we got here, Clint? Looks like we got us one 'o them hippies."

Clint, the bigger of the two, just blinked and stared. The talker had a big chew of tobacco he was working on. He pushed back his hat with his thumb and grinned.

Chris knew what was coming. Already the rage was beginning to kindle deep inside.

The talker leaned forward and spit a brown stream that hit the old man's moccasin foot and splattered onto Raven. He locked eyes with the talker and stood up. He wiped his hand on his jeans and using his thumbs readjusted the set of the shoulder straps of his backpack.

'Talker' wiped the back of his hand across his wet

mouth and uttered, "What's the matter, boy, din't ya like that? That's the way we treat hippy Injun lovers 'round here. Now, git!"

The simmering rage flared into a white hot fury. Raven smiled and replied, "I'll go, but not before you wipe your slobber off the old man's foot."

The redneck appeared to swell with anger. He exploded into action as he lunged forward muttering, "Why you red nigger lovin'..."

Raven stepped forward and underneath the cowboy's roundhouse right and buried his fist in his ample beer belly. Hot, fetid air and tobacco juice burst from the cowboy's mouth. He dropped like a rock to the wooden deck, gasping for air. The second cowboy was already reaching for Raven when he unexpectedly pivoted and kicked him squarely in the crotch. The cowboy's eyes bugged as he grabbed himself with both hands. Chris followed with a short, straight punch to the exposed throat. Clint gagged and dropped to his knees beside his sidekick. 'Talker' was on his hands and knees, choking on his chewing tobacco.

Raven twisted his fingers into 'Talker's hair. Ignoring his choking and sputtering, he dragged him over to the Lakota, who hadn't even moved. Chris savagely used the cowboy's face to clean the tobacco juice off his moccasin.

Releasing him, Raven straightened and resettled his back-pack and blanket-roll. Both rednecks were gasping and choking. Through watery, impassive eyes the old drunk watched the proceedings.

Bending from the waist Chris hovered over the two cowboys as he said, "Look at it this way, boys, it could've been worse... I could have taken off my pack. Think about that!"

The fire of Chris' rage diminished to hot coals as he turned to the old Sioux and thanked him in Lakota. The man's eyes momentarily came alive and he gave Raven a

WASICHU

brief nod before slipping back into a stupor.

Relinquishing the veranda's front stoop to the wheezing, coughing pair, Chris stepped back onto the county road and settled into his hiking stride. He moved faster now toward the distant presence of Bear Butte.

The old man kept his eyes closed. He heard the scuff of boots. The footsteps came to the doorway and stopped. The two cowboys were still coughing and clearing their throats. He heard a white man's voice say, "Hey, Harlan, come here, ya gotta see this."

The old Sioux listened to the clump of more boots and then the excited whispers of some other white men. Wheezing and more coughing came from nearby. When he heard laughter he thought it was directed at him. It became quiet. The same white voice spoke again, "Hey there, boys! You all been fightin'? Charlie, ya hear me? What's that brown shit all over yer face?"

The old one heard their derisive laughter. A large, gap-toothed grin spread across his weathered and wrinkled face.

THREE
~~~~~

The rising sun's fingers of light crept across the rolling terrain. In just moments the fingers changed and became an enveloping tide in a sea of illumination. Captured within this rising tide of light was the towering monolith, Bear Butte.

Christopher Raven stood at the base of the butte looking upward toward its summit far above. Standing there alone with his memories, Chris thought of his life before he had met Joe Spotted Horse. He remembered all the self-induced days of loneliness. This changed after his friendship with Joe, who had literally come into Raven's life as a savior. Joe's initial appearance was an explosion of emotional and physical energy that saved his life and sparked his new attitude toward others.

From time to time Raven pondered why he and Joe became so close. Perhaps it was because their life-styles ran a parallel course. Being an Indian made Joe something of a social outcast. Chris, being an orphan, had also felt the pressure of a sometimes cruel and unforgiving society.

Clutched in Raven's right hand was the figurine of a spotted horse that had been carved out of catlinite. The stylized horse was small, about two inches by one and a half. The pipestone was brick red in color with miniscule pale orange spots, and it was very old. Joe's father had passed it on to him as it had been passed on to the eldest son in their family for generations. Chris remembered Spotted Horse's reverence when he had told him about the sacred carving and of his responsibility to pass it on to his own son, Marlon. He recalled how Joe had vowed that when he returned from

'Nam he was going to do so.

Eyes misty, hand clenched tightly over the artifact, Raven thought of his friend's legacy and how much it meant to him. He also thought of all the time he had wasted since his discharge from the army. He dredged up the shameful memories of how his quick temper and stubborn pride had gotten him into numerous fights. It had been part of the reason why he had continued to move on, to drift. Yet, he never seemed satisfied enough in one place to want to stay there for very long.

While he drifted he was able to pick up a few bucks fighting at some of the local boxing clubs in the bigger cities. Boxing professionally helped him to channel some of his anger and frustrations. Since he had always loved the sport and had done a lot of amateur boxing in the army he figured that the rigorous training regime and the fierce action in the ring would be good for him. He had also studied martial arts during his army years. He had loved it, but after his discharge, the opportunities to compete disappeared along with his interest.

He looked again at the summit and resolved to return the artifact to Joe's son on the reservation right after the ceremony. Having waited so long to return the horse, he felt embarrassed to be showing up at such a late date.

A slight morning breeze swept in from the north, sending a chill across his shoulders and motivating him into action. Pocketing the artifact, he slung his back-pack over his shoulders and stepped out in the direction of the southeast trail that led up to the butte's summit, and Raven's ultimate confrontation with Joe's Gods.

While he walked, Chris smiled as he thought of some of his lighter moments with Joe Spotted Horse and his sense of humor. The incident that had him smiling had happened before Raven had met him. The story had been told to him by a paratrooper from Joe's old outfit. It was about a redneck

WASICHU

Indian hater 'back in the world,' by the name of Wilson. This guy had made Joe's life a living hell by mistreating him with racial slurs, war whoops, and the sneering use of the nickname, 'chief.'

Chris could still hear the sound of the hillbilly twang in the trooper's voice as he told him the story.

"Yes, sir, one night when Wilson was doin' his four hour stretch o' guard duty at the motor pool, he began hittin' on joints. Later on, he commenced to do a little noddin' in the back o' a covered truck. Well sir, all o' a sudden he woke up an' the way I hear'd it, his eye-balls were so wide open you couldn't have shut 'em with a pair o' vice grips."

At that point in the story Raven had to wait while his host went through a whole series of belly laughs and knee slaps. After he pumped another beer into him, he finally got him on track again.

"Yep, ol' Wilson's eyes were poppin' right out o' his skull. 'Cause in the poor light in the back o' that truck all he knew fer sure was that six-feet-plus o' naked, painted savage were sittin' astride him an' had a fist full o' his hair. He were wavin' the biggest ol' knife you ever did see right under Wilson's nose. Then Joe pushed that big sticker o' his right up against Wilson's hairline. I guess he must o' nicked him a little 'cause some blood had run in his eye. Well anyway, Joe only said four words to Wilson. 'Remember this night, wasichu.' Wilson passed out, fainted jus' like a girl... don't thet beat all? Ya know, from thet day on, Wilson never said another word ta Joe, an' they were in the same outfit fer another three, four months... not one word. If ol' Joe were ta walk within a few feet o' him, Wilson would turn as white as a Klansman's sheet an' beat it ta hell out o' there."

Raven laughed aloud as he recalled the glee expressed on the face of the trooper as he finished his story. He shook his head when he remembered how he'd made a night of it with Joe's troopers and paid dearly for it the following morning.

He was still chuckling when he adjusted his stride to accommodate the sudden increase in the incline. Off to his left he saw the A-frame tourist center swathed in morning sunlight. Seeing the building served as a reminder that later in the morning tourists would be using the very same trail to climb Bear Butte. The ceremony, he thought, wasn't going to take very long but he sure didn't want an audience.

Thinking of the ceremony made Chris recall their return from a particularly scary S.O.G. mission. He and Joe had gotten drunk and, like a couple of kids, had pledged their brotherhood by getting themselves tattooed.

Raven shifted his pack and opened his shirt. He hooked his thumbs behind the shoulder straps and leaned into the climb. Thinking of the black raven that Joe had tattooed on his chest made him foolishly glance at his own chest. Foolishly, because unless he was a contortionist he couldn't possibly see his own tattoo. The man had proved to be a true artist. While looking at Joe's artifact, the craftsman had done an exact rendering of the spotted horse carving just above Chris' heart.

It was on that same night that Spotted Horse had spoken of Bear Butte for the first time. He spoke of what a sacred, religious place it was to him and his people. He had told Raven some of their secret rituals; this included ceremonies and other things that stimulated his interest. Raven was fascinated. It had opened a whole new world to him. Spotted Horse had even talked him into learning the Lakota language. Chris had balked at first and had rationalized that he'd never use it. Joe had countered with the argument that he didn't have anything else to do in his spare time. Joe's final persuading factor had done the job. He said, "When you come to visit me on the 'Res' you will be able to impress the pretty ones with your fluency. I am sure that they will be amazed to hear a wasichu speak Lakota."

WASICHU

As the incline increased, Raven moved the back-pack higher, lessoning the pull on his shoulder straps. Still thinking of Joe, he increased his pace. The seldom used muscles began to stretch and strain, adjusting to their new duties.

As much as he tried, he couldn't ignore the little white signs that were placed at random along the winding, twisting path. With a shake of his head Raven said aloud, "Wonder what kind of idiots visit this place if the locals feel that they have to label everything and even point the way for up or down."

Getting caught up in his own silly thoughts, he mused about how nice it would have been if they had these signs in 'Nam. In his mind he could picture little arrow shaped white signs with various messages painted on them, such as: BOOBY TRAP, PROCEED WITH CAUTION or MINED AREA, STAY OUT.

Nearing the summit, his ludicrous mood left him. It was replaced by a resolve unlike any he had experienced before. When Raven had finally taken the steps to fulfill his promise to Joe, he had made a pledge to himself also that he would return the artifact and complete the ceremony in his honor. Now, his only concern was that he perform the ritual in the correct manner. He must do it the same as Joe's forefathers had done, but this ceremony was to be a eulogy in Joe Spotted Horse's honor, nothing more.

FOUR
~~~~~

At the top Raven rested. The breeze was noticeably stronger at the higher elevation. Pleased with his excellent conditioning, Chris noted that he was still breathing at a normal rate and was only lightly perspiring. Beginning with a brief exploration of the top, he noticed how the exposure to the sun and wind had stunted the growth of the trees and other foliage. He had experienced an eerie feeling right away. It was so quiet, the silence seemed to seep into his pores.

Shaking off the feeling, Raven moved through the stunted pine and rock formations. Closer to the edge his gaze absorbed the uninterrupted beauty of the vast prairie. On three sides the view was pretty much the same, gently undulating hills of tilled land, with only an occasional ranch house and a scatter of trees to break the sameness of the terrain. From the southwest side of Bear Butte he saw the rugged, wild profile of Paha Sappa, the Black Hills.

Staring at the towering hills, Chris thought of the many times that Joe Spotted Horse had spoken of them. He remembered the curious mixture of anger and reverence whenever he spoke of them. The anger was directed toward the white bureaucracy that had allowed the land to be stolen from his people. The reverence in his voice had derived from the Sioux belief that the Black Hills belonged to their gods.

Although many people might have a problem dealing with Joe's passion for an incident that had taken place so many years ago, Raven did not. Besides all of the reading that he had done on the North American Indians, his relationship with Spotted Horse had really opened his eyes and had set him on the right path toward understanding the

Sioux and their way of life. An example of Lakota family pride was told by Joe. Raven could still picture the intensity flowing from Spotted Horse's ebony eyes as he told of how his fourth generation grandfather had defeated and killed a chief of the Mandans in individual combat. Because of the custom of the times, Joe's grandfather was able to take his defeated enemy's name for his own. This he had done and had immediately been renamed Spotted Horse.

The first time Chris had heard the story he had been amazed. How in the world, he had wondered, did a people with no written history manage to do that?

Putting all thoughts of history aside, Raven moved closer to the western edge of the summit. He found a natural little alcove among a cluster of rock that formed a ledge that was like a small amphitheater. Behind the ledge there loomed several gnarled and weathered pine.

Instinctively Raven knew that he had found the right spot for what he was about to do. Removing his back-pack he carefully set it down, making sure that he didn't bump it against any rocks. He had handled the pack with extra care so that neither the ammunition nor the movable parts of the weapon inside would get banged around.

As Chris unrolled his blanket-roll, Spotted Horse's pump shotgun from Vietnam rolled out. It had been broken down into three pieces, but even so, from the tip of its snub-nosed barrel to the curve of its exposed hammer, it looked every bit the vicious weapon it was. If someone were to ask Raven why he had risked smuggling Joe's shotgun from 'Nam, he might have been able to come up with a few valid reasons; in truth, he didn't know why. At the time he just felt he had to do it.

While removing the other items from the blanket-roll and pack, his mind drifted back and forth between the function of the items he was assembling to use in the ceremony and thoughts of Joe and their friendship.

WASICHU

Taking five cherry-wood sticks from his pack, Chris moved around within the alcove's perimeter and forced four of them into the ground in the four directions, forming a squared rough circle. The fifth was driven into the dirt in the middle of the circle, representing the center of the universe. The four directional sticks made the circle about twenty feet in diameter.

In his mind, Raven could almost hear Joe as he once again gave his soft-voiced instructions. He recalled how Joe's voice shook with the passion and emotion of a true believer as he described the importance of each and every detail in performing a ceremony. When speaking of the four directions Joe had said, "One stick must be facing west for courage; another to the north for strength; one toward the east to gain wisdom; and the final stick placed toward the south for spiritual growth."

Chris had been enthralled listening to Joe as he diagramed the step-by-step procedure of the ritual. It wasn't so much the sacred ceremony, as it was the man explaining it. He really believed!

Joe had explained the use of the cherry-wood and how, "On each of the sticks a strip of cloth must be attached: white for north, yellow for the east, black for the south, and red for the west. These four colors represent the four major races of our world."

Raven was torn from his remembering by a sudden gust of wind. Looking at the sky, he could see movement among the many clouds. The sun was shining and the air was balmy, yet Chris had a feeling he had best hurry and get it over with.

Taking the pipestone talisman from his pocket, he carefully placed it in the center of the circle. He then looked around and quickly began to undress. While doing so, he concentrated on clearing his mind of everything except that pertaining to the ensuing ceremony. Once again he reminded himself of how adamant his friend had been that each detail of the ritual be followed exactly. Chris decided that this ceremony was going to be done right, the way Joe would have insisted that it be done.

Naked, he ignored the sudden rise of 'goose flesh' caused by the rapidly cooling air and began to move about in the circle, performing those little details that Joe had deemed as being so important. He removed everything from his pack that was needed and placed the pack and his clothing outside of the circle. Raven carefully tied the colored cloth strips onto their respective sticks. He placed a wooden bowl, with an offering of dried fruit inside, near the center stake.

Shaking out his blanket he briefly wrapped himself in it, luxuriating in its sudden warmth. He had purchased the blanket two days ago, knowing that a new blanket was mandatory for the ceremony, buying that particular one because it was a duplicate of the old Hudson Bay trading item. The bright red color had also attracted him.

After spreading the items out and repositioning the offerings, he absentmindedly placed Joe's shotgun near them to hold things in place. The wind gusts began to increase. Raven moved about within the circle sprinkling tobacco. As he moved, his eyes would frequently seek out the pump-gun. Suddenly he stopped. Another puff of wind buffeted against him. He swayed momentarily and then scattered his remaining tobacco as though it was an offering to the wind rather than an important part of the ritual.

Exasperated, Chris stepped quickly over beside Joe's shotgun. The three parts appeared to gleam malevolently up at him. He couldn't understand what it was about the gun that was bothering him. He stood there for a moment longer, staring at the back-pack. Raven was thinking of the one hundred prepared shotgun shells, the reloading kit, plus the powder and caps that were nestled inside and wondered if maybe they should be further from the circle. Looking at the shotgun again, he wondered if maybe he should assemble it. Realizing that his thinking was really getting goofy, he threw his arms in the air in frustration.

Shaking his head, Raven suddenly grinned. Looking down at his nakedness and at the forgotten blanket trailing from his hand, he rationalized that a man just naturally gets confused if he has to do a little thinking without his pants on.

Dismissing his uneasiness as simply a case of nerves because of his determination to do it right, Chris hurried through his procedures. He noticed that the wind had really begun to pick up. Ominous black clouds had moved in blotting out the early morning sun. Moving with a new found sense of urgency, he hurried to the center prayer stick and deftly picked up the pipestone horse carving. Gesturing toward the center stick, Raven muttered a quick prayer to Earth Mother. Using the same prayer, he repeated it to Sky Father. Clutching the blanket to him with one hand, and carrying the horse carving in the other, he moved quickly to the remaining four stakes. The wind's velocity had increased so much that Chris had difficulty standing immobile long enough to say the short prayer. Thunder began to crash and boom with the ominous portent of an artillery barrage. The noise was becoming deafening!

Having finished with his prayer at each of the four directions, Raven looked up at the rolling clouds. As the thunder hammered at his ears, he thought of Joe and how he referred to thunder as Thunder Beings, warriors of the Sky Father. He then remembered that the Thunder Beings were used by Sky Father for showing displeasure. Suddenly, he knew what it was that had bothered him about Joe's shotgun. Metal of any kind was prohibited from being inside the sacred circle! Raven made a sudden move toward the gun and then stopped. Realizing what he was allowing his mind to accept, he chided himself. Even while being nearly blown off his feet by a violent gust, he thought, there is no way that

BARRY BRIERLEY

I am going to believe that this storm was caused by the Sky Father's being pissed at me for having metal in the ceremony... no way! He quickly made his way to the center and replaced the artifact with the other offerings.

Another gust of wind nearly wrenched the blanket from his grasp and swept him off his feet. The clouds were moving so fast they seemed to tumble into each other. The stunted trees encircling his little amphitheater were whipping to and fro as though frenzied. He had never in his life seen a sky so full of impending violence.

Adding to the din of the thunder, lightning began to strike out on the prairie. Putting his hands over his ears, Raven felt the first tentacles of fear clutch at his stomach. The fear blossomed as he watched the stabs of lightning strike with crackling explosions of sound all around Bear Butte. Their violent thrusts lit the darkening sky with intense flashes of illumination.

He stood frozen to the spot unable to move from the circle. Suddenly there was a blinding flash of sparks and flame and a thunderous explosion!

With the pungent stench of sulphur in his nostrils, Raven felt his body leave the ground, being launched through the air as if shot from a catapult! Pain knifed through his shoulder as he struck a pine bough and then another, falling through the branches until he abruptly hit the ground. The air exploded from his lungs. Chris was still struggling to breathe when his senses were enclosed in a shroud of darkness.

The colors were breathtaking. The dancers, all men, were dressed in beautiful costumes; skins that were bleached to near white and pale yellow, softly tanned and adorned with brightly colored beads and woven quills. Many feathers, shells, elk teeth and colorful stones were in abundance among their paraphernalia. The dancers appeared to be

WASICHU

suspended, floating in air yet still able to move with fluid grace.

It was like watching a film without sound. The vivid colors and graceful movements formed a collage of primitive pageantry and savage artistry. Soon the images began to fade. Then they returned and with their image came the sound of chanting. Their color and movements were in perfect clarity until the singing and chanting began to fade. The images also began to fade until they were almost gone, when suddenly, superimposed over the fading dancers, was the bucking, twisting figure of a wild horse. First viewed from a distance, it slowly grew closer until it was squarely in front of him. Raven screamed.

It was Joe's pipestone horse that had come to life, lunging, kicking... drawing nearer with each twisting movement. A lump had formed in Chris' throat. He couldn't breathe! His heart felt ready to burst with each successive beat. It was so close that he felt suffocated by its foul breath, and so close that, had he been able to move, Raven was certain that he could have touched one of the red, glowing eyes.

Even though it moved and breathed as though alive it still retained its carved stone form. The dark red of its glossy surface intensified as an aura-like glow surrounded the menacing figure.

It gave one more violent, thrusting lunge, and then landed, standing astride Raven. Vapor exploded from the carved nostrils as the horror stretched its neck, stone teeth reaching, seeking . . .

Part 2
Lakota

FIVE
~~~~

Dakota Territory... Spring, 1876

The eagle screamed.

Raven opened his eyes to a blue world. Everywhere he looked was the startling blue of a flawless sky.

The eagle screamed again, entering Chris' field of vision from the left. With its six foot wing span fully extended, it hovered for a moment directly above him and then glided back to the left and out of view. My God, he thought, it can't be more than fifty feet above the ground. Then he remembered where he was. He recalled climbing the butte, the storm and the lightning striking near him. He cautiously sat up, flexed a sore shoulder, and checked himself over for other injuries. Finding none, he started to do a few stretching exercises, then stopped and stared at himself. Shit, he realized, I'm bare-assed naked! It then dawned on him that there could be a whole grade school class approaching the top of the butte at any moment.

With a cool breeze adding to Raven's motivation, he rushed to where he had left his clothing. While dressing, he had a feeling that something wasn't quite right. Things appeared different. It's the terrain, he mused, it seems changed somehow. It was as though there are more trees and brush in new areas and less in others. He felt confused and nervous about the new situation.

Standing in the one place, shirt half tucked into his jeans but now forgotten, Chris let his gaze sweep the summit. Suddenly, he whirled, eyes searching for danger. It was then he noticed that somebody had been there. Some of the things in the sacred circle had been moved. His heart seemed to stop beating. Joe's horse carving was gone! His sweeping gaze picked up the gleam of the shotgun parts and the canvas of his back-pack. He couldn't understand it. Why would someone steal a stone carving and leave an expensive shotgun and back-pack? It just didn't make sense.

Raven finished getting dressed. A quiet anger was building inside him as he moved around the area and repacked his gear. Suddenly, he saw some objects sitting on a rock shelf. He had been so intent on finding the horse carving that he hadn't noticed them. There were two handmade bowls and a small, intricately beaded fetish. It looked like a turtle. The beaded designs had been worked into beautiful geometric patterns.

Totally baffled, Raven hurriedly finished packing his gear. He quickly concealed the broken down parts of the pump shotgun in his horseshoe-shaped blanket-roll and strapped it to the pack. Shouldering the back pack, he immediately began to look for a sign, a clue, footprints or whatever. He needed something to give him some sort of direction.

His searching brought him close to the western edge of the summit. His nearness to the lip caused him to look up. What Raven saw made him gasp and stare so hard that he lost his balance and had to scramble back from the edge. Far below, next to a small lake, was a scattering of Indian tipis.

With a quick sigh of relief, Raven concluded that he was looking at tipis at a 'Buck skinner's Rendezvous... a club of black powder enthusiasts that periodically drive for miles with their families over weekends and holidays, getting together to live the way it was pre-1840. They would set up their tipis and only dress in clothing that had been worn during that era.

Chris sensed that the answer to the disappearance of the carving was in that encampment. In Raven's mind these people would be the ones who would recognize the value of an artifact such as the spotted horse. He concluded they had left the bowls and the fetish as a trade for their guilt.

Not wanting to waste a second, Chris spun away from the sacred butte's panoramic view and moved quickly toward the path that would take him off the butte.

Upon seeing the tipis, had Raven taken the time to really look at what was there, instead of seeing what he wanted to see, he might not have been in such a hurry to leave the butte. Had he really looked at that encampment he might have noticed the inordinate number of horses present and the total absence of motorized vehicles. If he had just glanced over the vast amount of prairie visible from that altitude, he would have been amazed. As far as the eye could see from Bear Butte's towering stature, there was absolutely no sign of human habitation except the tipis. There were no cars, no farms, not even a road or section of tilled soil. There was nothing to see but the prairie grasses, undulating in the wind, and the distant, rugged hills of a wilderness that existed one hundred years ago.

Moving through the rough terrain at the base of the butte, Raven struggled to grasp the reality of his situation. He shifted his pack to a more comfortable hang and tried desperately to find a reasonable explanation to the sights that he was witnessing. This can't be, he thought, I'm either hallucinating or I'm losing my mind.

Still moving westward, he passed the area where the paved county road had been less than an hour ago. Although he was confused and worried by all the changes and the unbelievably empty plain, Raven obstinately directed his strides toward the 'buck-skinner's' camp and his search for whoever walked off with the artifact. Trying to keep his mind on a tight track, he concentrated on the distant tipis and for the first time noticed that there weren't any vehicles in sight. But he did see a herd of horses on the north side of the camp.

Stubbornly refusing to acknowledge what he was and wasn't seeing, Chris mused aloud. "Wonder where in hell all their transportation is hidden. They can't all be that dedicated." He knew that some of the true traditionalists wouldn't even think of using lighter, or even matches, to start a fire. The dedicated buck skinners would use nothing but flint and steel. Even so, he thought, somebody has to have a car or truck stashed out of sight somewhere.

Closer now, he could see several horses with riders separating from the pony herd and a group of figures on foot converging with them. When the two groups came together, Raven couldn't make out any detail at all. With the horses and their riders milling about, a cloud of red dust was lifting. Because of the sun, all of the figures within the dust became abstract objects that shimmered and danced. The sight only added to Raven's state of disbelief.

Still moving in his soldier's gait, the early morning sun's warmth began to draw perspiration from his body. Birds were singing and flying here and there. He saw a lizard dart under a rock ledge. An eagle was a tiny dot far above him riding the wind. These were things Chris knew were real and, because they were, he made himself take note of them. Cataloging and digesting them, he did whatever was necessary to hang onto his fading sense of reality.

Being forced into a dangerous situation helped Raven retain his sanity as he was given focus and the opportunity to do what he was very good at... surviving.

Suddenly a horse and rider burst out of the dust cloud at a full gallop. Then another one rode into the open and, all at once, there were six of them heading straight for him! An immediate sense of impending danger plucked at his awareness. Shrugging out of his pack, Raven began fumbling with the blanket-roll straps and then stopped. He realized that he didn't have time to get the pump-gun out and assembled. Shit, he thought, I'm probably just paranoid. He

WASICHU

decided to wait for them, thinking that they probably just look threatening.

He suddenly heard a trilling sound coming from the camp, a noise that was coming from many throats. The strange sound caused the hair on the back of his neck to stir. He felt a trickle of sweat slide down his back.

The riders were quiet... no yelling, whooping, or anything. Apprehension began to twist Raven's stomach into a knot of anxiety as the riders became more visible.

He couldn't believe what he was seeing. "Jesus H. Christ!" he exclaimed.

They were now close enough for him to see their faces. He stared in disbelief. They were all Indians! With weapons in hand, eyes blazing, they were locked onto Raven like a thirty-six legged, heat seeking missile.

In the Indian camp, the old man who had first seen the lone wasichu coming from their sacred butte had mistaken him for a walk-a-heap (Bluecoat infantry) and had initiated the cry, "Natan Uskay (Attacker coming)!" Several warriors nearby had rushed to their horses. Those that were able grabbed whatever weapon was available, several had none.

It didn't really matter that some had no weapons, as their primary responsibility was to evaluate the impending danger to their village and to report the number of enemy approaching. They were also expected to engage the enemy and do whatever necessary to slow their advance.

It was easy to see how Raven was mistaken for a soldier. Since he was a soldier for most of his life, he walked like one, and he wore blue denim jeans and jacket. To an old man's tired eyes, blue is blue, and all the soldiers in his world wore blue.

Nervously, he watched them come. Then the anxiety was replaced with anger. Now was the time for action, not for analyzing his mental health.

When Raven had first seen the riders, he had just started down a low hill. Retrieving his pack, he quickly returned to the top of the incline as military instincts directed him. Fumbling with the straps on his pack, he thought, this time the high ground will be a distinct advantage. When the Indians' horses hit the base of the slope, the momentum would be forcefully slowed. Instead of simply riding over Raven, the horses would have to lurch up the hill at less than half the speed they had attained in reaching it.

Raven crouched over his pack and covertly watched them come. As he had predicted, when the six ponies hit the bottom of the hill, their speed was so dramatically decreased that Chris had enough time to remove his blanket-roll from the pack before they reached him.

The lead Indian's name was Wolf's Spirit. He was a proud, fierce, young warrior. In his eagerness to be the first to count coup, his arrogance caused him to be a trifle too reckless. He allowed his stallion to surge a couple of lengths ahead of the others. As his horse bucked and lunged up the slope, Wolf's Spirit saw the white man squatting, bending over something red and brown laying at his feet. His back was toward him.

In one continuous motion, Raven grabbed his three-and-a-half-foot blanket-roll, straightened, pivoted, and swung around as though he was Hank Aaron going for a high, fast ball. The make-shift bat, weighted down with Joe's dismantled shotgun, caught Wolf's Spirit square in the chest!

Just before the blanket-roll made contact with the lead Indian, Chris caught a glimpse of a surprised pair of black eyes framed by a dark and hostile face. Then they were gone, swept away with the momentum of the sweeping club.

The well-padded blanket-roll didn't seriously hurt the young warrior, but it took him off his horse and out of the fight.

WASICHU

When Wolf's Spirit's stallion lunged by, his haunch brushed against Raven, knocking him off balance. By the time he had recovered, the other five were all around him.

Dodging and weaving, Chris spun in a circle using his weighted blanket-roll like a medieval knight wielding his mace. It glanced off a pony's nose. The horse screamed! It reared over backwards throwing his rider! Raven struck another rider in the shoulder, the impact left him reeling and barely able to stay on his pony.

Moving, feinting, Raven choked on the red dust and became suffused by a towering rage. He swung the roll in an arc like a two-handed broadsword. Left, right, he slashed with a mindless ferocity! Suddenly they were all around him. Off their ponies, they reached for him as he slashed and stroked in each and every direction. All at once his roll was knocked out of his hands. He fought on with his fists, enjoying the jolt and pain when his knuckles met bone. Even when his adversary attempted to slide away from his consuming fury, Raven attacked relentlessly. Blood was beginning to ooze from his knuckles and other abrasions, but they were nothing that could incapacitate him. The cuts and bruises probably helped, more than hindered, by adding fuel to the fire of his rage.

Being nearly overwhelmed, Raven had to switch to a defensive style of fighting. Having managed to fight his way to a small outcrop of sandstone, he put his back against it. Using both boxing and karate, he put two more down. Shit, he thought, that made five down altogether and he counted at least four more to his direct front. With a sinking feeling inside, he saw even more riders coming from the camp. Refusing to let the reinforcements dis-courage him, Chris fought on. A glancing blow from a hatchet had him reeling until a vicious punch to the throat sent the warrior, choking and gagging, into the dirt.

When the two in front of him hesitated, Raven was

able to look beyond them at the thunderous arrival of a new development. The two warriors saw the new arrival and stepped back. The rider brought his horse to a sliding stop and effortlessly slipped from his back. Chris took one look and thought, oh shit, looks like I've really stepped in it now.

The new guy had to be at least six-and-a-half feet tall and tip the scales at about two-hundred-and-forty pounds. Dangling from his right fist was a war club that was four feet long. Fastened to the end of it was a stone the size of a cantaloupe.

The Indian, his gaze fastened onto Raven, strode purposely forward until he stopped a dozen feet away. Bruised and battered, Raven shifted his feet and readjusted his fighting stance.

The two men that had been in front of Chris, spoke to the giant in a language that was vaguely familiar. As they backed away the big warrior merely grunted. In a loud, resonant voice he exclaimed, *"Washtay, wasichu chickala* (Greetings, little white man)!"

Raven was utterly stunned. Lakota, he thought, he's speaking Lakota! His mind raced. The odds in favor of a half-naked stranger speaking to him in an ancient language, late in the 20th century, had to be nonexistent. The implied alternative was staggering.

"What in the fuck have I gotten myself into?"

Confused and disoriented, Chris was thinking out loud. If shock was a hammer he would have been driven into the ground like a flesh and blood spike. He had been so busy trying to stay alive that the strangeness of his adversaries hadn't made the impact on him that it should have. After hearing no English spoken, just Sioux, and after looking, staring, it was almost too much; the long hair, braids, loin cloths. For Christ's sake, he thought, there's even one brave running around buck-assed naked.

Raven straightened, took a quick step forward, and

WASICHU

locked eyes with the huge warrior. By physically moving, he was also mentally moving the enigma to the back of his mind and out of the way. At the moment he had a more immediate situation to deal with... namely, a six-foot-five situation... with a bad attitude.

Clearing his mind, Raven suddenly stepped forward and moved away from the rocks. The warrior crouched and brought his war club into a more ready position.

Raven began to slowly move to his right. When it looked as though the Indian would have to turn to keep watching him, Chris stopped and repeated the maneuver to his left. While moving, he kept an eye on the rest of the Sioux. The Lakota, as though they had read his mind, moved back and out of the way.

In an attempt to bolster his confidence, Chris began to talk to himself. "Well, looks like these guys think that you haven't got a chance in hell, don't it?"

As Raven talked he continued to move. The Sioux's eyes fastened onto him as though they were stapled there.

Not wanting the Lakota to know that he spoke their language, Chris used English. From what he knew about Indians he was pretty sure that they enjoyed a little bravado. The only problem being that he would have to back it up with performance.

He won't understand what I'm saying, he thought, but he will sure as hell understand my tone. Raven began to taunt the warrior.

"I may be as good as dead, but by God, I'm not going to die at the hands of this overgrown piece of shit!"

To the on-looking Sioux, Raven looked like a wolf pacing back and forth in front of a grizzly; continuing to move while looking for an opening to attack. The watching warriors had now been joined by women, and even children, to witness their champion warrior destroy the wasichu with the magical fighting skills.

Raven had other ideas. He continued to taunt. His confidence level soared as the adrenalin pumped through his veins.

"I'm going to take you out, Pal! Nothin' personal, but you have to go!"

While Raven continued his pacing maneuver, the big Sioux watched him like a cat staring at what was about to become his next meal. His only movement was his head as he followed Chris with his eyes, watching and waiting for him to make his move so that he could kill him.

Raven was hoping that the warrior wouldn't notice that with each change of direction he was moving fractionally closer. Also, with each swing to the right, Raven was moving just a little bit closer to the limit of the Indian's peripheral vision. Eventually, to enable him to keep Raven in sight, he would have to step back and to the left.

When he takes that step, Chris thought, his ass will be mine. If not, I could wind up with a butt-ugly haircut.

The Sioux had moved into a deeper crouch, swinging his monstrous war club up across his body and cradling it in his left hand.

Chris slowed his pace, thinking, he must have noticed I've been moving closer. He hoped he hadn't noticed the wider swing. He hadn't. When Raven was about four strides away, he did it. He took that step!

Before the step had traveled more than half its intended distance, Raven was moving with blurring speed.

As he launched his attack, the Sioux warning outcry, "A-ah!" leaped from Chris' throat.

His shout startled the Indian just enough so that there was a heartbeat of a pause, right in midstep.

That minute pause gave Raven the correct timing to complete his move. Before the Sioux's foot was firmly planted the fight was all but over.

Raven's step, pivot, spinning back-kick smashed into

WASICHU

the Indian's foot just below the ankle bone! The force of the blow, which kicked the leg back in the direction it had come from, completely destroyed the huge man's sense of balance. As he fell, hopelessly struggling to recapture his lost equilibrium, Raven completed his follow through and delivered a crushing, edged heel side-kick to the temple.

The swift, perfectly timed kick had landed before the Sioux's body hit the ground. As the huge man hit the dirt it set adrift a veil of red dust. Chris' fist penetrated the dust with a short, straight punch that landed on the exact spot of the temple where the kick had landed only seconds before.

Completing his punch, Raven automatically returned to a ready position. Standing over the Sioux, he looked down at the deep rise and fall of the massive chest and spat out the bitter adrenalin aftertaste and the word, "*Anho!*" (the Lakota utterance used when counting coup)

A sudden, guttural murmur came from the circle of dark-faced watchers, "Huhn, huhn."

The Sioux courage cry was like a chant with its lack of inflection and its gut deep resonance. The strange sound sent a shiver up Chris' spine. Looking away from the sea of hostile faces, the heady mixture of sweat, fear, and exhaustion caused Raven to sway momentarily.

The voice of a child, or woman, broke the silence.

"A-ah!"

Raven's head whipped toward the warning voice. What he saw was a kaleidoscope of images that flashed across his retina in a millisecond of time.

About one-hundred-fifty feet away was a group of horsemen who had just arrived. One rider was standing in his wooden stirrups, his right elbow at a right angle to his body. He was aiming a bow and arrow straight at him!

As though it was a series of frames seen through the lens of a slow-motion camera, Chris saw the Indian's fingers flare open as they released the arrow. The slender shaft leaped from the bow, the bow string slackened. Instantly the arrowhead filled his whole vision! Reflex! A searing pain burned above his left ear. His eyes closed and he fell. The last sound Raven heard was the eerie, guttural, "Huhn, huhn."

EXCERPT FROM THE JOURNAL OF CETAN CHICKALA (LITTLE HAWK)

The first time I saw the wasichu was the very day he arrived among my people, the Lakota.

It was a morning during the Moon of the New Grass, which the white people call April. He came at a time when we were wary of just about everyone. Our traditional hunting grounds were in constant threat because of the encroachment of the wasichus. Everywhere that our nomadic ways took us, we of Spotted Horse's band of Minneconjou, would find either Bluecoats or other wasichus, such as those who are forever searching for the yellow metal. Sometimes our land is filled with those who want to build permanent dwellings and tear at the breast of the Earth Mother with their metal knives.

We were camped beside a small lake almost within the protective shadow of Paha Mato, our sacred butte. It was at this time and place, when I was but twelve winters of age, that the wasichu entered my life and changed it forever.

I was guarding the pony herd with my friends at the northern edge of our camp when we heard the old one give the warning shout, "Natan uskay (Attackers are coming)!"

Several of our warriors, those that were camped closest to the horses, rushed in among them selecting their ponies. In spite of their haste, I was able to delay one of them long enough for him to tell me that a walk-a-heap soldier had been seen walking toward our camp from the direction of Bear Butte.

It was Kills Twice. The thin-faced young warrior said, "If there is one, there must be others. We must find out!"

As he reined his pony around and rode away I looked beyond him to the rising red dust on the open prairie.

The sun was in my eyes but by shading them with my hand I was able to see. Situated as I was on an outcrop of red sandstone I *was able to see quite well. There! I saw the Bluecoat. He was walking down a small hill. When our warriors burst into the open, leaving the pony herd and their dust behind them, I could hear the excited voices of some of the women as they made the trilling sound to encourage our warriors and to make their hearts large.*

I registered my gaze onto the wasichu. I was in time to see him stop and turn as if to run. But no, he moved quickly back to the top of the little hill. He removed the small travois-like load from his back and knelt beside it.

The warriors looked like they were going to sweep right over the top, but things don't always work out the way you expect them to. Their ponies slowed as they lurched and bucked their way up the hillock. The horse out in front was a large black stallion so I knew that his rider was Wolf's Spirit. Wolf was one of our band's most notable young warriors. He was almost on top of the crouching Bluecoat when, all at once, the wasichu straightened up and Wolf's Spirit went backwards off his horse! Then a pony fell down. They were all around the wasichu now, but I could not see because of the clouds of dust.

People were now rushing in among the pony herd making my responsibility meaningless. I leaped on my pony's back and forced my way past the running groups of people and in among the many lodges of our village.

I saw that one of our akacita was beginning to establish some order and to slow down those who were beginning to panic. Yet it was still necessary that I take care for many were running in all directions.

Akacita are warriors that are hand-picked by our council elders to oversee and keep order within our camps and while on the trail. They are much like the wasichu's police or the reservation police, which we later would call metal breasts. Instead of a badge or uniform, akacita wear a black stripe of paint down the right side of their faces that reaches from the eyelid to the jaw-line.

Why have we not heard any gunfire? Where are the rest of the soldiers? I could not understand. Gunfire and Bluecoats, you

WASICHU

cannot have one without the other. I stood on the back of my pony, Hawk's Wing, but I still could not see a thing except climbing dust.

I looked, but could not find my grandfather, Spotted Horse, anywhere. It was necessary for me to get permission to leave the village. I quickly rode to Grandfather's tipi. It was easily the most handsome lodge within the camp. With my grandfather's many deeds painted on the outer surface of the skins, it was also the most colorful. I pulled my pony to a sudden stop because the tipi flap was abruptly thrown back and a woman ducked through the opening into the sunshine. It was my mother. Her large, dark eyes met mine but then she looked away. Her gaze cast to the East where our people were up against the Bluecoats. In a voice loud enough to be heard over the noise of the village, she said, "If anyone were tempted to scout the wasichus it would be wise for him to do so carefully. The insect that bites the hardest is always the one that is hardest to see."

The last part, about the insect, was said to me over my mother's shoulder as she was walking away. I grinned at her receding back and turned away.

As I maneuvered Hawk's Wing through and around the remaining lodges between me and the open prairie, my mind once again rebelled at the Lakota tradition that prevented my mother and I from speaking directly to one another.

From the age of seven winters Lakota male children cannot speak directly to their mothers, they must use a third party. From that age onward a boy's upbringing and training is taken over by his father and other men of the tribe. It is a tradition that has been with us for so long that no one can recall when it started. I hate it! Two winters ago my father was killed by a Crow horse thief. The arrow had come out of the dark, piercing his heart and killing him instantly. Perhaps if my father were still alive this tradition would be easier to accept.

Clearing the village, I quickly urged my pony into a gallop. I was worried that I would be too late to share in the excitement. Hawk's Wing ran like the wind and in no time at all I was pulling him to a stop.

Near the bottom of the hill where I had first seen the wasichu, there was a gathering of people. Where were the wasichus? Our band had about thirty men of warrior age. While scanning the area, I guessed that there were fifteen or twenty of them spread out along a half-circle, mixed with women and children. I could see a few of our own wounded scattered around but no Bluecoats.

I could see only one wasichu and he looked like he was not going to be around much longer. He was battered and bloody and looked to be near exhaustion. It was his great misfortune that he was face to face with my good friend, Bear's Foot. Bear is the largest, the bravest, and the most ferocious Lakota that the Great Spirit, Wakan Tanka, has ever created.

Seeing the wasichu pacing in front of Bear's Foot reminded me of one of my father's stories. It was in January, Moon of the Frost in the Lodge, that he happened upon a great eagle that had surprised a rabbit in a clearing. The eagle, wings spread out in the snow, was crouched over its kill. A lynx was there thinking that the rabbit should be his. He was pacing back and forth in front of the eagle, looking for an opening so that he could attack, just like the wasichu.

I felt my breath catch in my throat. The wasichu does not have a weapon, yet he is stalking Bear's Foot. I could not believe it!

I was so enchanted by this display of courage, or foolishness, that I did not pay any attention when a new group of villagers joined the gathering. The lone wasichu held me completely enthralled.

Bear's Foot abruptly moved into a crouch. His giant war club was in a ready position. Suddenly the wasichu cried out and moving with the speed of the panther, spun in a circle and kicked Bear's leg into the air. Bear's arms flapped as he struggled for balance. His great club flew from his hand and he fell like a tree. As he fell, the wasichu kicked him again and then stood over him striking him with his fist. I could not believe what I had seen or what I was hearing. After humbling our greatest warrior, the wasichu had then shouted our cry for counting coup.

My held in breath left my body in a soft whoosh sound. I had forgotten that I had sucked it in. Bear's Foot, my friend... are you

WASICHU

still alive?

Standing over Bear, the wasichu's body was swaying like a broken branch in the wind. I was not surprised when the haunting courage cry of our people came from the many onlookers. We Lakota cannot resist paying tribute to great courage or superior fighting skills.

Bear's Foot's arm moved and he briefly raised a leg up before letting it drop back into the dust. I felt relief surge through my body. He was alive!

While my eyes were devouring the scene in front of me, a flicker of movement caught my attention. I looked to my right just as Sharp Horn stood in his stirrups and pulled the sinew string on his horn bow all the way to his ear. The sun glittered off the sharp, metal trade goods arrowhead. I became rigid with shock; he was about to kill the brave wasichu!

Without thinking, the warning shout "A-ah!" was out of my mouth before I could stop it. My shout had startled those around me. Ponies shied, bodies jerked; only Sharp Horn had not flinched. His concentration was so great that the only movement from him had been the releasing of the arrow.

The wasichu's head jerked to the right and he spun to the earth, landing on his stomach next to Bear's Foot. A vaporous film of red dust rose into the air. I drove my heels into my pony's flanks and he lunged forward as though raked by a grizzly. In three jumps I was there and off my pony, landing at my friend's side. Kneeling beside him, I saw Bear's eyes open and he tried to rise. He groaned and fell back to once again go walking in the night, which is what we Lakota call being unconscious.

By now others had joined me and they crowded in close to get a look at the wasichu who was such a fierce warrior. I saw that his clothing was not the same that the Bluecoats wear, but was made from some strange cloth. His hands and face were streaked with blood and dirt. I was reaching to touch the cloth when one of his hands twitched and slowly made a fist. When his hand had twitched there was a collective gasp from those nearby. Others had thought him dead, as I had.

While I watched this strange wasichu, I also listened. Many of the watchers spent time making conversation about the wasichu's strange clothing, while others spoke of killing him.

Suddenly, Sharp Horn was shoved aside, almost knocking me to the ground. Wolf's Spirit was standing there glowering at the inert wasichu. He pulled a long knife from his belt and stepped forward. His angry face and eyes challenged everyone that would meet his gaze.

"I say he dies!"

Behind me I could hear bodies moving and voices softly speaking. Then a soft, yet commanding voice rose above the crowd's quiet muttering.

"I say it is not for you to decide."

It was the voice of my grandfather, Spotted Horse. Wolf's Spirit ignored his advice and grabbed the wasichu by the shirt and jerked him off his stomach onto his side, baring his chest for the knife he had poised in his fist. Just as his knife hand started to descend, my grandfather's voice shouted, "Heyah (No)!"

This time there was no softness in his voice. It cracked with authority. Wolf's Spirit hesitated. The rage on his face abruptly turned to consternation as Spotted Horse stepped forward brushing him out of the way. Kneeling beside the wasichu, my grandfather pulled an object from his medicine bag. He leaned forward and held it next to the pale chest.

"Dho!"

With a great show of surprise, Spotted Horse rocked back onto his heels and stared at the wasichu. Swiftly I moved to his side. For the first time in my life I saw shock and confusion in his eyes. Clutched in his hand was the spotted horse carving that has been passed down to the eldest son for generations. Following Grandfather's gaze, I turned my head and saw what he was staring at. I felt my head spin. This cannot be. There on the wasichu's chest was a painting of our family's pipestone horse carving! It was accurate right down to the number of lighter spots on its body.

SIX
~~~

In a dream-like state, Raven saw flickering shadows over orange and yellow shapes dancing on a field of amber. Within the leaping planes of light, Joe Spotted Horse's face appeared. Joe looked older to Raven. He also looked confused and concerned. There was something strange about his appearance. Reflected light glanced off his braids and the otter-skin wrappings. The image had Chris confused. He couldn't make up his fever-addled mind. Was it Joe, or wasn't it? He looked so different and Raven was so tired... drifting, fading.

A new face appeared. Beautiful large eyes, black as onyx and bright as cut-glass, stared into his. Instantly he was drawn into their ebony depths. Her fingers touched his brow with the coolness of morning dew. They moved downward, slowly traversing his face until they found his chest. Her eyes followed her fingers as she lightly traced the pattern of the horse tattoo. He couldn't understand her mixed expression of awe and fear.

Slowly her image faded. She drifted back and away, becoming as one with the shimmering shadows, until they too disappeared and he was left with the lingering scent of sweet grass and sage.

Before opening his eyes, Raven knew that it was early morning. The birds were singing with that special early morning exuberance and he could hear the busy clatter of people preparing for their day. There was a difference though, a very large difference, and Chris was half afraid to explore the dissimilarity. He was beginning to be concerned about his health... his mental health.

With his eyes tightly shut, Raven fought to control a slowly escalating terror. He wasn't concerned about pain or death; those were his normal everyday adversaries. What frightened him was the possibility that he was losing his mind.

Calming himself, Chris slowly opened his eyes. He was in a tent. He looked again and silently corrected himself, a tipi. He knew at a glance that the dwelling didn't belong to any buck-skinner... that theory had gone out the window the second he had seen the brown faces of the Indians glaring at him from horseback.

He propped up on his elbows ignoring the sharp pain in his head. Raven looked about the large circular room in awe. The interior, he thought, is a lot like a Plains Indian diorama that he had seen in a museum some years ago. One big difference though, that one hadn't looked lived in... this one does! The discovery brought back a small trickle of fear in his belly. He fought it down and looked some more. It was full of tell-tale clues. There were objects that were obvious artifacts but were still being used. Most convincing of all was a half-finished war shield propped near his pallet, the paint still drying in bowls beside it. It was a museum curator's dream. Dreams, he mused. Was that a dream last night? The flickering light, the woman so beautiful, then he remembered the other face. "Joe Spotted Horse, are you here?"

Raven's whisper went unheard and his questions unanswered. It's not possible, he thought, but then I've been thinking that a lot lately. He hated having thoughts of Joe and their years together. Every time that he would remember, it would always wind up the same way. It would begin innocently enough but it would eventually tailspin into a countdown to when Joe was killed.

Raven eased back onto his pallet of robes and skins. He forced everything from his mind. His fingers absently stroked the long hair of one of the robes that was beneath him. Shutting his eyes again, Chris let his senses take over. It was easier than trying to make sense of a situation so totally unbelievable. My God, he thought, I don't even know if I'm a prisoner, guest... or 'fatted calf.'

Time passed as Raven lay there absorbing all the sounds and smells. By listening carefully, he could understand some of the conversation outside his tipi. Most of the voices were women and children, but once in a while he would hear the deep guttural responses of men. He felt pretty sure that he wasn't in any immediate danger. He noticed right away that he didn't have an armed guard anywhere nearby, unless there was one outside. At least, he thought, if I have to die they won't torture me. According to the stories that he had read about the Sioux, they all claimed that the Lakota rarely tortured any of their victims. They just kill your ass, he mused, and then carve you up like a side of beef. He shuddered in appreciation of his own black humor.

He heard the door flap open and shut again and sensed another presence inside the tipi. Keeping his eyes shut in the pretense of sleep, Raven strained to hear something that would give him an indication of his visitor's whereabouts.

Then he could smell him... the distinct scents of wood-smoke, leather and horse combined to tell him that his visitor was definitely not a woman. Chris heard a rustling right next to him but couldn't identify its source.

His heart felt like it was lodged in his throat. At any moment he half expected to feel cold steel pierce his flesh.

Feeling a light touch on his chest, Raven reacted with the lightning hand-speed that had saved his life many times in the past. His left hand grasped the intruder's wrist while his right fist cocked beside his ear.

This time, his quick reflexes weren't necessary. He was staring into eyes that were as black as midnight and a face as calm and serene as a woodland pond. Chris allowed the tension to leave his body but kept it close at hand.

Suddenly, he realized that he was staring at the face of Joe Spotted Horse. I may be going crazy, he thought, but at least I'm not seeing ghosts. That is the face I saw in the night. The man had Joe's features but was much older. He had the look of a man who was at peace with himself.

As Raven released the wrist, the Indian brought his first and second fingers to his lips, then moved them straight out from his mouth. He then gracefully pulled his hand back to his face with the index finger pointing up.

Hey, I know what that means, Chris thought, it's sign language meaning 'brother.' It was the first 'sign' Joe had showed him.

Using the word 'uncle' as a show of respect, Raven, in halting Lakota, said, "I am sorry, uncle, a mistake has been made."

The Indian's eyes widened in surprise, and a genuine smile lit up his weathered face as he nodded approvingly.

Slowly, he reached out and put his fingers on Raven's chest. Raven looked and saw that they were touching the tattoo.

In a voice that was vaguely reminiscent of Joe's, the Indian said, "There has been no mistake, my brother."

Taking a decorated pouch from around his neck, the old Sioux reached inside and removed a small object, placing it in the palm of his hand.

Raven was visibly shaken. It was the spotted horse carving! Newer looking, perhaps, but there could be no mistake it was the same pipestone talisman.

While Chris struggled to regain his composure, the Lakota carefully replaced the horse carving in its pouch. He looked up. When their eyes met, his gaze captivated Raven with its directness and the subtle glint of humor. When he began to speak, his oratory was so eloquent, Raven listened spellbound.

"When the cry was heard that someone was coming

from our sacred mountain, Paha Mato, I knew then that something wondrous was about to happen. I knew that you were not an enemy. I cannot explain to you how I knew, I simply did."

He paused for a moment, thinking.

"That morning there was a great storm. The Sky Father's Thunder Beings were especially vocal. It reassured my belief that something truly remarkable was about to happen. Wakan Tanka always gives us a sign before doing something miraculous. And then when I had followed the young warriors out onto the plain to where they had met you, and I saw your magical fighting skills, I knew."

Replacing the leather pouch back inside his beaded and fringed shirt, he stood up. He smiled down on Raven as he said, "Then also, when I saw you in single combat defeat one of our greatest warriors but spare his life, I knew for sure. You must be one of Sky Father's Thunder Beings sent to us in human form."

Once again, he paused and looked away as though seeking the right words. Raven couldn't help but marvel at the man's presence and the poetic rhythm of the Lakota language.

"These are trying times for the Lakota, the wasichus are everywhere. They want our land. They wish to steal the center of the universe and rend and tear at the breast of Earth Mother in search of their yellow metal. We will not let them do these things. We will fight! Even as I speak, many of our six tribes are already moving westward to a meeting place. Perhaps this war will not begin for many moons, but it will begin. Ours is but a small band of Minneconjou but when we join our brothers, Crazy Horse, Sitting Bull, Gall, and our Cheyenne friends, Two Moons and Spotted Wolf, we will be many times more in number than the Bluecoats."

Raven was becoming dizzy. His head wound throbbed even more as he came to realize what he had gotten into. Crazy Horse, Sitting Bull... the names were trapped inside with the beat of his pulsating head wound. Is it possible? His silent query was ludicrous. This is the year 1876? It can't be. His mouth became dry. My God, he thought... Crazy Horse!

The Lakota, obviously a chief, caught Chris' eye and continued, "I believe Wakan Tanka sent you to help us in our fight against the Bluecoats. Why he sent you as a wasichu, I do not know."

A sudden grin softened the old Sioux's weathered face as he said, "Perhaps he wished to see if the Lakota still have a sense of humor."

Turning to leave, he stopped and said, "Your belongings will be returned to you. I do not know what you are called up there . . ." He gestured toward the sky peeking through the tipi's smoke hole. "... but until you earn a name, we shall call you Wasichu."

Once again his smile brightened the tipi's interior as he said, "I am called..."

Before he was able to finish, Raven interrupted.

"Spotted Horse."

Being surprised, the regal, self-assured man came close to losing his composure. Having caught himself in time, Spotted Horse smiled and brought his hand up to the side of his face with two fingers extended. The sign, meaning 'friend,' was almost a parody of a two-fingered salute. He looked deep into Chris' eyes as he said, "Hohahe (welcome), Wasichu (white man)."

He ducked through the tipi flap, leaving Raven alone and awash in a sea of ambivalence.

SEVEN
~~~~~~

While straightening his pack, Raven looked up from his hunched position at the cloudless sky. He was squat-ting in front of Spotted Horse's tipi, sorting his gear. Strange yet familiar scents were in the village air.

In spite of it being a beautiful day and his sudden recovery from the head wound, Chris could feel the solid weight of depression pushing its way into his psyche. Returning to his task of assembling the pump-gun, he could still feel some stiffness in his fingers from the fight. And some of the scabs on his knuckles would crack and bleed but he had no serious ill effects. His brooding was beginning to overshadow any of the lasting physical discomforts. He thought of this new Spotted Horse and how his life had been spared. He thought morosely of Joe. By all rights, he reasoned, I should be dead alongside of Joe somewhere in Laos. Thoughts of Vietnam always caused something to tighten inside of him. Joe should be here, he mused, wherever the fuck 'here' is.

For a moment Chris stared dolefully at nothing. Taking notice of all the Indians doing their daily routines he suddenly straightened his slouching body. Children were running and shouting; men and women were laughing and talking as they worked. This is really stupid, he thought, I should be grateful for being alive. Angrily, he brushed aside his negative thoughts and resumed working on his gear.

All of his possessions had been returned to him in perfect condition. It was earlier that morning that Raven had awakened to find his pack and blanket-roll beside his pallet. They were unopened, yet appeared to have been brushed and cleaned. His clothing had also been cleaned and repaired.

Having been covertly watching the people moving around him, he had seen no sign of hostility directed toward him. He assumed that there must have been some kind of meeting. Spotted Horse, he mused, has probably convinced everyone that I'm not a threat. Most of the people ignored him, although judging from all the shy, sneaky glances thrown his way there was apparently a lot of curiosity.

After he finished cleaning and assembling the shotgun, Chris leaned it against the wall of the tipi. As he began to collect his things from the blanket, he caught some movement in the corner of his eye. Quickly turning his head, Raven had a glimpse of a small figure just before it disappeared behind a tipi. It was the same boy who had been watching him all morning.

As he put his gear into his pack, Chris thought again of Spotted Horse's belief that he was a Thunder Being. What could he do that would strengthen the chief's theory? He looked up at the huge expanse of blue sky. Emissary of the gods, huh? He stopped his packing. He thought that if he could change his visual image maybe it would encourage everyone to believe that he was other than mortal. Shit, he thought, maybe I can get out of this mess in one piece after all. Unless, of course, I'm not in a mess and I'm simply going insane.

Discarding the thought, Raven dug into his pack with a new enthusiasm. He pulled out a black silk scarf and clenched it in his fist, remembering. He had worn the scarf on every one of his twenty-two missions as an SOG Team leader during the war. His throat tightened as he thought briefly of Joe. Raven put the scarf on his head, pirate style, knotting it over his right ear. If they're going to continue to think of me as having been sent to them from the gods, he mused, I'm sure as hell going to have to change my 'look.'

Chris' blanket and canvas shelter-half were spread one on top of the other. Picking up his Randal fighting knife,

WASICHU

he stabbed the blanket in the approximate center and ripped a slash about thirteen, fourteen inches long. Satisfied that his head would fit through the opening, Raven slipped inside the tipi. He remembered seeing some tanned remnants of hides. As he turned to go outside, he saw through the door flap two leather-clad legs and the fringed hem of a dress scurry away. Rushing outside, he was in time to see an old woman looking back at him with fear in her eyes as she quickly moved away. Chris smiled at her. He could see that she hadn't taken anything and was probably just curious.

Starting in as big a circle as possible, Raven cut one long strip, creating a spiral into the middle of the circle. Doing the same thing to two more hides, he salvaged three long strips of leather. After trimming them to his satisfaction, he began braiding them together. While braiding, he noticed that several of the Sioux had moved closer and were watching his every move. Some of the women looked apprehensive. He couldn't figure out why. One old grandmother was staring at him with an expression of fear and awe. He just then realized that she had been the one snooping around his gear.

Gesturing and smiling, Raven coaxed her to his side. He handed her the braided end of his project, instructing her to hold it while he worked on the unfinished end.

In a gentle, quiet voice Chris asked, "Are you frightened of me, Grandmother? Am I breathing smoke and fire?"

For a moment he thought that she couldn't understand his somewhat clumsy Lakota. With her watery old eyes fixed on his face she said, "I saw you! I saw you kill those demons!"

Raven, surprised by her response, listened as she continued.

"We saw you cover them with your blankets and then stab and rip them with your big knife."

Having watched her weathered face throughout her tirade, he was astonished to see the absolute belief etched into her features.

Her old face softened as she beseeched him with rueful eyes and said, "Are they rubbed out yet? Are there others, Wasichu?"

Seizing the chance to implant his new identity in their minds, Raven made a show of a big smile as he moved to the woman's side. Putting his arms around her frail shoulders, he spoke to her in a voice that was soothing, yet loud enough for those nearby to hear.

"No, Grandmother, there are no others; there is nothing more to fear."

As she moved away the old one gave Chris a gap-toothed smile.

He looked about and was pleased that his flamboyant style seemed to placate the others as well. Most of them had resumed their activities prior to the incident.

With an inward sigh of relief, Raven thought, if I ever get out of this... whatever it is that I'm in... I'll have to take a shot at the movies. A hint of a smile showed in his gray eyes as he murmured under his breath, "If I still have all my hair."

The braiding finished, Chris grabbed the shotgun and attached one end of the braided leather to the dividing bracket between the snubbed barrel and the tubular magazine. He then tied the other end to the pistol grip. Both were tied securely but were done in a manner that enabled them to rotate in different positions.

Alternating double-ought buckshot with steel ball ammunition, Raven loaded six rounds into the magazine and one in the chamber. As he slammed the chamber home the noise launched a flurry of activity. There was a mad scramble of people moving away from him. Chris stared. He saw a couple of warriors actually duck behind some cover.

WASICHU

He couldn't believe it. 'Oh shit,' he thought, 'I'm in for it now.' All at once, nobody was moving and all eyes were on him. Off to his right he saw two men with arrows notched and ready to go. Raven slowly set the pump down. Giving everyone a weak smile, he made an effort to look busy fussing with the rest of his gear. He looked calm, but inside his heart was hammering against his ribs with the intensity of a drunk's fist pounding a tavern door on a Sunday morning.

While pretending to be busy, he secretly watched things slowly return to normal. He especially kept his eye on the two with the bows and arrows, just looking at them made his head throb. The sudden danger brought out the levity in Raven as he thought of how near he had come to acquiring an Arrow shirt and a piss-pot haircut.

There was a quick movement to the left. With his nerves still on edge, Raven looked in time to see that the boy was back. He'd just caught a glimpse of his wraith-like figure as he disappeared behind two women stirring a giant pot. Putting the boy out of his mind, Chris continued to assemble his outfit.

Taking the pump-gun, he slipped its makeshift sling over his right shoulder and adjusted the gun's hang so that the butt stock was up underneath his arm only inches from his armpit. The hammer was facing forward and the pistol grip was just inches above his hand. While working out the final adjustments, Chris suddenly stopped as it had just dawned on him that the pump shotgun hadn't even been invented yet, and wouldn't be for another twenty years. He could feel a little excitement beginning to uncoil inside his body. Holy shit, he thought, if anyone messes with me they're in for a big surprise.

Raven put the pump aside and finished putting his gear away. He took his sheathed knife and stuck it between his jeans and lower back. When he shook out his blanket, he noticed that some of the Lakota were edging closer again.

Taking advantage of their renewed interest, Chris threw the blanket in the air, stepped under it and let its red folds slide over him. Abruptly, his black scarfed head popped through the precut opening. Placing his pack inside the door flap, Raven gathered up his pump-gun. He looked at all the dark faces watching him and he thought of a little Black marine he had known in 'Nam. He was famous for always saying, "Be cool, brother, be cool."

Chris made a flamboyant bow by bending from the waist and sweeping his arm across his body. He saw some white smiles and heard a few giggles from the women and children. Thus encouraged, he flipped the ends of his blanket back over his shoulders with an exaggerated flourish and strode away.

While he walked, he enjoyed the many sounds and smells. His roving eyes absorbed the varied colors. He saw the band's pony herd north of the camp and was reminded of Bear Butte. Looking east, he saw the butte towering above the plain in solitude splendor. With a sigh, Chris thought, my God, yesterday I was up there performing a eulogy for Joe Spotted Horse, and his great grandfather isn't even born yet. Now, do I have a right to be confused? Shaking his head, he mused. How in hell am I ever going to get used to this weird shit? He remembered reading that Albert Einstein said, 'Time bends around the universe in a curving line. On that line you can go backwards or forwards.'

Raven stopped and stood still for a moment. He shut his eyes. When they flashed open, their subtle grayness emphasized a new light shining from within. Still thinking of Einstein's theory Chris said, "Shit, who am I to argue with big Al? We're talking 'Brave New World' here."

With a new spring in his stride, Raven continued on his scout of the village. Right away he noticed the unique way the camp was laid out. It was arranged in a circle with the tipis not quite meeting on the eastern side. He thought of

WASICHU

the broken circle as bull's horns. Spotted Horse's tipi was located where the boss of the horns would be and opposite the tips where the horns don't quite meet. The area within the circle was like a clearing in a forest, just an open space. In the middle, a few boys were playing some sort of a game using bows and arrows.

The sight of arrows brought his hand up to explore the scab formed above his left ear. He thought of the warning shout that had probably saved his life and wondered if he would ever find out who had warned him. Whoever had done so, he thought, had in the very least saved him the embarrassment of having to walk around with an arrow sticking from his forehead. He made a mental note to ask Spotted Horse if he knew who that person might have been.

Taking the sling off his shoulder, Raven shouldered the pump-gun and moved on. His hungry eyes feasted on the many sights. Everything had certain clarity, a newness about it that was irresistible. There appeared to be no subterfuges, everything was as it appeared. Wistfully, he thought, if only Joe was here, God, how he would love it.

The smell of wood-smoke, horses and grass gave the air a pungent, fragrant aroma. His surrounding view revealed many tipis, each different from its neighbor. If not in size and shape, they were different in colors and designs painted on their exteriors. Some were ornately painted with horseback Indian scenes, others had geometric symbols, stripes and shapes, while all were decorated with unusual color combinations.

Nearing one of the points of the horn, Raven noticed that there were no longer any children or women around, just warriors.

Directly in his path was a group of eight to ten men, all seated, all engrossed in some type of game. Between a couple of tipis, several other warriors were watching from horseback. As Raven approached, two men stood up. The closest of the two was the big guy that Raven had cut down to size with the use of karate. The other slighter figure looked vaguely familiar. The rest of the group just stared. Their gazes conveyed neither hostility nor familiarity, but Chris could see the tension in their bodies and tightness around the eyes. This told him that he'd best stay alert, that anything could happen.

Was he imagining it or did he see a glint of humor in the big guy's eyes? Drawing closer, he saw the smaller man's face tighten like a clenched fist, anger smoldering behind his strangely familiar glare.

Switching his attention back to the big one, Raven was impressed with the man's presence. Unless he's a mean bastard, he thought, he probably has a lot of friends. Hell, he probably has friends if he is a mean bastard! One thing for sure, if I play this right he's going to have one more friend before the day is through.

Raven had learned early in life how to be a survivor. Growing up an orphan had taught him the value of physical support. Being in a new home or institution, if the support didn't come naturally Chris would make it happen.

At the moment Raven's instincts told him that he didn't dare wait. He needed some friends and he needed them now.

As he approached the big Sioux, he made eye contact and held it as he desperately tried to remember what name Spotted Horse had called the guy. Then, he remembered, yes... Bear's Foot.

Bear's Foot stood relaxed, his weight resting on one foot. Chris couldn't believe it, the guy reminded him of a young John Wayne. All he needed to do, he thought, was to put his hands on his hips instead of having his arms crossed. With that Lakota 'schnoz' of his, that'd do it! The 'Duke' in braids and casual Indian attire.

Raven stopped three feet away. He slowly placed the

pump on the ground between them. He brought his hands up to shoulder level making a big show of them being empty as a conjurer or magician would do.

For the first time, his eyes left Bear's Foot as he sought the attention of the other warriors. His gaze moved from face to face, gauging the group. There. Standing in the background was his shadow, the boy who had been watching him.

Returning his gaze to the huge Indian in front of him, Chris swiftly brought both hands down, behind his back and under his blanket poncho.

The move was so fast that his hands couldn't have been out of sight for more than a split-second. They reappeared with the knife in one hand and the sheath in the other. He was so quick that it was a parody of a gunfighter's fast draw. The group reacted with murmurs and exclamations of surprise. Except for a slight widening of his eyes and nostrils, Bear's Foot hadn't so much as twitched.

Raven continued to hold the knife aloft. Its twelve inches of blue steel glistened in the sunlight.

Without taking his eyes off Raven, Bear's Foot turned toward his friends nearby and said, "The wasichu wishes to impress us with his speed of hand. I was more impressed with his quick feet."

The warrior's joke brought an appreciable scatter of chuckles from his peers.

"Perhaps I should have used my quick feet to run away when I last met the great Bear's Foot."

Hearing their language being spoken, a collective gasp came from the Sioux. Bear's Foot's eyes had flared wide in surprise.

"Yes, I speak Lakota. But I do not know the ways of the Sioux. I did not defeat Bear's Foot fairly. I had to become an *unktomi* (a trickster) to win."

As he spoke, Raven's eyes were moving from one

brown face to another, beseeching each for their attention like a politician milking his audience.

"When I had first seen Bear's Foot standing there with his great strength and power, I knew that I could win only by using trickery."

Looking full into the warrior's face, Chris stepped forward holding the knife and sheath out to him.

"*Wonumayin* (A mistake has been made)."

The big warrior's gaze dropped to the great knife. When he took it from Raven, the six-inch bone handle disappeared into a hand that was nearly the size and color of a boy's baseball glove. Eyes shining in appreciation of the quality of the blade, he turned it over and over as he examined its every nook and cranny. Hefting it, Bear's Foot ran a sausage sized thumb along the edge. Blood welled instantly and he lifted his hand and impassively studied the cut. Abruptly he turned his head and stared at Raven as a gigantic smile spread across the broad face. He faced his friends and held the fighting knife up for all to see. He ignored the blood from his cut as it ran down his arm. He hefted the knife again and looked at Raven.

Besides the obvious joy over the gift, Chris caught a glimpse of something akin to softness move across the strong features and touch the expressive brown eyes.

With a quickness that made Raven thankful that their fight had never had a chance to develop, Bear's Foot's hand snaked out and grabbed him behind the neck. Shaking him lightly with one hand, he waved the knife overhead with the other. Droplets of blood were flying everywhere as Bear's Foot made a proclamation.

"Let it be known that this wasichu is my friend. Anyone that harms him is attacking me!"

To add emphasis to his words, Bear's Foot slammed his fist with the cut thumb onto his broad chest. Blood splattered across those sitting nearby. The warrior ignored the loud complaints and fastidious hand wiping that was coming from those that were splattered by his blood. He grabbed Raven in a friendly head-lock and said, "If this terrible thing happens to my friend, I swear by Wakan Tanka, that I will kill them and eat their hearts!"

In the next instant, Raven was released only long enough to be swept into an embrace that all but took his breath away. As he was engulfed in the heady scents of sweat, horses and leather, Chris looked to see the reaction of the others. Except for a few close by who were angrily brushing at the blood stains on their clothing, they were smiling and chatting. Some were nodding their braided heads in apparent approval while others simply resumed their previous games.

There was one warrior who stood out like a clansman at a Black revival meeting. He was standing perfectly still with his arms across his chest and his gaze was locked on Raven. Pure venom was streaking out of his black eyes. All at once Raven recognized him, it was the other Indian that had stood up with Bear's Foot!

Chris watched the young warrior turn and stomp away, throwing one hateful glance over his shoulder as he left. The last look caused something to click in Raven's memory... he could see again the hate-filled eyes just before the blanket-roll had swept him off his horse.

Before he had a chance to reflect on the mistake he had made by not including the younger one in his plan, Raven was released by Bear's Foot only to be smothered by the others with their back-slapping and hugs.

Putting the angry Sioux out of his mind, Chris felt for the first time in a long, long time that maybe... just maybe... he had found a home.

EXCERPT FROM THE JOURNAL OF CETAN CHICKALA (LITTLE HAWK)

As I watched Wolf's Spirit walk away, his back stiff with anger, I felt a sadness move inside of me. I do not know why, perhaps it is because Wolf's Spirit is one of our best warriors and I have always admired him. Now, because of his hatred for the wasichu and of Bear's Foot's befriending him, I could sense that there would be trouble.

Hearing my name called, I looked up. Bear's Foot, grinning like a coyote, was gesturing for me to join him and the wasichu. My heart began to beat strongly as I moved toward them. All day I had been spying on the wasichu, or Thunder Being, as some believed. I know that he had caught me watching him. I now fear that the time has come for my punishment. I am already being punished for having warned the wasichu and saving him from Sharp Horn's arrow. No, that is not right. I am not being disciplined for having saved him, but for having warned him. My grandfather was happy that he was not killed but I had no right interfering.

My punishment was severe. I no longer share the responsibility with my friends of guarding the pony herd. Instead I must stay in the village and play games and help the women. Bah!

As usual, Bear's Foot was talking when I approached them. My gaze fastened onto the wasichu. Seeing him up close after he had been cleansed made him appear less fierce than he was before. I noticed that he was only about a hand shorter than Bear's Foot, but was only about half as wide. His clothing gave him a strange look. And then there was that funny looking gun with no barrel. It looked like if you pulled the trigger, the bullet would dribble off the end and onto the dirt. I was trying to think what his manner of dress reminded me of when he abruptly turned his head and looked into my eyes. All thoughts left my mind. I was astounded. His eyes were the color of the clouds where the Thunder Beings lived! For a moment fear touched my heart as I thought, perhaps he was sent to us from the gods. His eyes were so intense that it felt as though they could pierce my skull and see what I was thinking.

He spoke to me.

"Cetan, Bear's Foot has told me that you are the one that shouted the outcry that saved me from the arrow. I wish to thank you."

I was so thrilled that the wasichu had not used the hated 'Little' in front of my name, I barely heard Bear when he spoke.

"I did not hear my little friend's warning cry." *Bear's Foot grinned before continuing with his confession.* "I was busy walking in the night searching for a lonely 'ishta' (female) to warm my blankets." *Braying like a mule with laughter, he continued.* "There is much gossip about the brash Little Hawk who is always putting his nose in a place where it can be twisted, so naturally I heard what happened."

Throwing his arm over the wasichu's shoulder, Bear shook the great knife with his other hand as he said, "I, for one, am grateful to Little Hawk. If it were not for him I probably would not own this grand knife. More likely, Wolf's Spirit would have used it to take your hair."

At the mention of Wolf's Spirit, I saw a new light enter the pale eyes of the stranger.

"Is this Wolf's Spirit that you speak of the warrior that was standing with you and then left?"

This time I had trouble understanding the wasichu when he spoke Lakota. It was probably because he was excited. Having noticed that the wasichu was serious, Bear began to look around. A few of the men remained but not Wolf Spirit. Those that were still here were playing 'hand', gambling with plum pits. Bear's Foot looked again before answering the wasichu.

"Yes," *Bear rumbled,* "but I did not see him leave."

Removing his arm from the wasichu's shoulder Bear's Foot faced him and spread his arms wide to accentuate what he was about to say.

"Listen, Kola (friend), I will tell you what happened when

WASICHU

the arrow made you go walking in the night."

Bear's Foot then told the wasichu about how Grandfather had stopped Wolf's Spirit from killing him. With many gestures and pantomime, my huge friend began to elaborate on what actually happened. As he became caught up in his story, his seriousness left him. He even had the wasichu laughing at his childish antics.

When Bear finished, all flushed with excitement, I said, 'Tell us, oh great storyteller, how do you manage to know so much about what happened? You were snoring so loudly that Grandfather had to shout so that Wolf's Spirit would hear him and lower the knife."

I gleefully watched the smile leave his face as he stared at me in mock anger.

"You little gnat's ass, I am going to lift your hair!"

Roaring like a grizzly, he lunged at me. The knife flashed as he took a swing, missing me by an even smaller part of a gnat's anatomy.

What followed was a lot like a bull buffalo trying to gore a camp dog. Even the wasichu joined in, offering Bear the use of his gun. Finally, after much laughter and running, Bear's Foot gave up. He stopped chasing me and let his bulk drop into the dust. Looking back over my shoulder as I walked away, I saw the wasichu giving Bear a helping hand. Bear's Foot was still watching me so I gave him a flip of the tail of my loin cloth before running off.

Many days passed. It was May or the 'Moon of the Shedding Ponies.' had not seen the wasichu recently. I thought it best that I stay away for a while. Perhaps he will not remember my having spied on him that day.

The days were getting warmer as our village prepared for our move west to join with the other Lakota. I was helping my second mother, Deer Walking, prepare jerky and pemmican for our travels. My second father, Short Bow, was off with some of the other men hunting.

I should explain about my second parents. Among the Lakota, all children have second parents. Since I am forbidden to *speak directly to my mother during my manhood training, with Deer Walking I will still have a woman's guidance as well as a man's advice as I learn to become a warrior and man. Since my father was killed, this practice has doubled in importance for me. My father's father, Spotted Horse, teaches me as does Short Bow. Still, it is not the same as learning from your father.*

Part of my punishment for having interfered with the wasichu is that I must help Deer Walking with the wasna (pemmican) instead of taking part in the manly duties that the other boys my age are doing.

Looking up from my work, I saw Wasichu approach. I panicked for a moment. I did not know if I should be embarrassed or if I should worry about being finally punished for spying. Since he had already arrived and there was no more time to do either, I left it in the hands of Wakan Tanka.

"Washtay."

His greeting was said with a smile and a nod for me and Deer Walking. Deer Walking smiled and lowered her eyes demurely.

The pale eyed one squatted down beside me and flipped his blanket back over his shoulders out of the way. We talked for a while. He asked me many things about our camp and why we do some things the way that we do. He asked questions about some of the people he had met. He said that some things he does not understand because of his poor understanding of Lakota.

These things that we talked about confused me. If he was one of Sky Father's Thunder Beings, I would think that he would know all of these things. If he is not a Thunder Being then who is he and how did he happen to have a painting of our horse carving on his chest? Why is he here? Perhaps if I was older I would be able to understand more.

We talked of Bear's Foot for a while and then he asked me about Wolf's Spirit. He had not seen him since the day he had walked away in anger. I told him that Wolf's medicine was bad and that he was probably avoiding a meeting between the two of them. The wasichu nodded.

WASICHU

A glint was in his gray eyes as he said, "I would think that is true after what Bear had said about what would happen if anything happened to me."

A smile appeared, lighting his eyes and animating his lean face. It made me think that the thought of Wolf's Spirit being worried about Bear's Foot made him happy. Rocking back on his heels, he adjusted the gun with no barrel on his lap, poked at the Earth Mother with a stick, scratched at his head under his black cloth and looked at me from the side of his eyes. I was getting very nervous by the time he stopped fidgeting and spoke again.

"Cetan, Bear's Foot has told me that the woman who cared for me after the fight is your mother. Is this so?"

While he was speaking, he looked at Deer Walking who was pounding meat a short distance away. It was then that I understood what he was asking. I told him that my mother, Blue Feather, had been the one that cared for him. I explained about having a 'second mother' and of the ways of the Lakota concerning such matters. I did not know why but I told him of my father's death. He was very understanding.

Rising to his feet he said, "Someday soon I would like to meet your mother and thank her for nursing me when I was hurt." He paused for a moment and began to fidget again. He looked like he had an itch somewhere but didn't know how to scratch it.

While I was waiting for the wasichu to scratch his itch, I noticed he was wearing a necklace of elk teeth. I remembered seeing the same necklace on Bear's Foot.

"Would you mind my talking with your mother?"

His voice startled me. And then he was looking at me with the same look he had when he could not reach his 'itch'. I did not know what to say. Why should I care if he talks to my mother? Oh, no, I thought, it is about the spying. Not knowing what to say, I smiled and shrugged my shoulders.

I saw a smile in his eyes as he reached under his blanket. He held out an object to me. Not knowing what it was, I carefully took it from his hand. Surprised by its weight, I examined it. It looked to *be of steel and deer antler.*

Taking it from my hand the wasichu grasped the shiny steel part with two fingers and pulled.

"Dho!"

I was very surprised. Seeing the knife blade appear I could feel my heart beating. It beat even more wildly when he pulled another blade from the other end. I watched closely as he showed me again how to awaken the sleeping knife blades. I was nearly overcome with joy as I thanked him for my 'two-knives' present.

The wasichu gave my shoulder a squeeze. He smiled and waved as he walked away. He looked back over his shoulder and called out, 'That is for being nosey!"

As I watched him walk away I thought, nose, nosey. I did not understand. He must like big noses. Come to think of it, Bear has a big nose. I explored my nose with my fingers. I felt curiously disappointed when I discovered that my nose, if anything, was too small.

Part 3
Okute

EIGHT
~~~~~~

Raven sat upon a small knoll north of their encampment and thought of the days that had passed. The band had been moving northwest for several days. Their pace had been necessarily slow because of the elderly and the very young. Horses, dogs and people were their only methods of transport. The dogs and horses transported goods by the use of a travois. This device was made from two lodge poles tied to the animal and the other ends are allowed to drag behind. A platform was made between the pole ends and goods could be transported in this manner. It was crude but effective. All in all, Chris was impressed with the amount of organizing and discipline that was involved.

The *akicita* were in charge during their travels and temporary camps. Raven remembered seeing an example of their power shortly after they had left the Bear Butte camp. A sub chief had directed his family away from the main group. He saw one of the *akicita* ride out to intercept them. Chris was too far away to hear what was said but it was obvious that they were arguing. The argument came to an abrupt end when the *akicita* used his quirt. The whip cut across the chief's face and neck. A short time later the sub chief's family rejoined the main procession.

Raven relaxed and let his mind wander. He was finding it much easier to accept that he was in some kind of time warp. Whatever it is that I'm mixed up in, he mused, it's very real. His hand moved of its own volition to his temple and probed the healing remnants of his wound.

Looking to the west and south he could see for miles. There was nothing at all to indicate the presence of man. All there was to see was the undulating prairie with its tall grasses and distant buttes.

Staring southward into what was probably Wyoming, brought back some childhood memories of living on a ranch... three years in a foster home where the people were more interested in having a hired hand than they were in having a teenage son. Actually, what they really wanted was the monthly gratuities from the state... and a hired hand.

Some of the memories were good times. Raven smiled as he thought of the old timer, Bill Doolin. Bill was always quick to point out that 'he weren't no relation o' that no good Oklahoma outlaw o' the same name.' The old cowboy had been hired to do the odd jobs around the ranch that Chris couldn't do, such as repair machinery and tack. He was supposed to teach Chris but somehow managed to never get around to it. Bill did teach Raven everything he knew about horses. Come to think of it, he mused, having old Bill around was the only thing that made his years there worthwhile. If old Bill hadn't been around to talk to and ride with, he probably would have run away.

What Raven remembered the most about Bill Doolin was his hands; they were brown and scarred, strong hands for such a frail old man. When the rancher and his wife were gone, he would watch old Bill work with his hands and listen to his stories of horses and men he had known. He would precede his stories with the same old line, "This here happened way back before all the damn fools moved in bringin' their machines and city ways."

Bill liked to talk about when he was a kid and how he used to hear stories about the old 'Hole in the Wall' gang of outlaws, especially Butch Cassidy. He had said that some of the old timers used to tell him that, Butch was still alive and would come and visit from time to time. Chris figured they were probably just stories, but when he was a kid they were fascinating.

WASICHU

Thinking of old Bill's stories brought Raven back to his present situation and of stories Chief Spotted Horse had told him about himself and his people. Listening to the old chief, he thought, was like being with Joe again.

Spotted Horse enjoyed talking about his youth and what it was like before their wars with the white man. One story in particular had impressed Raven.

At the time of the incident, Spotted Horse belonged to a warrior society where each warrior was obligated to perform at least one totally unselfish act over a period of so many moons.

Spotted Horse and some of his society brothers had heard that several *wasichus* were being held captive in the North country by another tribe of Indians. They came up with a plan. They rounded up all the trade goods and horses they could gather and headed north. It had taken them several weeks of travel and hunting before they found the right Indians. After much bargaining, they traded several horses, buffalo robes, and blankets for the white captives. The chief couldn't remember how many prisoners there were, only that they were all women and children.

After the trade was completed, those same Sioux that were later to be called 'bloodthirsty, merciless, cold and unfeeling,' returned to the south. They released the women and children at a U.S. Army post where they knew they would be well cared for. They asked for nothing in return and received nothing.

Spotted Horse had told Raven the story as an example of the many attempts by the Lakota to live in peace with the wasichu.

Chris stood up and stretched. Looking down on the pony herd, he watched the boys as they made a game of guarding the horses. He wondered when Spotted Horse was going to allow Little Hawk to rejoin his friends.

Chris smiled, thinking of how Little Hawk showed up

at his lean-to every morning. He liked to watch him go through his morning exercise routine. Invariably, other children would show up and emulate Raven's every move. He chuckled, picturing all the kids doing stretch exercises, shadow boxing, sit-ups, etc. Hell, he thought, even Bear, who shares Raven's lean-to, likes to watch.

Raven grinned as he thought, maybe I could get Little Hawk to invite his mother to come and watch. The grin faded as he thought of his failure to even talk to her. Twice he had taken Bear with him when he had tried to speak with her. Using what the Lakota consider good protocol, he had Bear approach her for him. Both times she had refused to speak and had turned her back to him.

Bear thought he had the answer to why she would not agree to speak to him. He remembered the tease in Bear's voice as he said, "Wasichu, your problem is very simple. Whenever you are near her you are like a wolf around a bitch in heat. Your eyes are devouring her and with your tongue hanging out, dripping saliva, you frighten her."

He remembered Bear's Foot's booming laugh. Bear later became serious.

"Listen, Kola. I think it might be that she still loves her husband. He has been dead for two winters and she has not remarried."

Grasping his two thick braids for emphasis, Bear had said, "Notice how she always has her braids hanging down her front, never in back?"

Putting his thick arm around Chris' shoulder, he had continued, "Among the Lakota, married women wear their braids in front and available women wear them down their backs. I do not think she is ready to replace her dead husband's memory. That is why there have not been Lakota warriors courting her. She probably won't talk to you because it is plain to see that you have ideas other than just speaking to her."

WASICHU

Mentally chiding himself for having a schoolboy crush on someone who was unavailable, Raven scooped up his blanket and began to walk down the hill. He stopped when he saw some unusual activity going on in the camp. Some of the people were hurrying toward the eastern edge of the village. Beyond the camp he saw the dust of horses and riders approaching from the east.

Instead of rushing down there he decided to stay put. Watching the riders, he wondered if one of them could be Bear's Foot. He and two others had left the band two days ago. He hadn't told Raven where he was going. He had simply said, with his usual grin, "If you want to be a Lakota you are going to have to look like one."

Raven was puzzled by the warrior's remark, but it wasn't the first time that he didn't understand something that Bear had said or done. The big warrior was more complex than Chris had at first thought.

Judging by the amount of dust being kicked up, there had to be more than three riders, he thought. While he waited and watched he thought again of Bear's Foot and the many facets of the man's personality. One of the things that had puzzled Raven was that Bear didn't have a wife, or even a girlfriend. In a society where polygamy was commonplace, it had seemed a bit strange. It was Little Hawk who had enlightened him. He remembered the somber look and the moisture in Hawk's big eyes when he had told him the story.

"Three winters ago Bear's Foot had a wife and a daughter. Then, as quickly as the cold breath of our winter god can snuff a campfire, they were gone. A Crow raiding party had stolen some of our horses and during their escape they had driven the ponies right through the village. Bear's Foot's wife and daughter could not get out of their way quickly enough and were trampled by the running horses. In his grief, Bear left our band and did not return for over three moons."

When Little Hawk finished his story, Raven was sad for his friend, Bear's Foot, yet the boy's sensitivity and eloquence had a remarkable soothing effect.

They were now close enough for Chris to see two of the riders. They were herding several horses. As soon as he saw the third rider, he knew that it was Bear's Foot. He was easily recognized because of his size and the yellow elk-skin shirt he was wearing.

They rode into camp like returning heroes. Everyone was yelling; the women were making that curious trilling sound. At first Raven didn't understand. Then all at once it hit him. They had been on a horse stealing raid! My God, he thought, and here I had been thinking about how Bear had lost his family on the very same type of raid.

Mentally pushing aside the morbid coincidence, Raven began to wave his blanket overhead to get Bear's attention. Excited for his friend, he began yelling as he whipped the red poncho to and fro.

They were riding around the open area in the center of camp, yippying and yelling. It sounded as though the whole village was celebrating. Although segregated by his elevation, Chris still felt in tune with the elation and excitement. He saw Bear stop his horse and lean down to talk with someone, who then turned and pointed up at Raven. When Bear looked, Chris waved his blanket.

He watched for a moment as Bear's Foot rode over to the two men who had been with him on the raid. He recognized Wolf's Spirit but not the other one. He had wondered why he hadn't seen the young warrior around.

Raven had just started down the hill when he saw that Bear's Foot was on his way up. He stopped, deciding to wait for him. He saw Bear teasing the boys in the pony herd as he rode through. When he started up the slope, Chris saw that he was leading another horse. Smiling to himself, Raven thought, he can't wait. He has to show me his new prize.

WASICHU

Swinging his horse broadside to Raven, Bear's Foot stared down at him wearing a solemn expression. His voice was gruff as he said, "*Hau* (Hello), my friend, do you like my catch?"

Bear's horse had been blocking Chris' view of Bear's 'catch'. When he saw him, he felt his breath lodge in his throat... a beautiful, black appaloosa stallion. Yet, only the spotted rump showed the appaloosa trait. He was a big horse. With his wide chest, powerful hindquarters and long legs, Raven knew that he was looking at a lot of speed and agility.

Chris paused in his study of the animal only long enough to throw his friend an envious grin and say, "What a horse!"

The stallion held his fine head high. His wide nostrils were pink from running. Raven noticed his eyes were wide from all the excitement. He thought he saw a little fire gleaming inside the dark orbs. Somehow, he knew that when all the excitement was over, that tiny spark in his eye would still be there. Raven stepped back, shook his head in awe, and said, "That is a horse."

In his gruff voice, Bear's Foot said something else. Thinking that he hadn't translated his Lakota correctly, Raven asked, "What did you say?"

"I said, do you think he is too much horse for you, Wasichu?"

Chris stared into his eyes, looking for the tease that was so often there. Bear's Foot, grinning from ear to ear, thrust the lead rope into Raven's hand. Raven was speechless. As usual, Bear didn't have that problem.

Dropping his smile he said, "You did not think that I, the greatest warrior in the Lakota Nation, would give you a necklace in exchange for my grand knife? You are a warrior my friend, and a Lakota warrior must have a horse. You now have one." This last sentence was said in such a matter-of-fact way that to question any part of his statement would be to risk insulting his giant friend. Raven, moved by the wondrous gift, blindly thrust his hand toward Bear's Foot.

Clearing his throat, he hoarsely said, "Thank you."

Bear grasped Raven's hand in the manner of arm wrestling, not the conventional handshake. A bonding look passed between the two that said much more than words.

Reining his horse away from Raven and his newly acquired appaloosa, Bear walked his horse down the slope a short distance, stopped, then abruptly turned his mount around and short-hopped him back up the hill. The grin was back on his face when he reined in next to Raven.

"I forgot to tell you. The owner of your horse did not wish to give him to me." Slapping the sheathed Randall knife at his belt, he said, "When I showed him this, he was happy to give me his mountain pony."

With those innocent words ringing in his ears, Raven watched Bear's Foot's big hand delve into a stained leather bag hanging by his knee. The object he pulled from the bag caused Chris' new horse to jerk his head, nearly freeing himself. Hanging by its hair from Bear's fist was a human head! The horror, not two feet from Raven's face brought with it a flash from the past of dead babies, mutilated bodies, heads mounted on stakes, and all the other nightmares that were a part of Chris' Vietnam experience.

Raven couldn't look away. The long black hair was twisted and matted. Its eyes had rolled back so that only the white showed. Just above the jagged, gore smeared neck the mouth was set in a rictus grin of death. "See, he is still smiling." grinned Bear's Foot.

Throwing his head back he whooped with laughter, then spun his horse around and raced him down the hill, holding his grisly trophy high as he raced for the village.

Raven's held in breath left his body with a whoosh. With the expired breath, came a whispered "Jesus H. Christ."

NINE
~~~~

The following morning when Chris had gotten up, Bear's Foot had already left their dwelling. Chris was elated because Bear would have been merciless with his teasing. All of the riding that Raven had done the day before had nearly crippled him. He felt swamped by a multitude of aches and pains.

If he were to facetiously make a list for Christopher Raven's World of Pain, the top of the list would be reserved for the inside of his thighs. He actually felt better walking with his legs spread apart.

After hobbling about like an arthritic, old cowboy, he was able to loosen up enough to run through part of his exercise routine. Afterwards he felt much better and was more optimistic about his chances of surviving the day. He grabbed his saddle and limped over to his horse, hobbled nearby. With a mounting sense of anticipation, Chris began to saddle him, taking his time so that they could get reacquainted and establish a rapport

Bear's Foot had dug up this old McClellan army saddle from somewhere. It had been neglected, but by using some of the simple tack repair skills he had learned from old Bill, Raven was able to make it serviceable. Tightening the cinch, he swung up and carefully settled onto the hard, old army rig. As he lowered himself, he couldn't help but fantasize about the soft, fuzzy, thick bicycle seat cover he had used as a kid.

The night before, Chris had decided on a name for his horse. He decided to call him 'The Black' after Walter Farley's horse in his book, The Black Stallion. He's not all black and he's not an Arabian, but, Chris thought, he sure as hell can run like his namesake.

Steering The Black northwest, Raven let him move at his own pace. As they moved north of the camp he remembered that Little Hawk was going to be guarding the women berry pickers near there. Chris urged the horse into a faster gait and swung more to the east.

He was thinking that if he could find them he would let the boy ride The Black. Raven could tell that Little Hawk was dying to ride him, but he had wanted his horse to get used to him and his style of riding.

Riding east to the tree-line, he then followed the trees south until he was about a half-mile north of the Sioux camp. Turning north again, he was just south of where the trees ended and the prairie began. He knew that was where the berry pickers should be found.

Between Raven and the tree-line was a gradual incline of open ground that was intersected with several gullies. Just in front of the trees there was a deep ravine.

Looking south, he could see the hill he was on yesterday. It was directly between him and the camp. All that could be seen of the village were plumes of smoke from the morning campfires.

Letting The Black pick his way, Raven moved up the incline toward the trees several hundred yards away. He relaxed, enjoying the easy rhythm of his horse's pace.

Thinking of Little Hawk made him smile. Spotted Horse had finally relented and given the boy some responsibility again. His smile broadened when he realized that Little Hawk wouldn't appreciate being a baby-sitter for a bunch of berry pickers.

He was about a hundred yards from the trees when he pulled The Black to a stop and listened. Faintly he could hear voices shouting. Jabbing his heels into The Black's ribs, the horse lunged forward as though shot from a bow.

WASICHU

He knew that the berry pickers had to be in some kind of trouble. Lakota women do not make noise when away from the protection of the village. The Sioux have too many enemies who would love to catch their women away from the men.

By the time the stallion had covered half the distance, Raven was seeing splashes of color among the trees. Drawing nearer, he saw some of the women staring down into the deep ravine bordering the trees. The gully ran parallel to the tree-line. Women were throwing rocks down into it and shouting curses.

Leaving The Black at the base of the final gradient where large boulders were strewn about, Raven scrambled his way to the top. Having already shed his blanket he unlimbered the pump-gun and slid to an abrupt stop. Looking down into the gorge, Chris felt the hackles raise on the back of his neck. In spite of the fear spreading through his body, he was able to absorb the situation with one terrified look.

The gully below was strewn with a scatter of sage and rock. A single dead sycamore stood tall amid the otherwise stunted terrain to the west. About half way to the top of the tree there was a splash of color. The bright bead-work on Blue Feather's dress stood out like a beacon among the dead wood. Her arms and legs were wrapped around the main trunk of the brittle tree, and she was hanging on as if her life depended on it. It did!

Directly below her, a huge grizzly bear was tearing slabs of bark from the trunk of the tree as he tried to dislodge her from her precarious perch. The noises coming from the bear were so horrible that Raven hesitated before making any move.

He could hear Blue Feather shouting, but her voice was smothered with the noises of the bear, and he could not understand what she was saying.

"Sonofabitch, it's the kid!"

In his horror, Raven had spoken out loud. Little Hawk had suddenly appeared from behind some rocks. About forty feet from the monster he was throwing stones at it, trying to get its attention! Beyond the tree and part way up the bank of the gully, Chris caught a glimpse of two brown shapes as they scurried through the brush. He grit his teeth and exclaimed, "Shit, she's got cubs!"

Sliding and stumbling, Raven raced down the side of the ravine. Struggling to keep his footing, he could hear Blue Feather screaming at Hawk as he tried desperately to draw the grizzly's attention.

All at once he bounced a rock off the bear's snout. Roaring her rage, the bear spun off the tree and went for Little Hawk! One second she was against the tree and the next she was on all fours running straight for the boy. Little Hawk froze!

Raven bellowed, "Hawk, this way!"

He saw the boy suddenly break loose from his fear and sprint toward him. At that very instant he felt a rock come loose beneath his foot. As he struggled to maintain his balance, Raven's foot tripped over another stone. His momentum caused him to do a summersault and land flat on his back in the middle of the gully's dry stream bed. The impact forced the air out of his lungs!

A black curtain had dropped in front of his eyes. Nausea hit him; he tasted vomit. His vision cleared, but his head throbbed and his stomach churned as he gasped for air. The shotgun was gone! Scrambling on all fours he swung around, searching. There, by the rocks!

Blindly lunging for the gun, he was horrified by the realization that they were so close he could hear grunts of effort coming from the bear as she gained on Little Hawk.

Raven felt the cool walnut of the pump-gun's pistol grip slap into his palm. Spinning and rolling to his knees, he looked up and was staring straight into Little Hawk's terror filled eyes. The boy and bear were so close together that it looked like the grizzly was on a leash!

Still on his knees, Raven could see that Hawk was in the way! They were only about thirty feet away and closing fast when Chris yelled, "Drop down!"

Little Hawk, eyes swimming in fear, kept coming. Suddenly he tripped and slid on his belly in the gravel!

He was still sliding when Raven's first blast echoed off the gully walls. The load of double-ought buck caught the bear square in the face, blinding her. Her roar of pain and fury was deafening as she slid to a stop, spraying dirt and gravel over Little Hawk's feet.

Raven's second shot, a steel ball, struck the gaping jaws as she reared up. The projectile punched through the roof of her mouth destroying the brain and exploded a chunk of something wet and grisly from her skull! The third and fourth blasts were pumped out so close together that they sounded like one. The concentrated fire blew a hole in the sow's chest the size of a bowling ball.

Still upright the grizzly hemorrhaged, fell forward, and died. A pall of dust rose like pink smoke.

Raven's ears were ringing; his nostrils burned with the acrid stench of cordite. His eyes were riveted onto the motionless bear. With his body taut as a strung wire he was totally focused, and his gaze did not waver until the settling dust dulled the luster of the grizzly's eyes.

Finally satisfied that it was over, Chris lowered the hammer on the pump and rocked back onto his heels. He felt totally drained. He stared.

He was shaken loose from his dazed status by the dirt-covered form of Little Hawk rising shakily to his feet. Looking stunned, he stumbled forward. Raven stood up just as the boy rushed into his arms. A few sobs shook his thin frame and then he was quiet as his arms tightened around

Chris' waist.

Raven held him tightly. He shuddered to think of what could have happened. He remembered that when he had yelled at Hawk to drop down, he had done so in English and didn't have time to switch to Lakota. Raven wasn't a very religious man but he thanked God for Little Hawk's timely trip and fall.

Hearing shouts and that peculiar trilling, Chris looked up. The women were grinning and waving their arms and baskets overhead as they stood poised on the rocky lip of the ravine. He gave them a brief wave and thought of Blue Feather as he held her son's trembling body.

In the fifty odd yards that spanned the distance between the dead sycamore and Chris and Little Hawk, the floor of the gorge was covered with deadfalls and huge boulders. Therefore, it came as no surprise to Raven that he heard Blue Feather before seeing her.

The tinkle of the hawk's bells that rimmed the hem of Blue Feather's dress was getting progressively louder.

Those bells she habitually wore on all of her clothing was music to Raven's ears. He was so enamored with her that the mere sound of them would make him long to be near her.

She had been running and was slightly out of breath. She stopped, stared at the bear, then turned her gaze on her son. Little Hawk released Raven and ran into her arms. Chris saw the sunlight glint off a tear forming in the corner of her eye as she embraced her son.

Watching them as they caressed and held each other, Raven was pleased that the Lakota were flexible enough to make exceptions concerning their traditions. While he watched the outpouring of love, Chris experienced something new. Whatever it was that they had, he wanted to be a part of it. Never before, in his whole solitary life, had Raven ever wanted to be a part of someone else's family.

WASICHU

Little Hawk broke loose from his mother's embrace and began talking with unbelievable speed. The words just flew out of his mouth while his animated hands and arms were telling their own version in pantomime. Raven could only pick up a word or two but still had to laugh at the boy's vibrant enthusiasm.

He glanced at Blue Feather. She was staring at him. Her dark eyes caught his and held them. Raven couldn't have looked away if his life depended on it.

Little Hawk, having finished his story, stopped talking. He looked from one face to the other. He was grinning but looked puzzled.

Raven was the first to speak.

"Are you all right?"

Blue Feather still held his gaze. She nodded and said, "Yes, I am well, as is my son, but only because of you."

Her soft and lilting voice was a caress to his ear. Their gaze was so harmonious and intimate that Raven was becoming uncomfortable. Just hearing her voice was adding fuel to an already blazing fire.

I've got to get out of here, he thought, or one of us is going to be embarrassed. I wonder what the Sioux equivalent is for a cold shower... maybe a jump in the lake.

Raven's lustful reverie was interrupted by a shout from above. Raising his eyes, he saw the southern rim of the gully lined with eight horseback Sioux with the resplendent figure of Bear's Foot in the lead.

White grin flashing across his dark face, Bear shouted, "Hau, Wasichu! We heard so much gunfire we thought some Bluecoats were trying to win a battle against our berry pickers!"

"*Eyhee* (Alas), it was but one bear. Had we known that you were nearby, we would have summoned you. You could have sat on her and saved me many bullets and the bear a lot of suffering."

Much teasing and finger pointing at Bear's Foot followed Chris' joke.

Undaunted, Bear replied, "It is true then, all that shooting for one bear?"

Before Raven could answer, Blue Feather shouted, "*Han* (Yes)!" her voice ringing with emotion.

Gesturing dramatically, with her thumb pointed right at Raven, she said loudly, "He is the shooter of the great bear... he is no longer Wasichu, he is Okute (Shooter)!"

With his new name still sounding in his ears, Raven watched the warriors as they repeated it. Then they raised their weapons overhead and shouted, "Okute! Okute!"

The unexpected praise sent a thrill coursing down his back. Seeing all the smiles and hearing Little Hawk and Blue Feather join in, caused Raven to swallow hard on the lump in his throat.

EXCERPT FROM THE JOURNAL OF CETAN CHICKALA (LITTLE HAWK)

My encounter with the great bear brought me much honor. It brought even more for my friend, Okute. Never have my people seen a gun shoot so fast or with such deadly results.

Those that were there or within hearing are saying that perhaps Spotted Horse was right. Maybe this wasichu was sent to us from the gods. His gun sounded like very loud thunder which is the type of weapon that a Thunder Being would probably have.

I do not think that Okute is a god. I know that he is a great warrior and is very different from other men, but he is still just a man. My mother also thinks that the wasichu is a man. She has not spoken of this with me but it shows in her actions. Before the great bear, my mother would not speak with Okute. Now she will go out of her way to cross his path. It is almost as if she were a young maiden again. I have noticed that she now wears her braids down her back like a girl and has been spending a lot of time in her mother's tipi. I say 'her mother's tipi' because her father was killed by a wounded buffalo many winters ago.

After my father had been rubbed out, the tipi had become her home again, but she never used to spend so much time in there. Once, when I was walking by, I sneaked a peek inside. She was sewing something. I did not have time to see what it was because she caught me. She turned to my grandmother, White Star, and said, 'The coyotes are becoming more brave. If we do not watch out they will spy on us and cause all kinds of mischief.''

Embarrassed at being caught spying like a skulking Crow, I had quickly run away. Still, my mother's actions were very puzzling. Okute has been acting strange, also. Whenever I see him, he is laughing and joking. He even lets me ride The Black whenever I want to.

It was confusing to me until the other boys began to tease me about Okute courting my mother. I did not believe it. Our band was small; if someone was being 'courted' everyone would know about it. Perhaps the people were deliberately keeping the news from me. Later that day the teasing reached a point where I could no longer ignore it and I did something that I later regretted. Well, sort of regretted.

We were playing a game called Throwing-Them-Off-Their-Horses. It is like fighting a battle without any killing. We boys choose sides and line up opposite each other on our ponies. Then we charge each other, yelling and screaming, and we grapple and push, trying to knock the others off their horses. Those that fall off their horses are considered to be rubbed out.

Whenever we played this game we tried to make it as much like a real battle as we could. Sometimes we even played naked. In a real battle, many of our warriors would fight wearing nothing but a loin cloth because they believed that they were much quicker without clothing.

An older boy named Red Pony was saying some bad things about Okute and my mother. He was deliberately trying to anger me. It was like I was a thorn in his hand that he had to keep picking at, poking and prodding to get the poison out. Finally he succeeded.

Being a member of my battle group, he moved his pony up next to mine and stuck his big nosed face by my ear as he said, "I wonder if the wasichu has taken your mother into his blanket yet. She looks like she would welcome a chance to be in anyone's blanket!"

A fury took hold of me. I do not know if it was because of what Red Pony said about my mother or if it was the thought of her taking another husband. I do know that later Red Pony wished that he had left me alone.

I leaped from my pony toward him, attacking with the ferocity of a mountain cat. He quickly leaned backwards thinking that I would fly by between him and his horse's neck. He was right. I did miss him. But, as I flew by, I grabbed one of his braids. Although he was a much bigger boy, he did not have a chance. Because of my weight and my determination not to let go, Red Pony was jerked off his pony as though he had been slapped off by a grizzly.

WASICHU

I landed in the dirt on my hands and knees. Red Pony was not so fortunate. Maybe it was because I never let go of his hair until he hit the ground, but whatever the cause, the results would not change. He hit hard landing flat on his back in a pile of horse droppings. He was dazed! I was astride him in an instant and put my two-blade knife at his throat. Red Pony's eyes got real big when he felt the knife. Reaching behind me I found a clump just the right size and quickly jammed it into Red Pony's mouth. All the boys began laughing and pointing. I was still too furious to see the humor in this situation. I simply wanted to punish him. In a moment though, I realized that he did look pretty silly staring at me with a horse turd sticking out of his mouth.

Still full of anger, I mounted Hawk's Wing, deciding it was best to leave. My friends were still laughing as they watched Red Pony rise to his feet while spitting with great ardor. I noticed that he did not look toward me as I left.

Later that day my second parent, Deer Walking, told me that my mother wished to speak with me. Expecting my grandfather and Short Bow to be with her, I was surprised to find her alone in her mother's tipi. I was expecting a tongue lashing for my having attacked Red Pony.

Her gaze never left my face as she gestured for me to sit down beside her. Dropping her gaze, she said, "I know we are not to speak directly to each other as you near warrior status, however, I feel that we must."

She looked up. Her eyes captivated me with love and concern that I could see swimming in their dark depths.. Her voice had a serious quality that I had never heard.

"I do not know where to start with what I want to say to you. So let me begin from here."

Her eyes still held mine as she brought her left fist up and pressed it against her heart.

"I love you very much. Your father is no longer with us, yet I will always love him, and I will always cherish his memory and our time together."

113

I felt a lump forming in my throat as I remembered my father and of the many things that we had shared.

"The time has come for us to be a whole family again. Okute and I wish to marry. He knows that he will not replace your father, but he wishes to be your friend."

She lowered her eyes. Her fingers were entwined in her lap as she awaited my response.

I looked upon her great beauty and realized that my mother was still a young woman. What right had I, a boy of twelve winters, to decide whether or not my mother should be happy? I was proud that she loved me so much that she was willing to give up her happiness rather than cause me any pain.

Placing my hand on her shoulder, I waited until she looked at me before I said, "Mother, Okute is a great warrior and a true friend to me. How could I be against something that will only make both of us more happy?"

As I continued to talk I saw that tears of happiness had begun to pool in her eyes.

"I know that part of the reason that I am here is because of what I did this afternoon. I will not say that I am sorry for what happened, Red Pony got what he deserved. I will promise that it will not happen again."

With a grin beginning to take shape, I said, "'I know for sure that Red Pony will not cause any more trouble. He will not wish to taste my anger ever again."

As I laughed aloud at my bad joke, my mother studied me with a puzzled expression. She must not have heard all the details concerning my bad behavior.

Reaching behind her she then brought forth something wrapped in soft doeskin. Placing the small bundle between us she said, "This is what I have been doing while you were busy sneaking around like a coyote."

She carefully unwrapped the doeskin revealing a pair of moccasins, beautifully decorated with beadwork and quill. It was then that I understood why she did not want me to see her working

WASICHU

on them.

Among the Lakota, for a woman to make a pair of moccasins for a man and then to place them on his feet is the same as saying that she plans to wed that person. For the man to keep them and to wear them publicly is to say that he is accepting her for a wife.

"These are for Okute, if he will take them."

I moved closer to her and placed my hand on hers. I felt a closeness with her that I had not experienced for a long time.

"Mother... if he does not accept your moccasins he would be a fool, and the last thing I would ever accuse Okute of being is a fool."

My mother silently agreed and letting my mind roam at will, I thought of the day Okute came to us and of the many things that have happened since that time. His closeness with Chief Spotted Horse, his brother-like friendship with Bear's Foot, and how he saved me from the grizzly. All these things make it seem that he has been here much longer than two moons.

I suddenly asked her, "Do you ever wonder where he came from? He never talks about his family or places he has seen and remembered. It is like this is the only place he has ever been."

Her eyes widened and asked, "Tell me. Do you think that Okute was sent here by the gods?"

I thought for a moment.

I was flattered that she would ask her son of thirteen winters such a serious question... well, almost thirteen.

"I have not once thought of the wasichu as anything but a man. He is a great warrior with strange weapons and mighty fighting skills, but he is still a man. Besides, he is always asking me things about the Lakota. Would he not know these things already if he was a god?"

Her gaze softened as she nodded her head and pulled me close. I did not pull away, but I thought of doing so. What if someone were to take a quick peek inside and see me being cuddled like an infant? My fears were unfounded for my mother soon released me. I left for Deer Walking's lodge with happy thoughts flitting about in my head.

TEN
~~~

Wanting to be alone, Raven left the camp. Their new campsite was on the edge of a small lake and was surrounded by rolling grasslands, except for a small stand of pine and juniper along the northern exposure.

Once clear of the village, he walked along the edge of the lake. Since there was a slight breeze, he knew there shouldn't be many insects.

Walking at a leisurely pace, he enjoyed the quiet beauty of what was probably a Montana sunset. All at once he had a powerful longing. He couldn't imagine what had triggered it but he knew there wasn't a thing he could do about it. Damn, he thought, I'd give just about anything for a Big Mac, a large order of fries, and a Coke. A quiet chuckle slipped past his lips. It's funny how it's the little things that I miss the most... salt, coffee. It would be nice to see a ball game, or maybe have a few beers. The things that he'd always taken for granted are the things he missed the most. It was the same deal in 'Nam, he mused, only this time my tour of duty has been extended indefinitely.

A couple of hundred yards from the camp he came to a strip of pine and juniper. After he carefully scouted the area, he moved into the trees. He found a small clearing near the edge of the water. Knowing that he could never be too careful, he stood motionless in the trees and watched and listened.

Time passed and with it went the orange and purple sunset. He waited. The last of the red sky disappeared and darkness ruled. When his eyes had adjusted to the dark, Chris moved into the clearing. He stayed motionless for a short period of time. Satisfied that there was no danger, he removed his poncho. Spreading the blanket on the grass, he laid down, keeping the pump-gun close at hand.

    Raven relaxed and let his mind drift. He thought of the Sioux, his people now. They really are my people now, he mused. I have to admit, I have never been happier. His thoughts turned to Blue Feather. He knew there was no turning back now. Bear had told him that the only thing left of the series of rituals was the public show of acceptance by both parties and the presenting of gifts to Spotted Horse. Once that was over, they would married. And, unless something unexpected happened, he would have a son. He worried briefly that Little Hawk might resent him, but pushed that thought aside and felt the excitement begin to build.

    Yesterday, Bear had approached him carrying a large, folded blanket. The big warrior handled it as though it was made out of glass. The blanket was half red and the other half blue. The colors were divided by a strip of gold cloth. Crossing the intersection of gold was a belt of intricate beadwork. The geometric designs were created by the use of red, white, blue, and green beads.

    Bear had been very serious in his explanation of what was expected of Raven in his upcoming ceremony.

    "Listen, Kola, I borrowed this courting blanket from another friend. I want you to listen to what I have to say."

    Looking up at the stars, Chris tried to remember the details of the ceremony. At first he had thought the ritual silly, but after having experienced it he found it to be hauntingly beautiful.

    At dusk Bear and Raven had strolled through the village side by side. Their destination was Blue Feather's mother's tipi. Bear's Foot was dressed in a manner befitting a chief. His elk-skin shirt was beautifully beaded and fringed and the bottom half of the shirt had been painted a vivid green. He was wearing a red loin cloth and fringed leggings trimmed in horse hair and ermine pelts. In his hair were three

WASICHU

eagle feathers. His braids were wrapped in velvet-soft otter skin. With his great size and bearing he looked every inch a king.

On the other hand, Raven felt absolutely ridiculous in his outfit. It had all started when Bear had wanted Chris to play a courting flute outside of Blue Feather's lodge. He had flat out refused. As a compromise, Raven had consented to be costumed in this way. He was wrapped in the courting blanket from head to calf. His eyes and nose were the only parts of his face that were visible.

They had stopped several yards away from Blue Feather's tipi. Raven hesitated, so Bear's Foot with a softly intoned *'Huhn'* for courage gave him a little shove. The 'little' shove propelled him toward the tipi as though he had been launched from a giant slingshot. Regaining his balance and his courage, Chris began to pace back and forth in front of Blue Feather's lodge. He silently thanked God that the Lakota rite was done at night, rather than in revealing daylight.

He remembered thinking, what if she doesn't come 'out? What can I do about it? A little voice inside his mind had said, "Nothing... if she doesn't want you there isn't a thing you can do about it."

Raven's little mind games could have gone on forever, except that all of a sudden, she was standing there in front of the tipi's door flap. Her beauty was a wild, natural image such as that projected by reflections on a mountain lake in the early morning's soft light.

Her dress was made of bleached doeskin, appearing snow white in the evening's weak illumination. It was richly designed with elaborate quill-work and her skirt and bodice were covered with elk's teeth and hawk's bells.

Although unable to take his eyes off from her, Raven continued to pace as instructed. Her eyes followed his in a manner that was both endearing and hypnotic. Heart pounding, he allowed his pacing to draw him within a couple of feet of her beaded moccasins. He stopped directly in front of her. Then he reached out and grasped her wrist and pulled. He saw a flicker of something in her eyes. She resisted his pull. Instantly, a twisted knot of apprehension formed in his stomach. He pulled again. She held back. Raven's heart sank. Then, with a smile that dazzled his senses, she relented and allowed herself to be enfolded into his blanket.

    Chris shook himself loose from his woolgathering and raised up on his elbows. He cradled the pump-gun and thought of Blue Feather. He could almost sense her body next to him as it had been the night before. Her smell of sweet grass and sage had lingered in his nostrils half the night. He smiled, recalling that when he had taken her inside his blanket people began to come out of their tipis.

    In his whole life Raven had never felt so foolish as he had standing with Blue Feather wrapped tightly in his blanket, while scores of people milled about making a concentrated effort not to look at them. If he hadn't known better Raven would have thought that it was a planned village effort to 'police the area' and to clean up the grounds surrounding the many lodges. Everywhere Chris had looked there were people making an obvious effort not to look at them, but of course, they were all secretly watching. Being a wise but devious man, Bear's Foot hadn't told him about that part of the ceremony.

    Raven was falling asleep. As he slipped away, his last lucid thought was a frivolous one. With all those people watching, how was it possible for him not to have been able to make eye contact with even one person?

    Suddenly he was awake. He didn't know what had awakened him, but one of his senses must have triggered his inner alarm system. Raven had no idea how long he had slept. He was thankful for the moonlight. It revealed that if there was danger it wasn't close at hand.

WASICHU

A slight, indiscernible sound caressed his right ear. Raven soundlessly moved his body onto his right side so that he was facing the source of the sound. He clutched the pistol grip of the Winchester pump and thumbed the hammer back to half-cock. The sound came again. He couldn't quite make out what it was... then suddenly he knew... hawk's bells.

Rising to his feet, Chris stared toward the direction of the camp. In a moment he saw the slim form moving gracefully through the pine trees. He called softly in Lakota, "*Washtay, Niyaha To* (Blue Feather)."

She came into the clearing with the grace and bearing of a princess. With each gliding step her bells were making their tiny musical sounds. She stopped so closely in front of him that he could smell her. The sweet grass and sage scent was making his head spin. They stood close together, not touching, and looked into each other's eyes. Chris was enchanted by her large almond shaped eyes, the high cheekbones perfectly fitting her oval face. The arched brows, the graceful curves of her full lips... he was enthralled.

"I have come to you, Okute."

Her voice, with the soft intonation of the Sioux language, came to Chris as though carried on the wind.

"I am here," he said. "I will always be here for you."

Slowly he brought his hands up and placed them gently on the sides of her face. She tilted her face up, looking deep into his eyes, as he brought his mouth down to hers. She jerked her head back and away, her eyes full of wonder and shock.

Raven quickly added, "Don't be afraid. I would die before I would hurt you."

Cursing himself for being an idiot, Raven suddenly realized that maybe the Sioux didn't know about kissing. She probably thought I was going to bite her, he mused.

"Among us wasichu, two people that love each other bring their lips together."

Her large dark eyes were fixed on his face throughout his brief explanation. He couldn't read her expression except that she sure looked interested.

Then Blue Feather brought her hands up to the sides of his face and pulled it down. Surprised with her abruptness he flinched. Holding his face firmly, she carefully placed her lips on his. Raven put his arms around her and pulled her to him. Her lips and hands remained on his face and he could feel her soft body mold against him. Chris felt her lips trembling as her breath quickened. Her hands dropped to his chest. All at once she pushed against him. His sexual appetite having been truly whetted, Raven resisted. Blue Feather immediately stopped pushing. She looked deep into his eyes while gently placing her finger tips on his mouth. She stepped back. He released her even though he wanted her so badly that it was painful. Then he realized why she had pushed him away. With his eyes locked with hers, Chris couldn't see exactly how she did it, but the hawk's bells stopped tinkling. When he looked, he discovered she was totally naked.

In their urgency, Blue Feather's help turned into hindrance as they struggled to remove Raven's clothes. Finally, Raven stopped and let her finish what they had started together.

He was so enamored by her closeness and the softness of her skin that at first he didn't understand the sound of defeat in her voice as she exclaimed, "*Ey-hee!*"

As Blue Feather dropped to her knees in frustration, he realized that she was generations away from having experienced the zipper.

Smiling to himself, Raven unzipped his jeans and quickly removed them. Seeing that her eyes, instead of watching him, had followed the mystery of the zipper, he quickly shook off his bruised ego along with his last article of clothing and fell to his knees, also.

WASICHU

Softly, with great tenderness, Chris reached out with his hands, cupping her face. Her eyes bore into his with undisguised passion as she reached out, searching, finding then clasping him within her small fist. Surprised by her strength as much as her initiative, Raven felt his knees tremble as he took her satin smooth body into his arms and they toppled over onto his blanket. His left hand reflexively shot out softening their fall. His right hand, groping for her upper arm, found instead, her breast. An involuntary "*dho*" escaped her lips as his questing finger-tips caressed the rigid nipple.

In an instant their bodies were entwined. Her velvet soft body covered him with a blanket of writhing, hot flesh. The heady scents of sage, wild flowers and passion filled his nostrils while Blue Feather's softly pliant form filled his hands. An involuntary gasp escaped both their mouths as she brought her legs up and slid astride him. Raven, with his hands buried in the softness of her hips, lifted and slowly lowered her, transfixing her with his passion. A soft cry was heard as she settled down onto his body. For a brief heartbeat of time neither moved. Then, in a movement as old as life itself, they slowly, gently succumbed to their rising passions and plunged into the depths of their desire. They struggled frantically, fiercely striving to reach the surface as they climbed, soared and finally rode up through the barrier into ecstasy.

A sudden intake of air was followed by a sigh of pleasure as Blue Feather and Raven clutched each other with passion's strength. Breathing deeply they gradually eased into each other's welcoming arms.

ELEVEN

They awoke in the predawn stillness wrapped in one another's arms. Although alone, they whispered as they spoke of their future and of Little Hawk. She told Raven of their talk and of the boy's incident with Red Pony. Raven was amazed at Little Hawk's maturity and laughed uproariously as Blue Feather related the details of his revenge over the older boy. They stayed closely entwined until the sun's first rays broke above the eastern horizon.

He watched as the light filtered through the branches of the pines, painting a filigree of gold on her umber form. His eyes absorbed her beauty as she spoke quietly of the many things that needed to be done before they established their place within the band's society. While they talked, he continued to watch the light play across the fields and valleys of her lithe body. All at once Raven realized that Blue Feather had stopped talking. Seeing the question in her eyes, he smiled and tapped his temple with a finger as he said, "I am sorry, a mistake has been made. You are so beautiful that I am memorizing every detail of you so that I can take you with me, up here."

A radiant smile lit up her face and she scrambled to her knees. Blue Feather captured his face between her hands and kissed him as though she had been kissing since she was sixteen.

When she stopped, Raven shook his head in mock amazement and exclaimed, "You sure are a fast learner!"

Blue Feather, her voice husky with emotion said, "I love you, Okute. For you I will do anything."

Raven's voice broke as he replied, "And I love you."

Quickly, as though to hide his embarrassment, Chris began to dress. Smiling, he said, "If I don't hurry, Bear's Foot will leave on the scout without me."

Bear and Raven, along with two other warriors, were going to travel west and scout for Bluecoats, following the route to the gathering place of the tribes.

Blue Feather began to dress, also. She tried to make a game of it, racing to see who could finish first. She was giggling like a school girl and had him soundly whipped until she saw him zip up his pants.

She stopped, dropped her bodice, and stared at his fly. Seeing her stare, Chris stopped and didn't move. I don't believe this, he thought, it's like a burlesque routine. Struggling to suppress his laughter he watched her reach toward the exposed top of his zipper. Just as her fingers were about to touch the zipper's tab, Raven's hand shot out and captured her hand in a firm grip. Startled, she attempted to jerk her hand free. Her gaze leaped to Raven's face and saw his boyish grin and heard his laughter. Pleased that he was so happy, but not really understanding why or what was so funny, she joined in and shared his laughter.

Still chuckling to himself, Raven was about to put on his hiking boots when Blue Feather abruptly stopped him. She held out a restraining hand and then ran the few steps to the edge of the clearing. The tinkle of her bells worked their magic on Raven as he awaited her return. In an instant she returned carrying a small bundle.

The sun, having fully risen, encompassed her as she knelt in front of him. He watched the sunlight as it picked coppery highlights from her hair as she slowly opened the package.

Chris was struck speechless by the beauty of the red and black moccasins. Watching her as she carefully placed them on his feet, he sensed that they were more than just a gift between lovers.

WASICHU

He strode proudly about the clearing enjoying the lack of weight and the unbelievable comfort of his very first pair of moccasins. Returning to Blue Feather he lifted her into the air and grinned up at her as he said, "I love them. I will cherish them forever."

He carefully sat her down. Her dark eyes stared intently into his, and she said, "I am happy that you like them, my husband."

He stared as though he believed that he hadn't heard her correctly. Blue Feather quickly explained the Lakota custom, finishing with the words, "If you want me for a wife you must wear the moccasins publicly. We will then be considered husband and wife."

Dropping her eyes, she continued, "If you do not want me, you will publicly remove them."

His face expressionless, Raven nodded slowly and said, "This is a very serious matter. I will have to think about my decision."

Seeing her crestfallen face, he swiftly added, "I am teasing! I am your husband. I will always love you."

She trembled as his pale eyes seemed to send a message to her very soul. Suddenly, she threw herself into his arms. They embraced for a long moment.

"I must go. Bear's Foot will be waiting."

Breaking their embrace, Raven turned away. He quickly scooped up the blanket poncho and grabbed the pump-gun. Tying the laces of his hiking boots together, he slung them over his shoulder. Turning to leave, he stopped and looked at Blue Feather. He grinned as he said, "Perhaps when I return I will show you the mystery of the zipper."

Her full lips spread in a dazzling smile. There was a glint of mischief in her eyes as she replied, "Once you reveal the mystery of the zipper, perhaps you will allow me to explore what is hidden behind it."

Raven then strode off in the direction of the village.

His moccasins were so light he felt like he was walking on air. But then, maybe it wasn't the moccasins that made him feel so light of foot.

TWELVE
~~~~~~

Raven walked The Black along the northern edge of the village. Bear's Foot had told him that he would meet him on the western side. Watching the sun's brightness wash over the tipis he hoped that he hadn't kept him waiting.

Everywhere he looked there were people already up and about. Every lodge he passed, the people would smile and speak to him. He had an entourage of children petting The Black and playing their games as they walked beside him. It was pretty obvious that everyone knew about him and Blue Feather. I guess small towns have always been this way, he mused. Some of the villagers had openly admired his moccasins, others would look and grin. Young girls felt that they were worthy of at least a giggle or two. It appeared that he was being accepted by all. If not, he reasoned, he wasn't going to worry about it. As far as he was concerned, nothing was capable of changing how they felt about each other.

Still thinking of Blue Feather, Raven felt a small hand join his own on The Black's lead. Little Hawk's inscrutable brown face peered up at him. The small face with his mother's large eyes appeared very serious. He looked at Chris' moccasins, then lifted his gaze to his face. His expression gave nothing away. Relinquishing his hold on the lead, he let Hawk take over and just walked beside him. Raven was momentarily at a loss for words. Suddenly he stopped and turned the boy toward him. Little Hawk stared directly into Raven's eyes. Worried, Chris remembered reading somewhere that, 'The eyes are the windows of the soul.' In this case he hoped that it wasn't true because Little Hawk's appeared to be completely devoid of feelings.

Speaking in a halting, self-conscious manner, Raven

said, "Hawk, I love your mother very much and I will never let any harm come to her. You are almost a man and will soon be able to take care of yourself. But if ever you need me, I will be there for you."

Chris extended his hand as though to shake. Little Hawk looked at his hand, then lifted his gaze to his face. All at once Little Hawk stepped forward and his small body slammed into Raven's, his arms wrapped around his waist, clasping and squeezing. He barely had a chance to hug him back before the boy was off and running. Little Hawk stopped about fifty feet away, spun around and faced him. With the sun at his back it wasn't possible for Raven to see the boy's expression and it wasn't really necessary. When he heard Little Hawk's words, their meaning covered the distance between them instantly.

"Have a safe journey, Okute! My mother and I will await your return. Do not worry about her for I will be at her side at all times."

As Little Hawk ran away and disappeared behind some lodges, Raven had to blink repeatedly to relieve the sudden burn from some invisible sand that was causing his eyes to tear.

It had been several days since he had last seen Spotted Horse. He was talking with Bear's Foot and several other Sioux when Raven and The Black approached. Of the five that made up the group, Chris only recognized four. The fifth was a burly, mean-eyed Indian with an equally mean looking boil on his cheekbone.

Seeing Bear's Foot's greeting, Chief Spotted Horse faced Raven and gave him a welcoming smile. As always, he felt a jolt whenever exposed to that smile. Joe, you bastard, he thought, 'why aren't you here? I miss you.'

Spotted Horse's eyes dropped to Raven's feet and the smile disappeared. His gaze lifted and he asked, "What is this?"

WASICHU

Out of respect, as well as curiosity, the other men stopped talking. All eyes were turned toward Raven and the chief.

Spotted Horse's dark eyes studied Raven's gray ones. Raven returned the chief's serious look.

"Tell me, Okute, are you taking this woman for a wife . . .?" He asked the question with his arms crossed over his chest, indicating love. "... or are you just taking?"

On the word 'taking' the chief shot both his hands out to grab and then jerked them back.

Letting the pump dangle from its sling, Raven decided to add a little drama of his own by crossing his arms across his chest as he replied, "She is my wife. There is not a man alive who could take her without feeling her butcher knife or my gun at his head."

The old chief grinned widely and stepped forward, embracing Raven as he said, "I am happy for you, my son. She is like a blood daughter to me."

"She will always be safe, Spotted Horse. This I promise you from my heart."

Bear's Foot let out a blood-curdling whoop that probably turned a few heads in Sitting Bull's camp over the western horizon. Bear then leaped upon Raven, pummeling him on the back while trying to embrace him at the same time. Grinning, Raven turned away and experienced a mild shock. Standing squarely in front of him was a smiling Wolf's Spirit.

The young Lakota stepped forward. Offering his hand white man fashion, he said, "Wonumayin (A mistake has been made). Okute, I have wronged you. At first I had thought that you were simply a wasichu looking to get whatever he could get from us Lakota. Now I know that I was wrong. You are a great warrior, a Thunder Being sent to us by Sky Father to help us fight the Bluecoats."

Taking the offered hand, Raven put his other arm

over the young warrior's shoulder and turned to the chief as he said, "It must be as you say, Spotted Horse. I must have been sent by the gods. How else could I be so fortunate? I have the most beautiful woman in the Lakota nation as a wife and I have two of our bravest warriors for friends."

This last remark brought a derisive grunt from the unknown warrior who was fussing with his wooden saddle. Ignoring him, Chris turned to Wolf's Spirit as he said, "If a mistake has been made, then I am the one who made it. If it is truly being offered, I will cherish your friendship."

With those words, Chris offered his hand once more. Wolf's Spirit grinned, nodded, and shook his hand. The other warrior of their party, Kills Twice, shook his hand also. Without any further conversation the scouting party waved their goodbyes to Spotted Horse and pointed their horses westward.

Part 4
Enemies

THIRTEEN
~~~~~~~~

    While traveling, most Indians would ride single file. Whites would usually ride side by side, enabling them to talk with one another. The Indian way made more sense in a country where danger could be behind the next hill or around the next bend. By traveling single file there is less dust to be seen by hostile eyes and there is also a much smaller target if two enemy parties were to accidently meet face to face.

    Raven found himself to be third in their file right behind Bear's Foot. Wolf's Spirit and Kills Twice brought up the rear. All Raven knew of Kills Twice was that his fierce looks belied his great sense of humor and winning smile. Leading the procession was Standing Elk, the surly one with the boil. Bear's Foot had told Chris that Elk was a Hunkpapa, one of Sitting Bull's men who had been sent as a messenger to Spotted Horse.

    All day they rode. Alternating between a walk and a canter they moved across the rolling prairie. The country was beautiful, festooned with wild flowers and multiple grasses. Scattered clumps of pine and cedar made emerald castles atop some of the rolling hills. Chris noticed that the prairie grass was so tall in some areas it brushed the bellies of their ponies.

    The area they were moving into had become more noticeably rugged. Here and there, granite and sandstone abutments were sticking out like blemishes on the face of the prairie.

    When color began to illuminate the western sky, Raven was relieved. By the time they decided to camp for the night, his legs, butt, and lower back were aching from so many hours in the saddle.

After stiffly climbing down from The Black, Raven took his razor and moved down by the stream to shave and wash up. As he moved the straight edge across his face, he thought of old Bill down in Wyoming. Bill had given Chris the ivory handled razor as a parting gift. Now, nearly every time he used it he thought of Bill. He found of late that he had been thinking of the past, or future, whatever the hell it was, less and less, but once in a while old Bill would pop up.

He had been scraping away at his beard, thinking about the old cowboy, when he realized that he wasn't hearing any camp noise from the other four. Turning around, he saw three sets of eyes staring at him. Smiling to himself, Raven realized that they had never seen anyone shave before. Bear's Foot, who had already been through the 'shaving bit' with him weeks ago, was busy working an edge onto his fighting knife. The other three stood there and stared.

Raven was dry shaving, no water or soap; just the razor's keen edge scraping off the bulk of the whiskers. It was a noisy, raspy way of shaving that only sounded painful. Most of the twelve years that Chris had been in the army were spent in the field where there was rarely access to hot water, so he had learned to improvise.

Having plucked their facial hair for generations, shaving was foreign to most Indians. The blanket Indians that hung around the forts and the ones on the reservations probably knew about shaving, but to the wild ones it was something new and strange.

Finally, Raven said to the curious group, "What's the matter? Have you never seen a man skin himself before?"

Ignoring the three bewildered faces, Chris resumed his shaving.

When he heard Bear's Foot's bray of laughter, he smiled, knowing that as long as his friend was laughing, everything had to be all right.

WASICHU

At first light they breakfasted on jerky and some wild berries. Eager to get under way, they ate as they made their individual preparations. He chewed happily away on his meat as he dug into his *par fleche* (Indian saddle bags) looking for something cooler to wear. He pulled out an old purple tee-shirt and put it on.

While stroking The Black's velvet muzzle, he noticed again the notches on his ears. When he had first noticed them he had asked Bear about it. He remembered how Bear had clapped him on the back and assured him that he had the best type of horse he could ever have. The notches indicated that the bearer is fully trained in both war and the hunt.

His musing was interrupted by a loud "*dho!*" from Bear's Foot. His exclamation of surprise startled both him and The Black, who skittered a little away from him.

Raven had heard his approach, but the sudden noise caused him to instinctively bring the shotgun up. Seeing the sudden reaction, Bear stopped and stared.

Dropping the muzzle of the pump, Chris saw that Bear was still staring. He wasn't staring at the shotgun but was intently staring at Raven's chest. Damn it, he thought, I keep forgetting that some of the little things I take for granted are things that they've never seen before

On the front of Raven's tee-shirt was an imprint, a silk screening of the Minnesota Viking's logo, along with their mascot, a stylized profile of a Norseman, yellow braids and all. It was done in bright gold and white. Even though it was an old tee-shirt, the purple background made the colors really stand out.

Bear's Foot and Wolf's Spirit both stepped up to Raven for a closer look. Wolf's Spirit was infatuated. A big grin was on his face as he touched the imprint.

Raven thrust The Black's reins into Wolf's Spirit's hand, stuck the shotgun between his knees, and peeled off the shirt. The lump-faced Hunkpapa yelled angrily, "*Hopo* (let us go)!"

Ignoring Standing Elk, Raven thrust the tee-shirt into Wolf's Spirit's hand.

"I'll tell you what it says later... it's yours!"

Looking up beyond Bear's Foot's smiling face, Chris saw Standing Elk astride his pony, scowling ominously and wearing a narrow-eyed, pissed-off expression. For obvious reasons the Hunkpapa really irritated him.

Waving and smiling from ear to ear, Raven said in English, "Well, fuck you very much, you lump-faced son-of-a-bitch."

Just to upset him even more, Chris decided to take the time to explain the shirt design to Wolf Spirit.

Not having a written language, it came as a shock when he told them the big word was *Minnesota* (Lakota word for 'many waters').

In explaining further, he said, "The blond guy was a great warrior from the land called Minnesota, and the horn on his headdress came from one of his enemies called the Los Angeles Ram."

They stared at him, speechless.

Raven mounted The Black and fumbled in his bag for another shirt. Wolf Spirit stepped forward offering his hand white man style. Raven gave it a quick shake as Wolf said, "*Okute le mita pila* (my thanks, Okute)."

Surprised by all the fuss over a tee-shirt, Raven just smiled and gave him a nod.

He let The Black walk him over to join the others as he rummaged through his rawhide bag trying to find a tee-shirt without any design on it.

FOURTEEN
~~~~~~~~

They had been moving northwest for several hours when Standing Elk brought his pony to an abrupt halt. Turning his head he cupped his ear and listened.

A faint popping sound could be heard. Any military man who had ever been in combat could recognize distant gunfire. Raven's comrades were no exception.

The four began talking Lakota much faster than Chris could understand it. All he was able to pick up at the moment were bits and pieces. He could tell that the shots had come from the northwest, but not used to judging distances in open country, Raven had no idea how far away they were from the gunfire.

Eventually their Lakota quieted down, and Chris was able to follow what they were saying. Standing Elk told them that Sitting Bull's encampment was still a full day's ride away. They all agreed that the shots could have been intended for some of their people who were hunting or out scouting for Bluecoats and decided that they had best investigate.

Wolf's Spirit and Kills Twice galloped their ponies out to the flanks and moved on ahead of the others as a double point. Raven watched them as they rode away, getting smaller and smaller until they were out of sight.

Time passed. Then, in the distance, they saw a rider coming toward them riding hard, whipping his horse as though he was being pursued by a horde of devils. As the rider drew closer, they saw that it was Wolf's Spirit and reined in their horses. Seeing his friends, he pulled his mount to a stop and turned him into a spin while twirling a blanket overhead.

Not knowing their signals, Raven was a heartbeat behind the others in putting his heels into his horse's ribs. The three joined Wolf's Spirit and he whipped his stallion with his quirt so that he could lead them. While they rode at a ground covering lope, Wolf's Spirit relinquished the lead enough so that he could talk to Bear's Foot. He was evidently upset; his eyes were flashing with restrained fury. Chris was only able to pick up a word or two. He heard 'men killed' and 'prisoner.' 'Dead horses' were also mentioned, but the word that captured all of Raven's attention was 'wasichus.' Wolf's Spirit had spat the word out as if it was the foulest thing ever to pass his lips and then had used his quirt again to pull ahead.

In a short time they came to a long hill covered at the top with pine trees. It was several hundred yards long and maybe two-hundred feet high. As they approached its base they saw Kills Twice emerge from the trees near the top and run downhill toward his horse. Seeing the warrior's urgency, they were able to converge at his horse.

Winded and with urgency Kills Twice said, "We must hurry. Two are dead already and more will die shortly."

Kills Twice stayed with their horses while the rest of them carefully but swiftly made their way to the top of the ridge. They glided around trees and other obstacles with the grace of wolves as they eased up to the far edge.

Flat on his belly, Raven cautiously peered around the base of a resinous tree trunk and looked down into a small valley. The first thing that he saw was a dead Indian; then another. Three horses were down and the closest one had an Indian's leg pinned beneath it. Another uninjured warrior stood close by and was guarded by several armed white men. Judging from their beadwork and hair styles, Raven assumed that the Indians were Sioux.

Chris counted eight raiders. One of the whites was

WASICHU

squatting next to the pinned warrior. Two of the gang were rounding up the surviving Sioux horses while another was busy scalping one of the dead Lakota. The remaining four were loosely gathered around the captives and seemed to be arguing about what to do with them.

The outlaws were white except two of them looked to be of mixed blood, either Indian or Mexican.

Bear's Foot and Standing Elk backed away from the edge and began to have a heated discussion. From what Chris could make of it, Standing Elk simply wanted to spread out and open fire on them. Bear was concerned that they might shoot the prisoners. Raven's mind raced. He peered around the tree and looked the terrain over. He tried to see everything at once and still not miss anything. While he was in 'Nam Raven's ability to do the latter had been a gift that had kept him alive more than once. He pulled back and hissed, "*A-ah*."

Bear and Standing Elk looked up.

"While you two are babbling like two old women, those men are going to die."

Almost as a punctuation mark to Raven's words was the flat, hard explosion of a pistol shot! The startling noise sent everyone scrambling back to the edge.

Standing over the pinned warrior was a man in a duster with a smoking revolver dangling from his fist. The Sioux, shot through the leg, must have been in terrible pain. The one who had shot him was nudging the wounded leg with his foot. Even from their poor vantage point they could clearly see that the leg was broken.

The other Sioux exploded into action. He was attempting to reach his friend's tormenter. He must have known that he didn't have a chance of reaching him, but for what he lacked in size he made up for with speed and guts.

From somewhere in his clothing he had pulled out a knife. As he made his move he brandished the knife, causing two of the men to stumble back out of his way. As he flew by, a third man tripped him. Before he was able to get up, another man stepped forward and glanced a rifle barrel off his head. He lay there dazed.

While they were tying the Sioux's hands, Chris noticed how different he was from the other Indians. His skin was lighter than any Sioux that Raven had ever seen. His hair was also different, a dark brown, rather than the blue-black of the other Indians. There was something else, too, but Chris couldn't put his finger on it. He quickly scooted back from his tree and was joined by the others.

Before anyone could say a word, Raven said, "Listen, this is what we are going to do."

He told them his plan, making sure that each knew his role once the shooting started. He wanted the two with rifles, Bear and Standing Elk, to stay on the ridge where they had a good field of fire. The other two, Wolf and Kills Twice, were to work their way around the small valley and get in position on the other flank. When he told them to go, they hesitated.

Standing Elk's sneering face ignited a slow-burning fuse and Raven's anger began to smolder. It was in his voice and his eyes as he said, "You will go now. No one is to fire until they hear my shotgun."

Wolf's Spirit and Kill Twice looked at Bear's Foot.

Keeping his voice low, Raven exclaimed, "Go now!"

Both warriors went rushing down the hill toward their horses.

Chris was already moving down the back side of the hill when he heard an explosive outburst of Lakota from Standing Elk. His words were spoken too fast and too low for Raven to follow, but he paused when he heard Bear's harsh "*Heyah!*"

Seeing the anger on the Hunkpapa's face and Bear's stricken look, he wanted to ask what it was about, but he

WASICHU

couldn't take the time. He ran quietly down the hill to The Black. He quickly dug out his blanket poncho and put it on. Swinging up on his horse he pointed him in the right direction and dug his heels into his ribs. As he rode he reloaded the pump with double-ought buckshot.

Rounding the point of the ridge, he saw that he was still hidden from the outlaws by an adjoining finger of raised terrain that was at a right angle to the hill that Bear and Elk were on.

Pulling The Black to a stop, he dismounted. Moving to his horse's head, Raven stroked his silken muzzle and breathed into his nostrils. It was an old Indian trick that Bill had taught him to make the horse more familiar with Raven's scent, calming him as he is reassured that he is with his owner.

Raven made his preparations for what was to come. Checking the pump-gun one last time, he muttered, "Lock and load, you fuckers, we're about to rock 'n roll."

Underneath the poncho, he adjusted the sling on the shotgun. Then he twisted the blanket so that it concealed most of the gun, leaving only the muzzle exposed. The less they know about this gun, he thought, the better off I'll be. After taking several deep breaths, he began walking into the open, leading The Black.

Raven had decided that once the shooting started he would be more effective fighting on foot, and he really didn't know how The Black would react around loud gunfire. Besides, he mused, I know my capabilities in a fire fight while on my feet, but not on a horse.

His whole plan depended on at least three of the killers riding out to meet him, to see who he was and to discover what he was doing there.

Raven led The Black around an outcrop of rock and into full view of the outlaws. He felt a tightening in his gut when he realized what he was going up against. Thinking quickly he psyched himself up. Remembering his extensive training and countless combat situations, his confidence level began to soar. I'm a professional fighting man, he thought, and as far as combat is concerned, these dudes are a bunch of Neanderthals.

Raven began to experience that peculiar tingle of anticipation as he prepared himself for combat. Just remember, surprise is everything, he cautioned himself.

Chris figured he was about two-hundred yards away when he heard someone shout. Six pale faces turned toward him. He stopped. At that distance he couldn't read their expressions, but he had stopped to give them time to decide what they wanted to do. He didn't want someone panicking and opening up on him with a rifle because he was too close. But, on the other hand, he needed to bring them close so that the pump-gun would be effective.

By not posing an immediate threat, he thought that they might get curious and come closer to talk. They needed to be certain that he was alone. Once they did that, he mused, they'd probably kill me for my horse and gear. Under his breath he murmured, "But, you're going to find out that it's not as easy as you think... you murdering sonsabitches."

He watched as several of the men mounted up. A big man wearing a duster and riding a paint seemed to be the leader. He wondered if he was the one that was torturing the Indian. One of the riders kicked his horse into motion and rode away toward the two gang members who were with the captured horses.

Raven silently implored them. Come on, come on! Let's get it on! He was beginning to sweat. He'd love to be able to take the blanket off but he knew he needed it. Underneath the blanket, Chris let the shotgun hang by its sling as he tried to keep his gun hand dry.

Tugging on The Black's reins Raven moved forward again, wanting to get as close to the captives as possible

WASICHU

before all hell broke loose. He grasped the pump's pistol grip and made himself ready.

He felt an immediate respite when he saw four of the men wheel their horses and walk toward him and made his last stop. As he readied himself, he thought, thank God, no long range sniping. He waited. Under the poncho his thumb eased the hammer back until he felt it settle into full cock.

He hoped that from a distance he would look like some raggedy-assed drifter who had just stumbled into an unknown situation. Had the four riders been closer, they surely would have reached a different conclusion.

Raven's eyes were everywhere. They were looking above and to his right front, seeking out Bear and Standing Elk, and they were looking to the left, praying that Wolf and Kills Twice were in position. They were also looking beyond the oncoming outlaws to the captives and their two guards.

Then the time came when his cold, gray gaze focused in on the approaching four. As he had silently predicted, they spread out until they were four abreast. He began to assess which of the four was the most dangerous. Moving from left to right: first was a big, dirty hunter type, armed with a large-bore, single-shot rifle; next was a slim, narrow-eyed, two-gun packing hard-ass; the third was the leader, a big, one-eyed, mean looking bastard who was already grinning and probably had a gun underneath his long linen duster; and the last man, on Raven's right, looked to be of some mixed blood and was the most relaxed of the bunch. That could mean, he thought, that he's the most dangerous. Chris took note of the new looking, lever-action Winchester resting across his thighs and how he kept his hand wrapped around the stock and trigger.

They pulled their horses to a stop about ten yards away. Then they quietly sat on their horses and stared. The one-eyed leader still had his yellow grin working so Raven grinned back.

A trickle of sweat was working its way down Chris' back. He could feel the tension working on him. He ignored it. He would have sworn that he could feel the adrenalin pumping through his veins.

For such a big man, the leader had a high, twangy voice that sounded almost shrill when he asked, "What you doin' 'round these parts, mister? Don't ya know that the red niggers are painted an' are s'posed to be all over these here hills?"

Wanting to push him a little, Raven replied, "Well, it seems to me that I could ask you the same thing, right?"

The white scar that ran through the leader's left eye turned crimson as he said, "Listen here, mister, you ain't in any position to be askin' me any sassy questions!"

Raven was about to answer when all of a sudden 'Yellow Grin's' shoulder blossomed with an explosion of red and he lurched hard to the left, followed instantly by the booming report of Standing Elk's Spencer rifle.

Numerous things then happened in a splinter of time. Raven's first shot caught the two-gun man square in the chest, knocking him backwards out of his saddle. His handgun, having already been leveled, flew out of his lifeless fingers.

A bullet snapped by Raven's ear as he turned and pumped a load of buckshot into the breed's horse, hitting him in the face and neck. The horse screamed and went down, taking his rider with him.

'Yellow Grin's' pinto lunged forward. The big horse's shoulder hit Chris, spinning him around. He felt the hunter's heavy bullet rip through his blanket. The pinto raced by with the leader reeling in the saddle. Completing his spin, Raven's third shot took the unhorsed breed full in the face just as he was leveling his rifle for his second shot. His head exploded in a red mist and splatter of gore.

He jacked in another shell. His peripheral glance

picked up the hunter who had reloaded and was about to let fly. Throwing his body down and to the left, Chris never even heard the man's shot.

As he turned and fell, he fired in the hunter's general direction. It was a wild attempt to throw his aim off. Raven got lucky.

Some of the buckshot must have hit the man's horse. It was bucking and screaming as the big hunter, cussing and swearing, was trying desperately not to get bucked off and still manage to get another round in his breechloader. Rising to his knees, Raven shouldered the pump and shot the man in the chest. The big rifle fell out of his hands as his bucking horse dumped his body down into the dusty grass. He lay there unmoving, looking like a pile of old clothes.

Scrambling to his feet, Raven began punching more shells into the pump's heated frame and tried to look everywhere at once. He looked east where the leader's horse had taken him. Nothing was in sight. Chris figured his horse had apparently taken him around the outcrop and he had just flat out split.

While his gaze swept the small valley he heard only a few sporadic shots. It must be all over, he thought. He looked quickly toward the captives. Bear's Foot and the light-skinned Sioux were crouched behind a dead horse watching the horses mill around out on the prairie. Raven grinned as he noticed that the wounded Lakota had been pulled free of his dead horse and was returning the favor by sitting on him. Near him were the bodies of the two guards. They looked more like two piles of refuse than they did bodies.

Suddenly, two pistol shots broke the temporary quiet. They came from the cloud of dust that was rising from the churning hooves of the pony herd. From up on the hill, Standing Elk's rifle boomed and the resulting puff of smoke drifted into the pines.

For the first time since dropping his reins, Chris looked for The Black. He felt relief when he saw him standing not ten feet away from where he had left him. His ears were perked and he was staring straight at Raven. It was as though he was asking, "Can we go now?"

Quickly mounting, he swung The Black around so that he was facing the dust cloud and ponies. He still hadn't seen Wolf's Spirit or Kills Twice. Just as he was about to move in that direction, a rider burst out of the hovering dust. Chris thought, looks like one of the bad guys might make it. A booming explosion came from the ridge, causing a spray of dirt to erupt from the ground near the horse and rider. He dug his spurs in and it looked like he was going to get away, but another rider appeared. It was as though he materialized right in front of Chris' eyes. He had an angle on the first rider and was closing fast.

For the first time in his life, Raven heard the blood-curdling war cry of the Sioux. It came from the wild-riding, second rider... Wolf's Spirit!

The outlaw must have realized that he wasn't going to outride his pursuer. He reined his mount to a jarring, sliding halt and began to fire his pistol at the oncoming Wolf's Spirit.

What followed next was an amazing display of horsemanship. His horse running at full gallop, Wolf's Spirit slid from one side to the other, zig-zagging his horse abruptly back and forth. He never gave the man a clear shot at him or his horse. When Wolf was about seventy or eighty feet away from the rider, he suddenly swung his horse broadside and launched an arrow from beneath his stallion's neck.

Even from where Raven was watching, he could clearly see the arrow transfix the man's body. He was facing away from Raven so he could see a full twelve inches of bloody shaft sticking out of his back. He remained in the same position he was in when the arrow struck, body upright, pistol extended outward. The shock of the impact froze him in position as though he had turned to stone. That posture was not to remain, however. Wolf, in the instant that he had released his arrow, had swerved his horse and pointed him directly at the wasichu. In seconds after the missile had struck, Wolf's Spirit was there. As he swept by, his open hand smashed into the face of the dying killer, toppling him off the back of his spooked horse and into the dusty dirt. Wolf's Spirit's wild, "*Anho!*" carried clearly to Raven's ears.

Spinning his horse in a tight circle, Wolf returned. When he dropped from his horse near the body, Chris saw the sun glint off his scalping knife.

Raven's gaze swept the rest of the valley, making sure that it was really over. With the exception of the one-eyed leader, they had bagged them all. And, Chris thought, as hard hit as that Cyclops sonofabitch had been, he wasn't going to last for very long... at least not without some quick medical attention, he mused, and where in hell's he going to find that around here?

Chris heard Kills Twice before he saw him. He came whooping out of some tall grass brandishing a fresh, dripping scalp. He steered his racing pony over to Wolf's Spirit and the two of them rode their ponies at a breakneck pace, swinging their scalps overhead. Raven turned away. Whether they were showing off, celebrating, or just being young, it didn't really matter to him. At the moment he was experiencing adrenaline withdrawal. His hand shook as he wiped the sweat off his face. With the pump balanced across his knees, he whipped the blanket over his head and stuffed it behind the cantle. He sat for a moment as the tremors subsided.

Walking The Black over to where he had made his fight, Raven looked down on the two-gun man and the breed. The blood had already attracted countless flies. Gore was splattered everywhere. A picture of shock and disbelief was clearly etched into the gunman's face. The breed didn't have a face anymore, but then, Raven had seen it all many times before. He sat for a moment waiting for his nausea to dissipate, wondering if he should feel any regret because they were Americans. He had never killed a fellow countryman before. All of his battles had been fought on foreign soil against his country's enemies. He looked again at the bodies that had been smashed and torn by his shotgun.

His hands still shook slightly as he rubbed his face and eyes, doing so in a brisk manner as though trying to remove his doubts and fears. Sweeping his bandana off, he quickly raked his fingers through his hair, swung his leg over the saddle fork and dropped to the ground.

Leaning his forehead against the saddle's cool leather, he thought, this is really being stupid. Raven turned. He glanced again at the gunman, the breed and his dead horse, and then the dead hunter who still looked like a pile of old clothes. He shook his head and said aloud, "Regrets? I have one regret you fuckers... and that's the horse I had to shoot!"

FIFTEEN
~~~~~~~~~

Seeing the two young Sioux methodically stripping the dead, Raven looked down on his own victims. Something about the gunman's chest had caught his eye. Kneeling beside the body he saw a thin, black leather strap among the gaping holes in his chest. Flipping a short jacket aside he discovered a pistol nestled in a shoulder holster beneath his armpit. Now this is something I can use, he thought. As he stripped the shoulder rig from the body he felt a throbbing in his knees. Then he heard the hoof beats. Chris looked up in time to see Standing Elk ride by at a gallop, leading Bear's Foot's horse.

Raven hadn't heard his approach because of all the noise from the celebrating that Bear's Foot and the others were doing. Ripping the pistol and shoulder holster free, Chris stood up. Staring at Standing Elk's receding back, he could feel anger begin to smolder once more.

For the first time since it had all started, Raven had the time to reflect on Standing Elk's act of defiance. He had shot the wrong man at the wrong time. After Chris had fired the first shot Elk was supposed to shoot the breed, the man closest to him. This would have left Raven with three men side by side for the pump. The plan had been based solely on surprise. As it turned out, he was as surprised as his adversaries. And it nearly got him killed.

Too angry to finish what he had started, Raven threw the pistol and shoulder holster into his rawhide bag and swung up onto The Black. The horse shied and bucked.

Hanging on, Raven mentally lashed himself for losing his temper and forgetting that all Indian mounts are trained to be mounted from the right side. No wonder he fussed, he reasoned, it was probably the first time anyone had ever got on from that side.

Raven continued to chide himself as he trotted The Black toward the waiting group of Sioux. Bear's Foot saw him coming and stepped out to meet him. A huge grin was smeared across his face along with a broad stripe of vermilion that stretched from one ear to the other.

Chris slowed his horse to a walk while inside of him a battle was being waged. Part of him wanted to bypass his friend and go straight to Standing Elk. Another more civilized part of him wanted to stop and enjoy their victory with his friend Bear. Friendship won out.

Hanging on to his surging temper, Raven halted The Black and stepped down. His feet had hardly touched the ground before he found himself engulfed by Bear's Foot's cable-like arms.

Holding him at arm's length, Bear grinned and said, "My friend, never have I seen a more fierce fighter."

Raven couldn't help but return his grin. Bear's natural good humor was infectious.

Slapping the warrior on the back, Raven replied, "You also did some fine work. You saved the captives."

Bear nodded and steered Raven toward the others as he said, "Now, Kola, you will see what a great thing it is that you have done."

They stopped in front of the Sioux with the brown hair and lighter skin. Each man secretly scrutinized the other. What Raven saw was a Lakota of less than average height, lithe and sinewy in build. He had what looked like a scar from a bullet near his mouth and his hair, parted near the center, was loosely wrapped with red cloth into two long tresses.

Bear's Foot, grinning like a wolf, foolishly said, "Okute, this is one of the men that we rescued."

Chris smiled into the man's disturbing, hazel-colored eyes and then looked back at Bear as if to say, 'Well no shit, Dick Tracy!'

Bear continued, "His name is Tashunke Witko."

Raven felt a jolt like a thunderclap as he translated the name to Crazy Horse! The name raised goose flesh on Raven's arms. *Tashunke Witko* (Crazy Horse) was, along with Geronimo, probably the most famous Indian war chief in history.

Now he understood all the anxiety and tension up on the hill. They could very easily have lost their great leader to a bunch of killers, horse thieves, or whatever.

Feeling his gaze, Chris looked again into those strange eyes. He was suddenly aware of what it was that he had sensed earlier that was different about the man. It was his bearing. Although he dressed simply like a warrior, he carried himself with all the pride and dignity of a prince. There was a quiet aura of command surrounding him that was magnetic.

When he spoke, Crazy Horse's eyes came alive and hypnotic.

"Bear's Foot has told me of your many deeds during your short stay among the Lakota. After what I have seen today how would I not be impressed?"

Raven was surprised by his voice. It was as quiet and dignified as his demeanor.

His strange eyes inadvertently bonded Raven to him as he asked, "Why are you here, Okute? Where have you come from? You bring strange weapons and fighting skills to the Lakota... for what purpose? I do not understand."

Crazy Horse's questions were so unexpected that Raven didn't know what to say. He knew that he had to come up with something. Later, when he had time to think about it, he would be amazed at his spontaneity.

"In a land far, far away there lived a great warrior. He

was my friend, a brother. He was not a brother in blood but of the heart. This brother was killed in a battle far across the big water. He died with his fingers clasped in mine. My brother and I always fought side by side."

Crazy Horse's eyes studied Raven with a relentless intensity as he smiled and said, "You have not yet told me why you are here, wasichu. I do not understand."

Chris tore his eyes free from the chief's piercing gaze. While groping for an answer, he noticed buzzards were beginning to hover over the valley. Inspired, he found Crazy Horse's eyes once more and said, "Before I was able to prepare my brother for his journey, a giant eagle came and flew away with his spirit."

Raven paused for a minute, his mind reeled with the forced improvisation. The heft of the pump-gun reminded him of its presence and gave him a great idea.

"That night I had a dream. It was a vision of the great eagle flying to the land of the Lakota. It told me that I should come here to search for him."

Crazy Horse's eyes widened in surprise, and he exclaimed, "*Wakan*! The eagle is sacred to the Lakota."

Chris nodded. He knew from his reading that Crazy Horse was a great believer in visions and would fall for his story.

"When I find my brother I wish to return his greatest weapon to him so that his spirit will not be defenseless in the spirit world."

On impulse Raven thrust the pump into the chief's hands saying, "This is that weapon."

The Oglala war chief cradled the shotgun gingerly. With great care he began to examine its every detail.

Crazy Horse looked up from the pump-gun as he said, "We will help you find your friend's spirit. Perhaps, when you do find him you will choose to remain here and become as one with the Lakota."

WASICHU

Seeing a brief exchange of glances between Bear and the chief, Raven wondered if his friend had mentioned Blue Feather to him.

Inside, Chris breathed a sigh of relief. He had worried that his impromptu tale, with all its starts and stops, would sound phony. *Apparently,* he thought, *they figured that I was having difficulty with my Lakota.*

Placing his hand on Crazy Horse's arm, Raven said, "We must talk again at another time. Now, I would like to help your wounded friend."

The Oglala chief looked up and glanced at his friend, nodded at Raven, then returned to his contemplation of the pump's slide action.

Closely followed by Bear's Foot, Chris approached the wounded man. He was now sitting on the ground with his back against his dead horse. His broken leg was stretched out in front of him. The warrior had his eyes shut and was clutching his thigh above the bullet wound. When Raven knelt beside him, the Sioux's eyes shot open. When he saw the pale eyes and white face, his features twisted with hate.

Bear's Foot quickly explained who Raven was and that he was trying to help. The man's face softened as Bear told him Chris' story. Raven carefully removed the poultice that had been put on the warrior's wound. It was evident that the bullet had broken the bone.

Special Force's soldiers are taught field medical care but their training is pretty basic. Raven knew that without any sanitary medical supplies there wasn't an awful lot that he could do.

After Bear returned from The Black with a clean tee-shirt for a bandage and some water, Chris cleaned and bandaged the wound. He knew that his treatment was pretty crude, but he also knew that it was better than nothing.

Seeing Bear's Foot standing nearby watching, Chris asked him to find two or three straight sticks about the length of his arm. Feeling eyes on him, Raven looked and saw Standing Elk staring at him. He was wearing his usual sneer and his cold eyes were watching Raven's every move.

Bear, who had already turned to go, stopped and turned back upon hearing Chris' call.

Keeping his eyes fastened on Elk's face, Raven said, "If you think you can make this worthless piece of buffalo shit useful, take him with you."

In spite of Standing Elk's dark skin, Chris could still see the flush of blood behind it. The boil just below his cheekbone stood out like an overripe cherry.

With eyes narrowed down to slits, Standing Elk took a step in Raven's direction. His knuckles were white where his fingers wrapped around the shaft of his knife.

A short hard word from Crazy Horse stopped him in his tracks. He spun on his heel and walked toward the waiting Bear's Foot.

As Bear's Foot watched Standing Elk brush by, he said, "You know, I don't think he likes you very much!"

Standing Elk ignored him and stomped on by. Bear's Foot's patented shout of laughter followed in the wake of the warrior's angry passage.

SIXTEEN

Raven was just finishing the splint for the warrior, Tall Deer, when Wolf's Spirit and Kills Twice returned from a brief scout of the area.

The two warriors ambled over and hunkered down beside Chris and the injured warrior. Raven took one look and immediately had difficulty keeping a straight face. If he were to even glance at Wolf's Spirit, he would have to turn away and pretend to be coughing to cover up the laughter that wanted to pour out of him.

Wolf's Spirit was wearing the purple Viking tee-shirt that Raven had given him. It looked so ludicrous with his feathers and war paint that it took every bit of his will power not to howl with laughter whenever he would look at the young warrior.

Again, having to force himself not to look in Wolf's direction, Raven busied himself finishing up with Tall Deer's leg while the others talked about the fight. When he finished with the splint, he stood up. Tall Deer smiled up at him and said, "*Le mita pila* (many thanks), Okute."

Raven returned his smile and turned away. The smile left his face so suddenly it was as though it had never been there.

Standing Elk's bulky figure was standing a short distance away. He had his back to Raven and was busy examining Joe's pump-gun; putting it to his shoulder, hefting it. Chris had covered half the distance between them before even realizing that he had moved.

Standing Elk must have heard Raven's approach. He was still several paces away when he spun around, leveling the gun and pointing it directly at Raven's midsection.

His stride never faltered as Raven kept walking purposefully toward Standing Elk. The anger that was surging through Chris' body must have been evident on his face. When he was three short strides away he heard the disconcerting sound of the pump-gun's hammer being pulled to full cock. Raven's left hand snaked out and grabbed the fore stock of the gun. He felt, as well as heard, the hammer land on the empty chamber. He saw Standing Elk's eyes flare wide with surprise just before his straight, right-hand punch smashed into his face. Yellow puss erupted from behind his knuckles as Raven's fist burst the large boil!

Standing Elk's hands dropped away from the shotgun. Chris caught it before it hit the ground. The warrior's legs had turned into spaghetti and his eyes were as glassy as a pair of marbles. The Hunkpapa made a fumbling attempt to reach his knife, but he needed every bit of his concentration just to stay on his feet.

Raven's boxer instinct caused him to step toward the stunned Indian to finish him off. With his face streaked with blood and puss, Standing Elk abruptly sat down. His legs would no longer support him.

Then Crazy Horse was between them, appearing so suddenly, it was like he had been placed there by a conjurer's hand.

His strange, hawk's eyes cut into Chris like a pair of laser beams as he accused, "I thought that you were a friend of the Lakota. Why did you strike this man with your fist?"

As suddenly as it had arrived, Raven's anger was gone. It was replaced by an overriding desire to placate the charismatic war chief.

"Listen to me, *Tashuke Witko.* Because of this man's arrogance, I was nearly killed! Because of this same *heyoka* (clown), our plan for rescuing you and Tall Deer just about didn't work. We were very, very fortunate."

WASICHU

Bear's Foot interceded his considerable bulk between Raven and the chief. He interrupted with a strong, emotional outpouring of Lakota. He talked so fast that Raven had to guess what was being said. He assumed that Bear was summarizing their rescue plan for Crazy Horse.

As Bear finished with his explanation, Raven said, "Until a moment ago I was able to control my *witko* (crazy) anger, but seeing him with my brother's gun..."

As his voice faded away, Crazy Horse shrugged his shoulders and let regret show on his face. For several seconds the young chief stared into Raven's eyes. He placed his hand on Raven's shoulder and smiled as he said, "I have not thanked you for giving our lives back to us. Had you and my brothers not arrived, Tall Deer and I would surely have died and joined the others in returning to our Earth Mother."

Crazy Horse glanced at Standing Elk, who was still dazed and trying unsuccessfully to get to his feet.

Returning his gaze to Raven, he said, "Forget him, Okute. However, do not forget that he is Hunkpapa and is Sitting Bull's man."

The chief looked again at Elk and proclaimed, "He is very fortunate. Had I been you, I would have killed him."

With Crazy Horse's words still echoing in his ears he watched him turn away and instruct Kills Twice to build a travois for Tall Deer.

The young chief looked back at Raven and said, "We will return to the big village, Okute. When we arrive I will repay you for returning our lives to us."

He watched the Oglala walk away and marveled at the man's charismatic manner.

Looking overhead, he noticed the increase in carrion birds and realized that they should leave soon before the birds attracted some more two-legged buzzards.

Raven walked over to Standing Elk, who had now made it up onto one knee. He felt a tingle of some lingering anger as he bent over in front of him and slammed the slide back on the pump-gun, revealing the empty chamber.

Holding the receiver beneath Elk's nose, he snarled, "The first thing I ever learned about guns was that you never leave a loaded one around a child, especially a child that you cannot trust."

Raven straightened, rammed the chamber closed and walked away. Elk lost his balance and sat down with a thud. He was still having trouble focusing.

Bear's Foot walked over, poked the woozy Hunkpapa in the arm and announced, "Hey! Didn't I tell you that he did not like you?"

Bear's Foot's laughter echoed as he strolled away from the friendless Standing Elk.

SEVENTEEN

They collected everything of value that they could find that belonged to the dead men. Raven was able to pick and choose from the gear of the three men that he had killed.

Other than the breed's Winchester '73, the shoulder rig and all the forty-four ammo that he could find, Chris left the rest of the personal effects. He did take what money he could find. If he ever got to a town, he would be able to purchase something for Blue Feather and Little Hawk. He knew that if the Sioux took the coins, they would just make a necklace or two. And, most exciting of all, he found a bag of coffee beans.

They rounded up all the horses and, at Crazy Horse's suggestion, decided to drive the herd intact to the big encampment before dividing the spoils. The killers were left where they had fallen. They were stripped, scalped, and their throats were cut from ear to ear. The throat cutting was the grisly trademark of the Sioux. Bear said that it also would 'strike fear in the hearts of their enemies.'

Raven suspected that there was also some religious significance involved that Bear didn't want to bother getting into.

The scalping and mutilation was less shocking to Chris than many of the things that he had witnessed in his three tours in Vietnam. He had known guys that would risk their lives to be able to add another ear to their collection or to spend hours knocking gold teeth out of the mouths of the dead. There were some who wouldn't pass up an opportunity to lop some guy's finger off just to steal some cheap ring. As the man said, he mused, 'war is hell.'

They left the valley in the same direction that the Sioux had come. Two-hundred feet north of where the fight had taken place, there was a stream. Crazy Horse and his party had crossed the stream to enter the small valley. It was there that the ambush had been initiated.

The young chief had told him and Bear's Foot that as soon as they had left the water, the men had opened fire on them. The gunfire had come from three sides. Crazy Horse's mount had been hit almost immediately. Tall Deer's pony had been hit after the warrior had tried to rescue his chief.

Raven figured that the killers couldn't have been just horse thieves or they would have been more careful with their shooting. But, he thought, I'll probably never know. Hell, they could have been scalp hunters... he distinctly remembered that they had scalped the two dead Sioux.

For several hours they rode north through a land filled with a sweeping, wild beauty. The terrain was as diversified as it was beautiful. Grasslands and valleys, surrounded by granite or sandstone abutments, created a dazzling maze of grass and stone.

As the sun dipped behind a distant butte, they set up camp near a small stream. After the extra horses were corralled in a nearby box canyon, they hobbled their personal mounts and built a couple of fires. Crazy Horse produced some venison that had been left over from the day before. Those that were hungry cut some strips to roast while others tended their gear and looked over their newly acquired treasures.

After satiating his hunger pangs, Raven broke down the pump and began to clean it and his new weapons. As he worked, he thought it prudent to keep a wary eye on Mr. Standing Elk.

Since their earlier confrontation, the Hunkpapa warrior had kept his distance. Raven doubted that their situation would be resolved as his and Wolf's Spirit's had

WASICHU

been. Even Bear had said that it would be wise for him to keep an eye on Standing Elk until they were able to put some distance between them.

Having finished cleaning the pump and the rifle, Chris started in on the gunman's revolver. It had a six-inch barrel and worn, ivory grips. It was in excellent condition. As he hefted the gun, he admired the metal's oily, blue-black finish. This is one weapon, he thought, that has been taken care of. He figured that true craftsmen always take good care of their tools. With the care that this guy had put into his guns, Chris figured that he truly was the most dangerous of the four. Thank God, he mused, he'd taken him out first. He thought about that until his restless eyes picked up the stocky form of Standing Elk. Raven watched him while he worked and enjoyed the pre-dusk quiet.

After finishing with his gear, he leaned back and watched the last of the purple and red sunset disappear in the west. He thought of Blue Feather and pretended that it was his first thought of her. The reality was that he had been thinking of her quite often. My God, he realized, I've only been gone a couple of days. I must be really hooked, he mused. Just the thought of her made him smile. He relaxed and let his mind drift. He kicked back and tried to absorb some of the activities going on around him.

On the other side of the fire, Bear's Foot and Crazy Horse were having a quiet discussion. The fire was far enough away that he couldn't hear what was being said but he enjoyed watching them talk. The differences in their personalities were as glaring as their difference in size and appearance.

Bear's Foot was flamboyant and colorful, always ready to joke, laugh and live for the moment. Crazy Horse was quiet, reserved, a moody thinker and very charismatic. They were so different but still able to remain friends.

Raven became tranquilized by the drone of their

voices. The comforting sound of The Black accumulating mouthfuls of grass and tearing them free added to the contentment of the moment. Overhead, a night hawk swooped low during its diligent search for food. The combined sounds of the horses and the murmur of voices lulled Chris into closing his eyes. A vision of Blue Feather's face with her large, fawn-like eyes and soft, smiling lips beckoned quietly to him.

    He slept.

EIGHTEEN

~~~~~~~~~~~

He hadn't heard a sound but he knew someone was near. He could smell the scent that he now associated with Indians... a mixture of smoke, leather and horse. Eyes closed, he could sense the other's nearness. Underneath the blanket, he eased the Colt Forty-four out of its leather sheath. He kept his thumb poised on the lip of the revolver's hammer and waited.

A soft, sibilant whisper called his name.

"Okute."

Chris kept his eyes shut and struggled to keep his breathing normal.

"Okute, it is I, Bear's Foot. Please do not shoot me."

Opening his eyes, the first thing Raven saw was the wide, white smile on his friend's dark face.

"You were about to rub me out, were you not, you little weasel?"

The playful tone in Bear's voice encouraged Raven to play along and to join in his game.

"Of course not! How could I, a mere wasichu, hear the stealthy approach of the great bull buffalo?"

Grasping Raven's blanket, Bear's Foot whipped it into the air, exposing the metallic gleam of the pistol barrel pointed straight at his belly.

Bear's eyes got big and round as he loudly exclaimed, "*Dho!*"

He rocked back on his heels from his squatting position and shook his head as he watched Raven get to his feet and stretch.

"I must be getting old. Soon I will be having the herd

boys catch my pony for me and be forced to bribe others to chew my meat so that I can swallow it."

His three eagle feathers shimmered in the early orange light as Bear once again shook his head in dismay. He looked up at Raven and grinned as he said, "Crazy Horse wishes us to scout for him. He wants us to swing west before moving north to the great camp."

His gaze swung to the south and west. A serious note crept into his voice as he continued, "He wants us to watch for Bluecoats. We know that they are coming. We just don't want them to arrive sooner than expected. Crazy Horse and the others will continue on to the big village. Come, we should leave now."

Before Bear's Foot was able to get to his feet, Raven was at his side with a firm grip on his arm and shoulder, pretending to be helping him up.

Bear looked startled. Then he grinned, pushing Raven away. His booming laughter caused more than one pony to toss his head in alarm. Bear walked away, shaking his head and muttering to himself.

Raven and Bear's Foot were moving westward before Crazy Horse and the others were fully awake. Since there was only the two of them, they rode side by side, Chris on The Black and Bear on his large bay. Their elongated shadows pushed far ahead of them, leading the way. As they rode, their gaze constantly swept the terrain and the distant horizon. Occasionally they stopped to climb the high ground, increasing the range of their vision.

As the day wore on Raven noticed how the clouds appeared to be so low they created the illusion that, if he were able to reach just a bit higher, he could touch them.

"Big sky country," he muttered.

Later, they were traveling single file with Raven leading. Leaving an area of buttes and canyons, they moved into a country of rolling grasslands. The monotony of the plains was relieved by an occasional butte or low ridge.

Neither had spoken for quite some time, there being no real need for conversation. Each was comfortable with the other's silence. Chris reveled in the wild beauty of the land, in its wide open spaces and the freedom that it represented. Wildlife was everywhere. They saw deer many times, usually far ahead of them. Had they wished to take a chance on having their gunshot heard they could have easily bagged one. Once they had seen a small herd of antelope and had seen buffalo sign.

Chris' stomach growled. He was thinking of steaks sizzling over a fire, the fat dripping, hissing as it struck the coals. They had eaten some *wasna* (pemmican), but that had been hours ago.

"How about taking your bow out in case we see some deer," Raven said. He didn't know the Lakota word for deer so he used sign language, turning his hands and fingers into antlers.

Bear smiled and nodded. Balancing his rifle across his thighs, he reached behind his saddle and pulled his bow case and quiver of arrows free.

While stringing his bow he said, "I could hear your stomach, Okute. My paunch has also been making so much noise I thought there must be a *kaga* (demon) inside demanding that I feed him."

As Bear's Foot finished speaking he nudged the bay's ribs with his heels to bring him up alongside of The Black. Chris turned in his saddle to say something just as the bay's head had moved up level with him.

Just as Raven heard a loud 'thunk' the bay's eye bulged and blood sprayed into Raven's shocked face The grisly noise of the bullet's impact was followed instantly by the boom of a large caliber rifle.

The bay horse went down hard! Bear's Foot rolled free and came quickly to his feet. The bullet had hit Bear's horse below its right eye, dropping him as if his feet had been swept out from under him.

Raven quickly swung The Black between Bear and the rifleman. There was another booming shot as Bear's Foot dove for his rifle and rolled out of sight beneath a sandy knoll.

Chris dug his heels into The Black's ribs. The horse squatted and leaped forward as though he had been stabbed with Mexican rowels. In two heartbeats they were behind cover. Leaping from The Black, Raven crouched into a corner of a low hillock and cautiously raised his eyes above the level of the grass.

There was another loud gunshot. This time, Chris was able to see from where the shot had come. About a hundred yards north of them was a grassy ridge topped with pine. Right at the edge of the tree-line, Raven had seen a puff of smoke blossom and drift away.

Cocking his rifle Chris stood fully exposed and cranked out four rounds as fast as he could lever them. He had no visible target, so he spaced his shots to cover the area where he had seen the smoke. He dropped back down and glanced toward Bear's Foot. He was gone! Just seconds earlier he had been behind a clump of grass. Looking again, Raven could just barely see the tip of an eagle feather above the grass. Damn, he thought, how in hell can someone that size make him-self so small?

Sand exploded a foot from Chris' head. Both he and Bear's Foot immediately unleashed a barrage of rifle fire at the rapidly dissipating tell-tale smoke. As they watched and waited, Raven thumbed more cartridges into his rifle.

The sun felt good on the back of Raven's neck. Sand flies buzzed around his head as he sat on his heels Asian-style and waited. After an undeterminable length of time, Chris began to get restless. He yelled toward where he thought Bear's Foot must be, "I think he is gone. I will ride up there and make sure."

Bear's voice startled Raven. It came from an entirely different spot than he expected it to come from.

"If he is still there, I will make him crawl back into his weasel hole. Be careful."

As Raven ran for The Black, Bear rapidly levered shots at the distant ridge. Before he had fired his second shot, Chris was in the saddle. He kicked The Black into an immediate gallop and headed straight for the ridge.

Not wanting to give the shooter an easy shot, Raven employed a modified version of Wolf's Spirit's zig-zag approach. Nearing the ridge, he kept his eyes on the spot where he had last seen smoke. With every cut in his patternless zigzag, The Black would grunt and Raven could feel the long muscles between his legs bunching and flowing with a powerful grace. It was almost as if The Black could sense the urgency involved and had increased his effort.

He made it to the western side of the ridge and never heard a gunshot other than Bear's. Chris made a straight run toward the north side hoping to catch a glimpse of the sniper. There! Fresh pony tracks. He pulled The Black to a sliding stop and stared, feeling a sinking in his gut, at tracks that ran away to the north.

"Shit!"

Raven's exclamation said it all. He was gone.

Staring north, he tried to pick the probable route that he thought would give the shooter the quickest way out. The land stretched away with undulating, small hills and flat grasslands, with an occasional mesa to break up the flow. As far away as he could see, nothing moved.

Disgusted, Raven spun The Black around and trotted him up the gentle incline to the base of the ridge. About fifty feet from the top, he got off the horse, secured his rifle and readied the pump-gun. He figured that he had best look around in case there was more than one sniper.

Moving sporadically from cover to cover, Chris reached the crest and moved down the north side to where the shooter had made his ambush. Looking for sign, he found the spot right away. The grass was all flattened in an area around a scraggly pine that was growing out of some rocks. Raven looked but could not find any shell casings. For whatever it is worth, he thought, we know the bastard must load his own cartridges... otherwise why would he pick up his brass?

Looking out over the plain, Raven could see Bear's Foot's dead horse but not a sign of the warrior. A further search of the area revealed nothing, so he worked his way up to the top, taking the shooter's most likely route.

At the very crown of the ridge he found a single footprint. Chris didn't know much about tracking, but judging from the size of the print he appeared to be a big man, and he was wearing moccasins. Staring at the track, he wished that Bear's Foot was with him.

Before leaving the ridge, Chris looked north one last time. The country was so diversified that the sniper could be anywhere. He could even be nearby but just out of sight in a gully or behind a hill. Hell, he thought, he could be anywhere. He shrugged and moved down the slope to The Black.

While riding back to Bear's Foot, he tried to think who the shooter could be. The first assumption was the wounded outlaw who had escaped, but the more he thought of him, the less likely it seemed possible. He was wounded and was running in the opposite direction. Even if he hadn't been wounded, it seemed unlikely that he would take a chance of being deep in Sioux country by himself. Probably some bloodthirsty jerk, he thought, who was looking for some easy scalps or plunder.

Raven was shaken out of his ruminations by the sudden appearance of Bear's Foot. He was standing out in the open waiting for him. He was naked except for loin cloth and moccasins. In one hand was his rifle, the other held his four foot war club. Chris was again awed by the man's physique. Although he had never seen the man do any type of exercise, there was absolutely no visible body fat anywhere beneath the taut brown flesh.

Bear's usual congenial expression had been replaced by a visage full of cold, murderous intent. The planes of his face looked like they were chiseled out of marble.

Raven explained his findings while they loaded Bear's gear onto The Black. Bear turned to his dead horse, removed his rawhide bridle, and dropped to one knee beside him. He placed his hand on the bay's muzzle and lifted his face to the sky. He rose to his feet. Chris was amazed to see a tear slide down the savage face.

He glanced coldly at Raven and nodded toward the north as he said, "*Hopo!*"

With weapons in hand he ran past The Black moving with the effortless stride of the natural runner.

Raven, watching him run, muttered, "I have a feeling that guy's going to wish he never pulled that trigger."

They had been on the sniper's trail only a short time when Bear's Foot came to a sudden stop. Crouched over the tracks, he touched the earth and quickly brought his fingers to his nose, then his lips. He looked at Raven. A smile flickered briefly across his face but never quite reached his narrowed eyes.

"We have bloodied our Indian, Okute. He is wounded but not very badly. At least he is now carrying our mark."

Chris was perplexed. He asked, "How do you know he is an Indian?"

Bear's Foot didn't even bother to glance at him as he said, "His pony is not wearing the iron shoes that only wasichu's horses wear."

Without another word Bear was up and running

again. Following, Raven chided himself for not having noticed the lack of shoes. He thought of the blood spoor and wondered why there wasn't any sign of it on the ridge. It's probably there, he mused, only I didn't see it or the shooter hid it.

Chris kept a sharp lookout as he and The Black followed behind the warrior's loping figure. Bear's Foot had suggested that Raven watch out for another ambush so that he could concentrate on tracking.

They followed the trail for hours. Not once did the man's tracks waver from their northerly direction. Chris was forced to ease his hunger with more dried meat, but Bear was so intent on tracking that he didn't even bother to ease his hunger.

The country they were passing through was very rugged, with deep ravines surrounded by pointed hills. The trees looked almost black on the green knolls. With the jerky having only whetted Raven's appetite, his empty stomach caused him to view the countryside through a hungry man's eyes. The hills and ridges became mounds of green crème-de-menthe ice cream and the trees became dark chocolate topping. The brief fantasy quickly dissipated leaving behind an even larger void inside his stomach.

Raven could not begin to understand Bear's Foot's amazing endurance. Early on in their frenzied pursuit, he had traded places with Bear, but quickly came to realize that his friend could run circles around him. When they began losing time, they both agreed that Bear would stay on foot while Raven kept watch.

They continued to move northward. Relentless, they stopped only for water and nature calls. Bear's Foot was consumed with finding their enemy. They relentlessly followed his trail just as surely as Wi (the sun) followed its predestined path and climbed higher and higher into the cobalt sky.

NINETEEN
~~~~~~~~~~

As they topped a rise, the sky above the northern horizon attracted Raven's attention. A towering haze of tan and yellow dust stretched for miles. The source of the dust cloud couldn't be seen because it was too far away. With the backdrop of a bright blue sky, the dust cloud became a gigantic, ghostly apparition. Raven quietly sat The Black and stared in astonishment. He couldn't begin to fathom what was causing the strange phenomenon.

Bear's Foot stopped and looked back at Chris. He glanced at the sky to see what was causing his friend's strange behavior.

"We are almost to the main encampment. The dust is from the pony herd."

Bear's proclamation was staggering. Raven thought that it was incomprehensible to imagine the number of horses that it would take to create a dust cloud of that magnitude. Their numbers would have to be in the tens of thousands.

Eyes narrowed with suppressed anger, Bear's Foot continued, "It looks as though the weasel that killed my horse is running in a straight line for the village."

Still dazed by Bear's explanation of the dust cloud, Raven didn't bother to respond. A quick glance at the warrior's face revealed that he was still wearing an expression of ruthless determination.

Bear's Foot pivoted and broke into his usual ground eating lope. As he ran his eyes remained pinned to the earth flying under his moccasins. His total concentration was centered on following their adversary's tracks. When they drew closer to the great encampment, Bear's tracking pace slowed to a walk. The overall terrain had become more rocky and more difficult to track. Since the initial sighting of the blood trail there had been only one sign of fresh bleeding to help make the tracking easier, and that had been a long time ago.

Raven pulled The Black to a stop. Up ahead Bear had stopped and was bent over studying the ground. He had apparently lost the tracks. Raven silently kept watch as Bear's Foot dropped to all fours and painstakingly went over every inch of the craggy, rock filled trail. After a bit the warrior climbed to his feet and walked back to where Chris was waiting.

Bear's face didn't show the frustration that Raven knew must have been present when he said, "Okute, I must go and bring back a friend. Among the Oglala there is a tracker named Ptecila (Small Buffalo). This man can track an ant across a field of sand."

For an instant, Raven thought that he had seen a glint of the old humor in Bear's Foot's eye. When he looked again, the coldness had returned and the dark orbs had once again become those of a blood-thirsty hunter.

"To save time, I think it will be best if you wait for me here. There will be too many Lakota and Shiyala that will question your white face and we cannot take the time to explain. If we are to catch this weasel we must hurry."

Raven stepped down from The Black. Handing Bear the reins, he grabbed the pump-gun and said, "Take him. It also will save time."

Without another word Bear's Foot swung up onto the saddle. The Black gave a few half-hearted bucks in protest to Bear's additional pounds, but quickly settled down under his soothing hand and quiet words. Just before Bear nudged him into a gallop, The Black looked back at Raven. As he watched them ride away, Raven could have sworn that he

WASICHU

had seen a flicker of disgust in The Black's last glance. Perhaps, Chris foolishly thought, he recalled what Bear had done to his previous owner.

He had been waiting a long time and was beginning to get edgy. It wasn't a comforting thought to realize that within two or three miles was the largest gathering of free Indians ever assembled.

To pass the time, he had been sitting on a large, flat rock watching the birds and small animals scurry about in the brush and trees to his rear. Directly to his front there was a deep gorge and on the other side of it, was a tall cliff. Near the base of the cliff face he saw a gliding, red-tailed hawk.

Trying to put aside his nagging uneasiness, Raven lay back on the warm, flat rock. Resting the pump across his stomach, he relaxed as he watched the hawk. Fascinated, he observed its grace and beauty as the red-tail rode the thermals. Higher and higher it soared, in ever-widening circles, until it became a tiny speck high above the peak of the cliff. Not once, he noticed, did the hawk flap its wings. It had simply used air currents to reach its lofty height.

Raven suddenly sensed that all was not as it should be, something was wrong. His gaze whipped over the nearby hills, with their pine-topped summits, and quickly scanned over the rocks and brush for any movement. Then he realized what it was that was wrong. Not only was nothing moving... it was too quiet.

Slowly, being careful not to make any sudden moves, Chris sat up. He stretched and faked a yawn while his eyes secretly raked the area to each side and the gully to his immediate front. He saw nothing but he felt the hackles on the back of his neck stir with anxiety. Taking a firm grip on his nerves, Raven stood and turned in one slow, fluid move.

He froze.

There were four of them. All had weapons pointed straight at him, and they all looked like they knew how to use them and would be more than willing to prove it.

The pump was pointing down, nestled against his right leg. Chris' right hand was wrapped tightly around the pistol grip and his thumb rested lightly on the spur of the hammer.

Raven's first thought was that they didn't look like Sioux. Their hair styles were different and their skin was of a lighter shade. He knew that they had to be from the big village. It would be highly unlikely that any Indians, other than allies of the Sioux, would dare to be this close to a camp of such huge proportions.

Feigning a nonchalant attitude, Chris grinned. He stared into the midnight eyes of the tall warrior straight across from him as he joked, "*Washtay*! I certainly hope that you warriors are friends of the Lakota."

He got no reaction from his Sioux greeting. It's as though they're cast from bronze, he thought. What is this shit?

The Indian he spoke to was about twenty feet away. He was flanked by two men on his right and one on his left. Two had rifles and the other two had bows and arrows. With their blazing, hate-filled eyes they looked eager and ready for anything. The tall warrior's eyes darted toward the man on his right who was wearing a lavishly beaded vest.

'Beaded Vest' was a man of average height who looked to be in his mid-thirties. Noticing that he was the only one wearing any fancy clothing, Raven figured that he was their leader. All four of them wore their hair parted, loose on one side and tightly braided on the other.

Raven kept glancing at the Indian on his extreme left. He had noticed that the man's rifle was at full cock, pointed directly at him. What bothered him the most was that the Indian didn't look smart enough to be allowed to handle a loaded gun.

Raven made eye contact with 'Beaded Vest' as he

announced, "I am called Okute. I am of Spotted Horse's band of Minneconjou. My friend, Bear's Foot, borrowed my horse to ride into the village to find and bring back the famous Oglala tracker, Ptecila. I now wait for their return."

The unnerving silence continued as Chris speculated. Either these dudes don't understand Lakota, he thought, or they simply don't give a shit what I say.

Speaking in very poor Lakota, 'Beaded Vest' broke the silence. His voice was resonant with outrage.

"I am Deer Catcher of the *Shiyala* (Cheyenne). Even without your pale face I would know that you are a wasichu. You talk too much and say too little."

He paused for a moment as his black eyes continued to slide over Raven, as though he was from a sub-human species.

"Tell me why I should believe that what you say is true. You white hair mouths are famous for your lies and treachery. I think I should kill you so that you cannot tell others your lies."

Raven's oldest enemy, anger, spread like a grass fire through his body and erupted from his mouth with the quiet fury of a man with his back to the wall.

"Tell me, Chief Deer Shit, how do you think that I got here? Do you think that I flew here on a giant bird? Look at my tracks and you will see the truth."

Deer Catcher's eyes narrowed to menacing slits at Raven's angry, biting words. His warriors continued to be statues. Only their eyes were alive as they awaited their leader's command.

With hardly a pause, Raven continued, "Unless you want to die, I think that you had better look at my back trail. If your men can track better than they talk, they will see that I do not lie!"

Deer Catcher was so angry that his poor Lakota got much worse as he sputtered, "You talk kill me. You one, me many. You quickly will die!"

Chris had to force himself to show an outward calm. Inside, his fighting rage vibrated and quivered like a wild animal waiting to be released.

"Why do you think that I have been named Okute? Do you think that I merely sit around the lodge and bead moccasins with the women? No! I have big medicine. My shotgun shoots thunderbolts faster than you can blink."

Raven emphatically aimed the index finger of his left hand at the Cheyenne's face.

"You... will be the first to die!"

Seeing the Cheyenne's face turn into hard planes of red oak, Raven cleared his mind and prepared himself for the reflexive art of killing, or being killed.

"*Washtay!*"

Bear's Foot's voice bounced off the rocks. To Chris' ears, the big voice was like that of a savior promising eternal life. Relief washed over him as though dumped from a beaker of salvation.

Upon hearing the Lakota's voice, four pair of eyes swiveled in surprise. As the four heads turned toward the voice, Raven's shotgun swung up and leveled dead center on the *Shiyala* leader, Deer Catcher. The sound of the hammer clicking into full cock was heard by every living creature within a thirty-foot radius.

Nobody moved.

"Don't kill them, Okute! We may need them to help us fight the Bluecoats."

Although he couldn't see him, Raven was certain that Bear's words were accompanied by a huge grin, and that he was struggling to keep from laughing aloud.

The sound of several horses' hooves clicking on rocks and thudding into the grass followed Bear's tongue-in-cheek plea. He rode up behind the four Cheyenne looming over them from his big buckskin.

WASICHU

He began speaking rapidly to Deer Catcher in what Raven assumed was Cheyenne. With his eyes still riveted on the leader, Chris' peripheral vision saw the other three Cheyenne lowering their weapons. He could see the heat leave 'Beaded Vest's' eyes as he slowly lowered his rifle.

Sighing with relief, Raven lowered the pump-gun, then noticed Bear's companion. The Oglala's physique was in direct contrast to the big Sioux's bulk and height. He was a small, hunched figure seated on a smaller than normal pony. Ptecila was of a darker skin color than other Lakota and instead of his hair being parted, the top of his head was a mass of tousled curls. Looking at his hunched shoulders, dark skin, and curly top knot, Raven could easily see how he came to be named *Ptecila* (Small Buffalo).

Glancing back at Bear's Foot, who was still doing the talking, Chris saw a big change come over Deer Catcher. Physically, he appeared to have lost a couple of inches of pride and several pounds of inflated ego. Raven didn't know what Bear was telling him but it was certainly taking a lot out of him.

A soft, familiar nicker pulled Raven's gaze. The little Oglala and his undersized pony were gone, but in their place was The Black, who was staring at him. The stallion shook his mane, pawed the turf with a hoof, and snuffled loudly. The sunlight glanced off a black eye and briefly revealed the spark of fire, hidden within.

Raven stepped toward him. He called softly, "Ho, boy... ho there."

The notched ears stood straight up as The Black, neck arched and nostrils flaring, took a couple of short, hesitant steps forward. Hand outstretched, Raven walked slowly up to him. Nostrils quivering, The Black, silken muzzle reaching out, snorted over his fingers and pulled away. Chris casually moved up alongside of the animal and absentmindedly ran his hand along the sleek, muscular neck.

Looking beyond the smooth leather of the saddle, he could see Ptecila already at work on the sniper's lost trail. Leading his pony he was bent over, studying the rocky ground at his feet. All of a sudden he straightened, leaped onto his pony's back, and began moving in a northerly direction.

Raven called to Bear's Foot, "Hey, *Kola*, we should go. He has already found the tracks."

Bear turned his yellow horse to get a better view. There was a hard glint in the warrior's eyes as he said, "There is no need to hurry anymore, Okute."

Mystified, Chris watched his friend as he steered his buckskin toward the distant tracker. Raven was about to swing up onto The Black when Deer Catcher stepped up to him.

"*Wonumayin*, Okute."

Seeing the sincerity in Deer Catcher's apology, Raven grinned and stuck out his hand as he replied, "I, too, made a mistake."

Deer Catcher was momentarily perplexed by the proffered hand, but then grabbed hold and pumped enthusiastically as Raven said, "Bear's Foot has told me of the *Shiyala's* bravery and ferocity in war. My mistake was in not laying my weapon down and surrendering. If chance had not brought Bear back in time, I would surely have been rubbed out."

A smile brightened the Cheyenne's stern features as he released Raven's hand and said, "From what Bear's Foot has told me of you, I am not so sure."

Chris swung his leg over the saddle and gave Deer Catcher a small salute with the parting words, "We will meet again, Kola. When that happens we will be allies, not adversaries."

As soon as Raven pulled The Black alongside of Bear's buckskin he asked, "What did you mean when you said, 'there is no need to hurry anymore'?"

WASICHU

Bear's face was once again etched with lines of anger. Gone was the 'Duke Wayne' image. Instead his visage was purely savage. When Raven heard Bear speak, he wondered if the humor he had heard in his tone earlier had been imagined. His speech had acquired as many hard edges as his features.

"I spoke with Crazy Horse. He said that not long after we had left them, Standing Elk had approached him. He told him that since his people were on the opposite end of the big village, he decided that he was going to cut across country so that when he arrived at the village, he would be among the Hunkpapa."

As Bear's Foot paused, Raven felt like he'd been sucker punched. He hadn't once thought of Standing Elk being the sniper.

Eyes narrowed to slits, Bear's Foot leaned toward Raven. In a voice filled with menace he hissed, "We have a traitor among us, Okute. One who I will deal with personally."

Raven returned his friend's stare knowing that he was being told not to interfere. Standing Elk's fate was in Bear's Foot's hands.

His eyes never left Bear's face as he nodded and said, "*Waste* (good). Will you not have to prove that he is the one that ambushed us?"

A dazzling white smile transformed his brown face while his eyes still retained their murderous gleam.

The facetious thought, 'I wouldn't want to be in Standing Elk's moccasins,' made Raven look away so that Bear wouldn't misunderstand his smile.

"Have you forgotten that we have marked him? We have drawn his blood. If the wound does not show, I will find it. He is already a dead man!"

His last words were delivered with such a quiet vehemence that Raven nodded and turned away. His thoughts turned to something of far greater importance, his stomach. Food. Just thinking the word was making him salivate. They had been munching on jerky and pemmican earlier, but Chris needed more than that. He forced himself not to think about it and switched his attention to the hard working Oglala tracker. He was bent over his pony's neck, intently watching the pebbled ground as he relentlessly followed Standing Elk's tracks.

Raven's mind unexpectedly flashed back to the ambush. He now knew that the bullet that had killed Bear's horse had been meant for him. He remembered the hate in Elk's eyes when he had pulled the trigger of the pump, and recalled the Hunkpapa's fear when the gun's firing pin struck the empty chamber. Mentally shrugging aside his recollections, Raven decided that if Bear's Foot wanted to make this his own personal vendetta, it was fine with him. It was not a healthy time or place for an adopted white man to be killing an Indian for any reason.

About an hour had passed when Chris realized that they were practically at the encampment. The haze of the dust cloud had intensified to the point where it threatened to obliterate the blue of the sky.

As they drew closer, a subtle but steady murmur, like the distant sound of surf, permeated Raven's senses. He was astonished to discover that it was the sound of thousands of men, women, and children: talking, working and at play. It was a potpourri of mostly indiscernible sounds. A noise that was unlike anything Raven had ever experienced; an eerie sound that simultaneously beguiled and beckoned.

A sudden chill of apprehension washed over him. It only lasted for an instant before it was replaced by the thrill of adventure and Raven's insatiable curiosity.

They were moving up a gradual incline. At the top there was a scatter of pine and brush spread out along a rocky spine. Ptecila disappeared over the crest as Chris and

WASICHU

Bear's Foot followed doggedly in his small pony's hoofprints. Raven was enjoying the sharp scent of the pine when, all at once, he came to the apex of the hill. Reflexes alone caused him to jerk on the reins, stopping The Black. Raven felt as though he'd been kicked in the stomach.

Directly below them, a willow banked creek twisted away to the east and west. As far as he could see in both directions, the stream was engulfed on both sides by thousands of tipis.

A short wave of dizziness accompanied his churning stomach as he stared in absolute awe. It was without a doubt the most spectacular sight he had ever seen: the breadth, the sheer magnitude. The size of the pony herd alone was enough to take his breath away. The color, from the hundreds of painted tipis and the teeming picturesque people, was indescribable.

Following Ptecila's scuttling form, Raven was halfway down the clay embankment before he was able to look away from the incredible panorama. The Oglala was waiting for them at the edge of the first line of tipis. As they approached him, it was obvious that this was as far as Ptecila would go. There's no way, Chris thought, that he could follow tracks into the sprawling village.

Thinking of the hundreds of Indians in the village that would love the job of tanning his scalp was making Raven nervous. It made him remember a saying that had been popular in 'Nam. Grunts had facetiously used it to bolster their morale and nerve. 'Yeah though I walk through the valley of death I will fear no evil, for I am the baddest motherfucker in the valley.'

It wasn't working for Raven. Instead he was thinking, dear God what have I gotten myself into? He tapped his heels into the ribs of The Black and rode forward into the forgotten pages of history.

EXCERPT FROM THE JOURNAL OF CETAN CHICKALA (LITTLE HAWK)

This is the second day since I last saw Okute. Shortly after he and the others had left, we had taken down our lodges and had followed in their footsteps.

Our progress was very slow because a village travels only as fast as its slowest person. The very young and those that are too old or infirm to ride must walk.

During the move, my newly acquired friend, Red Pony, and I were busy keeping the pony herd together. Since we were a band that has been well led by my grandfather, we had many horses to watch and needed help from other boys and even some of the warriors. The warriors mainly stay on the lookout for enemies and animals that may become a threat to the herd.

Since the day I beat Red Pony in the fight during the war game, he has become my shadow. I do not know if he feels guilt over the things that he said about my mother or if he just wants to be my friend. It seems like I have lost an enemy but am forced to have another shadow. I am happy that he wishes to be friends, but he has become like a burr stuck in my hair that is too painful to remove.

While Red Pony and I sat our ponies and kept the pony herd moving along at a brisk walk, I thought back to when Okute had left. When I had heard that he was leaving with Bear's Foot and the ugly Hunkpapa I ran through the camp. I had told myself that I was hurrying because I wanted to see what other warriors were going along. Nearing my grandmother's tipi, I saw my mother there so I slowed to a walk. I did not want her to see me running around as though I was a small boy.

My mother was kneeling on a robe beside the lodge, combing her long, wet hair with a porcupine quill comb. She had apparently just returned from bathing in the lake.

Hearing my approach, she lifted her gaze to mine. I saw a

happiness dwelling there that I had not seen before. She smiled. It was as dazzling as the sun glancing off the lake's surface. She turned to my grandmother, who was punching holes in a skin with a bone awl, and asked, "Have you noticed anymore coyotes skulking about?"

Grandmother punched another hole and looked at me as she replied, "I do not know what we Lakota have done to anger Wakan Tanka, but I am sure that he put the coyote on Earth Mother's back for the sole reason of making our life miserable."

I was going to tell my mother about Okute's leaving, but after their insults and teasing, I was determined not to say a word. As I passed by, Grandmother looked up from her work with a twinkle in her rheumy eye. Furious, I turned away and as I started to run, I heard her tease, "Not only do coyotes skulk, they also run away."

I was jolted out of my daydream by a shout from Red Pony that surprised me so badly that I dropped the horse dance stick that I had been carving with my new knife. His sudden cry had also startled my pony, Hawk's Wing, causing him to buck and twist.

Red Pony was racing in pursuit of a few horses that had left the herd and run up into a maze of canyons. By the time I got my pony under control, I was eating Red Pony's dust. Drumming my heels against Hawk's Wing's ribs, I was determined that Red Pony would soon be choking on my pony's dust. Hawk's Wing was very fast. He had a very quick start and had won many wagers for me because of it. Quickly, we began to gain on Red Pony's horse.

I caught up with him at the first twist in the canyon. It was not a real canyon but was more of a dry stream bed with tall banks on either side. The stream had dried up years before.

Because of the willows and cottonwoods scattered along its twisted length, we had to be careful. There were low-hanging branches and dead trees lying everywhere.

We had almost caught up with the ponies when the canyon made another sharp turn and we found ourselves staring directly into the lowering sun. Amidst the swirling red dust of our runaway ponies, loomed a man on a large, spotted horse. With the sun behind him, he was a dark, menacing presence.

WASICHU

Because of our speed and the sharp turn, we were upon the man so suddenly that there was no time to stop. Since there was just enough room for a single rider to pass on either side, Red Pony, who had a slight lead on me, took the left as I took the right. I saw the white of an eye and the sun glance off a long pistol barrel as it swung down in a slashing arc. There was a sound like a burst melon as the gun smashed onto Red Pony's head, knocking him backwards off his horse. Horrified, I knew that my friend was dead.

Instinctively, I threw myself onto the far side of my pony. With my left hand twisted into his mane and my left heel hooked over his rump, we flew by so closely that my foot brushed the man's leg.

After we thundered by, I pulled myself upright again. My ears were still full of the terrible sound the pistol had made when it struck Red Pony. I jerked Hawk's Wing to a sliding stop. All thoughts of my friend's health were gone immediately. Survival instantly dominated my thoughts as I realized that I was trapped! My optimism plummeted. I discovered that I was in a box canyon. Already I was among the runaway ponies at the end of the canyon. The hills had squeezed in, making escape impossible in that direction.

I wheeled Hawk's Wing in a circle and turned to face my enemy. On the surface, I tried very hard to appear unafraid. Inside, I was fighting a rising panic that was threatening to take control.

I could see the enemy clearly now. He had turned his horse so that he was facing me. The sun was hitting him full in the face. He was a big, dirty wasichu. He sat his horse relaxed except for his left shoulder, which he carried hunched up toward his ear, letting his arm hang at his side. There was a large red-brown stain that looked like dried blood on the same shoulder of his long coat.

He showed his yellow teeth in a smile while a single eye gleamed at me from the shadow of his wide-brimmed hat. He had a high-pitched voice like a woman, and he spoke words to me that I did not understand. He gestured at me with his pistol, wanting me to come to him. I was terrified! I ignored him and told myself, think! Huge moths of fear began fluttering their wings in my stomach. Only one way out! And that way was past the wasichu. Thoughts were flitting around in my head like a bird trapped in a cage.

Calmness then came over me. It covered me like a cloud passing in front of the sun. I knew exactly what I was going to do. Seeing Red Pony's body lying crumpled in the sand convinced me that the white man would not dare to shoot me. He knew that a gunshot would bring my people to him as surely as a bee to its honey.

Taking a deep breath, I nudged Hawk's Wing into a walk. I headed straight toward him. I still had my two-blade knife clutched in my right hand. Secretly I switched hands and lowered my head as though in defeat. With my head down, I continued to watch him. For the first time I noticed that he had only one eye. There was a long white scar running through it. That is even better, I thought, if his left arm is as useless as his eye then I have a chance.

I was about four pony lengths away from him when he showed his evil, yellow smile and gestured for me to hurry. Suddenly, I dug my heels into my pony's ribs and screamed the Lakota war cry, "Hokahey!" Hawk's Wing leaped forward with the quickness of a mountain cat! Straight as an arrow, we shot toward the surprised wasichu sitting on his big horse. His horse nervously began to move his feet, trying to move backwards. I moved my head to the left side of my pony's neck and moved my body in the same direction. I wanted him to think that I was going to pass him on the left, as Red Pony had done.

With only two bow lengths separating us, I swung Hawk's Wing hard to the right! Startled, the horse reared back onto his hind legs, throwing the wasichu completely off balance. As I swept by, my left fist, tightly clutching my two-blade knife, struck upwards. I had been aiming for his injured shoulder. Instead, my sharp blade plunged into his lifeless appearing arm. He howled and yapped like a coyote as my steel grated on bone! My knife was nearly wrenched from my hand by the momentum of our passing.

New howls of rage followed me as I bent over Hawk's Wing's neck and shouted words of encouragement in his ear. The wasichu's roars of fury only increased our speed. Hawk's Wing blew around the twisting turns of the canyons like a whirlwind.

WASICHU

My heels pounded against my pony's ribs as I forced him to an even faster pace. I could feel tears coming from my eyes and drying on my cheeks in the wind. Just as surely as I knew that Red Pony was lying dead in the box canyon, I knew that his murderer was getting away. Without a doubt, I knew that by the time I returned with a war party, the wasichu would be gone.

"Hear me, Wakan Tanka. I pledge to you that I, Little Hawk, will avenge my friend. Okute and I will find this white man and kill him. I swear it!"

Having said the words aloud I felt better, yet my heart was still on the ground because of what had happened.

As we broke out of the canyons and into the open prairie, I could see our pony herd far in the distance, silhouetted against the orange and red of the setting sun. Once again, I urged a tired Hawk's Wing to increase his stride as I wiped the drying tears from my cheeks. The warriors would need a man to guide them to Red Pony, not a boy.

TWENTY
~~~~~~~~~~

The late afternoon sun beat down on the trio of riders as they moved slowly into the village. Under his blanket poncho, Raven was soaking wet with sweat, but it went unnoticed. At the moment, he was staring, watching incredulously as Ptecila followed Standing Elk's tracks right into the village thoroughfare. At least, he thought, he is going slow so maybe he's human after all. Damn, my hunger must be making me silly and sarcastic. Maybe it's not hunger, but fear, putting foolish thoughts in my head.

Just seeing the volume of people present was enough to justify his speculation. It was like being in the middle of a mall, he thought, on the Saturday before Christmas. Many people crossed in front of the little Oglala. Those who noticed that he was tracking did their best to avoid destroying his spoor. Not once did Raven see Ptecila raise his gaze. It was as if the maze of conflicting signs had some sort of mystical power over him. Bent from the waist, eyes glued to the ground, the curly-headed tracker led them deeper into the Hunkpapa camp.

Being last in line, Chris noticed how Bear's Foot, on his big buckskin, completely dwarfed the Oglala. It was interesting how a Sioux of such a small size had carved out a useful and very specialized niche for himself in a society that Raven had thought was an extremely macho domain. The lines between white and red were running more parallel than he had thought.

They stopped. Ptecila squatted down to examine some sign. From his vantage point on top of The Black, Raven watched the Lakota as they scurried here and there with their everyday chores and games. Their apparent lack of concern bothered him. If these people are worried about the army they sure weren't letting it show in their daily activities. It puzzled Raven because he had read that the whole purpose of this gathering of the tribes was to lure the Bluecoats in and then drive them from their land once and for all.

Ptecila started them forward again. Where was the apprehension? If they knew that the army was on its way, there should be some anxiety. Where in hell was it? Maybe, Chris thought, the chiefs don't tell the people everything, sort of a 'need to know' basis like it was in 'Nam. Now, there's a scary thought.

Once again Ptecila stopped them. They had come to a spot where the paths intersected. Because of its size and the space available, the village wasn't laid out in the usual Lakota manner. Instead of the usual orderly circle, they had simply grouped according to tribe and raised their lodges on either side of the stream.

Raven pulled The Black to a stop. Ptecila was down on one knee, moving his fingers lightly over the tracks. Taking advantage of the halt, Raven nudged his stallion up alongside of Bear's buckskin. The Black nipped the yellow horse on the shoulder. The buckskin jumped to the side, snorted, tossed his black mane and rolled a wild eye. Bear ignored the horses. He was busy putting on a long, fringed shirt. Raven wondered if his big friend was making a fashion statement or if there was a reason for wanting to sweat. Raven had thrown the folds of his blanket back away from his arms so it hung like a cape, but he was still sweltering.

Raven asked Bear's Foot why none of the people appeared to be concerned about the Bluecoats. It was obvious that Bear was engrossed with adjusting something under his shirt and was trying to keep an eye on Ptecila. At first, Chris thought that he wasn't going to answer. When he did, he was so preoccupied that he didn't bother to turn and face him. Raven assumed that he was thinking of how he was going to handle the confrontation.

"All that I have heard, Okute, is that a few suns ago the people had a Sun Dance. This is a very *wakan* (holy) ceremony. The principle dancer was the great medicine chief, Sitting Bull. Wolf's Spirit told me that after he had endured the 'one hundred cuts' and had danced, he had stared into the sun, seeking a vision. The chief eventually collapsed. When he was revived, Sitting Bull told of a vision... he saw many Bluecoats falling into camp upside down with their hats falling off."

Bear turned and looked at Raven with a cold smile.

"This is the very best of signs, Kola. It means that we will have a great victory over the Bluecoats." Bear's attention was once again drawn to Ptecila who had waved, and then had walked on ahead tugging on his pony's lead.

With his braids swinging to and fro and his curly head casting left and right for sign, he looked like a bird dog on a hot trail. As they closed the gap separating them from Ptecila, it became noticeable that the pedestrian traffic was thinning out fast. There was more space between the lodges.

Not more than a hundred feet from where he had discovered the tracks, Ptecila stopped and remounted his pony. He wheeled his mount and came back to Bear's Foot. Raven watched as the two exchanged a few words. He noticed that the tracker was older than he had first thought. Up close, his face was finely etched with a maze of wrinkles. Chris reasoned that he had probably thought him younger because of his size. He was gesturing emphatically but Raven could only pick up a few words. He did manage to pick up enough to understand that with his job finished, Ptecila was returning to the Oglala camp. Bear thanked him and was clearly praising his skills. With a quiet show of affection the big warrior put his arm around Ptecila's shoulders and gently squeezed. With a grin for Bear's Foot and a shy wave at Raven, the Oglala rode away.

Bear sat quietly on his horse for a moment, thinking. His face was turned away. He stared at the ground as if Earth Mother had the answers to his queries. Raven patiently waited for him to get his thoughts together. Eventually his head came up. He gestured for Chris to join him. In a voice full of an emotion that Raven couldn't quite figure out, Bear said, "You are about to meet a great man, but he is a man that I do not entirely trust. I want you and that thunder-maker of yours to protect my back. I would not want any Hunkpapa knives stuck in it."

He looked away momentarily. Both he and Raven watched the people going about their business. Most of the villagers were oblivious to their presence, but a few wary glances were thrown in their direction. "Most of the Sioux in this camp are Hunkpapa so this is no small thing I am asking of you, kola. You will make enemies."

Raven absently stroked The Black's satin neck.

"You are foolish to even ask. You must know that I will always be there to protect your back."

Bear's Foot studied Chris' face for a moment. The intensity of those ebony eyes made Raven squirm inside. He felt he had to move, do something... anything. He pulled the pump-gun up and laid it across his thighs. For just an instant, Chris caught a glimpse of softness as it warmed the coldness of Bear's gaze.

The tiny glint in his eye had been so fleeting, Raven couldn't be sure that he'd seen it. If it had been there it's gone now, he thought. Bear's Foot's no nonsense killer mask was back in place. Raven had the ominous feeling that it was going to take the spilling of blood to remove it. Bear's Foot gave Raven a cold smile and tapped his buckskin's side. As they moved forward, Bear suddenly looked over his shoulder and remarked, "It is time to see if Hunkpapa hearts are as brave when they are face to face with their enemy."

TWENTY-ONE
~~~~~~~~~~~~~

They walked their horses past two more lodges. Right at the edge of a spacious open area was a large, elaborately painted tipi. Its placement was obviously one of importance. Tethered behind the lodge were three horses. The one in the middle belonged to Standing Elk.

Walking his horse around to the front of the tipi, Bear slid off his back. Raven eased The Black in near to Bear's horse. He stayed in the saddle but maneuvered the stallion around so that the shotgun rested across his thighs, pointing in the general direction of the lodge. Because of the drape of his blanket poncho, only the eye of the muzzle was peeking out from beneath the red folds.

"Washtay!"

The neighboring camp noise quieted as though a giant hand had somehow turned the volume down.

"*Tatonka Iyotake*, it is I, Siha *Mato* (Bear's Foot). I wish to speak with you."

Raven was having difficulty catching his breath. *Tatonka Iyotake*, translated, became Sitting Bull. Bear had said 'great man' but Raven had no idea that it would be 'him.' He felt winded... his lungs just didn't want to function properly.

While Raven struggled to catch his breath, he could hear muted conversation coming from the tipi. Suddenly, the flap was thrown back on the skin dwelling. A tough-looking warrior emerged. His upper body was bare and his dark skin was puckered and ridged with white and pink scar tissue. The many scars gave emphasis to the man's powerful looking physique. Even his face was covered with the horrible scars. A large white ridge of tissue ran from the corner of his wide mouth to his ear. His burning gaze watched them closely as he lifted the tipi's door flap for someone else. In his other hand there was a hatchet.

As the second man stooped to come through the opening, Chris noticed that his hair was plaited into three braids, one of them going down the middle of his back.

When he raised his head, Raven felt a twist in his gut. With the single eagle feather standing straight up in back, Sitting Bull looked exactly like his famous photo. The same glaring eyes from the photo were pointing straight at Bear's Foot, but he refused to be intimidated.

A second bodyguard came through the flap. Chris barely glanced at him. His focus was on Bear and those around him. He saw Sitting Bull sway and his two guards quickly stepped up and gave him support. At first Raven didn't understand, but then he remembered Bear's Foot telling of the Sun Dance and the chief's ordeal.

Sitting Bull's mouth opened as though to speak, then closed. It opened again, but at that very instant Bear's Foot stepped forward so that his great size was only inches from the chief's body.

Both of Sitting Bull's guards stepped forward and had Bear pinned between them. The chief's two bully boys were now in control. If Bear made any sudden, hostile moves, they were in perfect position to cut him down.

With his immense height, Bear's Foot was in a control situation of his own. The chief had a strong, blocky frame but only average height. Without stepping back he was forced to look up at Bear's Foot. Sitting Bull could not afford to lose face by stepping away. His lofty position as leader of the Hunkpapa was political, not hereditary, so he had to stare up at six and a half feet of pissed off Minneconjou and hope that his 'boys' could handle the situation.

WASICHU

Impasse. Raven silently applauded Bear's tactic, although he had no idea where he was going with it. He could see a thin line of perspiration forming on Sitting Bull's upper lip. The scarred warrior on the left began to heft his hatchet while the other Hunkpapa's hand began to slither up under his shirt. Then for the second time that day the dry metallic click of the pump-gun's hammer pulled to full cock immobilizing everyone within hearing.

The two bodyguards had turned to stone. In the unnatural quiet, Raven's voice carried a great distance, even to the small crowd of curious onlookers.

"Slowly turn and see what I have for you."

Their hostile eyes searched and found the shotgun muzzle peeking out from beneath the red blanket. Their eyes flicked over the blanketed figure mounted on the tall buffalo runner. The muzzle of the shotgun looked as big as the mouth of the Bluecoat's cannon. That bothered them less than the huge grin that was spread all over the wasichu's face. Bear's Foot's rumbling baritone broke the mounting tension.

"Where is Standing Elk? I must speak with him."

Sitting Bull, head thrown back, met Bear's Foot's stare with a glare of his own. The chief's stocky frame swayed slightly but his lips remained sealed.

A rustling sound came from within the tipi. All eyes zeroed in on the door flap as a dark head emerged.

Standing Elk was wearing the same sneer he had on his face the last time Chris had seen him but with a little difference that was visible in the set of his eyes. Their constant movement just didn't fit the sneering expression. A blanket was draped over his left shoulder and arm in the manner of a chief. His arrogant bearing added to the phony illusion as he stood face to face with Bear's Foot.

"What do you want of me, Minneconjou?"

Standing Elk spat the words out as though they were

a mouthful of bitter berries.

Bear's Foot raised his hands in mock surrender.

"I have only come to say hau (hello) and to ask you a question."

His words were still ringing in Raven's ears when Bear's Foot quickly stepped forward. He grasped the startled Standing Elk's hand and began pumping it enthusiastically in a vigorous parody of the handshake.

While shaking Elk's hand, Bear's Foot continued to grin at Sitting Bull and Standing Elk.

From the instant Bear's hand grabbed his, Standing Elk's stoic expression had changed. His dark face had paled several shades and wore a pinched, unhappy look.

Raven watched from his high perch on The Black. He carefully scanned the crowd for hostile faces. Most appeared to be merely curious, but he sensed a collective feeling of expectancy. They knew something was going to happen and they were waiting for it.

Seeing the pain in Elk's eyes Chris figured the wound must be in the left arm or shoulder. Elk was trying desperately not to flinch but was grimacing with every shake of his hand.

Taking note of the onlookers, Bear's Foot raised the volume of his voice a couple of notches as he said, "I wanted to ask you something, Elk. When you shot at Okute and me from behind a tree, were you trying to hit us or my horse?"

Bear had stopped pumping Standing Elk's hand, but he continued to hold it as he met Sitting Bull's bitter gaze and announced, "Beneath this warrior's blanket there is a bullet wound placed there by Okute or myself. The Oglala tracker followed this man's blood trail to this very lodge."

An angry murmur rose and hovered in the air above the curious bystanders.

Reacting from some unseen signal, Sitting Bull's bodyguards stepped away from their chief as he impassively regarded his warrior, whose hand was still trapped within Bear's Foot's huge paw. The Chief's glaring eyes roamed the crowd as he probed for a clue to their mood and to assess their reaction to the situation.

Ignoring Standing Elk's occasional tug as he tried ineffectively to free himself, Bear began to play the crowd. He spoke of Ptecila's great prowess as a tracker. When he exhausted that subject, he moved on to a detailed description of the ambush, the tracks leading north, and Raven's brush with the Cheyenne.

Chris had the amusing thought that Bear was either trying to put the crowd to sleep or he was waiting for Standing Elk to bleed to death. Whatever he was doing, Raven could not be attentive as he was too busy trying to watch everyone at once.

Sitting Bull's boys appeared satisfied that Bear posed no immediate threat to their Chief, but Chris still felt the weight of the scarred warrior's stare.

Bear was summing up his monologue when Raven saw Standing Elk's free hand dip underneath his blanket.

"Aa-ah!"

Raven's warning startled everyone but Bear. His reaction was so swift that he must have been waiting for it. The warning cry was still echoing when he made his move. The fringes on his shirt leaped and swirled as he jerked Elk's hand and pulled the warrior to him.

Sunlight burst from the metal object clutched in Standing Elk's right hand. At first, Chris had mistakenly thought it was a knife. Then his retina relayed the correct image to his brain. It was a revolver!

Spectators backed away from the danger. Voices were raised in exclamations of surprise and fear.

Before Standing Elk could point and shoot, Bear's Foot had changed from the jerk and pull into a spinning pirouette that practically lifted the Hunkpapa off his feet.

Bear continued his swing. It was a deadly version of the game, 'crack the whip.' There was a blinding flash from sun kissed metal as Bear's Foot's fighting knife suddenly appeared from beneath his shirt.

Bear came to a sudden unexpected stop! Standing Elk would have fallen if it weren't for the *Minneconjou's* superior strength. Bear jerked the big man to him as though he were a child. With a sound like a cleaver striking a side of beef, twelve inches of razor-sharp steel slammed between Standing Elk's ribs.

A gasp of air erupted from Elk's gaping mouth! His eyes bulged as he struggled for the very breath of life.

Bear's Foot released the captive hand, jerked his knife free, and stepped back. An explosive grunt from Elk was smothered by the crowd's utterance of the guttural courage cry.

"*Huhn, huhn!*"

To Raven's ears the haunting sound seemed to come from the throat of the Earth Mother rather than from the mouths of the Lakota.

For an instant that seemed forever, Standing Elk was frozen in the same position as when he was struck. All at once his knees buckled and the prevailing silence was shattered by a thunder clap of noise as the pistol discharged into the earth at his feet. Standing Elk stiffened. Through the hovering cloud of acrid smoke, Raven watched as the warrior fell forward like a stack of dominoes. As he fell, his blanket preceded him, exposing a jagged, bloodstained furrow, up high on his left arm. Arms still at his side, he landed face first in the village dust. Standing Elk's body gave a few convulsive twitches and lay still. Blood began to ooze from beneath him and immediately soaked into the prairie dirt and grass.

Bear's Foot lifted his eyes from the prostrate form. Sitting Bull was staring at him with a murderous gaze. He met the chief's stare.

"*Wonumayin!*" Bear said.

Pointing with his thumb to the body at his feet, he continued, "This is the man that made the mistake. It was made when he tried to kill Okute and me from ambush. He also made a mistake by bringing his guilt and my revenge to the lodge of the great Sitting Bull. That is all I have to say."

A scatter of voices sounded the courage cry but stopped when Sitting Bull's baleful gaze swung in their direction. Still silent, he paused.

The chief, moving carefully in his weakened state, stepped over next to Standing Elk's body. He stared down at him for a moment and then bent over and lifted the blanket, exposing the bullet wound. Finally he dropped the blanket and straightened, facing Bear's Foot.

Contrary to his present physical shape Sitting Bull's voice was strong. It shook with suppressed outrage as he said, "*Siha Mato*, you have had your revenge. Now you must leave us!" He threw a withering look at Raven as he added, "Take your wasichu with you. We have no need of a hair mouth among the Hunkpapa."

Returning Sitting Bull's glare, Bear's Foot replied in a quiet voice, "*Hecheto aloe* (it is finished)."

Getting no further response, Bear turned and walked to his horse. Raven sat his horse as though sculpted from marble. But his gray eyes, narrowed against the sun's glare, saw everything.

Sitting Bull's two watchdogs drew most of his attention, especially the scarred one. He couldn't figure out why his hackles would not lie down. Whenever his hot eyes landed on him, Raven felt like he was in the cross-hairs of a sniper scope.

Without so much as a glance at Chris, Bear swung up on the back of his buckskin and began to walk him in an easterly direction.

Raven slowly turned The Black and followed in Bear's Foot's wake. His back tingled in anticipation of violence while his ears cringed from the loud silence. At any moment he expected to hear the twang of a bow string or the shrill screech of a war cry. Beneath his poncho, his body was drenched with perspiration as he moved steadily eastward and away from the Hunkpapa.

TWENTY-TWO
~~~~~~~~~~~~~~

After half a mile of weaving in and out of tipis and other dwellings, Bear's Foot pulled up and slid to the ground.

They were in a small clearing on top of a small knoll. The tipis stretched far to the west and east. Chris stared to the east and wondered where the Minneconjou camp was located, speculating when Spotted Horse's band would arrive. From the corner of his eye he saw Bear's Foot coming toward him.

Bear stared up at Raven. His expression was hard for Chris to read. He looked angry.

"Okute, get down."

Feeling a small tug of apprehension, he swung his leg over the fork and slid to the ground, landing squarely in front of Bear. Instantly, a pair of arms like girders of steel pinned his arms to his side. They felt as though they had been welded there. He looked into black eyes as cold and deadly as a shark.

Still clasping Raven in the vice of his hug, Bear's Foot smiled. Chris was dazzled by the transformation. When he realized that his friend was just playing games, he began to get angry. Be fair, he cautioned himself, Bear's probably elated that he's still alive after the scary encounter with the Hunkpapa. Hell, he reasoned, he's probably still jacked up from adrenalin.

"My friend, I have stopped here so that I can thank you for keeping the knives from my back."

"Bear, I am hot, hungry and tired. If you do not let go of me, you are going to need protection from me."

Seeing the seriousness in Raven's expression, Bear's smile slipped a little, then he threw his head back and laughed.

"I have you now, Okute. There is nothing that you can do about it."

To add emphasis to his boast, Bear gave a little extra squeeze. Raven could feel his anger escalate right in step with the pain in his arms.

Damn it, he thought, the man really doesn't know his own strength. He knew that Bear's Foot would never intentionally hurt him, but he was hurting him now.

"How would you like to be the only warrior in the Lakota nation with one foot?"

Still holding Raven tightly, Bear pulled his head back and gave him a derisive, leering smirk. The scoffing smile left his face so unexpectedly that Chris had to grin.

Bear stretched his neck to peer over his own biceps and looked down at his left foot. Resting solidly on his oversized foot was the muzzle of the pump.

With perfect timing, Raven cocked the hammer the exact second that Bear's Foot saw the gun.

At the click of the hammer, Bear's Foot's eyes opened wide so that even his nostrils flared! Unable to stop himself, Raven began to chuckle... then he laughed out loud.

Bear's Foot scowled. He stared hard at him for a second, then he was laughing with him. Bear released him and they both suddenly collapsed, falling to the ground. Irrepressibly, they were rolling on the grass laughing.

The Black and Bear's buckskin stared at their owners, rolling in the weeds and grass. Both were flicking their ears and snuffling. The Black stepped off the knoll and began grazing. With a final glance at Bear's Foot holding his stomach and laughing, the buckskin shook his black mane and quickly joined The Black.

Raven sat up, whipped the hot blanket off and sat

WASICHU

there, gasping for breath as he brushed away tears from laughing so hard. Bear's Foot was a few feet away, holding his stomach as the laughter still poured out of him. Soon the smile left Raven's face as he looked out over the flowing river of tipis. His gaze slid to the southeast as he pulled the sweaty bandana off his head. Perspiration had plastered wisps of dark curls to his broad forehead. The longer he stared at the southeast, the less distinct became his surroundings. The hard planes on his face softened while the pale eyes grew wistful.

His voice was softer than a whisper as he asked, "*Niyaha To* (Blue Feather), where are you?"

TWENTY-THREE

The blackness of the North Vietnam night was illuminated by the staccato muzzle flashes of the NVA's AK-47's. The iridescence of their green tracers swept in a deadly arc over the tall grass.

The whites of his eyes were the only part of Raven's face that was clearly visible among the green and black camouflage grease. Intermingled with the gunfire, he could hear excited, Vietnamese voices all along the perimeter.

An NVA patrol had caught up with him and his eight-man team at a very inopportune moment. They were on the very edge of their designated pick-up area. The slick was due at any moment and Raven had to get his men further into the LZ before it got there. Then he, somehow, had to talk the chopper pilot into dropping into a hot LZ. All he could do was hope and pray.

Feeling fingers gripping his sleeve, Chris spun away and brought his Swedish K-SMG up and was tightening on the trigger. Just in time, he saw the familiar grin of Joe Spotted Horse.

"Jesus Christ! Have you got some kind of fuckin' death wish, or what?"

Chong, Raven's RTO (radio man), was new to the team so he wasn't used to Joe's suddenly appearing out of thin air. He was staring open-mouthed at Spotted Horse, his Asian eyes as big and round as any Caucasian.

Before Spotted Horse had time to answer, the other members of his unit cut loose with a deafening fusillade. Their concentrated fire was homing in on the tree-line where the bulk of automatic weapon fire was coming from.

Because of the clamor, Joe had his mouth right up to Raven's ear as he shouted, "I gave orders to lay down some solid cover fire! I thought you would want us deeper into the LZ!"

Raven nodded emphatically and yelled, "You got that right!"

Giving Raven's sleeve a tug, Joe jumped up and moved swiftly into the tall grass. While running, he pumped several rounds from his gun toward the flashing muzzles among the trees. The resounding boom of the shotgun sounded out of place mixed in with the highly mechanized 'sewing machine' clatter of the AK-47's.

Raven and his RTO scuttled into the elephant grass, pausing only long enough to rake the tree-line with their automatic weapons. The enemy tracers immediately found where they had fired from, but by then they were already deep into the LZ, running for their lives. Then another automatic weapon zeroed in and the air around them snapped and hummed with menacing gunfire. Suddenly, the RTO went down. Raven took one look and swore. He slung his Swedish K, stripped Chong of his gear, threw him over his shoulder and ran. His radio man had caught one in the head and several in the back, killing him and destroying the radio.

The NVA gunfire unexpectedly stopped. The only sound was the swish of the tall grass and breathless gasps of exertion as the S.O.G. team dashed toward the center of the LZ.

Seeing two of his men hesitate and look back at the tree-line, Chris bellowed, "Move, move it! Shag ass!"

Even with the added weight of his RTO, Raven ran as though the hounds of hell were snapping at his heels. He could hear the rest of the team ripping through on either side of him. He never dreamed that running through grass could make so much noise. Joe was several meters out in front and when he broke clear of the grass, he stopped and prepared to provide cover if needed. Then they were all there, running for the dubious cover of a small hollow surrounded by a collection of dead trees.

Everyone slid into and around the natural depression and found cover wherever they could. Spotted Horse looked at Raven, who had eased his burden to the turf and checked to confirm that he was dead. Raven looked up and returned his gaze. Each knew immediately that the other's thoughts were the same as his own. Joe was the first to voice their fear.

"It's the chopper, man!"

Chris nodded and exclaimed, "You're right! The dinks quit firing so the 'slick' (Huey) won't know the LZ's hot!"

Eyes narrowed with concentration, Joe looked back toward the trees and said, "Soon as we load up they'll rip us to pieces. Shit!"

"Shit is right. When Chong got his, the radio got zapped, too."

Clearly audible was the rhythmic thudding of the approaching chopper as it zeroed in on the homing strobe light. Joe grabbed Raven's arm just as the Huey appeared. It hovered above. Dirt and other debris swirled and flew from the violent churning of the craft's rotors.

Raven yelled at the closest man, "Shut off the fucking strobe!"

The man couldn't hear him, but he got the message from Raven's agitated hand signals. The light went out. The landing lights brightened as the slick descended.

Pulling Chris closer to him, Joe shouted something unintelligible, and ran over to one of their mercenaries. Raven saw him yell in the man's ear and grabbed his AK-47 and thrust his pump-gun into the empty hands.

Stunned, he watched as Joe sprinted toward the tall grass and the waiting NVA. Just before he reached the elephant grass, Joe raised his hand. The light from the Huey glanced off a metal object clutched in his hand. The 'clacker' detonator! Raven's mind tumbled as he struggled with mixed emotions. He knew what Joe was planning, and it scared the hell out of him. Helpless, he watched him disappear into the grass.

At the edge of their LZ, they had rigged claymores in all the most likely approaches as a line of defense. Joe was going to attempt to detonate the claymores just before the NVA cut loose. If he times it right, Chris thought, he can set it off and be inside kicking ass with the AK before they can recover from the blast.

The Huey dropped to within a few meters of the ground. The gunner was gesturing emphatically! Needing no further encouragement, the men threw Chong's body on board and scrambled in after it. Raven grabbed the last man and shouted, "Tell the pilot all hell's about to break loose. Joe's going to detonate our claymores then shag-ass back here. Got it? Tell him to wait!"

As he spun away, Raven grabbed his arm and yelled, "You tell that sonofabitch that if he doesn't wait I'll shoot him down myself! Believe it! Now, go!"

The last of the team were climbing on board when the claymores went off. The huge explosion of red and orange fire lit up the jungle and drowned out the noise of the Huey. Automatic rifle fire followed immediately. There were several long bursts, then nothing. All that he could hear was the syncopated din from the revolving rotors. The side gunner was jumping up and down screaming, "Come on, Sarge! Come on!"

Ignoring him, Chris silently implored, 'Come on, Joe. You better not be counting coup, you goofy bastard.'

The gunner's nerve broke, and he screamed, "Fuck you, man! We're splittin' right now!"

Eyes riveted on the tall grass, Raven ignored the

raging gunner and prayed. Just as he heard the tempo of the rotors increase, he saw a shadow break free from the grass and sprint toward them. Head down, Joe was racing for the chopper like a broken field runner that could smell the end zone.

Raven threw his weapon through the door as eager hands dragged him on board. At that moment, the NVA survivors opened up. He felt the chopper shudder as several rounds hit it.

Spinning to the door, he saw Joe's sweat-drenched face grimacing with effort as he ran. Somewhere along the line he had stripped for speed. His assault rifle and other gear were gone, as was his shirt. All he was carrying with him was a driving will to survive.

Everyone in the chopper was screaming! Some were shouting encouragement; others were panicking. They were yelling, "Up, up! Get our ass out of here!"

Ten meters, five... bullets were kicking up dirt on both sides of him as he pushed himself faster.

The pilot, frantic because they were taking too many rounds, began to lift off. Joe leaped!

Raven caught him by the arms! They clung to each other as the Huey left the valley floor. Someone threw his body over Chris' legs for support. At that very instant an NVA gunner found Joe. Several rounds slammed into his back and legs! The impact nearly wrenched him out of Chris' hands. Their grip slipped until they were locked together by mere fingertips.

A wave of vertigo washed over Raven. They were fifty meters above the trees and climbing.

Chris stared in helpless horror at the bloody holes in Joe's chest. Joe's lips parted in a bloody smile as he pulled his fingers loose from Raven's.

TWENTY-FOUR
~~~~~~~~~~~~~~~

"No!!!"

The cry erupted from his lips as he sat up on the buffalo robe. His naked chest glistened with sweat in the moonlight.

Horrified, Raven could still see Joe's face as he fell. The image was becoming smaller and smaller, then gone.

Moonlight filtered in through the tipi's smoke hole. The pale light softly illuminated the dusky interior and soothed his trembling soul.

He shuddered and tried to dislodge his memories of the dream, but this time they wouldn't go away. It was a recurring dream that he hadn't had in months. Of course, it really wasn't a dream. It was a very real re-enactment of the moments leading to Joe's death. He had often tried to understand why he continued to relive those hated moments. Maybe, he reasoned, it was the dreams that had finally pushed him into doing the ceremony.

He vividly recalled when he had first had the dream. It was the night following the day he had turned in Joe's personal effects. That was when Raven had taken the artifact and the pump-gun.

Chris shut his mind to thoughts of the past. Or is it the future, he wondered? Letting himself drift, he watched the stars of the Montana night shining through the lodge's smoke hole. What is real? Can I really be here, he queried? For the hundredth time, he thought, maybe it's all a dream.

He felt a stirring next to him. Blue Feather's lithe form raised up beside him. She leaned back on her hands and studied him with her fathomless black eyes.

"What is it my husband?"

The light from above and the coals from the evening fire played together along the copper contours of her body. Unbraided, her long, glossy hair spilled across her shoulders, partially covering her nakedness.

Chris felt tightness in his throat. If I'm dreaming and this isn't real, he thought, then God help me. I want it to be real.

Raven smiled in lieu of answering and tentatively touched her shoulder. Her skin was like warm satin. He imagined that he could feel her blood pulsing beneath the flawless skin. His fingers slowly traced a meaningless pattern as they moved down across the surface of her body. Carefully he removed a strand of ebony hair from her breast.

While the moon kissed her cheek and shoulder with lips of blue light, Raven tenderly touched the globe of her breast. With fingers light as down, he explored the soft contours, the turgid erectness of her nipple.

Where before he had imagined the blood pulsing beneath her skin, he could now feel it pulsing hot and rigid between his two fingers.

Her breath quickened with desire. He heard her voice like a whisper of the wind.

"Okute."

Looking into the black depths of her eyes, he could see the smoldering passion of her need.

Fighting to hold back his own driving passion, Chris took Blue Feather into his arms. His hands explored the silken planes of her back, while her fingers clutched at the lean ridges of muscle across his wide shoulders.

Ever so slowly, as though she was made of the finest china, Raven lowered her onto the buffalo robe. As he gently positioned his body above her, Blue Feather could see the love in his eyes and was surprised by a tenderness that she had never experienced before. Tentatively, she opened her legs, feeling as though this was their first time. As he entered her and they became one, she gasped. His breath brushed her ear as a sigh of pleasure escaped his lips.

They released their pent up passions in a mindless explosion of movement and sound. Moving together, their bodies performed a rhythmic dance. The perfection of their union was so complete that when they neared the culmination of their desire, their passion fused and became one. They attained the ultimate sensation amidst a symphony of moans and cries as their ardent hungers were fulfilled.

TWENTY-FIVE
~~~~~~~~~~~~~~

The dawn's first light turned the skins covering the lodge poles translucent. A mosaic of rose and amber hues lit the interior, giving it a warm, cozy atmosphere. The smoke hole above gave access to contrasting rays of brilliant sunlight back-dropped by a bright blue sky.

Raven felt a small pang of disappointment. Blue Feather was gone. Placing his hand on the robe beside him, he could still feel her warmth, captured there within its curly surface. It gave him comfort to know that only moments before she had been there at his side.

Putting his hands behind his head, Chris let his thoughts drift back to the events of the previous day.

He and Bear's Foot had been with the huge pony herd when the news came of Spotted Horse's arrival. The news was brought to them by Wolf's Spirit. He rode up to them on his stallion, looking resplendent in bright yellow and green leggings and wearing the purple and gold Viking tee-shirt. Concealing his smile, Raven joined Bear in greeting the young warrior.

Besides the news of the band's arrival, he had other news as well. Chris had been given three of the pony stealer's horses. Crazy Horse, in a typical show of his generosity, had also given him two of his own ponies.

Bear had told him that Crazy Horse should be a wealthy man by now. Instead of amassing his wealth, he gave away all his extra possessions to those in need. It was one of the reasons that he was so widely loved and respected.

With a verbal show of youthful exuberance, Wolf's Spirit had told them that on the previous day some Cheyenne scouts had seen a large army camp of Bluecoats far to the south. They had said that there was no cause for immediate alarm because the army had many walk-a-heaps (infantry) with them. It would take them many days to reach their camp because the walk-a-heaps would slow them down.

After discussing the options the three of them decided that the next morning they would scout them in person. Shortly after Wolf's Spirit had left, Bear's Foot set out to speak with Spotted Horse about a purchase price for Blue Feather.

During their time together away from the band, Bear's Foot had explained to Raven what steps were to be taken to officially marry Blue Feather by Lakota custom.

Since her father had died several years ago, and she had no older brothers, Bear had thought it would be very appropriate to approach her former father-in-law.

Their haggling must have been brief because inside of an hour Chris was staring into Bear's smiling face as he told him the news.

Spotted Horse, realizing that Raven didn't have any buffalo robes (the standard price being five buffalo robes and other trinkets) had decided that he would accept one horse. Doing business with his heart rather than his head, Raven decided that one horse was too cheap for Blue Feather. He would give two... and maybe a couple of other things.

Chris stretched and got up. As he began dressing he remembered the joy of yesterday when they had reunited.

He was riding The Black and leading a long-legged bay and a sturdy looking pinto when he had found her. She was busy erecting poles for their lodge and didn't see his approach. He was to find out later that the tipi that they were putting up belonged to Blue Feather and was part of her dowry.

The two women helping her started to giggle and averted their faces when they saw him.

Seeing her friends giggling like a couple of little

girls, Blue Feather turned to see the cause of their unusual behavior. An expression of unbridled joy lit up her face.

"Okute!"

Before Chris had a chance to dismount she ran to him. Beaming up at him, she grasped his stirrup with both hands as though to hold him there.

She was wearing an elaborately fringed doeskin dress that had been bleached to a near white. It was lightly beaded in russet and blue. Her usual hawk bells rimmed the hem and bodice, giving the dress a personal touch.

Leaning down from his saddle, Raven cupped her cheek with the palm of his hand. She nestled her cheek against his hand. Her lips secretly brushed his palm.

Chris noticed her braids and decided to tease her.

"I see that you are wearing your braids in the front again. Have I been courting a married woman?"

With a teasing lift to her voice she said, "I also have been seeing a married person, only he has yet to realize that he is married... to me."

With his limited Lakota, Raven wasn't too sure that he understood her meaning, and when he did understand he was embarrassed.

He wasn't used to playing word games with women in any language and he was beginning to get the feeling things were no longer under his control.

Raven was certain that the whole encampment knew the reason for the two ponies waiting patiently behind him. In his embarrassment, the horses seemed to loom as large and noticeable as a couple of elephants.

To make things worse, Blue Feather sidled up to The Black and said with a mischievous glint in her eye, "I see you have some horses with you."

She began stroking The Black's neck.

"Is The Black becoming so old and crippled that you need to bring spare ponies with you?"

Raven saw The Black roll his eye and give her a derisive look.

Regaining some of his confidence, Chris tapped The Black's ribs with his heels and they moved forward.

Blue Feather stepped back with a look of concern on her face. Had she gone too far with her teasing? She wondered.

Looking back over his shoulder, Raven teased, "If you must know, I am using these ponies to purchase a wife, one who I am sure I will have to beat every day with a stick."

He softened his taunt by giving her a slow grin as he rode by.

Her laughter followed him all the way to Spotted Horse's lodge.

Raven was still smiling over the remembered words when the door flap was thrown back and Blue Feather entered. Having just returned from bathing, her waist length hair was wet and gleaming. She looked radiant.

"Hau, you look like a beautiful otter that has come all the way from the water to play with me."

She laughed and moved quickly into his arms. Looking up at him with an impish gaze, she said. "If I had come to play, the game I would choose would not be played in the water."

Laughing, Raven pulled her tightly to him and buried his face in her damp neck.

After a bit, Chris released her and hurriedly finished dressing. Pulling a faded black tee-shirt over his head, he looked up to see Blue Feather standing before him holding a beautifully tanned elk-skin vest. Smiling, she gave it to him.

He slipped it on. It was longer than a conventional vest, hanging to just below his waist. On each side there was a deep, roomy pocket with a short, lightly-beaded flap. Puzzled over the pockets, he queried, "How did you know how to make these?"

WASICHU

Smiling, she hurried over to his pile of gear and grasped one of the side pockets on his field pack.

"See, it was easy."

She dug inside the pack for a second and came out with several shotgun shells clutched in her fist. She dropped them into the right hand pocket then patted it. As there is no word for pocket in Lakota, she said, "These are for carrying the bullets for your thunder-maker."

Raven swept her into his arms and twirled her around so fast that her feet left the ground. When he set her down again they were both laughing breathlessly.

Suddenly serious, Chris framed her face with his hands and kissed her.

"*Le mita pila* (thank you)."

Pulling her to him he held her close for a moment. Her arms encircled his waist and held him tightly.

Pulling away from her clinging softness, he said, "I must go. Bear's Foot is waiting. Today we scout the Bluecoats."

She brushed her fingertips gently across his lips and laid her hand against his cheek.

"I, too, must leave."

She smiled briefly, slipped deftly under the skin flap and was gone.

Raven could hear the camp coming to life outside. He slipped on his beaded moccasins. Blue Feather had again put them on his feet the night before, culminating the ceremony that had made them man and wife.

Another day closer to Custer, he mused. The thought of having to fight the U.S. Army saddened him. He knew that as soon as he was seen among the Sioux he would be labeled a traitor and renegade. Somehow it just didn't matter. These were Joe's people and now they were his.

Struggling out of his new vest, Raven quickly buckled on the shoulder rig. He checked the revolver to make sure it was loaded and slipped it back underneath his arm. Putting the vest back on, he pocketed some extra ammunition, ducked under the door flap, and stepped out into the bright early morning sunshine.

TWENTY-SIX
~~~~~~~~~~~~~

Blinking from the sun's glare, Raven returned greetings from neighbors and others passing by.

The camp was already a nest of activity. Women were carrying firewood or water while children scampered here and there, looking for mischief. A few men were working on their weapons nearby. Other warriors were strolling around talking and laughing. Like soldiers in any army, he thought, they're killing time in between battles.

All at once he saw Spotted Horse. He looked like the Pied Piper with his new following of children and the insatiably curious. Raven grinned with his memory of the marriage ceremony and of the chief's face when he had tried on the mirrored sun glasses. Chris had thrown in the shades as a gift along with the horses. He never dreamed they would be such a sensation. The only time he had seen them off the chief's face was when he was letting someone look through them. Spotted Horse, not having seen Raven, moved on with his entourage trailing behind.

Blue Feather was nowhere to be seen. About twenty feet away, Little Hawk was hunkered down on his heels, watching him. Behind him, The Black and Hawk's Wing were grazing on buffalo grass.

Seeing that Raven had noticed him, Little Hawk stood up. Clutched in his left hand was his new bow.

Last night, Raven had heard the story of Little Hawk's adventure with the wasichu. He had been amazed at the boy's quick thinking and courage, especially after having witnessed the murder of his friend. Little Hawk's second father, Short Bow, was so impressed that he had given the boy his own personal bow and arrows.

Most Lakota boys are given their first real bow and arrows at the age of twelve. Short Bow had been in the process of making Little Hawk a bow when the incident had occurred. In his eyes, Little Hawk had acted like a true warrior and need not wait any longer for his bow, so he gave him as a gift, his own personal bow.

Raven and Short Bow weren't the only ones that were impressed. For a boy of twelve to count coup on a live enemy was exceptional. Many Lakota were already saying that someday he could become a great warrior.

Raven stood in front of the boy and looked down at the small face. He knew what was coming. There was no pleading in his eyes just a touch of tightly controlled anxiety.

"I wish to come with you, Okute."

Saying nothing, Chris studied him for a moment. He thought briefly of his mother but dismissed the thought. He knew that this was his decision.

"I can see of no reason for you not to come... as long as you do as you are told."

Little Hawk, fighting hard to conceal his joy, quickly mounted his pony.

"Come, Okute, I will take you to Bear's Foot."

Enjoying the warmth of the morning sun, Raven climbed up on The Black.

Maneuvering their way through the lodges, Chris noticed that there were an inordinate number of warriors around. More Sioux had been arriving every day. He saw a couple of tipis with their skin coverings rolled up part way that were billeting four or five men... no women, just men. Good God, he thought, if there are many lodges like that one, there must be thousands of fighting age Sioux and Cheyenne along the stream bed.

Because of the east-west sprawl of the camp, their southerly ride through the camp was brief. Soon they were clear of the lodges and climbing the canyon's shallow slopes.

WASICHU

At the top, Little Hawk led the way westward along the lip of the gorge.

Raven looked to the south. The land rolled and dipped. Conical hills topped with pine spread out as far as the eye could see. With distance and the naked eye, it appeared to be a rolling, unchangeable landscape. Having traveled over part of it, Raven knew that from a distance the terrain was deceptive. There were canyons, valleys, and grasslands out there.

Moving around the top of a rocky bluff, Chris saw Bear's Foot and Wolf's Spirit sitting beside their horses a couple hundred yards away. By the time they reached them, both warriors were mounted and ready to go.

After exchanging greetings, Bear's Foot and Wolf's Spirit began to joke with Little Hawk and fuss over his new bow.

Besides being the band's principle hunter, Short Bow was a true craftsman as well. so the warriors' praise of Hawk's bow was honest praise. But Chris was sure that some of it was calculated to make the boy feel accepted on his first scout.

They moved out in single file. Bear led, followed by Raven, then Little Hawk, with Wolf's Spirit bringing up the rear.

Heading southward, they traveled silently through the many hills and valleys. In places the new grass was so green it appeared iridescent. As the miles fell behind them the sun rose higher and higher, bringing with it an increasing warmth.

Resisting the temptations of deer and other game, they ate jerky and pemmican to save time. Raven stuck to the jerky. He didn't like the greasiness of the ground meat and berries. It was just as well, his friends wolfed down the pemmican as though it was a thick juicy steak.

They interrupted their travel every couple of miles so

that one of them could climb some high ground and scout the surrounding countryside.

The hours flew by and eventually they arrived on top of a long plateau that overlooked a large valley. Below them was a natural amphitheater. It was formed by low bluffs on three sides. These bluffs all but surrounded a curving willow and juniper-lined river which formed into a big bend. From their vantage point they could see at least three different streams, tributaries of the shallow river. Two streams ran northerly, one south. Scrub oak could be seen mixed in with the juniper.

Four sets of eyes searched the southern expanses and found nothing. At the moment nothing was moving but the ribbons of water and a host of birds that seemed to be everywhere.

Slowly they worked their horses down the slopes to the valley floor. They passed through a myriad of wild roses. Their pink blossoms blanketed the valley floor. The green of the abundant grasses mixed with the pink and green of the wild roses gave the valley a peaceful wild beauty.

After watering their horses, they crossed the shallow river and quickened their pace. The sun was high and they were anxious to sight the enemy.

The river was about an hour behind them when they saw a small herd of buffalo off to the east. Wolf's Spirit let out a whoop as his big black horse lunged into the open, away from the trail. In two jumps the stallion was in full gallop.

A shout from Bear's Foot caused Wolf's Spirit to pull his horse into a skidding slide, switch directions and return toward them all in one smooth maneuver. Once again Raven marveled at the young Sioux's horsemanship. Bear's Foot's hard voice lashed out at Wolf's Spirit.

"There will be time for *tatonka* later. For now we must find the Bluecoats."

WASICHU

Obviously embarrassed, the young warrior brought his left hand up to his brow and reclaimed his spot at the tail end of the line.

It wasn't the first time that Chris had seen a gesture like the one Wolf's Spirit had made. He hadn't thought about it before, but among the Sioux it seemed to be a show of respect or an acknowledgment of authority.

The trees had thinned and the land was beginning to flatten out. For miles they had been on a gradual incline. It now looked as though the rise topped off a couple of hundred yards up ahead. Bear urged his big sorrel into a gallop and moved ahead toward some trees to see what was ahead. He stopped short of the crest and approached it on foot.

They waited about fifty yards away as Bear eased up and peered over the edge. He instantly turned and made the sign for enemy.

Leaving their horses by the sorrel, they quickly wormed up beside him.

Less than a mile away was a long, seemingly endless column of horseback soldiers with a few wagons. They were flanked on either side by two large groups of Indians.

Raven was puzzled. How in the hell did they get this far so fast? They were unbelievably lucky, he thought, that the column wasn't heading straight for them. Had it been they would have run into their advance scouts a long time ago.

The column was angled to the right, the northwest. The angle was just enough so that they would miss their hill.

Leaving Little Hawk to keep watch, the three slithered down below the rise for a quick council. Bear's Foot opened the council with the query that was on all of their minds.

"Where are the walk-a-heaps? Did they leave them behind to have traveled so far, so quickly?"

A look of consternation crossed Wolf's Spirit's face.

"By this time tomorrow they will be nearing our village!"

Wolf's prophecy was still echoing in their ears when Little Hawk's voice rang out.

"*Dho! Wasichu mani* (walking white man)!"

Scrambling to his side they were in time to witness the climax of a small drama taking place among the Bluecoats. One of the rider's mounts started bucking and kicking, forcing him to leave the column. Suddenly the rider and beast parted company; the rider landed in a heap while his mount, a mule, sprang away.

While one of their Indian allies chased his wildly bucking mule, the soldier brushed himself off and picked up his gun. It was a rifle, not a cavalry carbine. The man was infantry, not cavalry! Bear said it for them all.

"They have their walk-a-heaps riding mules!"

Bear punctuated his outburst with a slap on the back that nearly catapulted Little Hawk over the hill.

"You have the eyes of your namesake, little friend."

Beaming at Bear's receding back, Little Hawk joined the others as they hurried to their ponies.

As they mounted, Raven said, "When they reach the stream, my bet is that they will follow it due north to the headwaters at the big bend."

"I think you are right, Okute. We must hurry but we must be on the lookout for their scouts. The Crow dogs and Shoshone could be anywhere."

Careful not to leave any rising dust in their wake, they hurriedly moved north. Once they felt safe from immediate detection, they heel-tapped their ponies into a gallop. By alternately galloping and walking their ponies, they crossed the varied terrain as quickly as possible.

TWENTY-SEVEN
~~~~~~~~~~~~~~~

The day had become hot with very little breeze. By midafternoon they were about halfway between the valley of the roses and the village. All were anticipating the water hole they knew was but a short distance away.

When they arrived at the water, they surprised four Cheyenne scouts and a big-nosed Oglala named Little Hawk. The four had just come from the village.

The instant that Bear heard the Oglala's name, his head whipped around until his eyes landed on the boy. He grinned at him and turned back to the scouts. In a brief monologue, Bear's Foot told them of the Bluecoats and of them being mounted on mules. They grew excited and began talking animatedly among themselves.

Bear told the big-nosed Sioux, who appeared to be the leader, that since they had the fresher horses perhaps it would be best if they returned to the village with the news of the Bluecoats.

Nodding his assent, the Lakota waved his arm to the north and shouted, "Hopo!"

He and his Cheyenne friends spun their ponies around, and in a surge of swinging quirts and rising dust, they were off.

Dismounting, the four walked their horses to the inviting sun dappled water.

Removing his vest, Raven splashed water onto his face and neck, relishing the soothing coolness as it ran down his chest. Rubbing the water out of his eyes, he saw Bear's Foot staring at Little Hawk. He was staring with the same intensity that a cat watches a mouse. Little Hawk tried in vain to ignore him. Bear, with his eyes still locked on the boy's face, walked over to him. With eyes grown as big as *heecha* (the owl), Little Hawk stood his ground.

The big warrior, bending from the waist, put his face within inches of the boy's. Raising a hand that was the size of a picnic ham, Bear clamped a finger on either side of Little Hawk's miniscule nose and squeezed.

"I just want to see if it is going to grow as big as the other Little Hawk's nose."

Little Hawk quit struggling, as though resigned to his fate.

Bear's Foot, still grinning from ear to ear, looked to his other friends to see if his humor was appreciated.

It was all the time Little Hawk needed. Using a full two-handed swing, he hit Bear's Foot under his raised arm with his heavy horn bow. He hit him so hard that the big man let out a howl loud enough to have brought a pack of wolves running to investigate.

As Little Hawk escaped to his pony, leaving Bear's Foot bent over clutching his ribs, Raven and Wolf's Spirit brayed like a couple of jackasses.

With the sound of Hawk's Wing's hooves drumming in his ears, Bear's Foot glared at his two friends until he too had to join them in their laughter.

The only sign of Little Hawk's having been there was a settling trail of dust leading northwards.

TWENTY-EIGHT

About two miles north of the watering hole, Little Hawk rejoined his friends. He had hid himself in some rocks. He waited until they filed past and then had joined them by bringing up the rear. He had thought it a good idea to stay clear of Bear's Foot for a while.

They arrived at the village just before dark. The sun was setting, displaying a vivid backdrop of red, orange and purple. Bear's Foot gestured to the northwest where hundreds of Sioux were gathering. Several fires were adding their own blaze of color to the steadily increasing gloom of dusk.

Turning to Raven, Bear's face was serious as he unsuccessfully tried to hide his excitement.

"Council fires... the old chiefs are trying to decide what we should do about the Bluecoats."

They agreed to meet at the council later. Bear and Wolf's Spirit waved and turned their horses to ride away. At the last minute, Bear turned in his bone saddle and scowled at Little Hawk. The scowl turned into a grin as he followed Wolf's Spirit down the slope. Chris and Little Hawk found another trail down the incline. When the ground leveled, they rode through the lodges at a canter, eager to get home.

Blue Feather must have seen them coming down the canyon's slopes as she was waiting for them. Her joy was written all over her face as the two of them rode up to the tipi.

As he climbed down from The Black, Blue Feather moved to Raven's side, her small brown fist nestled into his open hand.

"Hau, my husband. Did my son do well?"

Out of the corner of his eye, Chris saw the boy pull himself erect in the saddle.

"He did better than well. He was the first to see the walk-a-heaps riding mules."

"Waste (good), I am very proud."

Little Hawk, all business, reached for The Black's reins.

"Okute, with your permission, I will pasture The Black with some other ponies away from the main herd. The grass is long and thick in this place."

"Thank you, Hawk, you did well today. I too am proud of you."

Grinning like the Cheshire Cat, Little Hawk rode off leading The Black.

Blue Feather then tugged at Raven's hand and stepped toward their lodge.

"Hohahe (welcome to my tipi), my husband."

In the darkening dusk, her smile was like a beacon drawing his trail-worn body into the comfort and security of her closeness.

While Raven ate a delicious stew of venison and wild vegetables, Blue Feather filled him in on the day's events. In particular, she talked about the excitement generated by the news of the Bluecoats.

"When the herald came by this evening with the news that the soldiers are much closer, people started running everywhere."

In each village of the Lakota there is a herald, a town crier, who walks through the village daily calling out the news.

"Spotted Horse and some of the other older chiefs calmed everyone and told them not to worry that there would be a council to decide what to do."

Raven thought, if Indian politics are anything like

WASICHU

white politics, the council will probably last for hours.

"Soon I must go to the council, but first I will rest."

As Chris lay back on his blanket, Blue Feather snuggled up next to him and placed her hand on his chest.

"Sleep, Okute, I will wake you long before the *shakowan* (council fires) go out."

I should get up and go to the council right now, was his last thought before sleep smothered his senses with darkness.

TWENTY-NINE

It was dark when Raven arrived at the council fires. Hundreds of warriors were gathered in a rough circle. Those closest to the fires looked to be the older, more experienced chiefs and warriors. The outer circles were made up of the younger, more excitable braves.

Moving through the crowd, Chris could feel the tension exuding from their bodies. Their emotions seemed to have developed form and were hovering in the air.

He could hear low voices and whispering coming from everywhere.

An old chief was standing near the center of the gathering. All the others nearby were seated. He was speaking loudly and emphatically. It was his opinion that they should wait until the many Bluecoats attacked before starting a fight.

Several men nearby raised their voices, protesting against waiting. Others around the circle joined in. All those voicing an opinion said pretty much the same thing.

"Fight them now before they get to the village."

Silently, Raven agreed.

He began to work his way through the congested bodies, looking for Bear's Foot's towering figure. As he moved toward the outer ring, he fervently hoped that all these Sioux knew who he was or had heard of him.

Finally he stepped clear of the last row and began to move through the shadows.

A large warrior deliberately blocked his path. He was naked except for breech-clout and moccasins. His face was in shadow, but Raven immediately recognized the scarred torso... Sitting Bull's bodyguard!

"What are you doing here, wasichu? Spying for the Bluecoats?"

Having never heard him speak before, Raven was shocked. His voice had a raspy discord, like dragging a piece of broken glass over rusty metal.

Then he noticed the deep lacerations where puckered scar tissue covered most of his neck.

"Where is your pet bear? Is he not here to protect you?"

As he spoke, the warrior stepped forward, moving his face out of the shadow. Moonlight played across a menacing leer that twisted the jagged scar by his mouth.

For Christ's sake, Raven thought, am I back in high school or what? In English he said, "Hey, man... fuck you and the horse you rode in on!"

Raven chuckled at his own spontaneous wit in an attempt to control his temper.

Scar crouched and stepped forward. His hand went to the knife sheathed at his waist.

He said, "Why are you laughing, wasichu? I will cut out your liver and eat it!"

Raven was planning his first strike to Scar's damaged throat when a familiar voice interrupted his concentration.

"Are you looking for me, Scar? I am here."

Bear's Foot's deep baritone rumble had come from behind the man. Scar stiffened and stood up straight. Rather than turn around, he continued to stare at Chris.

Bear, directly behind him, put his mouth near his ear as he said, "I am here to protect you, not Okute."

Reaching over Scar's shoulder, he held four fingers the size of bratwursts in front of his disfigured face.

"In as many suns, I have saved the lives of four Cheyenne, and now you, from my little friend. Wakan Tanka must like you or chooses to save you for the Bluecoats."

WASICHU

He dropped his hand and gestured with it to Chris.

"Come, Okute, Crazy Horse will speak soon."

The man called Scar did not move from Chris' path. He made no move to stop him, but continued to hold his stare as Raven brushed by him to follow his friend.

They moved up into the crowd just as the old chief was sitting down.

"I meant to ask you before. How did he get all these scars?"

Bear turned his brown face to Chris, smiled and said, "*Mato* (bear). *Mato* wanted to eat Scar but Scar did not want him to. Scar rubbed him out with his knife."

The crowd was getting anxious. Several voices called for Crazy Horse. Raven didn't hear them; he was stunned.

Holy shit, he thought, I just about tangled with a guy that killed a bear with a knife... and in this country, 'bear' means grizzly.

After thinking about it, Chris decided that it was a story cultivated by Scar. He was probably mauled, he thought, and left for dead. Shouts coming from the crowd quickly regained his attention.

"*Oo-oohey* (It is time)."

The shouts came from many different places throughout the gathering. A growing hum of voices rose from the hundreds of Sioux and Cheyenne. Occasionally different voices called out, "*Ocastonka!*"

"What are they saying? I do not understand."

Bear waved his arm expansively in front of him. He nearly removed a brave's eagle feather in the process.

"It means, 'His name is everywhere!' The young warriors are asking for Crazy Horse."

Looking around at the hundreds, maybe thousands, of people, all waiting to hear Crazy Horse speak, caused the hackles on the back of Raven's neck to tingle. For the first time he was seeing an example of the man's legendary, charismatic power.

Crazy Horse rose from among the seated chiefs. A hush settled over the assembled throng. All talk was extinguished, as fast as water thrown on a fire.

The most notable thing about Crazy Horse was his aura of quiet dignity. He had a no frills, no flash, style.

Chris noticed that nearly all the chiefs seated within the inner circle were elegantly attired. It was at that moment that Raven saw Spotted Horse.

He had to clap a hand over his mouth to keep from laughing aloud. The old chief was resplendent in his beautifully fringed and beaded doeskin, full headdress, and handsome mirrored sunglasses.

After convincing Bear that the 'hand over his mouth' wasn't because he was going to be sick, Chris continued with his observations. Most were wearing elaborate head gear of some sort. Some like Spotted Horse wore the long beautiful, many-feathered war bonnets so commonly attributed to the Sioux and Cheyenne.

Crazy Horse, as usual, was very simply dressed. He was wearing two hawk feathers. His dark-brown, wavy hair was parted on the side. Unbraided, it hung in two long twists on either side of his chest, loosely wrapped in red cloth. Leggings, fringed shirt, and red loin-cloth completed his dress. The only ornaments he wore were a bone breast plate decorated with orange and light blue beads and a pair of quilled moccasins.

In a quiet voice he began speaking to the council of chiefs. His words were to the point as he told them of his plan.

"A strong force of warriors should leave for the Rosebud tonight. It is there that we should find them. We must drive the Bluecoats away. Warriors will also be needed to stay here in the village to guard the women, children, and old ones."

WASICHU

While a new wind of excitement swept over the crowd, Raven puzzled over his mention of the 'Rosebud.' It sounded familiar. Suddenly he remembered. There had been a big fight before the Custer massacre, but there hadn't been too much written about it. He couldn't remember the name of the general involved but he knew that later on he became famous for fighting Apaches.

Chris cleared his mind, brushing away his rambling thoughts. Crazy Horse was speaking again and this time his words were directed toward his fighting men.

"This will not be like when we fight other Indians. We cannot be satisfied with just counting coup. Three Star's Army is coming here to kill us. The only way that we can fight them and save our village is to kill also!"

Crazy Horse unexpectedly walked over to his place in the circle and sat down.

Pandemonium ran rampant through the crowded gathering. As far as the spectators were concerned, the council was over. People were leaving in all directions. The air was charged with electricity as many raced to their lodges to prepare for battle.

Raven could feel the excitement beginning to tingle throughout his body. When Crazy Horse had mentioned Three Stars, it had triggered his memory. General George Crook! Many believed him to be the best Indian fighter ever produced by the U.S. Army.

Chris faced Bear and asked, "Do you know that Three Stars is the best Indian fighter the Bluecoats have?"

Bear's eyes glittered as he replied, "Do you know that if I see him, he is going to be a dead Indian fighter?"

He then threw his head back and laughed uproariously at his own wit as they forced their way through the thinning crowd.

Already Raven could smell burning sweet grass floating in the night air as warriors began to purify themselves before going into battle. They would burn braids of the grass and with their hands they would cup the smoke into their faces and over their heads.

Young Wolf's Spirit and the comical, hatchet-faced brave, Kills Twice, joined them as they broke away from the crowd and moved toward the Minneconjou camp.

Bear's Foot moved ahead then stopped and faced his three friends before he spoke.

"Do we go with Crazy Horse?"

The three exchanged looks and grinned. This time Raven said it for all of them. He used the war cry taught to him by a Sioux in another lifetime.

"Hopo, it is a good day to die!"

Part 5
Rosebud

THIRTY
~~~~~~~~

All through the night the thunder of thousands of hooves reverberated off shallow canyon walls, splashed along the banks of the Rosebud, and sliced through the long grass and shaggy brush of the western hills.

The Cheyenne chief, Spotted Wolf, led a large force of his Cheyenne to the east, where he was joined by young Two Moons and his equally large group of Sioux and Cheyenne. Converging, they moved along the banks of the river, following it south toward its headwaters in the Valley of the Rosebud.

To the west, American Horse and He Dog raced their ponies along the plateaus and ridges leading a large number of eager Sioux and Cheyenne.

Other smaller groups of Sioux were whipping their ponies and pointing their noses south. These were the malcontents, the young hot-heads who refused to follow the chiefs and older warriors.

From the middle of the sprawling village, a column of four hundred men moved down through the pine topped hills and valleys. Serpent-like, the long column snaked its way southward. They rode four abreast with the *akicita* (police) riding on the flanks and at point. One man led them... Crazy Horse.

Altogether they were more than a thousand warriors looking like centaurs from hell, as they rode relentlessly southward. Eyes glittering with resolve, hands and bodies bristling with weapons, all were mixed with one common goal... kill the Bluecoats or drive them from their land.

From his vantage point near the front of the middle column, Raven had time to study and observe his leader.

Crazy Horse did not look like an Indian chief about to lead hundreds of warriors into battle.

He was wearing his usual two hawk feathers in his long, unbound hair. Around his neck was tied a short cape of some type of spotted hide. Except for breech clout and moccasins, he was naked. Pale dabs of paint called hail spots were patterned over his body and face. Clutched in his right hand was a Henry lever-action rifle. The moon's blue light reflected off the Henry's brass receiver as Crazy Horse raised it overhead, slowing the column to a walk.

Raven had decided to rest The Black and had chosen the dead gunman's dapple gray for the night's run. He seemed to be the most sure-footed and sturdy of his dwindling stock. Chris remembered how dependable he was around gunfire.

The *akicita* moved up and down the column cautioning the men to refrain from talking or making any unnecessary noise. When the morning star appeared, they came to a halt in one of the many shallow canyons. Pine-topped plateaus flanked them on either side.

Raven could feel the excitement moving through the hundreds of horsemen. Waiting for their scouts to report back, many of the warriors dismounted. They applied war paint and tied up their horse's tails. Most had done these things earlier but retouched or added some refinement to their paint, not having time to do so earlier.

Stepping down from his horse, Raven looked over at his three comrades. The momentary chill he experienced, looking at his friends' transformations, was obliterated by the ludicrous sight of Wolf's Spirit. He was covered from head to toe in black, red, and yellow paint, except for his upper body. This part of his anatomy had been reserved for the now infamous purple and gold Viking tee-shirt. Except for the shirt and moccasins, he was stark naked.

Bear's Foot was gigantic, in a full, eagle feather war

bonnet. Naked, except for loin cloth, he had painted himself with broad, vermilion stripes on his body and legs. Black paint was spread across his forehead to a point just below his eyes like a mask. He had also dipped his hand in red paint and had cupped his chin, splaying the fingers up across his face. The effect was chilling.

Even with his lesser physique, Kills Twice looked equally as frightening. The upper half of his face was red, while the lower was splashed with yellow ochre. The rest of his body had been dabbed with vermilion.

The moonlight changed the many colors on the men, horses, and equipment. The blue light made the colors even more garish. It was a spectacle that caused Raven to pause and stare at the dwindling reality.

Even the discipline among the host of savage Lakota was unreal. Who would believe, Raven thought, that four-hundred men would be so disciplined as to remain absolutely silent for several hard-riding hours. It just didn't seem possible. In the army there was always that ten percent that never got the word or chose to ignore it. But then, he mused, anything could be possible when you're in a time and place that shouldn't be believable in the first place.

Clearing his mind, Chris dug out a hunk of dried meat and hunkered down on his heels. Refusing to allow his mind to become unsettled, he chewed his jerky and stoically waited for whatever was to come.

THIRTY-ONE

The sky was just starting to lighten when suddenly there was a shout. Hundreds of eyes began searching, hunting. Directly to their front, less than a hundred yards away, a wolf was silhouetted on top of a low ridge.

Then there was another shout. "Crow!"

The wolf grew larger until he became recognizable for what he was, a horseback Indian wearing a wolf skin headdress. Then two more warriors joined the first.

No longer a need for quiet, challenges were called out as warriors used their quirts on their ponies hoping to head off the enemy scouts. Wolf howls answered the Lakota taunts, as the Crow disappeared behind the ridge.

As quick as some of the Sioux were, there were none as swift as Crazy Horse. His spotted pony was a solid two lengths ahead of everyone else.

Gone was the orderly column, the quiet ranks. Now it was a race.

Every Indian was mounted and flying in pursuit in a matter of seconds. They rode together from the canyon floor to the top of the slope. Ahead of them they could see the enemy, quirting their ponies as they tore down the long plateau.

The sun peeked over the distant horizon as gunfire shattered the morning serenity.

Crazy Horse had given up his lead by sliding off his pony and firing several rounds at the escaping Crow. One of them threw up his arms and pitched off from his horse. Another slumped over his pony's neck, both fists buried in its mane.

The young chief was about to remount as Raven and Bear's Foot had come abreast of him.

As they approached, Chris saw him scoop up two handfuls of dirt and throw it on himself and on his horse.

Later, Bear's Foot explained that many years before, Crazy Horse had a dream that told him how to prepare for battle. The dirt, hail spots, his manner of dress, all had been prophesied in the dream.

Wolf's Spirit and Kills Twice, in their eagerness to close with the enemy, had surged ahead.

The race continued for several hundred yards without the Sioux gaining much ground. It ended with the enemy scouts disappearing from view down an incline. As the closest of the Sioux swarmed down the same incline, more shots were heard. Then they heard firing from the right front and a scattering of shots far to the left.

When they reached the spot where the Crow had dropped out of sight, Raven could see that they were at the northern end of another long plateau.

Looking down at the fleeing Crow scouts, he couldn't help but notice the wild beauty of the scene.

He paused as the others moved around him and down the slope. On the level ground below him, the ponies' legs couldn't be seen in the tall grass. They appeared to flow rather than run through grasses that parted for them like a green sea. The Crow, their long hair ripping behind them, spread out, leaving a pattern of darker trails in the grass.

"*Hokahey! Hopo hokahey!*"

The Lakota war cry assailed Raven's ears from near and far. His heart seemed to pause, missing a beat, as he saw a large force of enemy Indians surging up onto the plateau at the southern edge.

Chris was swept down the slope with the others. War cries leapt from eager throats; heels and quirts pounded pony flanks, as the two forces headed straight toward each other.

WASICHU

Surrounded by vivid, living color, it was as though he was the only black and white player in a Technicolor production.

The two opposing bands came together with an indescribable clash of sounds. A cacophony of gunfire; screams, shots, and thousands of pounds of horseflesh meeting head on. Dust and swirling, wheeling horses were everywhere.

Raven, his eyes burning from powder, smoke and dust, singled out an enemy Crow. Before he was able to shoot, the warrior disappeared behind a wall of struggling Sioux and Shoshone.

Bear's Foot's form materialized out of a cloud of dust. He shouted at Raven, and charged in amongst a quartet of Crow. Horses reared; war clubs swirled.

Before he was even aware that he was doing so, Raven found himself right behind him.

Bear's Foot's four-foot war club was swinging in a wide arc. Left and right, he struck, emptying two saddles.

The other two, struggling to control their ponies, swung wide, out of the reach of his lethal weapon.

Raven's pump bucked in his fist as a steel ball punctured the shield and chest of the Indian closest to Bear's Foot. The impact knocked him completely off his horse. Another Sioux leaped on the back of the remaining Crow. Momentarily distracted by the struggling pair, he lost sight of Bear's Foot.

Chris spun the gray around just in time to deflect a hatchet blade with the barrel of his shotgun. A hate-filled savage face appeared through the gun smoke and haze. Just as the hatchet started its second sweeping arc, Raven smashed the butt-plate of his gun into the snarling face. The Indian's pony swung his head around, and with teeth bared, snapped at his arm as he brushed past, dragging his unconscious rider behind him.

I don't believe this shit, Chris silently cursed, I have to fight their horses, too?

"Aa-ah, Okute!"

Wolf's Spirit's voice sliced through the rising clamor.

The warning cry snapped his head around just in time to enable him to twist his body to the right, causing the steal lance head to pass between his left arm and body, instead of splitting his chest as though it was a pumpkin. The slit-eyed face of the Shoshone at the other end of the lance didn't have a chance to show surprise as Raven's backhanded swing of the pump-gun crunched into the vertical white stripes that covered his dark face.

Digging his heels into his horse's heaving ribs, Chris rode back with the other Lakota as the two forces backed off from one another. It was strange. Neither side made any attempt to shoot at the other as they drifted apart.

In the lull, Raven could see, beyond the Crow and *Shoshone* that Crook's Bluecoats were frantically trying to set up some organized positions.

Because of the distance, they looked like a giant colony of blue ants spread throughout the valley floor, moving about on the slopes of the plateau.

Scattered throughout the valley, he could see other groups of Sioux swarming around the soldiers. To the east and west he could hear the popping of many guns.

Crow wolf howls and resounding '*hokaheys*' brought the two forces smashing together once again. The fight raged back and forth, neither side being able to force the other to give ground.

Raven, having resorted to using his handgun for the close hand-to-hand fighting, took a snap shot at a Crow wearing a soldier's hat. He missed, but more importantly, through the drifting gun smoke and dust, he spied a long line of infantry marching toward them behind their Indian allies.

WASICHU

Oh shit, he thought, if that isn't a skirmish line, I've never seen one before.

He knew immediately what the Bluecoat's plans were. Once they felt they were close enough to inflict the ultimate damage, they were going to have their Indian friends retreat. Leaving the battlefield to the enemy, and with the infantry's long range rifles, they would be able to cut the Sioux to pieces.

Frantically, Raven searched through the fighting, milling bodies looking for a slim form wearing a spotted cape. He saw Crazy Horse just as he ducked under the wild swing of a tomahawk and slammed the stock of his Henry into the chest of a wild-haired Shoshone. Eyes as fierce as a bird of prey, he listened to Raven's hurried explanation of what he had seen.

Quickly, he wheeled his pony, and whipping his spotted cape overhead, he shouted, "Yea-hey! Yea-hey!"

Warriors flocked to him and they fiercely fought their way clear. They regrouped north of the taunting Crow and Shoshone.

Once again, they charged toward their enemies, only this time, when the Crow came to meet them, Crazy Horse split his force. One group swung wide to the east, the other to the west.

Both groups of Lakota swung wide enough so that they were unable to make contact with the enemy Indians or the Bluecoat skirmish line. By avoiding the Indians and skirmishers, Crazy Horse's maneuver had enabled them to find and attack other Bluecoat units that were still struggling to get organized.

Out of the fighting for a moment, Raven slowed his horse and looked east toward where Crazy Horse had taken his group. At first he couldn't see them, but then he caught a glimpse of Bear's Foot's towering figure as he and Crazy Horse's bunch rode out of sight into a ravine.

Stepping down from the gray, he watched as the others in his group tore off into the valley, looking for another fight. He knew they wouldn't have to look for long. It sounded as though there were fire fights going on throughout the whole valley. From where he was, he couldn't see much of the action but he could sure hear it.

For the moment, Chris thought that the smartest thing he could do would be to rest his horse and to share his diminished water supply with him.

While walking the gray to cool him off, he reloaded his weapons and kept a watchful eye out for any unwanted company.

THIRTY-TWO

The sun was beating down full force. Because of the heat, he was glad he'd stripped down to vest and jeans. Sweat was already in his eyes and running down his chest. The thin, black stripes he had painted across his body were running together. He was glad he hadn't put any paint above his eyes and only a thin strip of red across his nose.

Suddenly, he heard a concentrated volley of gunfire coming from the other side of the plateau, about where Crazy Horse should be.

Raven leaped on his horse's back and dug in his heels. The gray lunged forward, heading toward the heavy rifle fire at a gallop.

Immediately he began to draw fire. Foot soldiers, with their long rifles, were everywhere. Cavalry units were milling about, trying to find some Indians that would stay in one place long enough for them to put together a charge.

Ignoring the sniping, Raven pushed his horse into its fastest gait, wishing that he was on The Black.

Ahead of him, he saw a long, curving line of Bluecoats laying down a steady rate of fire into a mass of Sioux who had apparently just come out of a ravine. Horses were down, screaming and kicking. He could see several dead or badly wounded Lakota. Suddenly, he realized these were Crazy Horse's group of warriors that the soldiers' had surprised.

As he pulled his horse to a stop, he noticed dismounted cavalry mixed in with the infantry.

Still studying the situation, he spied Crazy Horse, who was once again waving the spotted skin. Boldly, the young chief galloped the length of the Bluecoat's line, leaving himself exposed to the guns of the ranks of Bluecoats. Untouched, he again split his band; one group went east around the Bluecoats' right, and the other group west, straight toward Raven.

When Chris spotted the opportunity, he was so surprised, he stopped the gray in his tracks. The soldiers closest to Raven had left their western positions to move further to the right toward the eastern group. They had left their flank completely exposed and vulnerable.

The western bunch led by Bear's Foot was starting to swing in a more westerly manner away from the sniping soldiers.

The Lakota, their paint and feathers flashing in the sunlight, seemed oblivious to Chris' presence.

Waving his arm and trying to shout loud enough to be heard over the bedlam, Raven angled his horse toward the soldiers' exposed flank. At last, Bear saw him and swung his horse hard in the direction that Chis indicated.

The hard-riding Sioux followed Bear's Foot's sharp maneuver as though they had been practicing it every day.

Raven's gray was a jump ahead of the others as they homed in on the open flank like a thirsty horse to water.

He couldn't believe it. No one was looking in their direction! The nose of the gray was a mere thirty feet away before they were noticed.

A sergeant, sporting a big, black moustache, saw them first. He did a classic double-take and jumped to his feet, swinging his rifle up to his shoulder as he moved. It never got there. Raven's load of double-ought buckshot caught him in the chest. He was dead before he hit the ground.

Chris, followed by Bear and his wild bunch, rode their horses right over the kneeling and prone Bluecoats. Cries of shock, pain, horror and rage filled the air. For a brief

WASICHU

interval, the fighting was hot and fierce.

Once again, Raven used his pump-gun as a club. He flailed left and right with it. In his fighting rage, the dusty blue figures below him became less than men. They were now mere obstacles that needed only to be conquered, smashed or forced aside.

Bear's Foot was roaring like a grizzly as he wielded his stone-headed war club. He hit one trooper so hard that his head was nearly separated from its torso.

Horrified, Chris saw a white scout cut the throat of a wounded Sioux and then stab him in both eyes as he was dying. He must have sensed Raven looming behind him because he spun around. His tobacco stained teeth were bared in a defiant snarl.

Chris, his voice hoarse with rage, croaked, "You're dead, asshole!"

The last thing the scout saw, before the twelve-gauge steel ball removed the top of his skull, was a pair of eyes as cold and gray as a slab of marble.

Suddenly, the Bluecoats began to run. Some did so gracefully, in a textbook manner, by backing away while still loading and firing. Others just turned their backs on the Sioux and ran.

A cluster of die-hards were still fighting and holding their ground. Raven and a handful of warriors rushed them. Using their ponies as a wedge, they smashed into the group of soldiers, scattering them. A short time later, after being separated from their friends, they quit fighting and fled. One soldier remained. He was furiously battling a couple of Sioux. Chris wheeled the gray in alongside of him. The shotgun club was already starting its descent when the trooper looked up. A scared, beardless face stared up into his. Raven stopped his swing. The boy jabbed the rifle's muzzle up into Raven's ribs and pulled the trigger. There was a dry metallic snap as the firing pin landed on the empty chamber. Raven savagely resumed his swing. The heavy barrel crushed the boy's skull as though it were a melon.

Rubbing his sore ribs, Chris thought, so much for that stupid 'give a guy a break' bullshit.

Through eyes burning from the acrid smoke and gritty dust, he could see that the Bluecoat's function as an offensive unit had been destroyed.

Looking to the north, Raven could see new groups of Sioux entering the battlefield. To the south, he saw soldiers everywhere. Beyond them, up on the bluff, new arrivals were still coming in.

He sat the gray, unmindful of the occasional bullet that buzzed by, feeling dazed and morose. He thought of the young recruit's face just before the gun barrel obliterated it, and of the mustached sergeant's eyes as the buckshot smashed into his chest. He remembered the Indians up on the plateau that he had killed.

Suddenly, a wild-eyed Sioux, a stranger to Raven, came galloping toward him brandishing a dripping scalp. The Lakota slid his pony to a stop beside him.

His body and face were covered with sweat and streaked paint. His arms were covered with blood.

Sticking the bloody trophy in front of Chris' face, he let out a blood curdling war whoop.

Raven stared into his eyes, pulled back the hammer on the pump-gun, and shifted the muzzle. The Sioux became very still and quiet. Angrily, he jerked the scalp back and away from Raven's face, took another short look into the cold, pale eyes, and rode off.

Thinking aloud, Raven said, "Works every time!"

THIRTY-THREE

~~~~~~~~~~~~~~~~

A pall of smoke hovered over the Valley of the Rosebud. The fighting continued for several hours with neither side dominating. Reinforcements kept arriving for both sides.

Crook's complete column had not yet arrived at the camp when the fighting began. The soldiers continued to straggle in throughout the morning.

The Indian forces were constantly being supplemented by a steady flow of warriors from the big village. Many of the new arrivals were Hunkpapa and Cheyenne.

Being free of any military responsibilities, Raven had been able to be with any group that he wished. Fighting side by side with the Sioux, brought back some of his old soldier instincts. He began to look for ways to be of help.

Instinctively, he had remained close to Crazy Horse. The man truly amazed him. He was everywhere, and wherever he went, he immediately took command. His handling of the cavalry was especially impressive. Whenever the Bluecoats would manage to mount a cavalry charge, Crazy Horse would have his Sioux and Cheyenne retreat. This would repeat itself time and again until the cavalry was totally frustrated with its inability to engage with the enemy. When this happened and the troopers were tired and disorganized, Crazy Horse would attack. The Calvary, normally an offensive unit, would be forced to wage a defensive battle.

The man's courage and vitality was unbelievable. Over and over again, Raven had seen him leading his reckless Sioux in frontal attacks. Long hair flying out behind him, he and his spotted pony would always be well out in front, setting an example for those that followed.

During one of the firefights, Chris became aware of something that he thought could be useful. He had noticed how the soldiers immediately carried their wounded away from the action. After leaving the fight, Raven began speculating on how to utilize what he had seen. He thought that if the Indians would shoot to wound, instead of to kill, it could make a difference. Raven reasoned that by wounding a Bluecoat, it took two more soldiers out of the fight to carry the wounded man to the rear. Eventually two more men would have to move him to the field hospital, and the greater the number of men removed from the firing line, the greater their chance of winning.

Excited by the possibilities evoked by his idea, Chris whipped the gray into a lope and began searching for someone to persuade. Crazy Horse had left the immediate area so he had to find someone else.

After numerous aborted attempts at convincing several of the minor chiefs of the merits of his idea, he gave up. Either his Lakota wasn't good enough in his explanation, or they simply didn't want to listen to him. Convinced that his idea would work, Raven sought out the one man he knew of whom the Sioux would listen.

He waited. Finally his patience paid off, and he was able to catch Crazy Horse moving to another part of the fighting. Fortunately, they were in a pocket of land that was free of fighting so there wasn't any danger of snipers.

The young chief had several warriors with him. Among them was his friend and lieutenant, He Dog. Surprisingly, the big Hunkpapa, Scar was also present. Apparently, Sitting Bull had stayed behind in the village.

Raven quickly outlined his theory. A fierce intensity flowed from Crazy Horse's hawk-like eyes as he listened to the idea. Chris was very careful as he spoke his Lakota to be certain that he conveyed the whole idea correctly. When he had finished, Crazy Horse honored him with a rare grin. The smile puckering the scar on his face.

"Waste (good). I recall the fight in the little valley, Okute. Your plan was good in that fight. It saved my life and the life of another. Your plan sounds good this time, also. It will be as you say."

His eyes held Raven's as he raised his left hand to his brow. Putting his heels into his pony's ribs he rode off, his hair and short cape billowing out behind him. His entourage followed, quickly enveloped in his dust.

One member of his group didn't follow. Scar sat his pony in silence, his cold eyes raking Chris' lanky form. Naked, except for breech clout and moccasins, and in full war bonnet, he was even more frightening in appearance than Bear's Foot. He wore very little paint. With the scars all over his body, he didn't need any. He sidled his pony next to Raven's.

"This morning I watched you, wasichu."

The rasp and gurgle of his damaged voice chilled Raven. He felt goose flesh rising on his arms and legs.

"You fought the Bluecoats like a true Lakota warrior. *Wonumayin.*"

Surprised, yet pleased, Chis said nothing.

As Scar spun his pony and rode off, he gave Raven a final look with eyes that were as cold as a pair of marbles.

Watching him move away in his own dust cloud, Raven thought, I may not have gained a friend, but if I'm lucky, I might have lost an enemy.

THIRTY-FOUR

Raven was belly down on a low ridge. The sun winked off the numerous brass bullet casings around him. Careful not to let his bare hands touch the metal on his overheated Winchester, he set it down and looked around to assess the situation.

On either side of Chris, there were approximately a hundred and fifty Sioux and Cheyenne, stretched out flat along the ridge. Less than two-hundred yards from where they were at, were two companies of dismounted cavalry.

Raven and his allies had been exchanging fire with them for about fifteen or twenty minutes. The Bluecoats were in a firing line that extended along the lip of a wash that had been formed by the stream at their back.

The troopers had been keeping up a disciplined, steady rate of fire. The Indians' return fire had been more spontaneous but was still enough to keep the soldiers pinned down.

Raven thought that it must be pretty unnerving for the troopers to be in a situation like this, not knowing when more Sioux were going to show. They were probably too far north of the main fighting to get any support of their own. The constant shrilling of the Sioux eagle bone whistles was probably getting on their nerves as well. It sure as hell's getting on mine, Raven said to himself.

The whistles were designed to be used as a signaling device, but in this fight they were used as a good luck charm. Chris would be willing to swear that every other Sioux in the valley had one. He had been hearing them mixed in with the gun fire all morning.

On his left was the Cheyenne warrior, Deer Catcher. Raven hadn't recognized him at first because of his huge good luck device, a wooly buffalo horn headdress. Like the Sioux eagle bone whistles, many of the Cheyenne were wearing the headdresses for the same reason... a life preserving charm.

Kills Twice, on his right, raised up and let loose with a big Spencer, adding to the lingering powder smoke that was beginning to hang in the low areas between the two groups. Raven was beginning to think that this little stalemate was a waste of time. Even the firing was beginning to slow down. Because the Sioux had the high ground and better cover, the cavalry units didn't dare to mount up and ride away. The Indian gunfire would cut them to pieces before they'd gone a hundred feet.

Looking north, up the creek, Chris could see brush and stunted willows on both sides. Eventually the stream disappeared around a bend in the ravine. Carefully he studied the terrain. He couldn't see any sign of soldiers or Indians north of them.

Most of the fighting was southeast, or west of their current position. He knew for sure that there were at least three big fights going on. He could still hear the sound of heavy firing in the distance. Crazy Horse and his chiefs had done everything in their power to keep the three battles going so that the army units would find it impossible to reunite their forces.

Whenever possible, Crazy Horse had rallied his warriors and encouraged them to wound and cripple, rather than to kill. Raven didn't know if it was working, but the army did appear to have a lot more wounded than dead. At least, he reasoned, he's using my idea.

As Raven moved back from his firing position, both Deer Catcher and Kills Twice gave him a look as if to say, "What the hell are you doing?"

WASICHU

Swiftly, he explained that he was going north to see if there was a way for them to surprise the Bluecoats by coming down the stream through the willows. The Cheyenne mumbled something unintelligible while Kills Twice grinned and waved.

He pointed the gray north and followed the plateau for several hundred yards. The popping sound of distant gunfire seemed to be coming from all directions, but it was probably an illusion because of the many canyons and ravines emitting echoes.

Chris was relieved when he discovered that the area appeared to be unoccupied. Maneuvering his horse around a stand of tall pine, he came to a small ravine that twisted off the plateau and down to the creek. He moved his horse carefully into it. Slowly he let his mount pick its way down the gradient.

Without moving his head in an obvious way, Raven was looking everywhere; distant slopes, the tree-topped bluffs, the mouth of the ravine. A hawk was soaring above the canyon floor. In front of his horse's hooves, a covey of quail moved, flitting from cover to cover. Their plumage created a splash of color among the bleak rocks and dead brush.

Ahead of him, Chris could see the green of the grass and willows near the creek. Small clumps of pine and small trees dotted the landscape as he left the ravine behind.

As soon as he reached the valley floor, the gunfire of the cavalry and Sioux sounded much closer. The sharp bark of the cavalry carbine was easily recognized over the different sound of the Indians assorted fire arms.

His ears were still evaluating the gunfire when his peripheral vision picked up some movement far to his left front. Instantly his eyes transmitted the message to his brain. Soldiers! They were tiny blue figures, hundreds of yards away, up on the far tree-line of the plateau that paralleled his own.

While keeping the gray moving at a canter around a copse of pine, he kept a wary eye on them. Although he figured that they were too far away, he still worried that they might possibly reach him with their rifle fire.

At that very moment, he saw several puffs of smoke blossom among the blue figures. Sand erupted in a couple of places along the sandy bottom between him and the creek, followed by the hollow popping of the rifles. More smoke ballooned from the ridge. He didn't hear the gunfire this time. He felt the impact with his legs as the heavy bullet struck the gray. The bullet smashed through the horse's shoulder and into his chest. He lurched to the right into the tree-line. As his horse went down, Raven instinctively threw himself from the saddle in the same direction that the horse was falling. His attempt to get clear of the dying horse failed.

Chris felt his body crashing through the brittle branches of a dead tree. His fall ended as his head struck a thick branch. A cascade of stars replaced his senses.

THIRTY-FIVE

~~~~~~~~~~~~

The pungent smell of crushed pine needles was in his nostrils as he regained consciousness. The back of his head felt as though he had been hit with a hammer.

Opening his eyes, he saw pine boughs and a flawless blue sky. Something was wrong. Frantically he blinked his eyes and looked again. He was seeing double! He shut his eyes and shook his head. A jolt of pain sent a wave of nausea through his body. He was startled by a loud cawing noise and the rhythmic beat of wings taking flight.

He moved cautiously until he was able to prop himself up on his elbows. Slowly he reopened his eyes. Panic gripped him with an iron fist. His left foot was trapped underneath his horse! He shook his head again, ignoring the pain. Digging his fists into his eyes, Raven rubbed them vigorously. The double vision would not leave.

Chris concentrated on taking deep breaths. Pushing the fear for his eyesight out of his mind, he began to think of what he had to do. Desperately, he tried to disregard his pounding headache and take a quick inventory of his predicament.

Apparently, he had landed right on top of a dead tree. Pine trees surrounded him on three sides but there was open terrain to his front. His dead horse next to him created a barrier between him and the open area. His foot was trapped in the hollow between the horse's hip and body. At least it's not broken, he thought. There was no pain when he moved his toes, assuring him of no serious damage.

The continual popping of distant gunfire was a constant reminder to Raven of the ever-present danger. At any moment some Bluecoats, or a wandering Crow or Shoshone, could happen by.

He wished that he knew how long he had been unconscious. Looking up through the pine boughs, he tried to locate the position of the sun. But the double vision was driving him crazy, so he gave it up.

Leaning back with his weight on his hands, Chris muttered to himself, "Well, Stanley, this is another fine mess you've gotten me into."

He smiled sardonically as he thought, hell, Laurel and Hardy probably aren't even born yet!

Brushing away a pestering fly, he looked over the back of the dead horse at the green willows bordering the creek. He could see the distant ridge where the shots had come from, but because of his double vision, he couldn't tell if there were still soldiers up there or not. If there were, he knew that he was in even bigger trouble.

In a flash of gut-wrenching remembrance, Raven heard again the sound of the bird's wings as they took flight. He knew with absolute certainty that if anyone had seen the bird's sudden flight, they would know that someone alive was in the area and would investigate.

He began a search for his weapons. His pistol was still snug in its shoulder holster but there was no sign of the pump-gun or rifle. He could feel his heart thudding like a drum as he frantically searched for his guns.

Chris, feeling like an animal caught in a trap, quit looking and forced himself to relax. Calming himself, he leaned back on his hands. Slowly, a smile spread across the angular planes of his face. Reaching down through the dry, broken wood of the deadfall, his searching hand found the cool, unmistakable feel of metal.

Triumphant, he maneuvered the pump-gun through the maze of branches until he was able to feel its comforting weight across his lap. He cursed himself for being such an

WASICHU

idiot. How could he have forgotten that he had the pump hanging across his back by its sling? His back was even sore from when he had landed on it.

Setting the pump aside, Chris pulled out a knife and went to work trying to dig himself free.

Later, drenched in sweat and drowning in a pool of frustration, Raven leaned back and studied the situation.

Underneath the horse's body, there was a relatively soft bed of old pine needles. Normally it would be an easy job to dig himself out, but there was a problem. An exceptionally thick branch beneath his trapped leg was positioned in a way that prevented him from digging himself out. But he wasn't complaining. Had the gray's body landed six inches closer to him, it would have snapped his leg like a pretzel.

Chris gave up. He decided to think first, rather than just burn up his energy in what could be a hopeless project. He shut his eyes and thought of Kills Twice. Maybe he and Bear's Foot are talking about him right now, he mused.

His gaze moved to the other side of the creek. He watched the double image of a hawk glide low over the grassy plain. Wistfully he envied its keen eyesight and freedom.

Time passed. Raven had become a statue... an immovable object with pale eyes that watched and listened. He also prayed. He prayed that his damaged eyesight would still be sufficient to warn him of any impending danger.

The heat and the flies were beginning to work on his frayed nerves. He was fortunate that he was in the shade, but even so he could feel the sweat running down his body and soaking the top of his jeans. He thought of the army canteen that was probably lying under the horse. Ineffectively he wet his lips with a tongue that rasped like a cat's.

The willows along the creek were jumping and shimmering. He knew that it was his eyes but it looked like heat waves. Chris thought, it's hot, but not that hot. The double vision was decreasing but he was still getting distorted images.

For the first time, he noticed that he wasn't hearing the nearby gunfire from the cavalry or his friends.

Before he had a chance to wonder why, the startling, mournful howl of a wolf was heard over the distant gunfire from the battlefield. It came from up the creek on the northern side of the ravine.

Raven nearly jumped out of his skin when an answering howl came from directly in front of him on the other side of the creek. The second wolf call was only a couple hundred yards away.

Hackles raised on the back of his neck as he realized that they couldn't be real wolves. A real wolf, he thought, wouldn't be within miles of this shooting gallery.

Needles of reality pricked at his awareness, forcing him to face the bitter truth of his desperate situation.

Softly, he spoke aloud, "Chris, my man, those are Crow Indians out there and they'd like nothing better than to be able to stretch your top knot on a willow hoop, set it in the sun, find some shade, and watch it dry."

Raven leaned back on his hands for a moment and calmly thought of his predicament. As quietly as possible, he unloaded the pump-gun and replaced the steel ball shells with ones loaded with buckshot.

With only his eyes showing from above the back of the horse, Chris watched and waited. He blinked and squinted. Still there, he thought, but it does seem to be getting better. At least the double vision is nearly gone.

The musical song of a bird came from the creek. Another sounded from up the creek, in the north. Bird calls, he thought. They were much closer now and were using bird calls to keep in touch.

He knew that one of them was among the willows

beside the creek. The other Indian had to be near a formation of jutting rock and stunted pine off to his left. He waited.

While his damaged eyes swept the area, he continued to work on freeing his foot. After a short time, he became frustrated again and quit. It would really be stupid of me, he rationalized, to get all involved in freeing my foot while the goddamn Crow are busy lifting my scalp.

He used his bandana to wipe his face and neck free of perspiration, wishing that he could remove the smell of his dead horse just as easily. Now that the gray began to smell, the flies were becoming an even bigger nuisance.

While he waited, he removed several .44 cartridges from the pockets of his vest and began to arrange them in piles of six. Utilizing a piece of bark, he formed his piles on the smooth side. As he maneuvered the bark so that it was close to his right hand, he noticed that his impaired vision had improved to the point where the double image was gone and was replaced with a ghost-like shadow.

The thirst remained intact, however, and thoughts of a tall, frosty mug of beer or an ice cold can of Coke surfaced. He could almost see the beads of moisture forming on the frosty glass. His tongue involuntarily whipped out and slid over his dry lips. He silently berated himself as he thought, stop being such a baby, you've been thirsty before.

Raven cleared his mind and concentrated on his immediate danger. They're going to have to make some kind of move, he thought, they don't have any more cover to move any closer.

He rubbed his eyes and blinked them free of burning sweat. The brush and willows beside the creek had lost their bogus heat waves and were much clearer now.

Movement caught his eye. An Indian wearing a black hat was standing beside one of the willows. He was dressed in a cavalry shirt, blue leggings, and a red loin-cloth. He appeared to be staring straight at Raven.

Without moving his head, Chris flicked his eyes to the left, looking for the other Indian. When he looked back, the Indian by the willows was gone.

"Sorry folks, the rest of the band didn't show up. Well, we're going to rock 'n roll anyway." For some reason, talking to himself bolstered his confidence. "If you'll just sit back and relax, the show's about to get underway." 'I'm not no Jimi Hendrix,' he thought, 'but I can play you a tune on my slide-action, pump trombone.'

Raven's instincts told him that his visitors were suspicious. Something was making them aware that he wanted them to get close before shooting. Actually, he had no solid proof that they even knew he was there. It was pure gut instinct that had him second-guessing them, but it had never failed him before, so he wasn't going to ignore it now.

Being in the shade Chris had hoped he wouldn't be seen and whoever showed up would have just ridden right into the range of his pump. Now that they were here and weren't about to ride in close, he had to do something to lure them in. Brushing the sweat from his eyes, he wondered, just how smart are these guys? Even if they are smart, he mused, if I can convince them that I'm 'not too tightly wrapped' they just might do something stupid.

The Indian was back. This time he was on his pony and had a rifle propped on his thigh. Raven threw a quick glance to his left and noted that the other one still wasn't showing himself.

An idea promptly popped into his head. He smiled and tried to hold his excitement down until he'd thought the idea all the way through. The more he thought, the broader his smile became. It just might work, he thought.

Even though he knew that the Indian was out of the pistol's range, he started shooting at him anyway. He thumbed the single-action colt as fast as he could. The pistol shots shattered the relative quiet of the clearing.

WASICHU

Startled, the Indian kicked his pony into a sudden move back into the willows. The last two shots followed the Indian into the trees. He quickly reloaded. There was a thunderous return blast from the willows. The bullet smacked into some wood high above him.

Raven smiled. This guy can't shoot for shit, he thought. He swiftly fired three more rounds into the trees by the creek. The Crow, if that's what he was, fired an answering shot that was also wide of the mark. This time, Raven spied a puff of smoke as it rose above some bushes.

This dude is dumber than he thinks I am, he thought as he emptied his revolver again toward the willows. He deliberately took his time reloading.

Then, the one on his left showed himself! He rode his horse straight toward Raven and pulled him to a stop just out of pistol range. Raven emptied his revolver at him, not even trying to come close. The Crow by the creek decided to show off a little. He showed himself again and began to verbally taunt Raven. Without understanding his words, his meaning was clear. The other Indian, all decked out in a fully beaded war shirt, stood in his stirrups and levered three shots with his Winchester. Two of the bullets thudded into the gray, while the third snapped by overhead, nearly giving Raven a new part in his hair. "Holy shit, this guy can shoot," He screamed.

Chris peered over the top of the horse as the two warriors began calling back and forth to each other. The one with the hat gestured toward Raven and said something that made 'War Shirt' laugh. As 'War Shirt' laughed again he waved his hand toward Chris behind his make-shift fort and rattled some more lingo to his buddy.

That's enough of this shit, he thought, and thumbed three shots at the Crow on the left, causing his pony to side-hop to the right. Swiftly shifting his aim, he emptied his gun at the one with the hat. Powder smoke hung in the air between them as he muttered, "Come on. Come and get it."

They reacted as though they had heard him speak. Both riders abruptly whipped their ponies into a full gallop and were coming straight at him! The Crow wolf howl sent a shiver up his spine as he covertly watched them come.

Thinking that he was busy reloading, the two warriors came at him without a thought of being cautious. They had calculated the amount of time it took him to reload, and they knew that he could never complete the task before they were on him. They're probably already thinking about the victory dance, Raven thought, and of the grand story they will tell of their bravery. He had kept his head tipped forward as though concentrating on his loading, but was watching their every move. Like a predator cat, he was locked in on his prey as he watched and waited. The beat of their ponies' hooves was growing louder each second, fifty yards... forty... thirty.

The Crow on his left was bent over his horse's neck. His greased hair stood up straight in front in the favored Crow style. The rest of his hair flowed behind him like a black cloud. Raven could clearly see white ermine skins attached to his shirt seams, flipping and twisting in every direction. The other Crow was coming in, sitting straight in his saddle; his hat brim was flattened against the crown from the wind of his passage.

War Shirt was smiling when Raven shot him. The pump's blast was punctuated by the clatter of the slide-action as he jacked in another round. He was reeling, fighting to stay on his mount when the second load struck him under his arm and blew him off his horn saddle. Keeping the shotgun to his shoulder, Chris pumped again and swung to his right. The other Indian had slid his pony to a stop and was trying to turn him when Raven's third shot turned his surprised face into a bloody maw and blew him out from under his hat. His lifeless body hit the ground with a thud.

THIRTY-SIX

The acrid stench of cordite bit at Raven's nostrils. Except for the buzzing of the flies and the muffled sound of the milling ponies' hooves, it was quiet.

He pumped in another shell. The metallic clatter of the slide mechanism fractured the stillness of the clearing.

The sudden noise spooked the horses again. They began to trot aimlessly around the bodies of their previous owners. One of them was a long-legged dun who snuffled at one of the bodies and shied away from the blood smell. Shaking his head, he trotted away from the alarming scent.

Raven absently noted the high cantle and fork on the Indian's bone and horn saddle. He continued to watch the horses as they meandered around the clearing, aware that if there was anyone else around, they would be the first to know it. Shifting his gaze to the rocks and trees from where 'War Shirt' had come, Chris studied the terrain. He then scanned the lush green underbrush by the creek. Only the tops of the willows moved with the slight breeze.

The faraway crackle of gunfire still came from all around but nothing close by. Much of the shooting was coming from the southeast. Noticing that it was still quiet down the creek, Raven assumed that Kills Twice and the other warriors had gotten bored and went to look for easier prey.

Blinking his eyes repeatedly, Chris suddenly realized that his eyesight was back to almost normal again. He wasn't sure when it had happened. He had been so busy trying to stay alive that he had forgotten about it.

The relief he felt motivated him into trying to free his

leg again. He abandoned his watching and waiting and began to dig in earnest. Using his knife, he attacked the soft loam underneath his foot. The big branch was still hampering his efforts but he was making progress.

As he worked, he would occasionally pause to look and listen. He was aware that as long as the horses were grazing quietly, everything should be fine.

Wiping the dirt from his sweaty brow, he thought again of the canteen under the horse. He looked around as he morosely brooded about the water. The surrounding countryside was so still, it was like a painting. His eyes lifted and fell on the bright green of the willows. You idiot, he thought, forget about the canteen, the creek is right over there waiting for you.

Now that the two Crow were no longer a threat, all he had to do was free his foot and he could drink and bathe to his heart's content. He was about to start digging again when he heard something. He couldn't identify the sound but it was sort of a tearing noise. He looked at the horses. Both ponies had their ears perked up and were staring at the copse of pine behind him. The tearing sound had come from behind him!

Desperately, Raven twisted and turned, trying to see into the woods behind him through the labyrinth of the deadfall's branches. It was hopeless! He forced himself to calm down and relax. If he could get his foot free he was confident that he could handle just about any situation. Blocking everything from his mind but the task at hand, he went at it. In less than a minute, he was free! He rejoiced over his small victory. Except for a little soreness around the ankle, his foot was fine.

Raven immediately grabbed the pump-gun and spun around, facing the rear. He studied the green and black shadows as he fed three shells into the pump. Suddenly, he saw something... a shadow, a flicker of movement. It could have been anything... a bird, or squirrel. He eased the pump's hammer back to full cock. Chris' eyes darted left and right, searching for some more solid cover. Carefully stepping around and over the broken branches of the deadfall, he slid to his right and got behind a tree.

"Don't shoot us, Okute, we are not some egg-sucking Crow! Think of all the *ishta* (women) that would grieve this night!" Raven put his back to the tree and slid to the ground. The welcome sound of Bear's Foot's voice worked like a tranquilizer. It felt as though his bones had melted.

Bear's huge form loomed over Raven's reclining figure. Wolf's Spirit and Ptecila appeared behind him.

"Are you tired, Okute? How long have you been hiding here?"

With a grin Chris tried to ignore the badgering, but he noticed that the usual bite was missing from Bear's teasing. Something was wrong; he could sense it. Raven quickly got to his feet. He spied a skin bag glistening with moisture hanging at Bear's side. He snatched it and drank greedily. Forcing himself to quit, he capped the container. Half afraid to ask what was wrong, Raven stalled by saying, "For a moment I thought that I had guessed right when I suspected that there were more than two Crow after my scalp."

Wolf's Spirit, face beaming, stepped out from behind Bear's bulk as he replied, "You were right, Okute." As he spoke, he held aloft a black, long-haired scalp. It was so fresh that it was still dripping. Chris swallowed hard, 'now I know what the tearing sound was,' he silently exclaimed.

Bear's Foot stepped forward. Behind him, the Oglala somberly watched. Raven could feel his stomach begin to churn with dread. Looking past the lurid war paint, Chris could see the grave expression on Bear's face.

"What is it? What has happened?" Even in his own ears, his voice had a hollow sound.

Bear's Foot, his voice quiet, said, "We have news

from the big village, Okute. A small band of pony stealers found the encampment this morning. Their hearts were not brave enough to try for the main pony herd, but they did find the small one. They took them all. The Black was with them."

"Are Blue Feather and Little Hawk safe?"

"Blue Feather is safe. A boy guarding the herd was rubbed out." Seeing the expression on Raven's face, Bear quickly added, "It was not Little Hawk. He was not there when the raiders came."

Chris noticed the hesitation in Bear's Foot's voice.

"Talk to me. Where is Little Hawk?"

It all came out in a rush of Lakota. His rapid speech gave Raven some difficulty but he still understood.

"He is following the Crow dogs! Blue Feather said that he felt to blame because it was his idea to put The Black in the small herd. He is following their trail to catch up with them to steal The Black away from them."

Raven could feel his heart swell with pride in the brave little fool while, at the same time, his stomach growled with anxiety and fear for his safety. Bear had calmed down some when he added, "Spotted Horse had been at the other end of the village when it happened. When he returned and heard about Little Hawk, he set out on his trail at once. Hopefully, he was able to catch up with him."

Ptecila stepped up to Raven and put his wrinkled hand on his shoulder as he said, "Your woman sent me to find you, Okute. Together we will find the boy." Chris was moved by the words of confidence. He spoke of finding Little Hawk with the same certainty as if he had been speaking of Wi going down at night or rising in the morning.

Looking into Ptecila's wizened face, Raven placed his hand on his shoulder. He peered deeply into his black cherry eyes as he replied, "Yes, Ptecila. Together, we will find him, my friend."

THIRTY-SEVEN

Stepping clear of the pine into the sunshine, Raven looked up. The sun was almost directly overhead. It's time to get hustling, he thought, and cover as much ground as we can before dark.

Utilizing Bear's Foot's great strength, they were able to recover Chris' saddle from the body of the gray horse. They were also able to recover his canteen and rifle. While they were busy with that, Wolf's Spirit and Ptecila rustled up the three Crow horses. Raven decided on 'War Shirt's' log-legged dun.

While saddling, they kept watch so that they weren't surprised by any roving bands of Bluecoats or enemy Indians. They could still hear a steady roll of gunfire to the southeast, so they knew that the fight was still going on. Chris was careful to keep a wary eye on the bluffs, he wouldn't welcome anymore long-range interruptions.

After recovering the Lakota horses, they made ready to leave. Before mounting up, Raven led his horse over to where Bear's Foot was fiddling with his gear. Bear was about to put his war bonnet back on but stopped when he heard Raven's approach.

Seeing him standing there in his John Wayne stance with his painted face wearing its most inscrutable mask, Raven was certain that Bear knew what he was going to ask of him. "Hear me, Kola. I have no right to ask this great favor of you, but I must."

Beneath the black and red war paint, Bear's face showed no expression. He waited for Raven to continue.

"I cannot explain how I know what I am about to tell

you, but you must believe that it will happen. This fight is just about over, a few short suns from now there will be another big battle with the Bluecoats. It will be against different soldiers than these we fight now. This fight will take place beside the Little Big Horn River, the place that you know as the Greasy Grass."

Bear's Foot's eyes widened at his mention of the Greasy Grass, but he remained silent and the mask stayed in place.

"If I do not make it back in time for this battle, I desperately need someone that I can trust to stay with Blue Feather and to keep her out of harm's way."

Bear's black eyes softened and he looked down at his foot and kicked at a clump of buffalo grass. When he looked back up, Raven was amazed to see tears in his friend's eyes.

Bear's Foot then stepped forward and wrapped his big arms around him.

Chris had known that the Lakota were a volatile, emotional people, and tears were not considered unmanly. But seeing a fighting man such as Bear's Foot, his body and arms splattered with blood and his face fiercely painted for war, moved to tears, was startling to say the least.

After the brief rib-cracking embrace, Bear stepped back. Holding Raven at arm's length, he stared at him with piercing eyes. With a sudden wide grin, Bear said, "She will be waiting, Kola. I also will be waiting. I long to see my little friend again so I can teach him the difference between a war club and a bow."

Bear's Foot made a face that was a cross between a grimace and a smile. He rubbed his ribs in a pantomime of being in pain as he turned away.

As Bear turned away, Chris saw another tear forming and realized, for the first time, the depth of his friend's feelings for Little Hawk. Now, he truly realized the sacrifice his friend was making by staying behind.

WASICHU

Swinging up on the Crow horse, Raven glanced down and said, "I will bring him back, Kola."

Bear, his hands busy adjusting his war bonnet, looked up at him. His face was serious as he replied, "I know you will. *Huntka* (God of the East) will protect you."

He grinned, giving Chris another look at the man he had come to love and respect.

"If *Huntka* is too busy to bother with a wasichu," he gestured toward the pump-gun resting across Chris' thighs, "make some thunder. The Crow will run like rabbits."

They left him leaning on his war horse, still messing with his war bonnet. His sorrow wasn't evident in his parting wave, but Raven knew it was there nonetheless.

Ptecila took the lead. Their plan was to head south and then swing east. Earlier, as they had gathered his gear, Ptecila had told him his plan.

The pony stealers had stolen the herd and had driven them southeast. Not having knowledge of a compass, the tracker had elaborated, "The Crow thieves have pointed their ponies toward the Center of the Earth. If we travel to where Wi awakens, we should be able to discover their sign."

While learning the language, Joe Spotted Horse had told Raven of the Lakota belief that Mount Harney, the highest peak in the Black Hills, was the Center of the Earth.

They rode south, following the ravine as it gradually widened into the start of the valley of the Rosebud. It was obvious from the volume of gunfire they could hear that there was still some heavy fighting nearby.

Nearing the mouth of the valley, the evidence of the battle was everywhere. There were no dead bodies but the carcasses of horses covered the landscape like bloated boulders. Discarded weaponry littered the ground. The wink and glitter of brass empties was coming from everywhere. The sound of battle was escalating rapidly.

When they rode into the open near the headwaters of

the Rosebud, they came face to face with chaos. Everywhere that Raven looked he could see soldiers and Indians locked in combat. The clamor of gunfire surrounded them, smothering any desire to speak.

South of them and across the Rosebud, he saw a large number of Bluecoats fortified on top of the tall bluff. They were holding a large force of Cheyenne and Sioux at bay with concentrated rifle fire. In spite of the distance, the vivid display of color and the movement of the rousing action, caused Raven's heart to quicken with excitement.

Closer to them was a smaller band of Sioux that was sweeping down on the army's large horse and mule herd. Their attack was being met by a hail of carbine and rifle bullets. The soldiers guarding them were showing a tenacious determination not to be driven from their post. Just as quickly as they had attacked, the Indians broke off their attack and with many a derisive shake of weapons and shields, they rode off to find easier game.

The trio swung east, studiously avoiding the major fighting. Even so, they still heard the buzz and snap of occasional bullets searching for a victim. Some were close enough to motivate them into looking in all directions for a specific marksman.

To the northeast, Raven saw a group of mounted Bluecoats riding up a small valley toward a distant crest that was conical in shape.

A steady volume of gunfire was erupting from the hill's summit. It looked like the major fighting was taking place on the northern side of the hill.

One of the soldier's horses went down as though it had been pole-axed; its rider tumbled right over his head. Raven noticed that the other riders immediately stopped and rushed to the man. One of the men got down from his horse and offered his reins to the fallen man who was busy brushing himself off. The man, who had to be an officer,

WASICHU

took the other man's horse and mounted up, leaving the other to climb up behind a friend. The group resumed their ride toward the conical hill.

Closer now, Chris was able to see that they were all officers. But the man that had his horse shot out from under him was dressed like a civilian. He was wearing some kind of tan colored suit.

The realization hit him like a right-hand punch from George Foreman. He was looking at another famous George... General George Crook, Commander in Chief! It was his mode of dress that made Raven aware of who the officer was. Crook became renown throughout the army for always wearing canvas apparel during a campaign or while on maneuvers.

A thick cloud of gun smoke drifted between them, obscuring the distant horsemen. In spite of the heat of the day, Chris felt goose bumps rise on his arms. A rush of pride surged through his body. Generations separated them, yet Raven felt an inexplicable satisfaction in having served in the same army as a great soldier like Crook.

He was momentarily disheartened as he thought of the brave soldiers that he had killed. Although he now thought of himself as a Lakota, he had spent too many years in the army not to be saddened by the bizarre turn of events that had placed him on the opposing side.

Relieved to be soon leaving the battlefield, Raven threw a final look at Crook and his entourage. Through tendrils of smoke he saw them approaching the base of the strange-shaped hill.

As he watched the haze of smoke lift from the hill's rocky crest, Chris' mind cleared in much the same way. He suddenly remembered why the army was here. Their mission was to drive the Sioux from their homeland, or to annihilate them. His resolve hardened as he thought of the great Sioux nation as it was at that moment, and of what the future held for them. For the moment, his pride had turned to shame.

He was snapped out of his senseless brooding by a large force of Sioux that had come riding up behind them. They were moving at a full gallop and chanting what must have been some type of war song. Raven had never heard anything like it. When they drew abreast, Ptecila kicked his heels into his pony's ribs and shouted, "Hopo!"

At a gallop, the three joined the wild riding bunch and had to ride hard to stay with them. Immediately Raven's senses were assailed from all angles. The collective scents of horse and human sweat, dust and gunpowder, attacked the delicate membranes inside his nose. His ears rang with the constant din. The chant-like singing and the explosive gunfire, as they smashed through Bluecoat or Indian pockets of resistance that were foolish enough to get in their way, was stimulating.

Raven looked around at the fierce, proud faces. Their bodies were embraced by cartridge belts and draped with all sorts of weapons, shields and other paraphernalia. Vivid splashes of vermilion, ochre and black adorned every warrior. He experienced an exuberance he'd never had before. Gone were the conscience-riddled thoughts and regrets of moments ago. All that mattered was the euphoria. Raven felt a true sense of belonging and being a part of what was then considered to be 'the greatest light cavalry in the world.'

As they approached the outer limits of the battlefield, the nearby firing tapered off until it became practically nonexistent. Ahead of them the stream cut directly in front of their column and moved north. It was the same branch of the Rosebud down which Two Moons and Spotted Wolf had led their Cheyenne last night. They turned to follow the sweep of the stream. Ptecila led them away from their wild riding escorts and rode into the willows and scrub oak that bordered the Rosebud. As he joined Ptecila and Wolf's Spirit, Chris looked back at the Sioux column as it moved north, following the Rosebud. He couldn't help but speculate that they were probably going to join their comrades in the fight for the conical hill.

Raven wondered how the fight for the hill turned out. He knew that the battle itself would end in a couple of hours. Having stopped the Bluecoats from marching on their village, the Sioux and Cheyenne would return to their lodges and Crook would lick his wounds and return to the south.

His thoughts were interrupted by a soft grunt from Ptecila. The tracker led the way as the three moved into the shallow water. Raven looked to the east and thought of Little Hawk. He prayed that the boy would keep his distance and just follow the raiders. Maybe we'll get lucky, he thought, and Spotted Horse will catch up to him. Hell, maybe he's caught up with him already. All we can do is hope for the best. One thing for sure, he mused, with Ptecila tracking we will find him.

Steadily, they moved eastward into a rugged, rolling countryside. Turning in the saddle, Raven looked back toward the distant bluffs and tree-topped plateaus. To the indifferent ear, the faraway sound of gunfire was just a mysterious whisper on the wind.

Part 6
Decisions...

THIRTY-EIGHT
~~~~~~~~~~~~~~

The afternoon sun was hot on the backs of the three riders. Relentlessly they rode eastward. Bound by their common quest, they pushed on with little or no rest.

Raven was determined to keep his thoughts free of Little Hawk until they found the trail of the stolen herd. Whatever has happened to him was totally out of his control. Deep inside, he knew that the boy was alive and that they would find him.

Since they didn't have extra horses, they played it safe by alternating their pace from a gallop, to a canter, to a walk. By using this strategy, they were able to cover a lot of territory swiftly without the risk of ruining their horses.

Up front, Ptecila and Wolf's Spirit slowed their tired mounts to a walk. Slowing the dun, Raven studied the figures of his two friends. He reflected upon how deeply entrenched he had become in the lives of these wild and wonderful people. He hadn't been keeping track of the time, but he knew that he couldn't have been with them for more than three or four months. Hell, he mused, it hasn't even been that long. He shook his head in awe as he thought, I feel as though I have known these people all my life.

Wolf's Spirit looked back at Raven. He grinned and pointed to the northeast. The antelope blended so well with their habitat that Chris was only able to catch a glimpse of two or three white rumps as they disappeared over a distant rise.

Wistfully, Wolf said, "*Heton Cikala* (antelope) are like the wind. They are here one moment and gone the next." Sadness crept into his voice as he continued, "In truth they are much like the Lakota. Free to roam where they wish, the antelope go to where the grass is the sweetest and the most plentiful. We Lakota are free to wander also. We go wherever the *tatonka* (buffalo) go. He is our life, our grass. The wasichus will not be happy until all of our people are kept in pens like their spotted buffalo (cattle). I, for one, do not want to live to see it happen."

Raven was astonished by Wolf's Spirit's oration. He had never, in the past, heard him string more than five or six words together at a time.

Attempting to lighten his somber discourse, Wolf added, "We can only hope that the wasichu do not decide that we are good to eat. If that were to happen they would probably shoot us and then use our meat to feed the blanket Indians who are willing to live in their pens without walls."

Chilled by the young warrior's black humor, Raven had to force a smile as Wolf gave him a haughty look. Softening the look with a brilliant smile, Wolf's Spirit returned his attention to the surrounding hills. Chris was left with a strange sense of guilt over what he knew was eventually going to happen to these wild, proud nomads.

They had been traveling at the same steady pace for quite some time. Ptecila unexpectedly lashed his quirt across his pony's rump and surged ahead. After a short dash of a couple of hundred feet he pulled up. Eyes nailed to the ground, he began walking his pony in a southerly direction.

When Wolf and Raven arrived, they stopped. Spread out before them was the trampled trail of the stolen pony herd. The two grinned at each other and began following the beaten tracks south. Ptecila rode far ahead of them. While Wolf and Chris followed the main trail, the Oglala ranged back and forth on the right side. Later he crossed over to the eastern side where he earnestly studied the ground as he moved further south.

In no time at all they saw Ptecila's pony cantering toward them. When he arrived, the grin on the man's wizened face gave Raven's expectations a definite lift.

"He is still following them, Okute. Either the boy has Wakan Tanka looking after him or he has medicine far beyond his few winters."

Ptecila's curly head turned away. He gazed south for a moment, then looked at Raven as he said, "Little Hawk has chosen to follow the side of the trail where the pony stealers would not expect pursuit. If he lives, this boy will one day become a great warrior."

Little Hawk, Raven thought, does show a lot of common sense and toughness for a twelve year old, recalling his tenacious bravery with the bear, then his counting coup on the white man, and now this. This is the way legends are made, he mused. He grimaced as he thought again of the future that is waiting for the Sioux. Little Hawk probably won't be allowed to be a warrior of any type.

Ptecila interrupted his thoughts with more data.

"Spotted Horse's tracks are there also. His tracks are overlapping so Little Hawk is still ahead of him."

Having the pony herd trail to follow, they were able to travel with more speed. The rugged surface of the land changed. It became a rolling-grassland that still retained an elemental toughness. Periodically they would find little pockets and twisted canyons of rock and dead trees.

Shortly before sunset, Wolf's Spirit had thought that he had heard the faraway sound of gunfire. They had remained quiet and listened, but hearing nothing, they continued southward.

When darkness arrived, they still hadn't caught up with them. Ptecila didn't stop so Raven and Wolf followed in his wake. It was so dark that when a night hawk swept near, all that could be seen of him was the white patches under his wings, and still they moved on in the same general direction. They were able to cover ground nearly as well as before. From time to time, when they felt that they might have lost them, Ptecila would slide from his pony. His skilled fingers would feel the ground's surface, searching for the torn and scattered turf caused by the passing herd.

Time had been moving slowly until Ptecila returned from a scout with news. He had found their camp! Ecstatic with his success, he proclaimed, "It was easy to find. They had made no effort to conceal their campfires."

Raven was having difficulty trying not to interrupt. He wanted to ask questions but didn't want to ruin Ptecila's story.

"The most difficult part was finding their guards. Then I had to discover a way for us to watch them without getting caught. For once I was happy that Wakan Tanka had created me small; had I been larger the guards would surely have seen me."

Holding up ten fingers, Ptecila continued, "I saw this many Indians but there could have been more."

Raven's heart sank, thinking, that's too damn many.

"Did you see any sign of Little Hawk?"

"No, Okute."

Reading the expression on Raven's face, Ptecila touched his hand as he spoke. "I did not have time to look for him. The guard was moving toward me so I left and hurried back."

His nut-colored face brightened for an instant. He grinned at Raven.

"Perhaps they have not discovered him yet!"

Raven nodded as he thought, that would be too damn easy.

It took them some time avoiding the sentries, but eventually Ptecila got them to the top of a low hill that overlooked the camp from the west.

At first, Raven had looked frantically for Little Hawk. When he couldn't find him, he began to needlessly worry, so he stopped looking for the moment and forced

WASICHU

himself to concentrate on other necessities.

Quickly but discreetly, they studied the layout of the camp. The two fires were near a stream that ran down from the northeast toward the southwest. Trees and brush lined the creek's banks and continued on to the northeast where the ponies were corralled. North of the stream were the fires and roughly a dozen Indians.

Raven was exasperated. He was finding it nearly impossible to get an accurate count of the raiders in the dark. There could be others bedded down somewhere else, he thought, or there could be more guards than the two Ptecila had seen.

They would count them again when they were more settled. A long time ago Raven had learned, 'if the opportunity is there, count your enemy, that way there shouldn't be any bloody surprises.'

Most of the pony stealers were curled into their blankets. A few still sat around the fires. They're either telling lies to each other, Chris speculated, or they can't handle sleeping on the cold ground by themselves.

One of the figures hunched near the fire drew his attention. There's something about him, he mused. He wondered if he was seeing things. The man looked like a white man. He was wearing a hat, but so were several others. This guy, he thought, has a different look about him.

He pointed the man out to Wolf's Spirit and asked if he thought he was white. The young warrior took one look and rubbed his chin as he emphatically declared, "Han (yes). He has a hair mouth (beard)."

A short time later, Wolf's declaration proved true. The man looked at the stars and revealed a short cropped, black beard that covered his lower face.

"Look!"

Ptecila's quiet urgency and sudden gesture startled Raven. Following the Oglala's pointed finger, he quickly absorbed the scene.

Between the fires and the stream, a blanketed figure stood in the shadows. He was almost hidden by the darkness, as was the blanket-wrapped form at his feet. To Raven's optimistic gaze the form looked human. The others weren't so sure.

Wolf's Spirit slipped his bow and quiver of arrows over his head and carefully placed them on the ground. Slowly he began to back off their hill. Chris stopped him.

"Where are you going?"

Wolf's grin lit up his face as he replied, "I go to see if it is truly Little Hawk."

In the pale starlight, Wolf's bright smile shined like a beacon of hope. Raven gave his shoulder a squeeze and hurried back to look down on the huddled form. Damn it, he thought, it has to be him. He turned back to Wolf only to discover that he had already left. One second he was there grinning like his name-sake and the next he was gone.

Chris and Ptecila watched the camp and continued to try and come up with an accurate head count. There was no sign of Wolf's Spirit. Maybe, Chris thought, he took the shape of a wolf and became a spirit. After living for months in the nineteenth century, Raven was ready to believe anything. Especially when he was as tired as he was at that moment. I guess, he conceded, that he could safely feel that he'd put in a full day.

He wasn't sure how much time had elapsed but it seemed like an eternity. All at once, Wolf appeared beside them as though placed there by a conjurer's hand. Raven just stared at him in awe.

Wolf's Spirit's expression needed no words. The young warrior grinned and said, "It is him."

Relieved, Chris took a deep breath and sat down away from the crest of the hill.

"Is he all right? Has he been harmed?"

WASICHU

Wolf's Spirit rested his hand on Raven's shoulder. In a quiet voice he said, "The boy is either in a deep sleep or is walking in darkness. He is bound, hand and foot, so he must be unharmed."

The young Sioux smiled and gave Raven's shoulder a little shake as if to say, 'Don't worry he's all right.'

"They wouldn't have that Shoshone guarding him if he wasn't able to run away."

Chris knew that his relief was short lived. Knowing that the boy was alive and unharmed was one thing, keeping him that way was another.

While trying to think of a mode of attack, Raven had a hunch. He didn't think the raiders were leaving at dawn. Ptecila had said that there were no shod pony tracks traveling with the stolen herd. Remembering Bear's Foot's words, 'only white men have iron shoes on their horses,' convinced Chris that the wasichu was already here waiting for them. Why?

Raven studied the layout of the camp for a moment. Wolf's Spirit and Ptecila were talking in a low monotone nearby. It was pretty obvious that they were expecting him to come up with some kind of plan.

It was then that he noticed something that was to make his 'hunch' valid. The camp was too organized and too very well layed out for a one night stand. They're waiting for someone.

Chris, instinctively, sensed that he was right. The white man was probably there as a mediate, he reasoned, a go-between, someone to pacify them if they had a change of heart or got impatient.

Knowing that every moment was precious, Chris knew that he had to come up with a plan, and soon. When the tally is three against thirteen, he thought, there isn't any plan that's going to sound like a good one.

The more pensive Raven became, the more

convinced he was that no set plan was going to work. He would have to ride into their camp without getting blown away and get as close as possible to Little Hawk. From that point on he would have to improvise.

Perhaps, he thought, when going in, he should project some type of illusion, something that would be sure to convince his adversaries that he wasn't a threat to them.

Thinking of his lack of any real plan, Chris ruefully shook his head and appraised the campsite one more time. He thought quietly for a prolonged moment. It just might work, he mused. The biggest weapon in our arsenal is surprise. There is no way that the Crow, or whoever they are, would believe that three men would dare attack them.

If he were to place Wolf's Spirit in one quadrant and Ptecila in another, with instructions to raise as much hell as possible once the shooting starts... hell, he reflected, anything is possible. The Crow wouldn't have any idea who or how many they were up against.

Before giving his friends his proposal, Raven leaned back and shut his eyes. He was exhausted. Maybe, he hoped, we'll have time for a quick nap before the dance begins. Quickly, he went over the make-shift plan in his mind.

Finally satisfied, he stood up and began to remove everything on his person that could be recognized as having been made by the Sioux. He would keep on his vest as his blanket poncho would cover it, but moccasins and every other little thing must go or be out of sight.

Before turning to Wolf and Ptecila, Chris looked toward the east. Already a red-purple blush of color was backlighting the rolling prairie. Staring intently at the diffused light that announced the beginning of a new day, he softly whispered, "Hokahey, it is a good day to die."

EXCERPT FROM THE JOURNAL OF CETAN CHICKALA (LITTLE HAWK)

My face was pressed against Hawk's Wing's sleek warmth. The smell of his sweat was strong in my nostrils. I was lying flat along his back, as he grazed along the edge of the stolen pony herd, hoping to remain unseen in the starlit night.

A chill moved up my back and a great sadness overcame me as I thought of how, earlier, I had nearly been caught and how I had seen the scalp of a Lakota who was less fortunate than I.

Wi had not yet completed his journey across the sky so it was still light when the pony thieves had stopped to camp. It looked as though a campsite had already been set up before they got there. Dead wood for a fire had been brought to the spot and an area near the water had been prepared for the ponies.

The camp was positioned in an open area among a bunch of trees that were stretched out along the sides of a stream. As far as I could see, there were rolling hills covered with sagebrush and grass. I prayed to Wakan Tanka that whoever the bad Indians had fired at had gotten away. My prayers were not heeded.

When Wi had begun to slip behind the bosom of the Earth Mother, the searchers had returned. They were jubilant! They rode through the camp at a full gallop. One of the Crow was waving a fresh scalp overhead. They were laughing and whooping as they triumphantly traversed the campsite.

I remember how my heart had turned to stone, and I felt unable to breathe when a big-bellied man wearing a Bluecoat's shirt with yellow stripes on the sleeve, had waved a blanket overhead. The blanket had looked like one owned by my grandfather!

Now, as I lay across my pony's withers, surrounded by darkness and enemy Indians, I can still feel the relief I felt when I had remembered seeing an Oglala with the same blanket as my grandfather's. He must have been the unlucky pursuer. My grandfather, being chief of our band, no longer rides with raiding parties.

My thoughts were washed away as Hawk's Wing began to walk in among the herd. He had needed no urging from me. It was as though he too was looking for The Black.

Without lifting my head, my eyes moved from one indistinct form to another as I searched for a telltale rump that would have a splash of light gray with dark spots.

Suddenly, Hawk's Wing stopped and snorted loudly. My breath caught in my throat as a fierce, grinning face appeared at my side. Another, this one painted, rose from the ground on the other side. Quickly, I pulled back on Hawk, trying to make him rear up and spin. Strong hands grabbed at my arms as I desperately kicked my heels into my pony's ribs. Something hard struck me a glancing blow to my head. I felt rough hands pull me from Hawk's back.

Barely able to stand, I fought them. They laughed and jeered as I struggled. Even as I twisted and kicked in their hands, I knew they had been waiting for me. How did they know? Just then, another blow struck me alongside of my head and I quit struggling. As my legs failed me and I felt myself falling, I realized how they had found me. They saw my pony tracks! My last thought before I drifted away to walk in darkness was that I was a fool, a little boy playing at being a man.

I awoke to the sound of birds singing. Wi's gentle rays were caressing my skin. My hands and feet were bound with rawhide. Someone had poured water on the leather binding so that when Wi's warmth dried them, the leather thongs would shrink and cut into my flesh. Already I could feel the burning from my lacerated skin.

I opened my eyes to what was probably the last day that I would see the blueness of the sky, or to see the wind move across the prairie grass like ripples in a pond.

My heart lurched within my chest! There, less than an arrow's length away, sat a wasichu. Quickly, I looked around. I was still in the camp of the Crow. After seeing them up close and in the

WASICHU

daylight, they did not look like a Crow war party. They appeared rougher, more unclean. Several of them were seated near a fire eating, less than a stone's throw away. Others were standing nearby, laughing and joking, one of them playing with a scalp. My ears burned with humiliation and anger as I turned away.

The wasichu's blue eyes were watching me. He had been carving on a piece of wood. I saw that the knife he used was my own two-bladed one given to me by Okute.

"Hau (hello), Little Warrior."

His words thundered in my ears. He speaks Lakota!

I did not answer him. He gave me a tight lipped smile and began carving on his stick once more. Beneath his big hat, his hair was long for a wasichu and hung down his back in a single braid. The hair on his face was cut short. It had silver in it like mato (the bear). The color of his skin was almost as dark as mine, and he wore buckskins for clothing as I did. Unlike mine, his leggings were black with grease stains and had been mended many times.

"Boy, we do not have much time. You probably do not trust me, but if you want to live, you had better listen carefully to what I have to say." As he talked, the blue eyes looked straight into mine except for when they lifted to watch the Crow.

"I was hired to babysit these horse thieves until the one-eyed son of a she-dog who hired me can get his tail feathers up here. A while back somebody put a hole in him and he is not able to do any hard riding."

For the first time, I was afraid. Could the wounded, one-eyed wasichu be the same one that killed Red Pony?

He paused for a moment. His blue eyes twinkled as he said, "Just between you and me, I don't think he wants to be this far into Lakota country any longer than he has to. I am telling you all of this for a couple of reasons. First of all, I have done plenty of bad things in my life, but I have never gone along with killing women and children, and I am not about to change now. Secondly, I am not about to side with a bunch of low-life blanket Indians such as these. The man that hired me said these were Crow." The wasichu turned his *head and spit, "Most of them are Crow but renegade Crow."*

He stood up and stretched his arms out. One of the Crow renegades called to him. He answered in the same language and made some strange gestures that made the Crow laugh and turn away.

Dropping down to one knee, the wasichu grabbed hold of my hair and pretended that he was tormenting me with my knife. While he did this, he spoke quickly but in a quiet voice. I had to listen closely because his Lakota was not very good, not even as good as Okute's.

"You got one chance, boy, and I am it. When the man comes to buy these ponies he would probably watch them carve you up. He hates the Sioux! Now listen carefully.

"When he comes, he will come from that direction."

He pointed behind me toward the other side of the stream.

"Now, these buzzards will probably get all excited when they see him coming. They will think about all the money they will get for these ponies and how much firewater it will buy. Some will probably just sit and wait for him to come. Others just might ride out to meet him."

The wasichu unfolded both blades of my knife and with a quick glance toward the Crow, dropped it beside my tied hands. "When that happens, I want you to cut yourself loose and high tail it toward the pony herd. I will be there with horses and we will both make pony tracks out of here."

He stood up. Reaching behind me, he picked up a rifle that, unknown to me, had been leaning against a tree. It was a big rifle, of a type I had never seen. Turning, he stood with his back to me and looked at the rolling prairie that surrounded us.

In a voice so low that I had to strain to hear, he said, 'They were bragging that they caught you in the middle of the pony herd and it looked as though you were looking for a certain horse. Is that true?"

I swallowed and spoke barely louder than a whisper. "Yes, it is true, a big black stud with a white spotted rump and notched ears."
Without another word or glance in my direction, the wasichu walked

WASICHU

away. Because of my rising excitement, I was able to ignore the pain in my wrists and ankles as I grabbed my knife and hid it beneath the flap of my loin cloth. Watching the wasichu as he walked over to the pony herd, I noticed his walk was in the same manner as Okute, slowly, but with a look about him that made me think if necessary, he could move with the quickness of the lynx.

I looked beyond my captors to the faraway tree-covered hills. My thoughts were of my mother and how her eyes would shine whenever they looked at me or Okute. I remembered the great bear and how Okute saved my life, and how my mother, while quelling my youthful fears, gave Wasichu his Lakota name, Okute.

Now, once again, Wakan Tanka has put my life in the hands of a wasichu. Why, I wondered. I can only hope that this one has the same magic fighting spirit as Okute.

One of the Indians stood up and looked at me. He slowly wiped his greasy fingers on the blue felt of his leggings. Staring at me, he bent over and pulled his knife free from the bloody piece of meat he had been eating.

Now with my own eyes, I saw that all the pony stealers were not Crow. This one looked as though he was of mixed blood, half white and half Indian. All of a sudden I was afraid. My throat felt parched; the bite of the thongs was like fire on my skin, but I welcomed the pain and the discomforts. They reminded me that I was still alive.

The breed left the others and began walking toward me. Looking into the eyes of the warrior, all I could see was death... my death. My heart seemed to stop! Light headed, short of breath, I watched my murderer advance.

Suddenly, he stopped and looked to the east. Several of the Indians had stood up, weapons in hand. All heads were turned facing the sun. As I looked, I had to squint because of Wi's great power. A rider was quietly sitting his horse on a small rise at the very edge of the enemy camp.

I could not see his face. The sun was a fiery ball directly behind him, masking his face with shadow. What I did see was *enough to assure myself that if I lived through this day I would never forget it, not even if I lived to see a hundred winters. Squinting my eyes I looked again. Yes, I could still see the red of the blanket as it draped over the broad shoulders. The wind still blew enough to stir the black wavy hair, and in my mind I could see the cool gray of the predator eyes.*

Okute had come for me!

THIRTY-NINE
~~~~~~~~~~~~

Raven sat quietly on the tall dun; his pale eyes raked the campsite. Nobody moved. It was like a freeze frame in a motion picture. Even the horses were still.

From his vantage point on top of the small hill, he could see everything. Little Hawk was on his left near the stream, the Crow were in the middle, and the pony herd on the right. He waited.

In the predawn darkness, Chris had entered the dry wash north of the camp. He had followed the wash as it meandered in an easterly direction. It swung in a short arc that enabled him to arrive at the base of the low hillock unseen. He had stayed hidden and waited for the sun. When the sun was high enough to be at his back, he had appeared on top of the hill, as though by magic.

Raven knew that the illusion wouldn't last, but he had needed an edge, something that would make the Indians hesitate before taking any violent action. If they were to take any violent steps, he had another advantage; the sun was at his back. Any premature shooting and they would be staring directly into the sun.

Chris Raven's imaginary freeze-frame was suddenly released, and the reel began to rotate. There was movement on the right as the white man stepped away from the trees, emerging into the sunlight.

Raven sucked in a mouthful of air. Directly behind the man at the edge of the pony herd stood The Black. Right next to him, quietly grazing on a clump of buffalo grass, was Hawk's Wing.

What in the hell, he wondered, is going on? Chris

was baffled. Why would those two horses be singled out?

The white man faced the Indians, giving Raven a glimpse of a thick braid peeking out from beneath a wide brimmed hat. He said something to the staring Indians in a language that Chris couldn't understand. The Indians were still standing and sitting as motionless as a collection of statues. When the man finished his brief speech, Chris noted that most of the Indians seemed to relax. Some even sat down and put their weapons aside. A few hung onto their guns and continued to stare at Raven.

As the man ambled toward him, Raven was able to look him over real good. What's this guy want? His silent query remained unanswered as he studied his man.

He looked to be in his forties. His dark hair and beard were frosted with streaks of gray. From his weather-stained, gray hat to his tall, stove-pipe boots, he looked every inch a hard-nosed customer. Raven took special note of his weapons. Both the big rifle and the holstered revolver had the oiled sheen of guns that were well cared for. I'd better watch this guy, he cautioned, he's been over a hill or two in his day. The man stopped about ten feet away. He dropped the rifle butt first into the red dust at his feet and rested his hands on the muzzle. The man's blue eyes studied Raven in much the same way that he had been scrutinized.

Shifting his weight to one leg, the plainsman spit an amber stream of tobacco and said, "Mister, I think I know who you are. If I'm right, and you ain't got a whole passel of Sioux waitin' over yonder hill, then you're either crazy or you got more 'bark' on you than you got good sense."

While keeping a close eye on the Indians and trying not to let his surprise show, Raven replied, "What I want to know is what it was you said to them Crow."

The man grinned around his chew and said, "Well shoot, I just told 'em you were a friend of mine who knew I was goin' to be here and just dropped in to do some socializin' and maybe take a looksee at some of our horse flesh."

Raven was in a quandary. He didn't know what to think. He couldn't figure the man out. The man cradled his rifle's muzzle in the crook of his arm and pulled a plug of tobacco out of his shirt pocket. As he produced a knife and cut a fresh chew, Raven noticed his rifle was one of the large caliber, single shot, 'buffalo guns.'

With his chew balanced on the blade of the long skinning knife, the man paused. His steady gaze met Chris' as he announced, "The way I see it you're here for the boy." At the mention of Little Hawk, Chris felt his muscles tighten reflexively. "I noticed right off how you keep sneakin' looks in his direction."

After popping the new chew in his mouth and settling it in his cheek, the man continued to dazzle Raven with his one-sided conversation. "I reckon that big black stud over yonder belongs to you, too. Am I right?"

Raven said nothing, but underneath his blanket the ball of his thumb increased its pressure on the spur of the pump's hammer. He watched and waited, ignoring the sweat that was sliding down his chest.

"Peers to me, the problem we got here is how we goin' to get the boy, your horses, and still get away without gettin' ourselves kilt."

Chris was stunned! He couldn't believe that he heard him right. Who is this guy, what does he want? He was about to speak when the plainsman beat him to it.

"Back yonder, that bunch of red-tailed buzzards are probably wonderin' why I have to stand so far back from my friend. Saavy?"

Raven watched him closely, staring with a sharp intensity, as he said, "Come ahead." When he was about six feet away, Raven spoke one word. "Stop."

After the man got comfortable, leaning on his rifle

again, Chris felt it was time for some answers. He asked, "If what you guessed about the boy and me is true, why do you want to help? It just don't make any sense, pal."

The plainsman's eyes narrowed as he said, "What in the hell is a pal?" He shifted his cud and was about to say more when Raven held up his hand, stopping him.

"Wait! First there's something I think you should know. Underneath my blanket I have a twelve-gauge loaded with double-ought buck. It's pointed right at your head. For all I know you're playing with me until you have a chance to 'take me out,' or you're waiting for the others to get here."

At the mention of 'others' Chris saw the man's eyes widen a fraction. "If you are playing games, at the first sign of trouble, I'm taking your head off right at the neckline."

The blue eyes shifted from Raven's poncho and twinkled briefly before he looked away and spit. He looked south for a second. Looking hard at Raven, he quietly said, "Mister, first off, I ain't takin' you out any-where. I can tell by the funny way you got of talkin' that you ain't from hereabouts. Even so, you should know that out here folks learn to trust. You take a man at his word! My name is Caleb Starr. Like I told the boy over yonder, there ain't many bad things that I ain't done, but killin' women folk and young 'uns ain't on the list and never will be. Saavy?"

Raven thought, 'I don't believe this shit. I'm here with a shotgun pointed at the man's head and he's getting pissed off at me because I'm questioning his sincerity!'

"And another thing, don't you be callin' them gawd awful misfit Injuns 'Crow.' I lived with the Crow for more than ten years. I can't think of one Crow who I knew would be seen with any of these no good, bottle-suckin' sonsabitches." Caleb Starr turned aside and spit. Looking Chris straight in the eye, he asked, "Now, can I tell you what the boy and I got planned?"

Dumbfounded, Raven couldn't speak. He nodded.

FORTY
~~~~~~~

A thin coat of red Montana dust settled onto Raven's hiking boots as he stopped to watch Caleb Starr lead the dun over to the pony herd. Thoughts of what the man had told him were still bouncing around in his head.

They had decided to stay with Starr's original plan. He would get their horses ready and stay with them until Raven and Little Hawk made their run. He would then provide cover fire.

Wolf's Spirit was downstream to the west; Ptecila was on the southern side of the stream. The plan was that they would wait until they heard the pump-gun before attacking.

Knowing that his original instructions couldn't be changed, Raven just had to hope for the best and pray that they recognized Caleb Starr as a friend.

Hitching the belt of his resolve into a tighter more secure slot, Raven began walking. He put a ludicrous, careless roll into his stride and a silly grin on his face as he strolled toward the enemy camp and the waiting renegades.

During the night's planning, Raven had decided if the opportunity presented itself, he would pretend to be mentally impaired. Hopefully, it would give the Indians a feeling of false security and dismiss any thoughts of his being a threat.

Raven's concentration on his role-playing walk was interrupted by the recollection of Caleb Starr's description of the man that had hired him. It had to be the same man, he mused. How many one-eyed men, with a bullet wound in his left shoulder, are there in the territory? Recalling Little Hawk's near-death encounter with him, Raven vowed to himself that if he ever saw that yellow grin again, the man would be dead meat.

He was close enough now to see a few suspicious stares and hostile expressions. He grabbed the bandana at his neck and tried to wipe the sweat from his face without untying it. By lolling his tongue like a dog, he pantomimed being hot. He saw one of the Indians nudge the man next to him and grin.

I have to be careful, he thought, I don't want to over play this; they probably already think I'm an idiot, wearing a blanket in this heat.

Being careful not to look at Little Hawk, he concentrated on his silly walk until he came to the area separating him and the renegades. He stopped abruptly with the pretense that he hadn't noticed Little Hawk until that very moment. Suddenly he rushed over to him.

Seeing the blood on his wrists and ankles, Raven had to bite down on his rising anger. He heard an angry shout come from behind him.

Little Hawk's large, hope-filled eyes stared up at him. Chris winked and hissed, "Be ready, Hawk."

He could hear heavy footsteps drawing nearer. Stepping back, Chris kicked gravel and dirt over a surprised Little Hawk. A rough hand grabbed his arm, spinning him around.

Fighting to dampen his simmering rage, Raven forced the anger out of his eyes and looked into a face that could have been sculpted out of red sandstone. The hate and anger etched into the pitted face mirrored Raven's own hidden emotion.

Letting his jaw hang slack, Raven grinned foolishly. Throwing his head back, he laughed uproariously. 'Stone Face' dropped his arm and took a step back. The anger quickly fled from his eyes and was replaced by something that bordered on fear.

WASICHU

Chris stopped laughing. 'Stone Face' didn't move. Raven grinned and gestured toward Little Hawk, as he ran his finger across his throat, indicating cutting. Regaining his courage the Indian sneered and made a sudden movement that let Chris know he wasn't welcome near his captive.

Raven stumbled along behind 'Stone Face' as he sauntered toward the Indian's cohorts. He was having difficulty controlling his rage. The sight of Little Hawk's bruised and swollen wrists and ankles had ignited a smoldering fire inside him that was threatening to escalate into an inferno at any moment.

Still struggling for self-control, Raven walked in among as wild and murderous a looking bunch as he had ever seen. The pinch of the pump's braided sling biting into his shoulder bolstered his confidence and calmed his tingling nerves.

Keeping his jaw slack and his eyes empty, he squatted beside the nearest group. He made sure that the blanket concealed most of the pump. For all I know, he thought, one of these bastards could have been at the Rosebud yesterday. If so, they would most likely remember a fast shooting shotgun.

Catching one of the savages staring at him, Chris gave him a big, foolish grin, causing him to look quickly away. Others watched him but swiftly glanced away when he looked back at them. After a short period of time they ignored him.

Being careful not to draw attention to himself, he began to take inventory. Once, when he caught another staring, he again gave his empty smile and the warrior looked away. The count went quickly after that and when he'd finished, Raven's anxiety level had reached a new, higher plateau. Four Indians were missing. Just before first light they had counted thirteen, including Caleb Starr. One was probably with the pony herd, so that would leave three unaccounted for. Where the hell are they, he wondered.

While speculating about the missing three, his side vision picked up some movement to his right. His look caught a hard looking half-breed stuffing some black and silver hair into a stained bag. Shock exploded somewhere deep inside him.

Whatever thoughts were formulating in Raven's mind were never completed. A loud shout came from south of the creek!

A rider thundered across the stream. Water leaped in a glistening arc from beneath his horse's hooves as the sun glinted off the whiskey bottle he was holding aloft.

The Indian rider cruelly jerked his horse to a jarring stop fifty feet short of the camp fires. Waving the bottle overhead, he happily harangued his excited comrades. His big belly jutted out like the prow of a ship.

Recognizing the Indian's blue shirt with corporal chevrons from their earlier count, Raven figured he had probably missed the trio's departure when he was traversing the dry wash. Looking beyond the rider to the south, he thought, I bet I know who isn't too far behind.

The savage gathering of thieves had suddenly become animate. Raven watched as the talking and laughing warriors straggled toward Big Belly. The big warrior sat on his pony, brandishing his bottle and laughing.

Those that had their ponies staked nearby leaped astride them and rode south, accompanied by a chorus of yips and wolf howls. A few on foot ran by the big bellied horseman. In their anticipation of the available firewater, they had paused only long enough to gather their weapons.

Chris and Starr's plan, though desperate, was to wait until as many Indians as possible were out of the camp. Raven would then try to get as close to Little Hawk as possible before making a run for the horses.

Raven slowly stood up. Perspiration was sliding

down his upper body like the tributaries of a river. It's time, he thought. He felt a tingle of apprehension when he noticed that the big-bellied Indian was staring at him from his lofty seat on his pony. Two of the Indians, one wearing his hair Crow style, were standing at his stirrup trying to cajole a drink.

Raven's glance scanned the area. Nobody was paying attention to the boy. Beyond the three with the bottle, two more Indians stood by the stream and stared southward. Those five were the closest and presented the most immediate danger.

Still playing the simpleton Chris began to move obliquely toward Little Hawk. Letting his mouth hang open, he shuffled forward in his rolling gait. He stopped. Gawking at the ground, he picked up a stick and poked at an imaginary object. Dropping the stick, he shambled on, playing his role to the hilt. Underneath his poncho, the sweat was pooling at his waistband. The tension was building with each bogus move he made.

Chris was still about ten paces from Little Hawk when he heard a loud voice shout.

"Hey, white man! You stop!"

He had expected to be challenged but not in English. Had it been in any other language he would have feigned ignorance long enough to have reached the boy.

Raven stopped and turned; it was Big Belly, who nudged his pony into a walk toward him. Chris tried desperately to maintain his simple-minded pose. Beyond the slow approach of the Indian's pony he could see the other two arguing over something.

As he came closer, Raven's attention was inexplicably drawn to the horseman's dress. Above the man's high-top moccasins, his legs were bare and dusty. The dust looked white on his brown legs. The big belly stretched the blue army shirt so taut that it pushed over his cartridge belt and against the rifle resting across his thighs. He noticed the Sioux style braids and how the sun glanced off something hanging from the copper-colored neck. Raven stared. The Indian's pony brought the 'something' closer, then still closer. He stopped. Five objects gently swayed on a cord against the dark chest.

For a fleeting moment, all of Chris' senses were working at the peak of their potential. He felt the warmth of the sun on his uplifted face. The sharp smell of horse sweat nipped at his nostrils. He heard the soft exhale of 'Big Belly's' pony as he saw the light reflect off the fine hairs on its muzzle. Suddenly all that was left was a rapidly increasing roar in his ears. The fury was coursing through his body like fire through dry prairie grass. His eyes lifted to the cruel, angry face. The lips were moving but Raven heard nothing. He saw the narrowed eyes suddenly widen for an instant then disappear as the Indian's head exploded in a scarlet spray of blood and bone.

Startled by the pump's booming discharge, the pony shrieked and lunged forward. The headless body was twitching spasmodically as it slid to the side and toppled onto the ground.

The abrupt recoil and blast of sound released Raven from the debilitating captivity of his mind-numbing rage. He automatically pumped another shell into the chamber as he glanced at the objects scattered at his feet.

Separated by the shotgun's discharge, the broken cord sprawled in a serpentine manner. Strung along its length were four recently severed fingers. They had been positioned on either side of the familiar pipestone carving of a horse... Spotted Horse's amulet.

FORTY-ONE
~~~~~~~~~~~

For a time-stopping frozen moment, nobody moved. Then, only the skittering movement of Big Belly's horse marred the stillness of the scene.

Raven's voice, hoarse with emotion, broke the spell.

"*Inyanka* (run)!"

The one word thrown over his shoulder toward Little Hawk prodded 'Big Belly's' two friends into action.

With the quickness of a ferret, the Indian on the left whipped an arrow from its quiver, notched it, and had the bowstring drawn halfway to his ear before Chris fired. The solid impact of the projectile caused the Indian to stagger backwards, his legs buckling. The steel ball had entered just below the left armpit, smashed through the ribs, and pulverized the heart.

The other renegade lost his nerve. He ran to his left, trying to reach the shelter of some trees. He didn't get there! The mass of buckshot caught him in full stride and sent him skidding, leaving a crimson smear among the grass and sage.

Shots were now coming from the creek causing Raven to swivel sharply. An arrow whispered by his ear. He then felt a sharp blow to the calf of his left leg. The punch of the bullet spun him in a half circle and dropped him to one knee. Staying on the knee, Chris pumped two shots into the brush by the stream.

On the other side, he could see riders directing their ponies up an incline leading to the creek. He saw one of them throw up his arms and clutch at a feathered shaft protruding from his chest.

Ptecila, he thought. As he struggled to rise, he saw

the spotted horse carving lying beside his knee. Scooping it up, he quickly shook it free of its grisly companions and stuffed it in his pocket.

Another bullet from the creek snapped by his head as he struggled the rest of the way to his feet. Pain tore through his leg as he put his weight on it.

Hoof-beats came from his left. Over his shoulder, Raven was horrified to see that the boy was still there.

Little Hawk was desperately scuttling on his hands and knees in the direction of the pony herd. A warrior, bent over the bobbing neck of his pony, was almost on top of him. As he pulled alongside the stumbling boy, sunlight winked off the steel-bladed hatchet that was clutched in his upraised hand.

Swiftly swinging the pump into line, Raven stepped to his left. A bolt of pain shot up his leg. He fell! With horror-filled eyes, he saw the hatchet raised in readiness. Then, before it could descend, there was a thunderous explosion, and the Indian was blown off his horse, as though struck by a giant fist. Raven's relief was exhilarating. Caleb Starr and his 'buffalo gun' had joined the fight.

Favoring his left leg, Raven scrambled to his feet and hobbled toward Little Hawk. He silently cursed himself for being a fool as he forcefully punched several shells into the shotgun's magazine.

He hadn't realized that after being tied up for so long, the boy was going to have problems walking, not to mention running.

Beyond Little Hawk, he saw Starr burst into the open, spurring a long-legged roan. He had The Black and Hawk's Wing strung on a lead behind him.

As Raven jacked another round into the pump's chamber, he felt a solid tug on his poncho as a bullet searched for him. An arrow hissed by his ear as another thudded into the ground only inches from his foot. A bullet

WASICHU

kicked up a spray of dirt near Little Hawk's struggling form. The boy had bravely gotten to his feet and was stumbling toward Starr and the horses.

Giving Little Hawk some supporting firepower, Chris' pump bellowed and bucked in his fists. He unleashed three shots, as fast as he could pump the slide, into a group of riders near the creek. One rider went down, spooking a couple of ponies that began milling about in indecisive circles. The enemy gunfire quickly faded away as they heard a resounding, "*Hokahey!*"

Wolf's Spirit, crouched low over the neck of his big stallion, exploded into the open. With his horse moving at full gallop, the young Sioux recklessly charged the group of surprised renegades.

Fearing that his buckshot might hit Wolf or his horse, Raven didn't dare shoot! He stared, mesmerized.

Wolf's Spirit stood in his stirrups, his bow appeared like magic. One, two and three slivers of light were launched from his bow in as many seconds. A rider slid from his pony's back, a yellow shaft protruding from his chest. Another warrior reeled and fell, clutching at an arrow in his neck. A horse screamed and began to buck.

A shout from behind broke the spell and pulled Chris around. Caleb Starr raced by in a dusty splatter of dirt and gravel. Beyond him, Chris saw Little Hawk, mounted on his pony, leading The Black. Once clear of Raven, Starr haunch-slid his roan and stepped out of the saddle while his mount was still moving. In his right fist, he was carrying Raven's Winchester. Just before Wolf's Spirit closed with the renegades, the plainsman levered four ear-splitting shots into the massed riders.

"Sweet Jesus," Chris exclaimed, "Where in the hell are they all coming from?"

There were more Indians crossing the creek and joining the others than had originally been in the camp.

Caleb Starr stopped firing as Wolf's stallion smashed into the renegades smaller ponies like a four-legged battering ram. One horse went down in a flurry of flailing legs and hooves. Wolf's Spirit was fighting like a man possessed! He used his heavy bow like a war club. Striking left and right, he smashed his way, cutting a swath into their churning center.

"*Okute!*"

Little Hawk's shout spurred Raven into action. As he limped toward Little Hawk, he glanced south in time to see more riders appear through the haze of dust. Spinning away, he heard again the sharp reports of his rifle as Caleb tried to give Wolf's Spirit some more cover fire.

Little Hawk was grinning as he appeared, riding his pony through a cloud of dust and gun-smoke. For Christ's sake, Raven thought, you'd think that we'd already fought our way clear. In spite of his mounting misgivings, Chris grinned back.

The Black was a sight to behold. He was enjoying all the noise and excitement. As he drew near, Little Hawk released him. With his neck arched and his head held high, he trotted and pranced over to Raven.

Chris caught a glimpse of the fire in his eye as he grit his teeth and put his foot in the stirrup and stepped up. A wave of pain washed over him as he swung his wounded leg over the cantle and slid his foot into the other stirrup.

A crashing explosion made Raven forget his pain. Starr had switched back to his buffalo gun. A quick glance showed that Wolf was still slicing in and out among the confused and unorganized renegades. Raven was about to go help when Wolf's Spirit, unexpectedly, broke clear of the melee.

Chris was surprised by the big horse's speed. Wolf Spirit's big stallion burst out of the fracas as though he'd heard a quarter-mile starter's gun. His rising exultation was swiftly lowered when he saw several riders emerging from the red dust cloud behind the hard-riding warrior. There were three of them and they were whipping their mounts mercilessly, trying to head him off. They were coming at a slight angle, and it was helping them to gain rapidly on Wolf's Spirit.

Raven shouted at Hawk and commanded, "Stay with Starr!"

When his heels thumped into The Black's ribs, the horse's leaping response nearly caused him to lose a stirrup.

Caleb Starr had just swung a leg over his roan when Raven's shout reached him.

"Starr! Get the boy out of here!"

As The Black flew by, the plainsman grinned around his tobacco plug and spurred his horse toward Little Hawk.

Wolf's tenacious pursuers began shooting from their horse's backs, hoping for a lucky hit. Raven, being on a collision course with Wolf, had more reason to be worried about an accidental hit than he did. The young warrior was looking back and sliding from one side of his stallion to the other to present a more difficult target. Crouching over the bobbing neck, Raven could feel The Black's great muscles rhythmically bunching with each stride as the gap between them narrowed rapidly.

With less than forty feet separating them, he thought that Wolf's Spirit hadn't seen him coming. Suddenly, Wolf savagely pulled back on his rawhide rein, forcing the stallion into a slide. Before coming to a stop, he jerked his horse's head to his left and smacked his heels into his ribs. The stallion lunged to his left in response and surged into a gallop.

With his dark hair whipping in the wind and his red poncho billowing out behind, Raven burst through the stallion's lingering plume of rising dust, looking like an avenging devil. The Black's wild-eyed charge added to the illusion, as demonic, wheezing grunts could be heard with each powerful stride.

The three Indians were caught as they were trying to turn their ponies in time to stay with Wolf's Spirit's stallion.

Neck outstretched, yellow teeth bared, The Black exploded into their midst like a twelve hundred pound cannonball!

The first horse and rider he made contact with went down as though struck by lightning. The Black struggled to regain his balance. Instantly, pain shot up Raven's leg like a burning fuse. It detonated in his skull in an explosion of searing agony.

The following warrior had charged his pony into The Black, pinning Chris' injured leg in the process.

Through pain-fogged vision, Raven had a glimpse of blazing eyes encompassed by a familiar, pitted, stone-like face. Helplessly he watched as a steel hatchet descended toward his unprotected head.

At that very instant, The Black nimbly regained his footing and swiftly surged forward over the downed rider and horse.

Chris heard a scream as he lurched forward. He cringed as he felt a glancing blow on his left shoulder, followed by a burning pain. Enraged, knowing that the Indian's pony would be only a step behind, Raven grasped the shotgun with one hand and grit his teeth against his pain. Twisting his body, he swung the pump in a hundred and eighty degree arc. When the snub-nosed muzzle was pointed at 'Stone Face's' pitted chest, he squeezed the trigger. The twelve gauge's recoil nearly tore the gun loose from his hand. Chris watched with a savage glee, as Little Hawk's jailer was blown off the back of his pony.

Painfully, Chris pulled The Black to a stop. Slightly winded, he ignored his throbbing shoulder and sucked in more air while he looked for Wolf's Spirit. He couldn't see him but he saw the other renegade. He was sitting upright on his pony, futilely trying to extract a three foot reed shaft that had pierced his body fore and aft.

Unexpectedly, Wolf's Spirit entered into his field of vision. The wounded Indian had been between them, blocking his view.

Wolf's stallion was charging straight at the Crow, who didn't even look up. He must be in shock, Chris thought, as Wolf's Spirit's horse swept in close and the warrior's heavy bow smashed onto the Indian's exposed head. The blow neatly knocked him from the back of his pony, who suddenly bolted at Wolf's shouted, "Anho!"

With Wolf's coup outcry echoing in his ears, Raven quickly looked to the south. He could see a number of horses and riders milling about on the other side of the creek. He wondered why nobody had been firing at them or coming to their comrades' assistance. Raven was about to put his heels to The Black when a fusillade of gunfire erupted from trees and bushes by the creek. The hum and crackle of bullets flying through the air was everywhere! One of the Indian ponies went down, screaming and kicking.

Thumbing shells into his pump, Raven jerked on the reins, spinning The Black. He felt a bullet tug at his blanket. Another one snagged at his hair at the base of his neck. The bullet had come so close he'd felt the heat of its passing.

Just as he was about to urge his horse into flight, the shooting tapered off, then stopped. Looking back, he saw riders splashing across the stream, whipping their mounts into a gallop.

Raven was confused. At first only three of the bunch had pursued Wolf's Spirit, now it looked like the whole shebang was coming for them. What the hell's going on? His musing came to a sudden halt as soon as he spied the tall man wearing a tan duster, spurring a big pinto toward the head of the pack.

Through clenched teeth, Raven grated, "One-Eye! That sonofabitch has got them all pumped up again!"

Burrowing his heels into The Black's ribs, he yelled, "Hopo, *hiyu ho* (come on, let's go)!"

Wolf's Spirit shook the blood from his fresh scalp and leaped onto his stallion's back.

When The Black jumped over the nearby dead horse, Chris saw a fan of long hair and a crumpled body partially pinned beneath. Remembering the earlier scream, he saw that the rider's head was twisted at an unusual angle. He glanced back and saw that Wolf was bent over his horse's neck and was urging him on with his quirt. They began to pull away. In frustration, the pack began to fire at them. Eyes straight ahead, he could see Little Hawk and Caleb Starr waiting for them far to the north. Chris felt a sudden elation. We've done it, he thought, there's no way that they have the horsepower to catch us.

He looked back and felt his stomach twist into a knot. Wolf's Spirit's horse was running close behind, but without a rider!

Fifty yards to the rear, Raven saw the young warrior struggling to his feet. The right side of his body was painted red with his blood. Beyond him, he could see several of the riders whipping their mounts in anticipation of being the first to close with the helpless Sioux.

For a split second, Raven's mind went blank. The vacancy was filled by the horrible image of Joe Spotted Horse's bloody smile as he fell away from him toward the distant trees.

"No!!!"

The involuntary cry triggered his reflexes and he hauled back on his reins. He spun The Black as tightly as possible, and the big horse was in full gallop within three jumps. Sensing the urgency, the stallion lengthened his stride and zeroed in on Wolf's Spirit's lonely figure.

WASICHU

He was turned away from Raven, facing his enemy. His bow was gone. The only weapon he had was the knife clenched in his right fist. In spite of his wound, Wolf's Spirit stood straight and bravely waited, knife in hand, to fight to the death.

Seeing that the race was going to be close, Raven waited until he was about sixty yards from the riders. Ignoring the pain in his calf, he stood up in his stirrups. As he balanced, he saw Wolf's head whip around at the thunderous sound of The Black's approach. Squeezing with his knees, he brought the pump to his shoulder. He fired four times, as fast as he could work the slide.

He saw a horse and rider go down. Another Indian slipped from his pony's back and disappeared in the dust. A horse broke his gait and began bucking furiously, while his rider struggled to keep his seat.

Chris' wounded leg buckled and it took a desperate grab at The Black's mane to stay aboard.

Faced with Raven's withering hail of buckshot, some of the renegades had pulled in their ponies and were turning around and riding away. Three were still coming on hard, an Indian and two white men!

Raven flew by the astonished face of Wolf's Spirit and suddenly jerked hard on The Black's reins. Digging in with all four hooves, the big horse brought them to a dusty, sliding halt.

Still at full gallop, the three foolishly began to fire wildly. A bullet kicked up a geyser of dirt behind them. An arrow came the closest, nicking The Black's rump, causing him to skitter to the side.

Quieting The Black, Raven centered his sights on a belt sling that was holding the left arm of the man he thought of as 'One-Eye.' Just as he squeezed the trigger, the 'belt sling' disappeared as the punishing kick of the recoil obliterated his sight picture.

Chris' concentration had been so totally focused that he hadn't noticed that the Indian had been crowding his pony up alongside the one-eyed outlaw. The warrior was so eager to count coup that he had cut his pony right in front of 'One-Eye' at the exact second that Raven had pulled the trigger.

The Indian had been leaning over his pony's neck and caught the full load of buckshot in the face and chest. It blew him off the back of his pony so suddenly that Raven didn't even see him. It all had happened so fast that Raven thought that he had missed. 'One-Eye' was still coming!

The distance separating them had disappeared and the two outlaws frantically slowed their mounts and leveled their weapons. Smoke and fire suddenly belched from the pistol of the gunman on Raven's left. Firing from the hip, Raven pumped twice. The twin blasts thundered in his ears as he saw the first shot miss and the second send the gunman spinning from his saddle to fall into the churning red dust.

The pump-gun was unexpectedly wrenched from his tingling fingers as a terrible blow smashed into his side and the flat report of a pistol shot slapped against his ears. Raven was dazed, reeling in the saddle.

The impact of the bullet striking the gun stock had driven the steel frame into Chris' ribs, forcing him to grab at the fork of his saddle for balance. Only the braided sling had kept the pump from plummeting all the way to the ground. Wooden stock splintered, the pump-gun hung upside down suspended from Raven's elbow.

Before Raven was able to recover enough to move, 'One-Eye's' pinto had swung up alongside The Black. The two horses immediately began to slash and bite at each other like murderous adolescents, as Raven waited to die. His hands had become useless hunks of numb, tingling flesh. His mind faltered as he struggled to find a life-saving solution. Not willing to accept his imminent death, he stared helplessly into his murderer's malevolent gaze.

WASICHU

With the swiftness of the blink of an eye, an eight year old memory gave him a fleeting image of the NVA officer's cold black eyes as he leveled his automatic.

Smoke still snaked from the bore of One-Eye's long-barreled pistol. Leaning forward in his saddle, the one-eyed killer grinned. Reaching across his useless left arm, he suddenly raised the big revolver's muzzle level with Raven's head.

"Thud!"

Raven flinched! 'One-Eye' was violently slapped back into the cantle of his saddle! A large bullet hole had magically appeared in his chest. The killer's protruding eye was already glazing, as a dazed Christopher Raven heard the faraway boom of the riffle shot. The outlaw's body crumpled and slid from the saddle into the dirt. Chris stared at the blood-splattered rump of the outlaw's horse and blinked in disbelief.

Still somewhat sore and dazed, Raven grimaced as he twisted and looked beyond the grinning face of Wolf's Spirit. Far to the north, he could see two tiny, motionless figures sitting their horses on a little knoll. The smoke from the barrel of the buffalo gun was still dissipating above the larger of the two figures.

In a voice, weakened by emotion, Raven exclaimed, "Caleb Starr, you are one sharpshooting sonofabitch!"

FORTY-TWO
~~~~~~~~~~~~

After Wolf's Spirit's wound had stopped bleeding, Raven helped him secure a make-shift bandage. Luckily, the bullet had missed the kidney, glancing off a rib before tearing a ragged hole above the hipbone, as it exited. Chris marveled at their good fortune as he left Wolf to the adjusting of his bandage. For the first time since finding Little Hawk, he was able to relax. The feeling had painfully returned to his hands. Taking stock of his injuries, he knew they would heal. He facetiously thought that a little pain would remind him that he was just as mortal as anyone else.

Raven looked off to the south where the surviving renegades were preparing to leave then he glanced toward Little Hawk and Caleb Starr who were returning with Wolf's stallion. He let his gaze drift further north and thought of Ptecila. The little Oglala was supposed to rendezvous with them in the distant north if they became separated. He carefully removed the blanket poncho and let the breeze soothe his tired, overheated body. Examining his shoulder, he found the hatchet wound to be superficial. Must have chipped some bone, he guessed, 'cause it sure as hell aches.

Little Hawk and Starr arrived, leading Wolf's horse. As he gimped over to them, he saw that Wolf's Spirit was already there, greeting his stallion. Hand clasped to the bandage at his side, he threw Raven a quick grin. Then, glancing at Starr, he quickly arranged his face into the habitual, expressionless mask worn around whites.

Little Hawk was looking down at Chris as though he expected to be chastised at any moment. Raven thought that there would be time enough for that later. Also, he realized,

I'll have to tell him of his grandfather's death.

Little Hawk dropped his eyes and silently awaited his punishment. Smiling broadly, Chris gave the boy's leg an affectionate shake and squeeze. "I am happy to find that you are well," he said. Raven noticed that Starr smiled quietly at his words and spat off to one side.

"Following the pony stealers was a very brave but foolish thing... but, we will talk of that later. For the moment I am simply happy that you are alive and well." Little Hawk looked up and nodded as he seriously replied, "Yes, Okute."

Caleb Starr's gentle twang interceded with a quiet command in English. "Look yonder."

Raven followed his gesture and saw the last of the renegades leaving with the stolen pony herd. Looking back at Caleb, then back at the departing horses he said, "I suppose I should try to get our horses back, but to tell you the truth I don't have the energy."

Starr nodded in agreement, then spit. "Peers to me, there's always tomorrow..." He nodded toward Wolf's Spirit, who had a hand pressed to his bandaged side and was sitting his horse with his eyes shut. "... and that fine, young warrior there needs some rest to heal that wound."

Chris said, "You got that right." He stepped up close and offered his hand as he proclaimed, "Caleb Starr, I owe you my life and probably Little Hawk's as well."

As they shook hands, Caleb replied, "Mister, I'm just happy to have been here. Mind tellin' me your name?"

"Christopher Raven or Okute, take your pick."

"You know, Christopher, if someone was to tell me about this here ruckus, I wouldn't believe it. Two men takin' on fifteen, twenty ..."

Raven interrupted, "It was three... four including yourself. We had one warrior down south of the creek. We're hoping that he's waiting up north for us."

Starr nodded and accurately spat an amber stream of

tobacco juice between the twin uprights of his roan's ears.

Glancing at Wolf's Spirit, Starr proclaimed, "If'n half the Sioux hereabouts can fight like that boy there, I pity Gen'ral Terry and all the rest of his Yankee soldier boys."

Before Raven had time to respond, Starr continued, "Where's that repeatin' scattergun of yours?" Raven limped over to The Black and returned with the pump. He jacked the chamber open and handed it up to Starr.

The plainsman examined it with obvious admiration. He even fingered the splintered hole in the stock as he studied the wood. He slammed the slide up, shutting the chamber. Sighting down the barrel, he eased the hammer down and handed the pump-gun to Chris and remarked, "Damnation, boy, that there gun is really something. I ain't never seen the like."

Caleb reined his horse around, then stopped and looked back. He grinned at Little Hawk, nodded at Wolf's Spirit and raised his hand goodbye. Raven lifted his in return and Starr touched his spurs to the roan's flanks. As the horse cantered away, Starr's loud voice carried back to them, causing Raven to be thankful that his other friends didn't speak English.

"If'n you ever get tired of playin' Injun, Christopher, I got me a little horse ranch just south of Deadwood Gulch. Come up and set a spell so we can swap lies."

While hobbling over to The Black, Starr's last words 'playing Indian' stuck in his mind. Is that what I'm doing, he wondered, playing cowboys and Indians? He dropped his red blanket over The Black's withers and, being aware of the splintered stock, slung the gun over his shoulder. Painfully, he swung up on his horse and walked him over to join the others. His gaze followed the line of the stream as it moved east and then meandered north. Absently, he thought of their need for water to clean their wounds and for drinking.

Stopping beside Little Hawk, his eyes were drawn

east to the diminishing figure of Caleb Starr. Watching the distant horseman brought to mind many things. He had known the man less than an hour and he owed him two lives. Without his help, Raven was convinced that they never would have pulled it off. That shot that nailed 'One-Eye,' he mused, was the finest rifle shot I've ever seen.

Suddenly, his hand moved to the empty rifle scabbard strapped onto his saddle. With a grin he muttered, "Why, you old sonofabitch. You never gave me my rifle back."

He watched Starr crest a hill about a half mile away and then disappear down the other side. The thought entered his head without any warning. The thought had a voice. The voice whispered, 'Go with him. There is still time. In a couple of days you'll be at Bear Butte.'

Deep within his pocket, Chris felt the pipestone horse pressing against his leg. Was it his imagination, he thought, or could he actually feel heat coming from the carving? It seemed to pulsate against his thigh. In his mind, he could picture himself once again climbing the butte to its summit. He would perform the same ceremony; make the mistake, exactly as before. Would the storm's ensuing thunder and lightning propel him magically back to the future?

Unbidden, the voice returned. 'For what?'

He looked at the boy. A tired Little Hawk looked back at him, a bemused smile on his face. Wolf's Spirit was still dozing, sitting quietly on the back of his stallion. The Black pawed the ground and swung his head around and looked at him. Raven thought of Blue Feather. Would she be waiting with Bear's Foot by the Little Big Horn River? How far away is Custer? Is there still time to beat him there?

Returning his gaze to Little Hawk, he could see something hidden within the boy's large eyes. Was it just adulation, friendship? Perhaps it was something more. Raven felt a twinge in his leg as he turned The Black and faced the northwest. "*Hopo tiyata* (Let us go home)."

FORTY-THREE
~~~~~~~~~~~~~~

With his head still spinning over the finality of his decision to stay in the nineteenth century, Raven had led his friends in a final search of the battle site for Ptecila.

As they prepared to move north, they silently thanked Wakan Tanka that their search for the Oglala's body was time wasted. But they did pick up a few useful items from the things left behind by the renegades. Little Hawk was especially excited; he had found his new bow and arrows among the forgotten gear.

Too tired to look for anymore treasures, the battered trio left the area, moving north. In no time at all they left the rolling terrain and entered a vast plain intercepted with countless gullies and dry washes.

Raven let The Black pick his own trail while he doggedly worked at repairing the pump-gun's splintered stock. Among the useful things found at the scene of the fight, were some rawhide strips. With Chris busy binding the wood together on his shotgun and Wolf tending to his poultice, it was Little Hawk that saw them first.

They first appeared as a small dust cloud on the northwestern horizon. Wolf's Spirit figured that they must have traveled for a long time on the rocky bottom of a dry wash, or they would have seen their dust much sooner.

Too late now, Chris thought, if we can see their dust, they can see ours.

He watched Wolf's Spirit's face as he stared at the distant plume of dust. Raven flicked a covert glance at Little Hawk as he asked, "What do you think, Wolf, could they be Lakota?"

Shielding his eyes with both hands, the young warrior

studied the dust cloud before speaking. With his lean, dark face revealing nothing, he replied, "I do not think they are Lakota. The people have no reason to be this far south, or to be moving east."

Hearing his words, Raven felt hope tear loose deep inside of him and plummet into despair. Not allowing his concern to show in his face or eyes, he looked at Wolf's Spirit. Accepting the warrior's weakened condition, Chris knew what he would have to do. In his mind, Raven tried to formulate the correct Lakota before asking his question.

"Wolf, do you believe that those riders would know from our dust that we are more than one rider?"

From the corner of his eye, Chris saw Little Hawk's head turn quickly toward him.

Wolf's Spirit gazed into Chris' eyes with a searching intensity. Something in the warrior's look told him that he knew what Raven's intentions were. As soon as Wolf spoke, Chris knew that his guess was right. The young warrior's voice was as soft and respectful as though he was speaking to his chief.

"I do not think that they will be able to recognize the difference, Okute. We have been walking our horses beside each other like wasichus. There has not been much dust."

Just ahead of them was a deep dry wash that ran east and west. As they moved down its rocky side, Raven was pleased to see that it had a gravel bottom.

Little Hawk interrupted his planning. He was bursting with curiosity and excitement, and asked the one question that Chris didn't want asked.

"What are we going to do, Okute?"

Raven didn't answer.

"Are we going to outrun them?"

At the bottom of the wash, Raven stopped The Black and faced Little Hawk. Keeping his tone light and free of anxiety, he replied, "We cannot outrun them, Hawk. Our ponies would not last; they have already been run hard and walked long today."

Looking deep into the boy's snapping, black eyes, Raven had to battle a sudden rising tide of emotions. He cleared his throat and softly said, "We will have to take separate trails."

Before Little Hawk was able to say anything, he continued with his pitch.

"We do not have the time to talk this over, so this is what we will do. You and Wolf's Spirit will follow this gully west. I will continue on and meet with whoever is making that dust. We will rendezvous later, north of the Rosebud."

Sensing that Raven would rather deal with Little Hawk alone, Wolf adroitly maneuvered his stallion up the northern slope of the wash. He stopped just shy of the grassy top, leaving his head above the lip so that he could watch the distant riders without any danger of being seen.

Raven quickly unrolled his blanket poncho and busied himself, slipping it on so that he wouldn't have to face the imploring look in Little Hawk's eyes.

"Okute, they will kill you!"

Somehow, Raven was able to manufacture a large, convincing smile to accompany the bogus sincerity of his words.

"Listen Hawk, if I am alone they will not harm me. I am a wasichu. The Crow and Shoshone are allies of the whites. They will not dare harm me."

Before turning away from Little Hawk, Raven used the Lakota euphemism for ending a discussion.

"That is all I have to say."

He quickly turned his head, not wanting him to see the lie hidden in his eyes. He knew that the chances of him not being recognized were pretty slim. Someone would have been at the Rosebud, or ridden with the pony stealers that morning.

Chris chanced a peek. Little Hawk's head was down as he quietly sat on Hawk's Wing. Chris watched as Wolf's

Spirit, hand pressed against his poultice, gingerly walked his horse down the slope. He pulled him to a stop next to the somber Little Hawk. For a brief interlude the only sound came from the horses, as they softly blew through their nostrils and shifted their weight from one hoof to another.

Wolf's Spirit quietly announced, "They have turned toward us, Okute. It is certain that they have seen our dust."

Little Hawk looked at Raven. He did not see the look of understanding that passed between Raven and Wolf's Spirit. He only saw that his new father was preparing to die so that he and Wolf could live. He felt Wolf's touch on his arm and his quiet words.

"Come, Hawk. Okute's way is the only way."

Suddenly remembering, Raven thrust his hand into his pocket and pulled out the pipestone horse carving. Unceremoniously, Chris held the talisman out to Little Hawk. Tentatively, he took it from Raven's palm and met his gaze.

Seeing the pain in Little Hawk's eyes, convinced Chris that the unspoken implication of the carving being in his possession was clearly understood.

Raven then said, "As you know, your grandfather would have wanted you to have it. I will explain what happened when we meet at the Rosebud."

For a brief interval, their eyes met and held, and many unspoken words and feelings were conveyed. Raven longed to take the boy into his arms and comfort him, but couldn't, as there was not enough time. Instead he said, "I am sorry, Hawk. I must go."

As Raven wheeled The Black, he saw tears pooling in Little Hawk's eyes. He gently dug his heels in and the stallion lunged up the side of the bank.

Clearing the top, he looked to the north. The riders were still too far away to count but one thing was certain, they were heading straight for him. As he was about to leave the lip of the wash, he looked back. Wolf and Hawk were no longer there. Like magic, the two Lakota were gone. Raven shook his head in amazement at the Sioux ability to blend and become part of their terrain.

He dug his heels deeper into The Black's side. The big horse responded, instantly breaking into a lope. He headed straight for the growing dust cloud. He wanted to put some distance between him and his friends so that the enemy, after they had killed him, and had seen his solo tracks would have no reason for going further south.

When he was a couple hundred yards from the stony dry-wash, Chris slowed The Black to a walk. They were much closer now; he could almost make out individuals. He made a rough estimate of between twelve and fifteen... too many.

He loosened the revolver in its holster. The feel of the patina of oil on the metal's surface reminded him of 'Nam and of the countless times he and Joe had cleaned their weapons together, spreading the parts out on their bunks. In his mind, he could still see the diffused light reflecting off the oily parts disassembled on the army cots. He recalled the happy, boyish grin that was so often on Joe's face. It was especially there when he and Raven would banter in Lakota over some nonsensical subject.

Raven mentally put the images aside as he watched the riders, still several hundred yards away, deploy into a skirmish line. Even with their edges blurred by distance, Chris could see that they were Indians. He felt a brief pang of disappointment. If they had been soldiers, he might have been able to convince them he was on their side, or something; anything would be better than to be shot down like a rabid dog.

Trying to keep his thoughts light, in contrast to the heavy situation, he imagined a click and whir as his thought process searched for a way out of his dilemma. Looking his imaginary prospects straight in the eye, Raven could see that his predicament was virtually hopeless.

Speaking aloud to The Black, he exclaimed, "Well, boy, looks like we're going to rock and roll together one last time!"

He unslung the pump-gun and placed it across his thighs. He felt the sun's warmth against the nape of his neck and along the length of his bare arm. Gently, he stroked and patted The Black's sleek neck.

Sporadic visions of Little Hawk and Blue Feather erupted from his memory like cinematic reminders of the truly happier moments of his life. He also witnessed once again, the joy of giving as it spread itself across the broad face of Bear's Foot when he had handed him the lead-rope of The Black.

His memories were interrupted by a sharp pain in his leg as The Black instantly responded to his sudden urging by breaking into a sudden gallop.

He could see more detail now... blankets billowing, braids flying, the blue of an army shirt, leather thrums dancing in the wind. He cocked the pump, keeping his thumb on the hammer. He closed his eyes, feeling the rhythm of The Black's powerful strides. An image of Blue Feather appeared and shimmered before him. Her beauty made him giddy with longing. The illusion changed. She was riding; coming toward him now, flanked by Bear's Foot and Ptecila. He blinked. They were still there. His eyes were open! Raven simply could not believe what he was seeing. Lakota, they are Lakota! His mind staggered with the reality that a party of Sioux had actually come looking for them.

He was now close enough to see smiles and to recognize some of the warriors. A fleeting glimpse of Blue Feather's face was enough to remind him of what he must do. Practically overcome with joy, Raven jerked The Black's reins and wheeled away before he could see the anxiety he knew would be in Blue Feather's eyes. He knew that seeing him alone must be painful for her. She had to be thinking that Little Hawk must be dead.

WASICHU

The Black slid and hopped into the turn like a barrel racer. In two lunges, they were in full gallop again. He raised the pump-gun overhead and jerked the trigger. As the booming report bounced across the prairie, he pulled the stallion to a sliding stop and fired another loud, blasting gunshot.

He finally saw the black dots materialize from the prairie floor. Because of the distance, the lip of the dry-wash couldn't be seen, only the two objects that grew, like ghosts, until they were identifiable as Little Hawk and Wolf's Spirit.

Quickly slipping his blanket off, Raven began turning The Black in tight circles while he twirled the blanket overhead. It was the Plains Indian signal meaning 'come to me.'

Looking to his left and right, he saw Blue Feather and Little Hawk whip their ponies into a gallop and race toward him from opposite directions. Over the growing thunder of the ponies' hooves, Raven could hear the haunting, courage cry of the Sioux. Soon, he thought, we'll be going home.

AUTHOR'S NOTE

My story is fiction but extensive research had been done to make the Battle of the Rosebud as accurate as possible, yet liberties were taken with time periods within the battle.

With the exception of the obvious historical personages such as Crazy Horse, Sitting Bull, General Crook, etc., all the principle characters in my story are fiction. Any similarity to persons living or dead is coincidental. Except for Crazy Horse's rallying cry the night before the Rosebud Battle; the dialogue by Sitting Bull and Crazy Horse, within these pages, were created totally from my imagination.

Through research, I have tried to portray the Native American people as they were in those harrowing days when our nation was attempting to sweep away all obstacles in the path of our territorial expansion, while labeling it the 'advancement of civilization.' When will it end?

That is all I have to say.

BIBLIOGRAPHY

Armstrong, Virginia Irving, I Have Spoken (American History Through the Voices of the Indians), Swallow Press, 1971

Benchley, Nathaniel, Only Earth and Sky Last Forever, Harper and Row, 1972.

Brown, Dee, Bury My Heart at Wounded Knee, Holt, Rinehart and Winston, Inc., 1971.

Brown, Vinson, Voices of Earth and Sky, NatureGraph, Happy Camp, CA , 1976.

Connell, Evan S., Son of the Morning Star, Harper and Row, 1984.

DeBarthe, Joe, Life and Adventures of Frank Grouard, University of Oklahoma Press, 1958.

Finerty, John F., Warpath and Bivouac, University of Nebraska Press, 1966.

Hofsinde, Robert, Indian Sign Language, William Morrow and Sons, 1956.

Karol, Joseph S., Everyday Lakota (An English-Sioux Dictionary for Beginners) The Rosebud Educational Society, 1971.

WASICHU

Linderman, Frank B., Plenty--Coups Chief of the Crow, University of Nebraska, 1962.

Maurer, David A., The Dying Place, Dell Publishing, 1986.

Niehardt, John G., Black Elk Speaks, Pocket Books, 1972.

Neihardt, John G., When the Tree Flowered, Pocket Books, 1973.

Red Fox, Chief William, The Memoirs of Chief Red Fox, Fawcett Publications, 1971.

Sale, Richard, The White Buffalo (Lakota glossary), Simon and Schuster, 1975.

Sandoz, Mari, These Were the Sioux, University of Nebraska Press, 1961.

Simpson III, Charles, M., Inside the Green Berets, Presidio Press, 1983.

Vaughn, J.W., With Crook at the Rosebud, Stockpole Co., 1956.

Walker, James R., Lakota Society, University of Nebraska Press, 1982.

Made in the USA
Middletown, DE
01 April 2025